About the Authors

Rebecca Winters lives in Salt Lake City, Utah. With canyons and high alpine meadows full of wildflowers, she never runs out of places to explore. They, plus her favourite holiday spots in Europe, often end up as backgrounds for her romance novels because writing is her passion, along with her family and church. Rebecca loves to hear from readers. If you wish to e-mail her, please visit her website at: www.cleanromances.net

Elizabeth Bevarly is the award-winning, nationally number one bestselling author of more than seventy novels and novellas. Her books have been translated into two dozen languages and published in three dozen countries. An honours graduate of the University of Louisville, she has called home places as diverse as San Juan, Puerto Rico and Haddonfield, New Jersey, but now resides back in her native Kentucky with her husband, her son, and two neurotic cats (as if there were any other kind).

New York Times and *USA Today* bestselling author **Barbara Dunlop** has written more than fifty novels for Mills & Boon, including the acclaimed *Whiskey Bay Brides* series for Mills & Boon Desire. Her sexy, light-hearted stories regularly hit bestsellers lists. Barbara is a four-time finalist for the Romance Writers of America's RITA® award.

American Affairs
COLLECTION

July 2020
Manhattan Money

August 2020
Florida Secrets

September 2020
New Orleans Opulence

October 2020
Rocky Mountain Rumours

November 2020
Los Angeles Love

December 2020
New York Nights

American Affairs: New York Nights

REBECCA WINTERS

ELIZABETH BEVARLY

BARBARA DUNLOP

MILLS & BOON

First Published in Great Britain 2020
By Mills & Boon, an imprint of HarperCollins*Publishers*
1 London Bridge Street, London, SE1 9GF

ISBN: 978-0-263-29869-7

MIX
Paper from responsible sources
FSC™ C007454

This book is produced from independently certified FSC™ paper to ensure responsible forest management.

For more information visit: www.harpercollins.co.uk/green

Printed and bound in Spain
by CPI, Barcelona

THE NANNY AND THE CEO

REBECCA WINTERS

CHAPTER ONE

"MS. CHAMBERLAIN? You're next. Second door on the left."

"Thank you."

Reese got up from the chair and walked past the woman at the front desk to reach the hall. At ten o'clock in the morning, the East 59th Street Employment Agency in New York's east side was already packed with people needing a job. She'd asked around and had learned it was one of the most reputable agencies in the city. The place reminded her of her dentist's office filled with patients back home in Nebraska.

She had no idea what one wore for an interview to be a nanny. After changing outfits several times she'd opted for a yellow tailored, short-sleeved blouse and skirt, the kind she'd worn to the initial interview on Wednesday. This was her only callback in three days. If she didn't get hired today, she would have to fly home tomorrow, the last thing she wanted to do.

Her father owned a lumberyard and could always give her a job if she couldn't find anything that suited her, but it wouldn't pay her the kind of money she needed. Worse, she didn't relish the idea of seeing Jeremy again, but it would be inevitable because her ex-fiancé happened to work as a loan officer at the bank where her dad did business. Word would get around she was back.

"Come in, Ms. Chamberlain."

"Hello, again, Mr. Lloyd." He was the man who'd taken her initial application.

"Let me introduce you to Mrs. Tribe. She's the private secretary to a Mr. Nicholas Wainwright here in New York and has been looking for the right nanny for her employer. I'll leave you two alone for a few minutes."

The smart-looking brunette woman wearing a professional business suit was probably in her early fifties. "Please sit down. Reese, is it?"

"Yes."

The other woman cocked her head. "You have excellent references. From your application it's apparent you're a student and a scholar. Since you're single and have no experience taking care of other people's children, why did you apply to be a nanny?"

Reese could lie, but she had a feeling this woman would see right through her. "I need to earn as much money as possible this summer so I can stay in school until graduation. My academic scholarship doesn't cover housing and food. Even those of us born in fly-over-country have heard a nanny's job in New York can pay very well, so I thought I'd try for a position." Hopefully that explanation was frank enough for her.

"Taking care of children is exceptionally hard work. I know because I raised two of my own."

Reese smiled. "I've never been married, but I'm the oldest in the family of six children and did a lot of babysitting over the years. I was fourteen when my youngest sister was born. My mother had to stay in bed, so I helped with the baby. It was like playing house. My sister was adorable and I loved it. But," she said as she sighed, "that was twelve years ago. Still, taking care of children is like learning to tie your shoes, don't you think? Once you've figured it out, you never forget."

The other woman eyed her shrewdly while she nodded. "I agree."

"How many children do they have?" *Please don't let the number be more than three.* Although Reese wouldn't turn it down if the money was good enough.

"Mr. Wainwright is a widower with a ten-week-old baby boy named Jamie."

The news concerning the circumstances came as a sobering revelation to Reese. She'd assumed she might end up working for a couple with several children, that is if she were ever offered a job. "Then he's still grieving for his wife." She shook her head. "How sad for him and his little boy, who'll never know his mother."

Reese got a swelling in her throat just thinking of her own wonderful mom still remarkably young and vital, probably the same age as Mrs. Tribe.

"It's a tragic loss for both of them. Mr. Wainwright has arranged for a nanny who's been with another family to start working for him, but she can't come until September. Because you only wanted summer work, that's one of the reasons I was interested in your application."

One of the reasons? She'd aroused Reese's curiosity. "What were the others?"

"You didn't name an unrealistic salary. Finally, one of your professors at Wharton told me you've been on full academic scholarship there. Good for you. An opportunity like that only comes to a very elite group of graduate students. It means you're going to have a brilliant career in business one day."

To run her own brokerage firm was Reese's goal for the future. "That's my dream."

The dream that had torn her and Jeremy apart.

Jeremy had been fine about her finishing up her undergraduate work at the University of Nebraska, but the scholarship to Wharton had meant a big move to Pennsylvania. The insinuation that she was too ambitious led to the core of the problem eating at him. Jeremy hadn't wanted a future-executive for a wife. In return Reese realized she'd had a lucky escape from a future-controlling-husband. Their breakup had been painful at the time, but the hurt was going away. She didn't want him back. Therein lay the proof.

Mrs. Tribe sat back in her chair and studied Reese. "It was my dream, too, but I didn't get the kind of grades I saw on your transcripts. Another of your professors told me he sees a touch of genius in you. I liked hearing that about you."

Reese couldn't imagine which professor that was. "You've made my day."

"Likewise," she murmured, sounding surprised by her own thoughts. "Provided you feel good about the situation after seeing the baby and discussing Mr. Wainwright's expectations of you in that regard, I think you'll do fine for the position. Of course the final decision will be up to him."

Reese could hardly believe she'd gotten this far in the interview. "I don't know how to thank you, Mrs. Tribe. I promise I won't let him, or you, down. Do you have a picture of the baby?"

A frown marred her brow. "I don't, but you'll be

meeting him and his father this afternoon. Where have you been staying since you left Philadelphia?"

"At the Chelsea Star Hotel on West 30th."

"You did say you were available immediately?"

"Yes!" The dormitory bed cost her fifty dollars a night. She couldn't afford to stay in New York after today.

"That's good. If he decides to go with my recommendation and names a fee that's satisfactory to you, then he'll want you to start today."

"What should I wear to the interview? Do I need some kind of uniform? This is completely new to me."

"To both of us," came her honest response. "Wear what you have on. If he has other suggestions, he'll tell you."

"Does he have a pet?"

"As far as I know he's never mentioned one. Are you allergic?"

"No. I just thought if he did, I could pick up some cat or doggie treats at the store. You know. To make friends right off?"

The woman smiled. "I like the way you think, Ms. Chamberlain."

"Of course the baby's going to be another story," Reese murmured. "After having his daddy's exclusive attention, it will take time to win him around."

Mrs. Tribe paused before speaking. "Actually, since his birth, he's been looked after by his maternal grandparents."

"Are they still living with Mr. Wainwright?"

"No. The Hirsts live in White Plains. An hour away in heavy traffic."

So did that mean he hadn't been with his son for the

last couple of months? No…that couldn't be right. Now that he was getting a nanny, they'd probably just left to go back home.

"I see. Does Jamie have paternal grandparents, too?"

"Yes. At the moment they're away on a trip," came the vague response.

Reese came from a large family. Both sets of grandparents were still alive and always around. She had seven aunts and uncles. Last count there were twenty-eight cousins. With her siblings, including the next oldest, Carrie, who was married and had two children under three, that brought the number to thirty-four. She wondered if her employer had any brothers and sisters or other family.

"You've been with Mr. Wainwright a long time. Is there anything of importance I should know ahead of time?"

"He's punctual."

"I'll remember that." Reese got to her feet. "I won't take any more of your time. Thank you for this opportunity, Mrs. Tribe."

"It's been my pleasure. A limo will be sent for you at one o'clock."

"I'll be waiting outside in front. Oh—one more question. What does Mr. Wainwright do for a living?"

The other woman's eyebrows lifted. "Since you're at Wharton, I thought you might have already made the connection or I would have told you. He's the CEO at Sherborne-Wainwright & Co. on Broadway. Good luck."

"Thank you," Reese murmured in shock.

He was *that* Wainwright?

It was one of the most prestigious brokerage firms in

New York, if not *the* top one with roots that went back a couple of hundred years. The revelation stunned her on many levels. Somehow she'd imagined the man who ran the whole thing to be in his late forties or early fifties. It usually took that long to rise to those heights.

Of course it wasn't impossible for him to have a new baby, but she was still surprised. Maybe it had been his second wife he'd lost and she'd been a young mother. No one was exempt from pain in this life.

Nick Wainwright stood at the side of the grave. *In loving memory of Erica Woodward Hirst Wainwright.*

Thirty-two years old was too young to die.

"I'm sorry I neglected you so much it led to our divorce, Erica. Before we separated, I never thought for one moment you might be pregnant with our child, or that you'd lose your life during the delivery. My heart grieves for our little boy who needs his mother. It was your dying wish I raise him, but I feared I wouldn't know how to be a good father to him. That's why I let your parents take care of him this long, but now I'm ready. I swear I'll do everything in my power to be a better father to him than I was a husband to you. If you're listening, I just wanted you to know I vow to keep that promise."

After putting fresh flowers against the headstone, Nick walked swiftly to the limo waiting for him in the distance. He hadn't been here since the funeral. The visit filled him with sorrow for what had gone wrong, but with the decision made to take Jamie home, it felt right to have come to her grave first.

This early in the morning there was only his chauffeur, Paul, to see his tall, dark lone figure get in the back wearing a pale blue summer suit and tie. As he closed the rear door his eyes flicked to the newest state-of-the-art infant car seat he'd had delivered. Before the morning was out, he'd be taking his ten-week-old boy back to the city with him.

"Let's head over to my in-laws."

His middle-aged driver nodded and started the car. Paul had worked for Nick's dad, back when Nick had been in his early teens. Now that his father was semi-retired and Nick had been put in as head of the firm, he'd inherited Paul. Over the years the two of them had become good friends.

Once they left the White Plains cemetery where members of the prominent Hirst family had been buried for the past one hundred and fifty years, he sat back rubbing his hand over his face. In a few minutes there was going to be a scene, but he'd been preparing himself for it.

Prior to the baby's birth, Nick hadn't lived with Erica over the nine months of her pregnancy. Her death had come as a tremendous shock to him. Though he'd allowed her parents to take the baby home from the hospital, he hadn't intended on it lasting for more than several weeks. In that amount of time he'd planned to find live-in help for the baby. Because of his guilt over the way their marriage had fallen apart, he'd let the situation go on too long.

When Nick had phoned the pediatrician in White Plains who'd been called in at the time of delivery, he'd informed Nick that if he hoped to bond with his son, he shouldn't wait any longer to parent him on a full-time basis.

The doctor gave Nick the name of Dr. Hebert Wells, a highly recommended pediatrician who had a clinic on

New York's upper west side and could take over Jamie's care. Then he wished him luck.

Following that conversation, Nick had phoned his attorney and explained what he wanted to do. The other man had contacted the Hirsts' attorney to let them know Nick was ready to take over his responsibilities as a father and would be coming for Jamie to take him home.

Erica's parents had wanted Nick to wait until the nanny they'd lined up would be available. They wanted control over the way their only grandchild—a future Hirst who would carry on the family tradition—would be raised. That meant having equal input over everything, the kind of children he associated with and where he would attend school from the beginning through college.

But Nick wasn't willing to wait any longer. Through their attorneys he promised to consult them on certain matters and bring Jamie to White Plains for visits, but deep down he knew nothing he said would reassure them. Time would have to take care of the problem.

Nick's family, who lived on Long Island, wanted control of *their* only grandchild, too. But they were at the family villa in Cannes with friends at the moment, confident Nick would do what had to be done to keep his in-laws pacified.

"Erica's parents seem willing to keep him for now," his mother exclaimed. "It would be better if you let Jamie stay with them for the next year anyway. You can go on visiting him when you have the time. It's the best arrangement under the circumstances."

Nick knew the script by heart. His own parents had already found another suitable woman for Nick to meet when he was ready. They saw nothing wrong in letting Erica's parents oversee Jamie's care, a sort of consolation prize to remove their guilt by association with the son who'd divorced "the catch of the season."

Their attitude came as no surprise to Nick. He'd been an only child, raised in virtual luxury by a whole staff of people other than his own parents. What they never understood was that it had been a lonely life, one that had caused him great pain. He didn't want that for Jamie. But deep down he felt nervous as hell.

Though Nick might have been the whiz kid who'd risen to the top of Sherborne-Wainwright, a two-hundred-year-old family investment brokerage, he didn't quite know what to do with Jamie. The world of a two-and-half-month-old baby was anathema to him.

He'd visited him every Saturday, but was an unwelcome visitor as far as Erica's family was concerned. They had a well-trained, well-vetted staff, plus a private nurse to see to Jamie's every need.

Weather permitting, he would carry the baby outside to the English garden where he could get away from the officious woman in her white uniform. Otherwise Nick remained in the nursery, but he was superfluous in the help department. The staff had everything covered ahead of time. That in itself made it impossible for him to get close to his son.

As the old Georgian colonial estate came into sight and they passed through the outer gate, Nick determined everything was going to change, starting now. He alighted from the back of the limo. "I won't be long, Paul."

The slightly balding family man smiled. "I'm looking forward to seeing him. He's bigger every time we come."

That was the problem. Jamie was changing and growing with each passing day and Nick wasn't here to see it happen. The commuting had to stop so the fathering could begin.

Before he reached the gleaming white front door, Erica's father opened it. Walter had a full head of frosted brown hair and a golfer's physique. Erica's parents were handsome people, but his father-in-law's glowering expression brought out Nick's temper, which he did his best to keep under control.

"Walter?"

"Before I let you in, I want you to know Anne's in a highly emotional state."

"You think I'm not aware of that?"

The older man grimaced. "She asked me to tell yo—"

"I know it by heart, Walter," he broke in. "Though I can't go back and change the past, I intend to do the right thing for our son. I told that to Erica when I stopped at the cemetery a little while ago."

Walter's eyes flickered as if he were surprised by the admission. After a slight hesitation he said, "Come in the dayroom. The nurse has Jamie ready for you."

"Thank you."

After three years of marriage—the last year spent in separation while the divorce was being finalized—his in-law's home was full of ghosts from the past. In the beginning his wedding to Erica had been happy enough. Everyone claimed the lovely Hirst daughter was the catch of the season, but time proved they weren't meant for each other, and she'd spent a lot of her time here rather than the city.

There'd been unmet expectations and disappointments on both sides. The sameness of their existence had become so severe, they'd drifted apart. The last time they'd been intimate, it had been a halfhearted attempt on his part to rekindle what they'd lost, but the spark was gone.

He followed his father-in-law through the house until they came to the dayroom, a contemporary addition that had been constructed after Erica had moved back with them. No doubt to keep her busy with something to do while she waited for the baby to come.

Anne's series of decorators had filled it with pots of flowers and rattan couches covered in bright prints of pink and orange. The floor-to-ceiling windows overlooked several acres of garden and manicured lawns that were green and smooth as velvet.

His mother-in-law sat in one of the chairs, stiff as a piece of petrified wood. Nick's gaze flew to his son, who was lying in the fancy baby carriage. He'd been dressed for travel and was wide-awake.

Nick had no complaints about Jamie's care, but couldn't wait to take him away because he'd be damned if he would allow history to repeat itself for one more day. Nick had been emotionally neglected by his parents. Erica had suffered the same fate though she could never admit it and preferred living in denial.

There'd been a lot of damage done. He wasn't about to commit the same crime where Jamie was concerned.

"Hello, Anne."

She couldn't bring herself to look at him.

Nick walked over to the carriage, still awed by the

fact that he was a father, that he and Erica were responsible for Jamie's existence.

The baby had inherited Nick's long, lean body and black hair, but Nick saw hints of Erica's nose and bone structure in his face. She'd been an attractive, slim brunette of medium height like Anne.

"Hi, sport. Remember me?" Nick leaned over and grasped Jamie's tiny hand. One look at Nick and the baby breathed a little faster with excitement. He wrapped his fingers around Nick's index finger. The next thing he knew it went to his mouth, always to the mouth, causing Nick to chuckle.

So far his eyes were a muddy color and would probably go brown like his and Erica's. No doubt they would fill with tears when he took Jamie away and the baby discovered himself in strange surroundings. Better get this over quick.

Seizing the moment, he lifted the baby and propped him against his shoulder. "Come on, son. We're going to take a little ride in the car with Paul. Would you like that?"

Walter handed him the quilt and a diaper bag. His eyes sent a message to Nick that he'd better live up to his promises. "The nurse printed out Jamie's routine and the things you'll need after you get to your apartment."

"I can't thank you enough for watching over Jamie until now. I promise I'll bring him back next Saturday for a visit."

"We'll expect you." But Walter couldn't get Anne to lift her head.

"Anytime either of you wants to see him, just come by the apartment. If I'm at work, the nanny will let you in."

Anne's head flew back, revealing a face devoid of

animation. "Barbara Cosgriff can't let their nanny come to you until September. There's no reason to take our grandson yet." The reproach in her voice was palpable.

"There's every reason, Anne. I miss my son and am engaging someone else until then."

"Who?" she demanded.

"I'm not sure yet. My secretary has been interviewing applicants all week. By tomorrow I expect she'll have found several for me to talk to personally. She'll do a thorough vetting. That woman is worth her weight in gold and has never let me down yet."

"What does she know about being a nanny?"

"Though I realize you can't comprehend it, she's been an exceptional working mother for me and that has never changed since she came to work eight years ago. It tells me she'll know what to look for. Keep in mind that the nanny she finds will only be with me three months until the Cosgriffs' nanny becomes free."

That was what he was saying now, yet in fact he had no idea if he would hire the Cosgriffs' nanny at all! But that revelation could keep for another day. "I plan to work shorter hours this summer, so it won't be as if Jamie's alone with her twelve hours a day."

"If you'd taken more time off to travel with Erica, you could have saved your marriage."

No. Nothing could have saved it, Anne. But to get into a postmortem with her at this stage would be futile.

"Your penthouse isn't suited to having a baby there, but somehow you insisted on Erica living there with you so you could be close to your work. She needed a real home where she could entertain."

His temper flared again, but he managed to keep it

contained. "She made it into a place where she could invite her friends after the opera and the ballet. I offered to buy Sedgewick Manor in the Hamptons for her, but she preferred to stay with you because she said it suited her better. Jamie and I will manage."

Nick didn't know how yet, but he'd figure it out. He kissed the baby's silky head. "Thank the nurse for the notes. I'm sure I'll need to refer to them until I get used to the routine."

She kept her hands tightly clasped in her lap. "The nurse said he'll be ready for another bottle when he goes down for his nap at noon."

"That's good to know. We'll be back at the apartment by then." Hopefully at that point Nick would have heard from Leah Tribe about the new nanny.

"See you next Saturday. Remember you can call anytime."

Nick turned and walked through the house with his son, still disbelieving this day had come and he was leaving the whole dreadful past behind. It was like tearing off a straitjacket.

When Paul saw him, he got out of the limo. Together they put Jamie in his new car seat. Nick could have done it without Paul's help, but he was grateful for it because it would probably have taken Nick half a dozen tries to get the confounded thing right.

The older man studied his tiny features for a minute. "I see a lot of you in him, Nick. He's a fine-looking boy."

"Blame that on his mother."

Paul patted his shoulder. "I'll drive carefully."

"I'm not worried."

He put the diaper bag on the opposite seat, then sat

next to Jamie and fastened his own seat belt. As they started down the driveway, he looked around but only saw the closed front door of Hirst Hollow. It symbolized a closed life because both sets of parents had been emotionally unavailable.

You should have done this sooner, Wainwright.

But it was too late for more regrets. He needed to let the past go and concentrate on Jamie. When he looked down, he caught the baby staring at him.

Nick smiled and put out his hand so he'd grab it. His little fingers took hold with surprising strength. No tears yet. They hadn't been gone long enough for Jamie to miss the familiar faces of his nurse and grandparents.

He fought down the anger generated by his own lack of action up to now. Mired in guilt, he'd been slow to pull himself out of a depression that had its inception long before Erica's death. His estrangement from her had been one thing, but to realize his son barely knew him twisted his gut.

A chance remark by a client last week had wakened him out of his morose stupor. "With your wife gone, that new baby of yours must be a real joy to you. There's nothing like a child to make the pain go away." The comment made him realize he could be a good father.

Once his client had left the office, Nick had got on the phone to his attorney and let him know he planned to bring Jamie home where he belonged. After setting things in motion, he'd called in Leah to help him start looking for a nanny.

Nick studied the little scrap of humanity strapped in the infant seat next to him. Jamie was *his son.* Flesh of his flesh. It pained him he'd waited this long to go get him. Emotion grabbed him by the throat.

"I know this is a brand-new experience for you, sport. It is for me, too. You have no idea. I'm more the baby than you are right now and frankly, I'm terrified. You're going to help me out, aren't you?"

For answer, Jamie gave him a big yawn. A laugh escaped Nick's throat. He'd never been responsible for anyone before. Except that wasn't exactly true. When he'd taken on a wife, he'd promised to love her in sickness and in health, for richer or poorer, until death do us part.

He sucked in his breath. He'd only done the for-richer part right. But now that he had Jamie, he realized he'd been given a second chance and planned to do all of it right.

Nick had come along late in life, his parents' only child. No siblings to play with. They hadn't allowed him a pet because both his parents didn't want to deal with one. It was too hard, they said, when they went on vacation.

He had two cousins, Hannah and Greg, the children of his father's oldest brother. They rarely played together. It wasn't until after he and Greg were taken into the firm that he got to know him better. In Nick's loneliness growing up, he could see why he'd turned to books. Over time he'd found solace in his studies and work.

Erica had been a socialite wife like her mother, like Nick's. One eternal round of beautiful people enjoying their financially comfortable, beautiful lives. Not until Nick was part of the firm did his own father take an interest in him because he had a head for finances. But by then the damage had been done. They didn't have that emotional connection he'd hungered for from childhood.

He caught Jamie's busy feet with one hand and squeezed gently before letting them go again. Nick would be damned if he let the same thing happen to him and his son. Unfortunately two and a half months had already slipped by. Precious time that couldn't be recovered.

While they drove on, he opened the diaper bag and pulled out the instructions. Besides sending along some supplies, the nurse had left exact notes on her routine with Jamie, how much formula he needed, how often, nap times, that kind of thing.

He'd already arranged for the department store to deliver a crib and a new infant car seat that had come yesterday. As he thought over the list of things still to be done, his cell phone rang. Glad to see it was his secretary, he answered.

"Leah? Any success yet?"

"I've found someone I believe will suit you and the baby."

A Mary Poppins type only existed on film. "As long as she likes children and is a real motherly type and not some cardboard creation, I bow to your wisdom."

"I'll let you be the judge. She knows she hasn't been hired yet. I told her a limo would be by to pick her up at one o'clock so you could meet her and make a final decision."

"She can start today?"

"Yes. She needs a job badly."

Excellent. "What's her name?"

"Reese Chamberlain."

"Tell me more about her."

"If you don't mind, Nick, I've decided to take a leaf out of your book. You once told me you prefer to attack a new project without listening to any other voices first while you formed your own opinion. I think that's a good philosophy, especially in this case. She'll be standing in front of the Chelsea Star Hotel on West 30th."

Ms. Chamberlain really was in financial difficulty if she'd had to stay there.

"Tell Paul to look for the woman in yellow," Leah added.

"You're being very mysterious, if not cryptic. Give me something to go on."

"I'll wager she's not like anyone you ever met."

"That sounds promising."

"I hoped it would."

He made a sound in his throat. "Are you still accusing me of being a cynic?"

"I wouldn't do that. If I've made a mistake, call me later and let me know so I can keep looking for the right person."

"Do me a favor and phone Ms. Chamberlain. If she can be ready in forty-five minutes, we'll pick her up on the way to the apartment."

"She might not be available before time, but I'll see what I can do and get back to you." She clicked off.

Nick pocketed his phone, wanting to approve of Leah's assessment of the woman because there was no time to lose. Establishing a routine for the baby with the new nanny ASAP meant he'd sleep better nights. Any more weeks spent with his grandparents and Jamie would think the nurse in the starched uniform was his mother. Heaven forbid.

CHAPTER TWO

REESE had barely reached the hotel when her phone rang. She checked the caller ID and her stomach clenched. She might have known this job was too good to be true. Better to brave the bad news now and get it over with before she left for the airport. She couldn't afford to pay for another night here.

"Mrs. Tribe?"

"Ms. Chamberlain? I'm glad you answered. I've spoken with Mr. Wainwright. He's on a tight schedule and would like you to be out in front of the hotel in approximately forty minutes. Is that possible?"

She breathed a huge sigh of relief. "No problem at all."

"That's fine then. I'll let him know. Good luck to you."

"Thank you again."

After hanging up, she hurried to the dorm she'd shared with three other women. The one with Gothic piercings and purple streaks in her hair was still there stuffing everything on the bed into her backpack. She flicked Reese a glance. "How'd that interview go, honey?" Her Southern drawl was unmistakable.

"I think I got the job, but there's one more test to pass."

"I'd rather blow my brains out than be a nanny. They couldn't pay me enough."

Reese decided a response wasn't necessary. She only had a few items to pack in her suitcase and got busy.

The woman finished packing her things and turned to Reese. "It's been nice meeting you, honey. Y'all be careful now."

"You, too. Good luck finding your boyfriend."

"I'm going to need it." The door closed. Peace at last.

Reese went to the restroom to freshen up. One look in the mirror and she decided to put her hair back in a ponytail. Babies loved to tug on loose strands. Hers would be better confined. With the heat already building outside, messy limp hair and a flushed face wouldn't make the best impression. She had the kind of skin that splotched when the temperature soared.

After applying a fresh coat of lipstick, she left the bathroom, anxious to get this final interview over. With her purse and briefcase in one hand, and her suitcase in the other, she went downstairs to the lobby to check out. Unfortunately other guests anxious to get out sightseeing had the same idea. She had to wait in line.

There was a small crisis behind the desk. The computers were down. If the problem didn't get resolved fast, Reese was going to be late. Five minutes went by. She made the decision to go outside. Of course it meant losing her place in line. If her ride had come, she would ask the driver to wait while she settled her account.

Sure enough a black limo with smoked glass had

pulled up in front. As she hurried toward it, a uniformed chauffeur of middle age got out. "Ms. Chamberlain?"

"Yes. I'm sorry if you've been waiting. I'm still in line to pay my bill. Could I leave my suitcase with you? I'll run back inside. I shouldn't be much longer."

"Take your time."

"Thank you."

Ten minutes later she rushed back outside. The driver opened the rear door of the limo for her so she could get in.

"Oh—"

"Oh" was right, Nick thought to himself as the long-legged, ash-blonde female took the seat opposite him and Jamie. She brought a flowery fragrance into the limo with her. What was she? Twenty-five, twenty-six?

Her modest blouse and skirt couldn't hide the curves of a body well put together. She had to be five-eight in her bone-colored sandals and was so different from the image he had in mind of a plump, fortyish maternal type, he couldn't imagine what Leah had been thinking.

Maybe the wrong person had gotten in the limo, but she was wearing yellow.

"You're Reese Chamberlain?"

"Yes."

"I'm Nicholas Wainwright."

Her light blue eyes flared as if in surprise. "How do you do," she said in a slightly husky voice that for no particular reason appealed to him. When she saw the baby who'd fallen asleep, her eyes sparkled with life. She leaned toward Jamie, seemingly oblivious to Nick. "Oh—look how darling! All that black hair and those long, silky lashes against his cheeks."

Her gaze finally darted to Nick's. "I'm sorry to have kept you. Mrs. Tribe warned me you were a punctual man, and now I've already committed my first sin. But the computers were down at the hotel and I had to wait in line until they could check me out."

No New Yorker here or anything close. Midwest maybe? "So my driver explained. We're not in a hurry. Jamie's being very cooperative."

"He's a wonderful boy." When her eyes lifted, he could see they'd darkened with emotion. "I'm so sorry about your loss. If you decide to hire me, I promise to do everything I can to make your son as secure and happy as possible until your permanent nanny comes to live with you."

Either she was the greatest actress alive, or this was her true self. Leah was a shrewd judge of character. Something had to have appealed to his secretary for her to pick a woman whose age and looks were totally wrong for the position. She appeared too healthy to be a model, yet had the right bones and height. All Walter and Anne had to do—or anyone else for that matter—was get a glimpse of her and…

The limo was already working its way through traffic. Paul would have them deposited at the front of the apartment before long. Nick needed more information so he could decide if he would send her back to the hotel before they ever got out of the car.

"Room and board aside, what kind of salary were you expecting, Ms. Chamberlain?"

She named a figure below what he'd anticipated she would ask for. "Does that sound all right to you?"

"It's fine," he muttered, bemused by everything that

came out of her mouth. "Tell me what happens when you leave me in September?"

"I'll move back to Philadelphia."

His dark brows lifted. "Another nanny position?"

She studied him with a puzzled expression. "No. I'll be in school again. I guess Mrs. Tribe failed to mention that to you."

Something had been going on with Leah he didn't understand. Without all the facts, he was at a loss. "She probably did, but I'm afraid I've been preoccupied with the arrangements for my son."

"Of course. She said your in-laws have been helping out. There's nothing like family coming to the rescue in a crisis. The baby will probably have a hard time with me at first, always looking for you or his grandparents. Were you thinking of giving me a trial run? I'll do whatever. And please don't worry. If you decide to look for someone else, I have a backup plan."

He blinked in surprise. "I thought you needed a job."

"I do, but if all else fails, I'll fly home and my father will let me work for him this summer. It isn't what I want to do," she added, sounding far away, "but as I told you, there's nothing like family in an emergency. Dad's a sweetheart."

What had Leah said? *I'll wager she's not like anyone you ever met.*

"Where is home?"

"Lincoln, Nebraska."

So Nick was right. "What does your father do for a living?"

"He owns a lumberyard. I've helped in the office before."

"You're a long way from home. I presume college brought you to the East Coast."

"That's right. I'm a business major."

Nick's black brows furrowed. "Have you ever been a nanny?"

"No," she said forthrightly, "but I come from a large family and have done my share of tending children."

"Your mother worked, too?"

A gentle laugh escaped. "Oh, she worked—but not outside the home. Being the mother of six children is like running a major corporation. She's been on call 24/7 since I was born." Her eyes wandered to Jamie. "There's nothing sweeter than a new baby. All they really need is lots of love between eating and sleeping."

Suddenly the door opened. Paul stood there, reminding Nick they'd arrived. He'd been so engrossed in the conversation he hadn't noticed the limo had stopped. Unless he could come up with a compelling reason not to hire her right now, taking her upstairs would be as good as a fait accompli.

While he hesitated, a piercing siren filled the air, the kind that sent an alarm through your body. It was so loud it woke Jamie, who came awake startled and crying. Before Nick could turn to get the baby's straps undone, Ms. Chamberlain had already accomplished it and plucked him out of the car seat.

In an instant she had him cuddled against her shoulder. She'd moved too fast for it to be anything more than her natural instinct to comfort. "Did that mean old siren scare you?" Her hand shaped the back of his head. "It scared me, too, but it's all right." She rocked him, giving him kisses until his frightened cries turned into whimpers.

"Sorry," she said, flicking her gaze to Nick. "I didn't mean to grab him, but that siren made *me* jump and it was easier for me to dive for him than you. His heart is pounding like a jackhammer." She started to hand the baby to Nick, but he shook his head.

"He seems perfectly happy where he is for the moment."

With those words it appeared he'd sealed his own fate. Still bemused by what had happened, he turned to an oddly silent Paul who'd already pulled the diaper bag and her suitcase out of the limo.

The baby was gorgeous. He had the overall look and coloring of his dark, striking father, but it was apparent his mother had been a beauty in her own right. No wonder Mr. Wainwright seemed to brood even as he spoke to Reese. She hadn't the slightest idea how long he and his wife had been married. What mattered was that she'd only been dead ten weeks.

Reese had undergone her own crushing pain when Jeremy had broken their engagement, but at least they hadn't been married or had a child. She didn't even want to think about the white-hot pain Jamie's father must still be in. Reese couldn't figure out how he was coping.

There was nothing she could do to alleviate his anguish. But if given the chance, she would love his little boy and make him feel secure during the hours his father was at work. By the time fall came and the new nanny took over, his daddy would have put more of his grief behind him.

Last Christmas Reese had been in agony over her split with Jeremy, but six months had gone by and she was still alive and functioning better these days. Though it would take Mr. Wainwright longer to heal, she was living proof that you didn't die of a broken heart. But he wouldn't want to hear those words right now so she wouldn't say them.

"Shall we go up?"

His deep voice broke into her reverie. She turned her head, surprised he'd already gotten out of the limo. Reese took a quick second breath because it appeared he wasn't about to send her away yet. Feeling the baby cling to her had made the whole situation real for the first time. She discovered she wanted this job very much.

"Jamie seems to have quieted down," she commented.

"Thanks to you." The comment warmed her before he reached for his son. Though he was tiny compared to his father, they looked so right together in their matching colored suits. She surmised Mr. Wainwright was in his early to mid-thirties although age was hard to tell and could add years when one was grieving.

Realizing she would become morose if she kept thinking about it, she stepped out of the limo with her purse, determined to put on a bright face for Jamie. That was her job after all. She followed his father inside a prewar brick-and-limestone building. Evidently there'd been massive renovations because the interior exuded luxury. They entered the elevator and rode to the fourteenth floor.

When the doors opened, she glimpsed a penthouse the public only got to see from inside the pages of *Architecture Digest*. The apartment itself was a piece of modern sculpture with its tall curving walls and a sweeping loft where she glimpsed a library of books and statuary. At every turn she was surprised by a bronze étagère of Mesoamerican artifacts here or a cubist painting there.

Impressions of Old World antiques, objets d'art and moiré silk period pieces flew at her like colors through a prism. There was a grand piano and a set of gorgeous Japanese screens in one section. Everywhere she looked, her gaze fastened on some treasure. A grouping of eighteenth-century furniture faced the fireplace. She wouldn't know where to begin describing the layout or furnishings of this Park Avenue address.

Months ago she'd seen an article with pictures in the *Times* of a condo something like this one that had just sold for thirty million dollars. She supposed his wealth could have come through his business endeavors.

But his breeding gave her the sense that he'd been born into the kind of family whose wealth had been one of the mainstays of Wall Street for generations. Mrs. Tribe hadn't let on. If Reese had been in her place, she wouldn't have, either.

"Since you're from Nebraska and the wide-open spaces, you'll probably find the area out here more to your liking."

She followed him across the living room's velvety Oriental rugs to the span of rounded arched windows reminiscent of the Italian masters. He opened some sliding doors. When she stepped out on the terrace, she felt as if she'd entered a park complete with trees, hedges, a pool,and tubs of flowering plants placed around with an artistic flare.

As she walked to the edge, she had an unimpeded view of Park Avenue down to the Helmsley building. The whole thing was incredible. "I would imagine after a hard day at the office, this is your favorite room, too." She saw a telescope set up at one end beyond the patio furniture. When Jamie was old enough, he'd be enthralled by everything he could see through it from this angle.

"It can be pleasant if it's not too hot. I can't say I've spent that much time out here lately, but I do use the gym every morning. It's on the upper deck of my terrace. You'll see the stairs. You're welcome to work out if you want."

"Thank you."

She sensed he was in a dark mood. Lines bracketed his mouth. "Let's go back inside. I'll let you pick the bedroom you'd like, but perhaps you'd like to freshen up first. The guest bathroom is through that door."

"Thank you. I'm pretty sure Jamie's diaper needs to be changed. Could we go to the nursery first?"

He shot her an intense glance. "For now there's only a crib in my bedroom that was delivered yesterday. I haven't decided where he should sleep yet."

So Jamie *had* been at his grandparents' from the start. Why? "I see. Well, let me wash my hands first." She slipped inside the bathroom that looked more like an arboretum with plants and flowers. After washing and drying her hands, Reese joined him just inside the sliding doors and trailed her employer through the fabulous apartment to the master bedroom with a decidedly all-male look.

It had been decorated along straight lines and contemporary furniture with accents of greens and blues. Some graphics on the walls. No frills, no sense of femininity. Above all, no family pictures. Too painful a reminder? Maybe he kept them in the living room and she hadn't noticed.

The walnut crib stood at the end of the king-size bed. It had a crib sheet but no padding. The diaper bag had been put in the room along with her suitcase. Without hesitation she reached inside the bag for a diaper. Along with a dozen of them it contained a twelve-hour supply of small, individual bottles of formula, another stretchy outfit, a shirt and a receiving blanket. She pulled it out and spread it over the top of the bed.

"If you'll lay him on this, we'll change him."

He walked over and put Jamie down. "Okay, sport. This is going to be a new experience for all of us."

Mr. Wainwright wouldn't be the first man who'd never changed a diaper. "The baby's so happy with you, why don't you undo his outfit. We'll work on this together."

Reese smiled to herself to see the good-looking, well-dressed executive bending over his son to perform something he'd never done before. He seemed more human suddenly and even more attractive.

It took him a minute to undo all the snaps and free his legs. Reese undid the tabs on the diaper. "Lift his legs." When he did, she drew the old one away and slid in the new one. "Okay. Lower him and put up the front, then fasten it with these side tabs."

The baby's body was in perpetual motion. You could hear him breathing fast with animation. "He likes all this attention, don't you." She couldn't resist kissing his tummy after his father had finished. In truth her physical awareness of Mr. Wainwright had caught her off guard.

"Great job, Daddy. You did it so fast, he didn't have a chance to get you wet." His quiet chuckle pleased and surprised her. She'd like to hear that sound more often, then chastised herself for having any thoughts of a personal nature about him.

"While you finish dressing him, I'll get rid of this." She took the soiled diaper and headed for a door she could see across the room, thinking it was the bathroom, but it led to an office where he could work at home. "Oops. Wrong room."

"The bathroom's behind me. I didn't realize it was your destination." By now he was holding Jamie against his shoulder again. They really did look gorgeous together.

Reese averted her eyes and moved past him before opening the door to the elegant bathroom. She put the diaper on the marble counter, madly compiling a mental list of all the things they would need to make his apartment baby friendly.

After washing her hands, she came out again and said, "Do you know my whole family could fit in there comfortably?" His lips twitched. When they did that, he didn't look as stressed and was too attractive by far. "How many bedrooms are there besides this one?"

"There's one across the hall from my room, and one at the other end of the apartment."

"I've been thinking… Would it be possible to move your office to that other bedroom, or to somewhere else in the apartment entirely?"

He cocked his dark head. "Anything's possible."

"It's just that your office is the perfect size for a nursery because it has a door leading into your room as well as the hall. If you put Jamie in there, he'd be close to you. I assume that's what you want. As for me, I could stay across the hall where I could hear him, too. I don't know about you, but when I was growing up, I didn't like being isolated from my parents."

He stared at her so hard, she couldn't imagine what was going through his mind, but it made her worry she might have overstepped her bounds. "What do you think?" she prodded quietly.

"It's a brilliant idea, one I would never have thought of."

"Oh, good." Reese was amazed he would admit something like that. Most men had too much pride. She liked that quality about him very much. To her alarm, she realized, there wasn't anything about this man she didn't like.

Why hadn't his wife fixed up a nursery before the baby was born? Had they lived somewhere else? Maybe he'd only recently moved in here, but why hadn't he brought everything for the baby with him?

Whatever the answer, you would have thought his wife would have taken on the job of getting prepared for a baby, but she was gone now. All he had was Reese.

"I tell you what. If you want to stay here with Jamie, maybe you could ask your driver to take me to a store where I can get all the things we need in one stop? It'll take a limo to bring back everything we require in a single trip."

When he didn't respond she said, "Or else I'll make a list for you and you buy everything while I tend the baby? Later we can move furniture and get everything set up. It's kind of fun to do together. Jamie can watch us. He's very bright and alert. By tonight we'll have this place transformed and he'll know he's home with his daddy."

She watched him reach in his pocket for his cell

phone. "I'll call Paul and tell him to meet you out in front. He'll take you to a place where I have an account. Buy whatever we need. When you get back, the concierge will arrange to get everything upstairs."

To not have to worry about money would be a first in her life. Since it was for Jamie, she would take his father at his word and enjoy her shopping spree.

"After you've returned I'll ask the chef to send up a meal for us. Are you allergic to anything?"

Chefs, a doorman, a concierge, no ceiling on expenditures— One could get used to this instantly.

"No, but thank you for asking. Are there certain foods you can't tolerate, Mr. Wainwright?"

"No."

"What about the baby?"

"So far no problems that I know of."

"Thank goodness. Excuse me for a minute while I freshen up in my bedroom."

She reached for the suitcase and briefcase and carried them across the hall to the other bedroom done in an opulent Mediterranean decor. It had its own ornate en suite bathroom with two sinks. She would use one of them to bathe Jamie. Afterward she couldn't wait to wrap him up in the plush lavender towels hanging from a row of gilded hooks.

Reese looked around, incredulous that this was happening. Her thoughts darted to her employer. How was is it possible she'd be sleeping across the hall from the most fabulous man she'd ever met in her life?

After Ms. Chamberlain left the apartment, Nick fed the baby another bottle. He'd watched the nurse burp Jamie and had gotten that part down right. Once Jamie fell asleep, Nick laid him in the center of the bed and put the quilt over him. In the process he noticed the time on his watch. It was after three. The day had gotten away from him completely.

He reached for his cell phone and called the office. "Uncle Stan?"

"Where have you been? I need to discuss the Grayson merger with you. I've run into a snag and want your help."

"I'm aware of that, but it won't be possible today or tomorrow. Can't you talk to Uncle Phil?"

"He's at the dentist getting a new crown this afternoon."

"Then ask Greg."

"He doesn't know all the ins and outs. It's too tricky for him."

"Nevertheless I can't come in the office until Monday."

"That might be too late, Nicky." His father's younger brother had always been an alarmist.

"Sorry, but it can't be helped."

"Since when? I don't understand."

No. He wouldn't. His uncle and aunt had been childless. "Today I brought Jamie home for good."

There was a deafening silence. "I thought he—"

"He's been with his grandparents too long as it is," he broke in.

"But how will you manage?"

So far…better than Nick had thought possible. "I've hired a nanny." A totally feminine, beautiful, unexpected young woman. The image of her clutching Jamie to her while they were still in the limo—as if she was the mother—refused to leave his mind.

"I had no idea you'd even been looking for one. Your father never said a word."

"He and Mother were already in Cannes when I made the decision."

"I hear a decent one is almost impossible to come by. Is she over forty?"

His patience was running out. "Why do you ask?"

"Because anyone younger who still has their eyesight will do whatever it takes to get set up with you."

If Nick had inherited a cynical gene, it had to have come from his uncle. But in this case he wasn't worried. Leah would have done a thorough check of Ms. Chamberlain's background. He paid his secretary a salary that ensured mistakes like the one his uncle was talking about didn't happen.

"See you on Monday, Uncle Stan," Nick muttered before clicking off. Now to get busy dismantling his office. But before he did that, he changed out of his suit into something more comfortable.

To his relief, Jamie slept through the next two hours. By the time the concierge rang him at five and told him he was on his way up with Ms. Chamberlain, Nick had just wheeled the baby crib into the empty room.

He walked through the apartment to the entry and opened the door. Soon his nanny emerged from the elevator carrying bags in both hands. As she passed by him she said, "Merry Christmas." She was intriguing and amusing at the same time.

Behind her came the concierge pushing a dolly loaded with cartons. Paul brought up the rear with more bags. He winked at Nick, who was still reacting to her comment. "This bag goes in the kitchen. Then we have one more load," he whispered before heading for the other room.

"You've done the work of a thousand—" she exclaimed to Nick after the men had filed back out of the new nursery. "Jamie's going to *love* this room once we've whipped it into shape. How's he doing so far?"

She had such a vivacious personality, Nick was mesmerized. No wonder Leah had picked her. Ms. Chamberlain had to have stood out a hundred miles from any of the other nanny candidates.

"He's still asleep on my bed."

"I'll just wash my hands and peek in on him."

"While you do that I'll ask the kitchen to send up our dinner." He made the call, then started looking through the bags, curious to see what she'd purchased for one tiny baby. In a minute the concierge came through with even more cartons.

"Have fun putting all this together, Mr. Wainwright. Leave the empty boxes outside in the hall and I'll pick them up."

Nick thanked him and walked him out in time to ask the waiter to set up their dinner in the dining room. Halfway back to his bedroom he met her in the hall carrying Jamie in her arms. "This little guy was awake. I guess he could hear the noise and started to fuss. He needed a diaper change and let me handle it, but I think he wanted you to do the honors."

"Well, now that the deed is done, our food is ready in the dining room."

"That sounds good. If you'll open the carton that says *baby swing,* we can set it up in there and he can watch you while we eat. It will be perfect for him when we go out on the terrace during the day."

He hadn't seen one of those at the Hirsts'. "You want to swing?" Nick gave him a kiss on the cheek before heading into the nursery. Reese followed him and waited while he opened the carton.

"There should be some batteries taped to the inside of the lid."

"Batteries?"

"They make it swing and play music at the same time."

Though he moved millions of dollars around on paper every day, the world of a baby and all its attendant necessities had passed him by completely. Whether his boy needed a swing or not, he had one now. Thankfully it wasn't as difficult to put together as installing the base of the infant car seat in the limo. It had taken him several attempts before he'd managed to do it right.

"Let's go try this out."

"Your daddy's a genius to assemble it so fast, Jamie."

"Don't speak too soon in case it goes crashing down, taking my son with it."

"We're not worried."

He stared into her shimmering blue eyes, dumbfounded over Leah's find. "Then you should be."

CHAPTER THREE

WHEN Nick looked at her like that, Reese's heart began thudding for reasons she didn't dare explore right now.

She followed him back to the living room. The floor-to-ceiling French doors at the end had been opened to reveal a dining room that took her breath. First came the chandelier of Czechoslovakian glass. One of this kind and size was a museum piece. She thought the same thing of the massive Italian provincial hutch that lined the far wall.

Its shelving held handblown Venetian glass and stunning pieces of china no longer made. On the opposite wall was a long European hunt board with its distinctive stylized pheasants and peacocks. A still-life oil painting of fruits hung above it.

The window featured tapestries with tassels pulled halfway down depicting various pastoral scenes. When she could tear her gaze away, it fell on the rectangular table of dark oak dominating the room. She counted sixteen chairs around. The exquisite woodwork was complemented by the upholstery fabric, a blend of rich green and cream striping on velvet.

Two candelabras with lighted tapers flanked a breath-taking centerpiece of fresh flowers including creamy lilies and roses interspersed with greenery. The top of the beautifully carved table had such a highly polished surface, everything gleamed. Two places nearest the doors had been set where their dinner awaited them.

She finally looked at her employer. "I'm afraid whoever dreamed up this masterpiece of a room didn't have that swing in mind." He'd set it on a gorgeous Persian rug at the corner of the table.

"I have to give my wife credit for much of the apartment's decor."

So they *had* lived here together. How painful this must be for him. "She had incomparable taste."

He took the baby from her and fastened him in the seat. "Let's see if he likes this." When he pressed the button, it started to swing and played "Here We Go Round the Mulberry Bush." Jamie looked at his father. The baby acted happy and it brought a ghost of a smile to his father's lips.

Mr. Wainwright's eyes unexpectedly narrowed on her features. "Your contribution to the room keeps it from feeling like a museum. Shall we eat?"

Reese could imagine the apartment felt that way to him with his other half gone out of his life. But he had his adorable son staring up at him in wonder, as if his father was the whole world to him. That had to compensate for his loss.

Leaving him to sit at the head of the table, she took her place at the side just as the song changed to another nursery rhyme. It played a medley of ten tunes.

He removed the covers from their plates, sending a mouthwatering aroma through the room. "Help yourself to coffee or tea."

"Thank you, but I'll just have water." She poured

herself a glass from the pitcher and drank a little before starting in on her food. "This roast chicken is delicious."

"I'll tell the chef. He was plucked from a five-star hotel in Paris."

"The chicken or the chef?"

His deep laugh disarmed her. "Touché."

She laughed with him. "It explains the buttery taste I love. I'm afraid I'm as bad as Julia Child. We think alike. Butter is the building block for good food."

His dark eyes flicked to hers. The candlelight reflecting in them made the irises look more brown than black. Until now she hadn't been able to decide their exact shade. "You eat a lot of it out in Nebraska, do you?"

"We Cornhuskers never heard of cholesterol," she teased, laying it on a little thick. "In truth, all of us healthy farm girls thrive on it."

One dark brow shot up. "If I offended you, I didn't mean to."

She smiled. "I know you didn't. I was just having fun."

"That's a refreshing quality of yours, Reese. Mind if I call you that?"

His genuine warmth came as a surprise. She hadn't expected a truly successful, wealthy CEO like him to be so well-rounded. It was probably that quality as much as his brilliant mind that drew people to him and made him such a paragon.

"To be honest, I hate being called Ms. Chamberlain, *Mr.* Wainwright."

He smiled. "If that was more funning on your part, I still get the hint. Call me Nick."

"Thank you. I was afraid it wouldn't happen for a while."

Another chuckle ensued. "Am I that impossible?"

Reese was already too addicted to his potent charisma. "Not at all, but I'd like Jamie to know I have a first name. Ms. Chamberlain is kind of heavy for a ten-week-old." She put her fork down. "Speaking of the baby, I know it looks like I bought out the store, but everything I purchased was for a reason. Of course I'll take anything back you don't like or find necessary."

"I'll reserve judgment until tomorrow. We've worked hard enough today and need an early night."

"The only thing we ought to do before turning in is to fix up Jamie's crib."

"What's wrong with it?"

"Nothing, but it needs a mattress cover under the fitted sheet and a bumper pad to go around the edges so he won't hurt his head against the bars. And I bought a cute little mobile with farm animals that plays tunes. Anything with bright colors and he'll reach for it."

He glanced down at Jamie. "You know what, sport? I have a feeling Reese is going to spoil you rotten."

"That's the plan," she interjected. "You can't spoil babies enough because they're too cute." She leaned over to cup his cheek.

"Would you like dessert?" he murmured.

She felt his dark gaze on her, making her so aware of him, it sent heat to her face. "I don't think I have room for any, thank you. The dinner was wonderful."

Reese started to get up from the table, ready to take the dishes into the kitchen. She assumed it lay beyond the door at the other end of the dining room. But he said,

"Leave everything for the waiter. He lets himself in and out. So do the maids."

"I didn't realize." She remained in place.

"When you need a wash done for you or the baby, just put it in a laundry bag on the counter in your bathroom. You'll find them in the cupboard beneath the sinks. If you need pressing or tailoring done, phone them to indicate what you want."

She left her napkin next to her plate. "Do you always have your meals brought up?"

"No. Most of the time I eat out. Occasionally I fix something in the kitchen and sit at the island. While you're here, feel free to order whatever you want from downstairs. All you have to do is pick up the house phone and dial one for the chef's office, or two for maid service. They come in every morning. Your job is to take care of Jamie, nothing else."

"Understood."

"You're welcome to fix your own meals whether I'm home or not. Tomorrow there'll be time for you to look around the pantry and compile a list of groceries you'd like to have on hand. Dial three for the concierge. Give him the list and he'll see they're delivered."

He pushed himself away from the table and stood up to take the baby out of the swing. "Come on, Jamie. Let's see how long it takes your old man to put that mobile together."

"You've been given a reprieve on that one," Reese said, bringing up the rear. "The only thing you have to do is fasten it to the end of the crib and turn on the music. There's a small sack of batteries somewhere, but give me a minute to make up the crib first."

He moved fast on those long, powerful legs. She had

to hurry to keep up with him. When they reached the nursery, she found the item for him, then quickly got busy. After she'd tied the last part of the bumper pad, she reached for Jamie.

"I'll feed him while you set up the mobile."

She darted into Nick's bedroom and got a bottle of formula out of the diaper bag, sat down on the end of his bed and fed Jamie.

"You're a hungry boy." He drank noisily. His burps were noisy, too, making her laugh. When he'd drained his bottle, she wandered back into the nursery where she found Nick watching the mobile turn while it played a song.

He glanced at her as she walked in. "I know I didn't have one of these when I was growing up."

She nuzzled Jamie's neck. "I think you're going to like what your daddy just put up." When she lowered him to the mattress, the tune drew his attention, as did the plush animals going around and around.

"Look, Nick—his cute little body is squiggling with excitement. He loves it!"

"I think you're right." When she looked up, their eyes caught and held. The intensity of his gaze made it difficult to breathe. "If you want to call it an early night, go ahead. I'll get up with him during the night. Tomorrow will be soon enough to take care of everything else and set up a schedule."

Then he looked back at Jamie with so much love, Reese was spellbound. She got the hint. He wanted time alone with his son. Nothing could be more natural or more reassuring to Jamie who, would be spending tonight in brand-new surroundings.

"I'll say good-night then and see both of you in the

morning." As she reached the door, she turned around. "Thank you for giving me this opportunity. I'm very grateful. He's a precious boy."

Without waiting for a response, Reese slipped out of the nursery to the bedroom across the hall. After taking a shower and getting ready for bed, she climbed under the covers and reached for her cell phone to call her parents. It was an hour earlier in Lincoln.

"Reese? I've been hoping you'd call, honey."

"Sorry about that, Mom, but I've been so busy today, this has been my first chance to call. I've gotten myself a nanny job."

"Of course I'm happy for you, but everyone misses you."

"I miss them, but with the salary I'll be making here, I can concentrate my time on studying for the Series 7 and the Series 65. I have to take the test at the end of July before classes start again at the end of August. It shouldn't be a problem putting in the hours I need and still work around the baby's schedule." But she needed to get busy right away, which didn't give her much breathing room.

"You only have one child to look after?"

"Yes. He's ten weeks old. Oh, Mom, Jamie's the most beautiful child you ever saw." That was because his father was the most arresting male Reese had ever laid eyes on in her life. The byplay of muscles beneath his T-shirt revealed a fit masculine body. Working out in his gym on the roof every day was the reason he was so buff.

"What are his parents like? I hope they're nice. Do you think you'll all get along?"

Reese bit her lip. “There’s just the father. His wife died during the birth.”

“Oh, no—”

“It’s very sad.”

“What’s his name?”

“Nick Wainwright. He’s the CEO at Sherborne-Wainwright. It’s the kind of brokerage company every student at Wharton would kill for in order to be able to work there. Would you believe I’ve been installed in his penthouse on Park Avenue? If Jackie Onassis were alive today, she would gobble it up in a second.”

Her mom chuckled. “Be serious.”

“I am. Who ever dreamed I’d be an honest-to-goodness nanny in a household like his?”

“How old is he?”

“It’s hard to tell. Thirty-three, thirty-four maybe.”

“Well…you’ve got a terrific head on those shoulders and broke off with Jeremy for a reason. I don’t have to worry about you losing sight of your career plans just yet, do I?”

“Nothing could make me do that.”

“I believe you. Destiny has already singled out my brilliant daughter for something special. Tell me more about this financial prince of Park Avenue.”

“Mom—” Reese laughed. “Financial prince…what a thing to say.”

“Tell me the truth. Is he as gorgeous as Jackie’s son was?”

Her mother would keel over if she ever got a look at Jamie’s father. “There are no words.”

“Well. Coming from you, that says it all.”

Reese was afraid it did.

“Still, if I know my daughter, you won’t let anything

get in the way of your goal. I happen to know you're going to be a big name to contend with in the business world one day."

Reese's eyelids prickled. "Thanks for believing in me, Mom."

"Oh, I do! Just don't let those mothering instincts make you too attached to the baby. It can happen."

Reese knew it was one of the hazards of the job, but she'd deal with it. Jamie was an adorable little boy and it would be so easy to get attached to him, but Reese reminded herself that she would only be here for three months. "I love you. Give Dad and everyone else my love. I'll call you soon."

Once she'd hung up, she checked her phone messages. One was from her roommate, Pam, who'd gone home to Florida for the summer. Reese would call her sometime tomorrow.

The other call came from her study partner, Rich Bonner. He'd asked her to phone him back as soon as she could. He'd flown home to California for a break before returning to Philadelphia. Like her, he was preparing for his exams. They'd done a lot of studying together. Reese knew that Rich wanted more than just a platonic friendship with her, but she wasn't interested, not that way.

If she didn't return his call for a while, he'd hopefully get the hint. One of the problems with Rich was that he was highly competitive. As long as they remained friends, he had to be nice to her when she got higher grades than he did.

But Reese wagered that if she were ever to become his girlfriend, he'd start telling her how to live her life. Heaven forbid if she landed a better job than he did after graduation. Worse, what if she were married to him and he expected her to stay at home? Another control freak like Jeremy. Help. No more of that, please.

With a sigh, she turned off the lamp at the bedside and pulled the covers over her. Having taken Nick at his word that he would be getting up with the baby, she'd closed the bedroom door. Starting tomorrow night she'd put the new baby monitor in her room so she could hear him cry.

The day had been long and she felt physically exhausted, but exhilarated, too, because she'd found the kind of job she'd been hoping for, never dreaming it really existed. Now she didn't have to go home. Instead she could make the kind of money her father wouldn't be able to pay her by her staying right here in New York.

All she had to do was look after one little baby in surroundings only an exclusive group of people would ever know about or see. When Reese had mentioned Jackie Kennedy to her mom, she'd also been thinking of her son John Jr.'s Tribeca apartment.

It must have been over ten years ago she'd seen a few pictures of the interior following his death when she'd been a teenager. From what she remembered, it wasn't nearly on the same scale of splendor as Mr. Wainwright's fantastic residence. The architectural design for making the most of the light was nothing short of breathtaking.

Like the man himself. *Breathtaking.*

"Good morning, Reese." Nick put his newspaper down on the glass-top patio table. He'd seen her ponytail swinging as she'd stepped out on the terrace and closed the sliding door. In a modest pale orange top and jeans that still managed to cling to her womanly figure, he was going to have difficulty keeping his eyes off her.

"So *this* is where you are." She walked right over and hunkered down in front of Jamie, who was strapped in the swing wide-awake. He liked the motion, but Nick hadn't turned on the music yet. "I've been looking for you." She kissed his cheek and neck. "Hey—you're wearing a nightgown. Do you have any idea how cute you look?"

Jamie transferred his attention to her while he took little breaths as if he recognized her. Naturally he did. Nick could have been blindfolded but would still know her by her scent. It reminded him of wildflowers. This time she kissed his son's tummy, causing him to smile. "Did you sleep through the night like a good boy?"

"He had a bottle at two-thirty and only woke up again at seven-thirty."

"Well, good for you." She tickled his chin and got him to laugh out loud. "Five hours is terrific. The sixty-four-thousand-dollar questions is, how's Dad?" She shot Nick a direct glance. The iridescent blue of her eyes was an extraordinary color.

"Dad's all right for an old man. What about you?"

"I got a wonderful sleep and now I'm ready to help put that nursery together."

"Not before you eat breakfast or you'll hurt Cesar's feelings."

"Chef Cesar?" she teased.

"That's right. He made a crab omelet in your honor with plenty of butter."

"Did you hear that, Jamie? I guess I'd better eat it while it's still hot." She sat down opposite Nick and removed the cover on her plate. "Croissants, too?" Her gaze darted to the baby, who followed her movements while she ate. "We're going to have to go for a long walk in the stroller to work off the pounds I can already feel going on. But that's okay because this food is too good to resist."

Nick couldn't imagine her ever having that kind of a problem. "Coffee?"

"Please."

To his dismay he discovered Reese had another quality he liked besides her ability to have fun. She enjoyed everything and ate her meal with real pleasure. No female of his acquaintance did that, certainly not Erica, who was constantly watching her figure.

He found Reese a woman devoid of self-consciousness. For some men, it might be off-putting, but for Nick it had the opposite effect…a fact that troubled him more than a little bit. She was his nanny for heaven's sake!

After finishing her coffee, she looked across at him with a definite smile in her eyes. "Before we put our shoulders to the wheel—is there anything I should be worried about in the *Wall Street Journal* this morning?"

He chuckled. "Not unless you've been following news on the euro."

"Is it good or bad?"

Her question surprised him for the simple reason he couldn't imagine it being of interest to her, but she was being polite so he would return the compliment. "Overnight it staged a late surge in U.S. trading, rebounding sharply against the dollar. As a result it unwound the 'carry' trades and sent the Australian dollar and Brazilian real plunging."

Her well-shaped brows knit together. "Is that a critical situation in your eyes?"

"No, but it has some global economists rattled."

"Well, if you're not upset, then I'm certainly not going to be." She got to her feet. "If you don't mind, I'll carry him back to my bedroom and give him a quick bath. Then we're all yours."

Nick had no idea what to make of her. But as he watched her disappear with Jamie, he decided it didn't matter because his son appeared to be in the best of hands. Yesterday morning he couldn't have foreseen the changes that had already taken place since he'd picked her up in front of the hotel.

He gathered up the swing and headed for the nursery. After putting it in the corner, some impulse had him walking across the hall to her room. She'd left all the doors open, so he continued on through. When he reached the bathroom, the sight that greeted him brought a lump to his throat.

Reese had filled one of the sinks with water. While she cradled the back of Jamie's head in the water, she washed his scalp and talked to him in soothing tones. His son was mesmerized. Slowly she rinsed off the baby shampoo, then took a bar of baby soap and washed his limbs. With the greatest tenderness she turned him over and washed his back. He made little cooing sounds Nick felt resonate in his body.

Without conscious thought he reached for one of the towels and held it up for her. Their eyes met for an instant. She said, "While you dry him off, I'll find him a new outfit to put on."

Nick cuddled his boy to him, uncaring that he was still wet. He smelled so sweet. As he felt Jamie burrow into his neck, a feeling of love flowed through him so intense, he was staggered by it.

"What do you think?" she asked when he appeared in the doorway to the nursery, holding up three outfits. "The white with the tiger, the green with the fish or the navy with the Snoopy?"

"Maybe we should let Jamie decide." He turned him around in his arms and walked over to her. "I wonder which one he'll go for."

She laughed in anticipation, watching him closely. "His eyes keep looking at the dog."

"Every boy should have one," Nick declared. "Snoopy it is."

"Did you have a dog?"

"No. What about you?"

"We went through three before I left home."

Reese had the diaper ready. Nick lowered his son in the crib and put it on with no hesitation this time. She handed him the one-piece fitted suit with no legs. After he'd snapped it, he picked him up again.

"Let me brush his hair and then he's ready for the day." As she lifted her arm, it brushed against Nick's. An unconscious thing to be sure, the lightest of touches. But he'd felt her warmth against his skin and the next thing he knew it had swamped his sensitized body.

He hadn't been intimate with a woman since the last time he'd slept with Erica. That was the reason for this total physical reaction. *It had to be.*

"First things first," she declared. "There's a diaper pail around here somewhere with a scented deodorizer. Ah—" She opened one of the cartons. "Just what we need." After lining it, in went the diaper. Then she lifted her head, causing her ponytail to swish like quicksilver. "Where do you want the crib to go?"

He struggled to concentrate. "How about the far wall. The sun won't reach him there when the shutters are open, and it will leave both doorways free."

"Perfect." She moved things out of the way so she could roll it into position across the hardwood floor.

Nick settled Jamie back in his swing and they got to work opening all the boxes. While he put the stroller together, she stacked diapers, baby wipes, powder, baby cream, lotion and ear swabs in the changing-table compartments. After watching her bathe the baby with nonallergenic products, he realized there was a reason for everything she'd bought.

"I'm glad you took the Oriental rug away. I can't wait for you to see the baby furniture," she said as he reached for one of the bigger cartons.

Curious himself, Nick opened the box and discovered a child's antique white dresser with olive-green trim and a Winnie the Pooh hand-painted over the drawers. The next box held a child's chair in the shape of Piglet. A big Eyeore dominated the oval hook rug. In another carton he found a lamp whose base was shaped like a honey pot. The last carton was the biggest. When he opened it, he found an adult rocking chair with Owl as the motif.

"That's so you can sit in here and feed him while you rock him to sleep." She'd thought of everything. The set charmed him. *She* charmed him.

He took all the boxes out of the apartment and piled them in the hall. When he came back, Reese had placed the furniture around and had put a soft, furry Winnie the Pooh in one corner of his crib.

"You've turned this room into the Hundred Acre Wood. I like it."

She whirled around with an anxious look on her face. "Honestly?"

"I doubt there's another nursery more inviting. Jamie will grow up loving to be in here. Thank you for helping me." She was an amazing person who had the knack of making everything exciting.

"I haven't had so much fun in years."

Neither had he. The ramifications of that admission were beginning to haunt him. "It's noon. We need a break."

Reese nodded. "I think your son is ready for another bottle." She finished putting the outfits she'd bought into the dresser drawers.

"As soon as I wash my hands, I'll be right back to try out the rocker with him."

When Nick returned a few minutes later he found her putting more things on top of the dresser. Besides a large, colorfully illustrated edition of Winnie the Pooh, plus a leather-bound book that said *Baby's Memories,* she'd added a pacifier, a couple of rattles, some infant painkiller, a baby thermometer, his little brush and a box of tissues.

In an incredibly short period of time she'd written Jamie's signature on the face of his apartment. Now it was *their* home, father and son.

At the thought of what would have happened if he hadn't hired her, he experienced real terror because it had opened up an old window of time. For a moment he'd glimpsed the painful gray emptiness of yesterday. He wanted that window closed forever so he wouldn't have to know those emotions again.

Needing to feel his son's wiggly body, he drew him out of the swing and they sat down in the rocker. Reese had put the bottle of formula next to it. While Nick fed him, she placed a burp cloth over his shoulder. He felt her gaze and could tell something was on that fascinating mind of hers. "I'll be right back."

Before long she returned with her phone and started snapping pictures of him and Jamie, of the room itself. "I'll get these photos made into prints and start his scrapbook. My mom kept one for each of us and I still look at mine. When you get time, give me any photos you'd like to add."

"I'll do that." When he'd separated from Erica, he'd instructed the maids to put the wedding album and photos in the dresser drawer of the bedroom at the other end of the hall.

"While you're at it, if you have his birth certificate and the picture they took of him at the hospital, I could add it," Reese suggested. "There's a family tree in his book where I can put in pictures of you and his mother, and his grandparents. After he's older, he'll pore over them for hours."

Nick smiled as the ideas rolled from her. She seemed to really care about Jamie and his future. She was remarkable.

"Later on I'll see what I can dig up."

"Good." She took one more picture of the stuffed animal in the bed. "We'll call his baby book *The Penthouse at Pooh Corner*."

Nick broke into laughter. He couldn't help it, even though it startled Jamie, who fussed for a minute before settling down again. Her way of putting things was a never-ending source of delight.

In the doorway to the hall she said, "You two deserve some quality time together so I'm going to leave you alone. While you're feeding him, would you mind if I took a tour of your apartment?"

"This is your home for the next three months. I want you to treat it as such."

"Thank you."

Actually Reese's request was an excuse to go back to her room. She'd have all summer to admire the treasures in Nick's home and much preferred to do it when she had the apartment to herself.

The important thing here was to give him time alone with Jamie. Tomorrow he'd have to go back to work. Today was a gift he could enjoy with that adorable little boy who was an absolute dream to take carc of.

For the moment she needed to acquaint herself with his kitchen. The disposable bottles of formula the nurse had sent in the diaper bag would be gone in another couple of feedings. Reese had bought the same brand of powdered formula and a set of bottles yesterday. She needed to run them through the dishwasher.

When she reached the fantasy kitchen, she wished Julia Child had been with her so she could hear her go into ecstasy. Now *there* was a chopping block befitting a piece of veal she could slap down and pound the life out of before she turned it into mouthwatering *escalope de veau*.

While Reese was still in a bemused state, the house phone rang. It sounded so loud, she jumped in surprise and hurried to pick it up for fear it would wake Jamie, who was probably asleep by now.

"Hello?"

"Ms. Chamberlain? This is Albert, the concierge."

"Oh, yes. Thank you for your help yesterday, Albert."

"That was quite a collection of things you bought. How's the nursery coming along?"

"We've got it all put together."

"That sounds like Mr. Wainwright. Does the work of ten without thinking about it. I'm calling because his in-laws have arrived and want to come up. Is he available to talk to?"

Reese was pretty sure Nick wasn't expecting anyone, but that wasn't for her to decide. "Just a moment and I'll tell him to pick up the phone." She put the receiver down and hurried through the apartment to the nursery.

The baby had finished his bottle and lay against Nick's shoulder with his little eyelids fluttering. Reese hated to disturb them, but she had no choice. She walked around in front of him. He raised those dark eyes to her face in question.

"Albert is on the phone. He says your in-laws are downstairs and want to come up," she mouthed the words.

Nick brushed his lips against the baby's head before getting to his feet in one lithe male move. "I'll talk to him from the phone in my bedroom."

After he left with Jamie, she walked back to the kitchen. The second she heard Nick's deep voice, she hung up the phone.

The bottles were still waiting. She removed the packaging before loading them in the dishwasher. The lids and nipples fit inside the little basket.

Beneath the kitchen sink she found a box of dishwasher detergent that hadn't been used yet. She undid the seal and poured some in the dispenser. Pretty soon she had the machine going on the wash/dry cycle.

While she waited, she opened the canister of powdered formula and read the directions. Once the items were dry and sterilized, she measured enough instant formula into each, before adding the required amount of water.

Nick chose that moment to bring an attractive, well-dressed older couple into the kitchen. “Sorry. I was just making up Jamie’s formula.” She wiped her hands with a clean cloth.

Nick’s eyes glimmered with some emotion she couldn’t put a name to. “No problem. Reese Chamberlain? I’d like you to meet Jamie’s grandparents, Anne and Walter Hirst. They wanted to be introduced.”

“Of course.” She walked over to shake their hands. “It’s a pleasure to meet you.”

CHAPTER FOUR

REESE had once seen the original oil painting of Grant Wood's *American Gothic* in Chicago. It depicted a farmer and a woman with stern faces standing in front of a white farmhouse. In the man's hand was an upturned pitchfork.

Though Nick's in-laws were good-looking people, they could have been the models for the painting. Mr. Hirst wore an expression of dislike in his eyes as he said hello. She could imagine him coming to life to poke her with his farm implement. His wife remained stiff and mute. Reese felt for the brunette woman who'd lost her daughter so recently. Lines of grief were still visible on both their faces. Pain, pain, pain.

This had to be brutal on Nick, who was still trying to deal with the loss of his wife, too. He shifted Jamie to his other shoulder. Looking at Reese he said, "I explained that the three of us are still getting acquainted. Leave what you're doing and come with us while I show them the nursery."

There was enough authority underlining his words for Reese to know he expected her to join them. Why, she didn't know, but she did his bidding without question.

When they reached the nursery she heard a sudden gasp from Jamie's grandmother.

"What a surprise!" his grandfather said. "Where did your office go?"

"It's dismantled in another bedroom. As you can see, we're coming along thanks to Ms. Chamberlain, so you don't need to be concerned about the baby's welfare. Sit down in the rocking chair and hold Jamie. He just had his bath and a bottle. I doubt he'll be hungry for another couple of hours."

Nick handed her the baby. Reese held her breath, hoping he wouldn't start to cry having to leave Nick's arms. To her relief he just looked up quietly at his grandmother. It was a sweet moment. Jamie had a wonderful nature.

"I'll get a chair from my room for you, Walter." Nick was back in a second. "Now you can enjoy him together." With wooden movements, he sat down next to his wife.

By tacit agreement Reese left the nursery with Nick and they headed for the kitchen. "What can I do to help?"

Aware of his body close to hers, she was all thumbs. "I just need to finish off making up these bottles." Nick found the lids and tops and before long the task was done and eight fresh bottles had been put in the fridge.

"I had a feeling they'd make a surprise visit," he murmured, "but not before tomorrow."

What he meant was, he knew they'd show up when Reese was alone to see how she was handling their grandson. But by their appearance today, it was clear they hadn't been able to wait that long.

"They're missing Jamie," she said. "Who wouldn't? He's as good as gold. Not one tear yet."

Nick nodded. "I know. I've been waiting."

"Not all babies have his wonderful disposition. It should ease your mother-in-law's mind that he's adapting so well to the change in surroundings."

He trapped her gaze. "That's because you haven't given him a chance to get upset. When I put in for a nanny, I never thought Mary Poppins would actually pop inside the limo."

Reese's mouth curved upward. His comment took the chill off the remembered moment when his in-laws had first looked at her as if she was an alien. "I'm afraid there's only one of those."

Better that Nick saw Reese as a fictional character.

Unfortunately she couldn't say the same thing about him. Meeting him had caused her to view him as someone very real and charismatic in spite of his deep sorrow, or maybe even because of it. Not for a second could she afford to forget this was a man who'd just lost his wife. It hadn't even been three months. Reese needed to focus on Jamie and nothing else.

"To be honest, I was afraid I'd pop in that limo and find Captain Von Trapp surrounded by seven precocious children all needing individual attention at the same time."

His low laughter rang in the spacious confines of the modern kitchen. No matter how hard she fought against it, the pleasing masculine sound connected to every atom in her body. She caught Nick's gaze and something intense passed between them, stealing Reese's breath.

"Nick?" Both of them turned in the direction of his mother-in-law's voice. The interruption had spoiled a conversation she'd been enjoying, and something else had passed between them, too, that Reese wasn't prepared to think about just yet. "We'd like to talk to you for a minute please."

Her brittle words expressed in that demanding tone meant she'd heard them laughing together. Reese feared it had been like an affront to her sensibilities. This was awful. Nick shouldn't have come into the kitchen with her.

"Of course, Anne." He glanced back at Reese. "Excuse me. Why don't you call down and order sandwiches and salad for us. Have them set up our lunch on the terrace. Cesar knows what I like."

"All right." Reaching for the phone, she gave Nick's order to the kitchen and asked them to add a pot of coffee. The waiter was to bring their lunch up to the patio table.

Relieved to be alone at last, Reese tidied away the things she'd used in the kitchen until it was once again spotless, then she walked out to the terrace, the only safe place in the apartment at the moment. While she waited for the food to come, she looked through the telescope. Once she'd made some adjustments, she had a bird's-eye view of one part of the Big Apple. Starting tomorrow she'd take Jamie out exploring in the stroller. Central Park was only two blocks away.

Last year she and Pam had come to New York for a few days on the train, but they'd been short on time and money. They'd ended up seeing one Broadway show and spent two days visiting the Metropolitan Museum of Art. That was it. The equivalent of a grain of sand in the middle of the Sahara.

"Ms. Chamberlain?" She lifted her head from the

eyepiece and discovered a uniformed waiter with dark hair transferring plates from a cart to the table. His black eyes played over her with obvious male interest. He was probably in his early twenties. "I know I haven't seen you before. I'm Toni."

"Hello."

"I understand you're the new nanny."

"That's right."

"I work here Thursdays through the weekend."

"Do you like it?"

He grinned. "I do now. If you want anything, call down to the kitchen when I'm on duty and ask for me."

"I believe we have everything we need," a deep, masculine voice answered for her. Nick had come out on the terrace, surprising both of them. He had an aura that could be intimidating. Just now he sounded vaguely dismissive.

"Good afternoon, Mr. Wainwright." Toni took hold of the cart and left the terrace without delay.

"Was he bothering you, Reese?"

She shook her head. "He was being friendly. That's all." She walked over to the table with its large white umbrella and sat down beneath it. "Are your in-laws still here?"

He took a seat opposite her. "No. After Jamie went to sleep, they left to meet friends for lunch. Otherwise I would have invited them to have a meal with us."

"Do you think this visit has helped them?"

Nick took the covers off their dishes. She hadn't had a club sandwich in years. "I'm sure it didn't, but there wasn't anything they could voice a complaint about.

It's apparent that with you here, everything's under control."

But Reese knew they *had* made scathing remarks about her. If the looks Mrs. Hirst had given Reese in the kitchen could inflict damage, she would have been vaporized in an instant.

"Earlier Walter told me Anne was…fragile," Nick added, as if he were choosing his words carefully. "After the way they both behaved today, I can see they're still not happy with the idea of my bringing Jamie home. I should have made the break sooner."

Reese sensed he was in a brooding mood. "It's hard to make decisions when you're grieving."

"You have some knowledge of it?" He'd posed the mild question while devouring his sandwich.

"My fiancé and I broke up at Christmas. It hit me very hard, but I couldn't compare it to your loss. When you have a child born into the world, you don't expect to have to carry on without your wife."

A bleak look entered his eyes. "Erica was in good health until she went into the hospital. Her labor wasn't normal. By the time she got there, the placenta had torn and she'd lost too much blood faster than they could replenish it. The doctor performed a Cesarian before Jamie got into trouble."

"Thank heaven for that," she whispered. "He's a little angel."

He studied her through a veiled gaze. "Does that mean you're not ready to back out of our contract yet?"

"If you knew me better, you'd realize I'd never do that, but I'm assuming your in-laws don't have much faith in me. From their perspective I suppose it's understandable."

"I'm very pleased you're here to help with Jamie, so let's not worry about them. As you said, when a person is in mourning, their emotions are in turmoil. Nothing would help them but to have Erica back."

Nick was talking about himself, too, obviously. Reese didn't know how he was functioning. The best thing to do was change the subject.

"I've been thinking. How do you feel about my taking Jamie out and about in the stroller tomorrow? Just short little forays at first. Depending on how he does, maybe longer ones."

"That's fine. Later today we'll program your cell phone so you can call me or Paul at any time. When you want to take Jamie farther afield, arrange it with him. He'll drive you to spots where you can explore to your heart's content. I'll give you a remote to the penthouse to keep all the time. All I ask is that you check in with Albert coming and going. It's for your safety."

In other words, with Nick's kind of money he would be a natural target if someone decided to arrange a kidnapping. Only now was she beginning to realize what an enormous responsibility she'd taken on. "I'll be extremely careful with him, Nick."

"I have no doubt of it." He finished his salad. "I'll open a bank account for you first thing in the morning so you'll have funds to draw on."

"Thank you."

"We haven't discussed your hours yet. If I can depend on you Monday through Friday until five every day, then you can be free to do as you wish the rest of the time. How does that sound?"

Incredibly generous. "I couldn't ask for a more perfect arrangement. But please feel free to depend on me if something comes up in the evening or on a weekend and you need my help."

"If that should happen, I'll pay you overtime."

"That won't be necessary. Being allowed to live here in such luxury with all my meals paid for is like another salary in itself. I wouldn't dream of taking more money than we agreed on." She helped herself to the salad.

An amused gleam entered those dark eyes. To her chagrin her pulse sped up. The phenomenon kept happening the more she was around him. "Since we have that settled, are there any questions you want to ask me?"

"There's only one I can think of right now. Do you know when Jamie's supposed to go in for his next checkup?"

"The nurse indicated he saw the doctor three weeks ago. I'm going to be taking him to a new pediatrician here in the city named Dr. Wells. I'll give him a ring tomorrow and find out when he wants to see him. They'll send for his records right away."

"I think that's wise in case he needs another immunization soon."

He sat back in the chair to drink his coffee. One of the first things she'd noticed in the limo yesterday was that he didn't wear a wedding ring. In one way she thought it odd because his wife's death had been so recent. On the other hand, maybe he'd never worn one, or possibly he didn't like rings of any kind. *And maybe you're thinking about him way too much for your own good.*

"If there's anything you want to do for the rest of the afternoon, take advantage of the time, Reese. I plan to get a little work done around here and do a few laps in the pool."

"How can you do any work when your office is in shambles?"

A chuckle escaped his throat. "I'll worry about it later."

"The mess will still be there later. Why don't we tackle the other bedroom while Jamie's out for the count? I'll feel much better if we set it up for you. Don't forget I'm the one who managed to get everything knocked out of whack. Kind of like the little kid who comes along and destroys the puzzle you just put together."

His haunting smile turned her heart over. "Okay, let's get busy." He rose to his tall, imposing height. "But when we're through, I'll take care of Jamie until I leave for work in the morning."

"He'll be thrilled with all your attention."

Hurrying ahead of him, she walked through the apartment to peek on the baby, who was fast asleep. He looked so precious with his arms and legs spread out, his little hands formed into fists.

"Not a care in the world," Nick murmured near her ear, surprising her. She could feel the warmth from his hard body. For a moment she had the urge to lean into him and cling. Almost dizzy from unbidden longings, she turned away. But in the next instant she spied a glint of pain in those dark orbs and despised herself for being so aware of him when his thoughts had absolutely nothing to do with her.

Leaving them alone, she rushed out of the nursery and down the hall to the other bedroom. The room was a vision of white and café-au-lait with an exquisite white lace throw over the down-filled duvet.

White lace curtains hung at the huge window that gave out on a fabulous view of the city. There was a love seat with a jacquard design in the same colors and a white rug with a deep pile in a geometric design of coffee and beige.

When Nick came in she said, "This is a beautiful room. Luckily it's big enough to accommodate everything if we move the love seat against that other wall. What would you think if we put your desk in front of the window where you can look out? If it gets too bright you can always draw the sheers.

"And on the left here we'll set up your computer system. Keep in mind that if you get tired, you only have to take a few steps to the bed."

His hands went to his hips in a purely male stance. He glanced around at all his state-of-the-art equipment without saying anything. She wandered over to the window and looked out while she waited for him to make a decision.

"I've got a better idea." Reese turned to him, curious to hear what he had to say. She felt his penetrating glance. "I'm going to give up having an office altogether and work from a laptop in my bedroom when I'm forced to."

"I don't understand." She was incredulous.

"There are only so many hours in the day. If I can't accomplish what I need to do at the office, then I'll turn it over to someone else. I have my son to think about now." His explanation sounded more like a declaration, as if his mind had been somewhere else. "Please feel free to enjoy the rest of your day. I'm going out to the pool."

Reese had been dismissed. Now that their business was concluded, naturally he had other plans that didn't include her. Silly how bereft she felt.

Needing to shake the feeling, Reese went to her bedroom to start studying. But an hour later she realized she'd been going over the same section of work a dozen times and nothing was sinking in. All she could think of was a pair of dark eyes that set her heart rate fluttering.

What she needed was a good walk in the park to clear her head.

"Albert?" Nick approached the front desk at three in the afternoon. "Has Ms. Chamberlain gone out with Jamie yet?" It was Friday. He'd turned over some work for one of the office staffers to finish up so he could come home early and spend it with Jamie.

"She left maybe a half hour ago."

"Thank you."

Disappointment crept through him because it wasn't only his son he'd been longing to see. All week he'd found himself watching the clock. When it was a quarter to five, he'd called Paul to be out in front of the building to drive him home. Today he couldn't take it any longer and knew he had raised eyebrows when he'd taken off from work two hours before time.

He realized that their constant togetherness over those first two days had spoiled him. Now, Nick missed talking to Reese. She was the most alive woman he'd ever met. Intelligent. Her conversation stimulated him and there was no question Jamie adored her.

Since he had no legitimate reason to prevent her from doing what she wanted with her spare time, he usually took his son up on the roof to the gym and worked out in front of him.

Throughout the week she hadn't called down to the

kitchen for dinner once. That gave him no opening to join her. Apparently she liked fixing her own food and ate before he arrived, frustrating him no end.

Not able to take it any longer, he broke his own rule and phoned her. She answered on the fourth ring. "Hello, Nick? Are you phoning from your office?"

Her voice sounded tentative, if not a trifle anxious. He brushed aside the thought that he knew her voice so well already, knew how she was feeling simply from the tone of it. He had to remind himself that as much as he enjoyed Reese's company, she was only temporary in his and Jamie's life.

"No. Where are you and Jamie?"

"At the park. Is anything wrong?"

He sucked in his breath because it seemed there had to be some kind of emergency in order for him to be with her at a different time than the schedule dictated. The schedule *you* established, Wainwright!

"I was able to tie up work early and decided to spend the rest of the day with my son."

"I'll come right home then."

"That won't be necessary. Tell me where to find you."

Nick heard her hesitation. He didn't know if it was because she wasn't sure of her exact location, or if she didn't want his company. If it was the latter, was it because she was afraid to be alone with him? In his gut he knew she wasn't indifferent to him, but maybe she didn't want the relationship between them to move to a more personal level. He knew it would be a mistake to blur the lines between them, but Nick was becoming more and more enchanted with Reese.

He grimaced when he thought she might be in contact

with her ex-fiancé. Was it possible she still had feelings for him? Nick had too many questions for which there were no answers yet.

"We're in front of the Sweet Café watching the sailboats."

"Don't leave. I'll see you shortly."

Once he'd hung up, he shrugged out of his suit and changed into more casual clothes. To save time, he had Paul drop him off near the east rim of the pond.

A mild breeze kept the sun from being too hot. Tourists and locals came here in any kind of weather, but there were more people than usual milling about this afternoon. Quite a few of them were pushing children in prams and strollers. Nick scanned the area looking for Reese's ponytail. She didn't appear to be around.

One knockout blonde with hair attractively tangled caught his eye over by the water where she was examining one of the sailboats. She wore a filmy layered top in blues and greens over a pair of jeans defining womanly hips. Her slender yet rounded body reminded him of someone. He moved closer and suddenly his heart pounded with ferocity because he saw Jamie in the stroller in front of her.

"Reese?"

She whipped around, causing her wavy ash-blond hair to swish against the top of her shoulders. The change of hairstyle had thrown him. He couldn't decide which one he liked better. Her hair had the kind of texture he'd love to work his fingers into.

At first glance her eyes flickered, causing them to reflect the blue off the water. They seemed to search his for a long moment before she averted them and leaned over to pull Jamie out of his seat.

"Look who's here." The second Jamie saw Nick, he grew more animated and squirmed to reach him. "You know your daddy all right." Reese gave a gentle laugh as she handed him over.

Nick kissed his son, rocking him for a minute while he enjoyed the smell of her flowery scent on the baby's cheeks and neck. "Have you missed me today? I know I've missed you." He pressed a kiss to Jamie's tummy, provoking more smiles and laughter.

Today she'd put him in the green suit with the grouper fish on the front. In his tiny white socks and white high-tops, the picture he made tugged at Nick's heart. He was proud to claim him and grateful for the meticulous care Reese took of him.

He flicked his gaze to her. "Have you walked to the north end to see the Alice in Wonderland statue?"

She nodded. "It's wonderful. I particularly loved the Mad Hatter. I can't wait until Jamie's old enough t—" She stopped midsentence. He found it fascinating how an unexpected flush spilled into her cheeks.

"To *what*?" he prodded, already knowing the answer.

"I have a tendency to run on sometimes. Obviously I won't be around when he's older…it's just sometimes difficult to think about not seeing this little one grow up." Nick was gratified to find her this attached to Jamie already. In truth, for the past week he'd been imagining a future that included the three of them. Since the moment he'd brought her to the penthouse, he'd been happier than he'd ever been in his life.

He couldn't pin it down to any one thing or moment. All he knew was that she was on his mind to the point it was interfering with his concentration at the office. "Let's grab a bite while we're here. Have you eaten?"

"I hadn't planned to until we got back to the penthouse."

"Are you hungry?"

"I have to admit a salad and lemonade would hit the spot." No doubt she kept her expenses down by not spending money on food.

"I'm hungrier than that." Since the advent of Reese in his life, his appetite had grown. Food tasted better. The sky looked bluer. When he woke up in the morning, the world seemed filled with new possibilities. He looked down at his son. "What about you, sport?"

Reese answered for him. "I'm sure he wouldn't turn down a bottle. It's warm out here."

With Jamie against his shoulder, Nick pushed the stroller. Together they made their way to an empty table and sat down beneath the umbrella, welcoming the shade. As he looked around, it dawned on him he hadn't been here in years. He'd been so busy making money for the brokerage, this part of life had passed him by completely.

"Here's a bottle for him." Reese handed him a burp cloth, too.

"Thank you." His breath caught when their eyes met. "The waiter's coming over. Will you order me a steak sandwich and coffee while I feed Jamie?"

The baby nestled in his arm, eager for his formula. He was hungry and virtually inhaled it, then let out several burps loud enough to bring some other diners' heads around with a smile.

Laughter bubbled out of Reese. He loved hearing it.

"Your son would be welcome in some parts of the world where it's polite to burp after a good meal."

He continued to rub Jamie's back in order to get out all the air. By the time his eyes fluttered closed, their food had arrived. Nick lowered him into the stroller and put the canopy down to shield him from the sun.

While Reese ate her salad, he attacked his sandwich. "Did I tell you I'm taking him to his grandparents in the morning?"

She nodded. "I bet they can't wait to see him."

"Next time I'll take you with us."

A shadow crossed over her lovely face. "Why would you do that?"

"For one reason, you'll be ready for a change of scenery. For another, Jamie is already attached to you. Another week of enjoying your exclusive attention and he'll have a hard time being separated for a whole day. With you along to reassure him, things will go better." He could tell by the shadows in her eyes she was worried about it.

"Don't be concerned. You'll be free to walk around certain parts of the grounds. Hirst Hollow is open to the public on Saturdays. You'll be enchanted with the flower gardens."

Reese finished her lemonade. He could practically see her mind taking it all in, working up a protest. After she put her glass down, she didn't disappoint him. "No matter what, your mother-in-law won't be enchanted to see the nanny along for the ride, especially this nanny!"

"Anne's going to have to get used to it. You're an integral part of my household."

"But Jamie doesn't come from a normal household."

"Go on," Nick urged, drinking the rest of his coffee. He was curious to hear the words she was getting ready to spout from lips he suddenly realized he'd love to taste.

"You don't really want me to spell it out."

"You're wrong," he fired back. "I'm fascinated by everything you have to say on the subject."

"If I told you, it could be taken as an insult, and that's the last thing I would want to do when I've been given a dream job."

"At least do me the courtesy of telling me how my son's home is *not* normal. I have to work, and I need someone to look after Jamie—what's wrong with that?"

He was prepared to hear that he made the kind of money that separated him from the masses, but she said something else instead—something that touched on that painful area of his soul no one else knew about or understood.

"In the short time I've worked for you, I've learned that Jamie is a Hirst and a Wainwright, two blue-blooded American families."

"You mean we only breathe the rarified atmosphere of the elite upper class from England going back several hundred years? You're right, Ms. Chamberlain. Someone put it much better than I could. 'In our world men were better than women, horses better than dogs, and Harvard better than anything.'"

Her cheeks turned to flame, but she held his gaze. "I should never have brought this up."

"Why not? It's the truth. Did you know the

Wainwrights have had horses on Long Island going back at least two hundred years? Nothing's more important than pedigree and belonging to the right clubs. Not even marriages have as much significance as long as the principles belong to that exclusive world where the women provide the decoration.

"Everyone has rank, some higher than others. One is aware of his social placement at all times. That's only the outer shell we're talking about. Unlike the soft meat of the crab, their inner stuffing is even harder. It blinds them to the loving and understanding of their own children."

As he spoke, emotion darkened her eyes.

"Erica's and my family share an ancestry that has been in love with itself for generations. They've continued to hone the 'right' way to do things to a fine art while at the same time distancing their offspring by their criticism and lack of affection."

He heard Reese's sharp intake of breath before she said, "For that very reason certain things aren't done, like hiring an unsuitable nanny, someone like me."

"Correct. The way you hug and kiss Jamie all the time, you're probably the most unsuitable nanny in existence, which makes you perfect for the job."

Her delicately arched brows knit together. "That sounded like a declaration of war."

"War…divorce… Ultimately they're the same thing. It's time the cycle of neglect ended, starting with Jamie."

"So you're using me for a guinea pig?"

Nick nodded without shame.

"Mrs. Tribe mentioned that you'd be hiring another nanny in the fall. What about her?"

"Since my mother-in-law was the one who arranged for her in the first place, I'll let her fix the mistake. Barbara Cosgriff's another blue blood. She and Anne make up part of a very elite circle. The Cosgriffs won't be in need of their nanny by September, therefore, they're delighted to do this favor for my mother-in-law, who spoke for me without my permission, something she's good at doing."

"So whom do you plan to hire?"

"I'm not sure of anything yet, but it goes without saying that whoever she is, she'll be entirely unsuitable."

A small sad smile broke the corner of Reese's wide mouth. "You're a clever man gaining my sympathy so I'll be a willing accomplice."

"Let's just say that for Jamie's sake, I'd like your help. Are you with me on this?"

Her gaze darted to the baby, who was just starting to wake up. She let out a troubled sigh. "You're my employer. I need this job and I love Jamie, so I'll do my best for you."

Nick ignored the little dart he felt when she referred to him as her employer. He hoped she might be inclined to do it for him. Shaking this off, he pulled out his wallet and put some bills on the table. "You have another full week before I force you to face the dragon. Put the thought away until you have to deal with her."

"That's not so easy to do."

"But possible. Remember I've had longer practice at this than you." He stood up. "If you'll push the stroller, I'll carry Jamie back to the car. He loves his bath so much, I think I'll take him for a little swim and see how he does. Have you been swimming yet?"

She hurried to keep up with him. "I don't have a suit."

"But you *can* swim?"

"Yes."

"In my teens I did a lot of sailing. It's a sport I'd like to do with my son. If he's going to share that love with me, then he needs to start getting used to the water. Already he feels safe with you. The next time you go out with Jamie, buy yourself one. Consider it your uniform and put it on my account."

If she wanted to squirm her way out of that, *too bad.*

CHAPTER FIVE

ON SATURDAY, Reese tried to study, but finally gave up. With Nick and Jamie gone from the penthouse, she was at a totally loose end. After fixing herself a sandwich for lunch, she took off for Macy's at Herald Square.

The crowded ten-story department store contained everything including the unimaginable. One would have to be here days to see it all. She ended up spending hours walking around. Eventually she found some swimsuits on sale for her and Jamie.

With Father's Day coming up, she shipped her dad a small framed picture of New York showing Park Avenue. She slipped in a note telling him to hang it in his office.

While she was looking at the toys, she discovered a wooden hand-painted toy sailboat in sky-blue with a white canvas sail Jamie could give his father. It was the perfect size to fit on a desk or a dresser. The artist on hand personalized it on the keel for her with quick-drying black paint. *The Flying NJ.* When it was finished, she asked the salesgirl to gift wrap it.

Since she was in the right place, she purchased some doughnut toys and a colorful octopus that played classical music when you touched the tentacles. By the time she got back to the apartment, it was after seven.

As she turned down the hall to her bedroom, she almost bumped into Nick. "Oh—I didn't realize you were home." Her pulse raced out of control to see him standing there in tan trousers and a midnight-blue silk shirt. He looked and smelled marvelous.

His dark eyes took swift inventory of her in her jeans and layered top. "Looks like you've been having fun. Is there a bikini inside one of those bags?"

Her cheeks grew warm for no reason. "Yes, among other things."

"I hope you put everything on my account."

Reese shook her head. "Not today. Excuse me while I put them away."

He rubbed his hard jaw. "I don't know about you, but I haven't had dinner yet. Paul is going to drive us to Nolia's in Greenwich Village. The salmon and sea bass are to die for."

She bit her lip. He obviously needed to unwind after being with his in-laws. "Won't it make too long a day for Jamie?"

"He's staying in tonight. Rita, one of the maids who's been working here a long time, is going to take care of him while we're gone. I'm expecting her any minute."

Reese took a shaky breath. Going out to dinner with Nick alone wasn't part of her nanny job, but as the thought of turning down his offer entered her mind, she realized that she wanted to be with him so badly, she felt an ache to the palms of her hands.

"What should I wear?"

"Anything you feel like."

In other words, formal dress wasn't required. She was hot and sticky and needed a shower first.

"Don't take too long. I'm starving," he said in a husky tone.

She'd been hungry when she'd walked in the door, but with those words her stomach had too many butterflies to know what she was feeling. "I'll hurry."

Ten minutes later she joined him in the foyer wearing a sleeveless dress with a rounded neck in an allover black-on-white print. The summery outfit could be dressed up or down depending on her accessories. After brushing out her ponytail, she'd caught her hair back at the nape with a black chiffon scarf and slipped on low black heels.

When Nick saw her, the unmistakable glimmer in his eyes set a tone for the rest of the evening, making her feel feverish throughout their delicious dinner. A live jazz band prompted Nick to dance with her. He drew the eyes of every woman, young or old.

She thought of Cinderella, who got her chance to be spun around the castle ballroom with her prince. But in that childhood fairy tale, the author never described the feelings running riot inside the scullery maid who for one night had been transformed into a princess. The adult thoughts and desires of a woman weren't meant to be read by dreamy-eyed little girls.

Nick had told Reese he wanted her to experience some nightlife while she was in his employ. In her naïveté she'd given in to that temptation and thought she could handle it, but if he pulled her against his hard-muscled body one more time he'd feel her trembling.

"You're a wonderful dancer, Reese."

"Thank you. So are you."

"I could do this all night," he murmured near her ear.

Don't say another word, Nick. "If I hadn't walked around Macy's all afternoon, there's nothing I'd like more."

"I forgot about that. You should have said something sooner. We'll go."

Ever the consummate host who went out of his way to make her comfortable, they left the restaurant and rode back to the apartment in the limo. The maid was there to meet them.

"Jamie never made a peep."

"Thank you, Rita."

"Anytime." Her brown eyes flicked to Reese with interest before she left the penthouse.

When the door closed, Reese looked up at her incredibly handsome escort. "Thank you for a lovely evening, Nick. I must be the luckiest nanny in New York with the nicest employer and the sweetest little boy."

His eyes were veiled as he smiled at her. "We'll have to do it again."

No, no.

"Lest you've forgotten, Cinderella only had one night at the ball. It wouldn't do for the hired help to expect a repeat with the prince. Good night, Nick."

Reese left for her bedroom having meant what she'd said. To lose her head over this man when she was being paid to do a job for him would bring heartache—the kind she instinctively knew she would never recover from.

For the rest of the week she made certain she and Jamie were there to greet him when he walked through the door of the penthouse, but that was all. Once she'd told him about Jamie's day and answered any questions he had, she disappeared to get going on her studies.

On the following Friday she was studying on her laptop when she heard Jamie's distinct cry through the baby monitor. He hadn't built up to it. One minute it was quiet in the room. In the next, he'd let go as if he'd awakened with a nightmare, or was in pain.

He'd only been down for an hour since his one-o'clock bottle. She slid off the bed and rushed across the hall to the nursery. Alarmed to see him in so much distress, she picked him up to comfort him.

"Uh-oh—you're hot." She walked over to the dresser with him to get the thermometer. To date his health had been so perfect, she'd almost taken it for granted.

"Hmm…101.4. That's not good. Let's check to see what's going on." When she undid his stretchy outfit and diaper, she discovered he'd had diarrhea. "Oh—you've got a stomachache." She got him all clean again and put him in a fresh diaper and a shirt.

For the next hour she walked him around the apartment on her shoulder, singing every song she could remember to comfort him. He remained restless and whimpered, then let out another heartrending cry before she felt him have another loose movement.

Back she went to the nursery and cleaned him up once more. This time she applied some rash cream so he wouldn't get sore. When she picked him up again, he burrowed into her neck, still feeling hot.

Without hesitation she carried him to her bedroom and phoned Nick on her cell. This was the first time she'd called him at his office since coming to work for him. Though she hated disturbing him, she knew he'd want to be told.

"Reese?" He picked up on the third ring. "Is there a problem?"

"I'm glad you answered. Jamie's come down with diarrhea and is running a temperature of 101. He's going to need fluids to lower it, but I'm not sure what the doctor would prescribe."

"I'll phone Dr. Wells right now. How long has Jamie been sick? When I left him this morning, he seemed fine."

"I know. He woke up crying in the middle of his afternoon nap. My sister Carrie uses Pedialyte when her baby gets dehydrated, so ask the doctor about that. Since we don't have any on hand, I'll give him some water for now."

"I'm on my way out the door," he declared in a decisive tone. "I'd planned to come home early anyway." Secretly she was relieved. Normally Nick hid his emotions well, but this was his little boy who was ill. He must be as nervous as she was, if not more so. "While you try to get more liquid down him, I'll call the doctor then stop by the drugstore."

"Good."

"I'll be home soon."

After she hung up, she went to the kitchen for a bottle and filled it with cool water. Jamie seemed eager enough to drink, but by the time she reached the nursery and fed him a little, he threw up.

She put him in the crib and changed his clothes for a second time. His temp had climbed another tenth of a degree. She wet a cloth and sponged his forehead and cheeks.

Before long Nick entered the penthouse. "Reese?"

"In the nursery."

As he came through the door, Jamie threw up once more. It frightened him so much he started crying harder. After she'd wiped off his mouth, Nick pulled him out of her arms and cuddled him against his chest. "Hey, sport—what happened to you?"

Her gaze fused with Nick's. "Did you reach the doctor?"

"His nurse said he'd call me back. In the meantime we're to try and get liquids down him in small increments."

"I've been doing that, but after a minute, up it comes. It must be some kind of flu."

"Maybe the Pedialyte will stay down." Nick kissed his forehead. "The nurse said it was good to use. I got him cherry. He's a lucky little guy you're here for him."

Nick was always ready to praise her. It made her want to do everything right in his eyes. "I'll take it to the kitchen and put some in a sterile bottle." When she returned to the nursery Nick told her the doctor had called. "We're to keep a close eye on him. If we can't get anything to stay down, we're to take him to emergency. The hospital will keep him informed."

She nodded. By evening he'd thrown up enough times to convince her this was serious. His temperature never dropped. "He seems too lethargic."

Lines marred Nick's face. "Let's take him to the hospital. I'll tell Paul to bring the car around."

"While you hold him, I'll put some things in the diaper bag for him."

In a short time they left the penthouse. Paul drove them to the E.R. entrance and they hurried inside with Jamie lying limp against his daddy's shoulder.

One of the emergency-room staff showed them to a

cubicle. Right after that another person came inside the curtain. His tag said he was Dr. Marsh. He got to work checking the baby's vital signs. "How long has he been sick?"

Jamie didn't like being examined. His cries wrenched Reese's heart. "Since about two o'clock. It came on so fast I couldn't believe it. We've tried to get liquids down him, but he just spits it up and hasn't urinated for several hours."

"We'll have to culture him to find out if this infection is bacterial, but I'd say he's picked up Rotavirus."

"What is it exactly?" Nick's features had darkened in anxiety.

"A disease of the bowel that causes diarrhea and vomiting. Most children have had several incidences of it by the time they're five."

"How would he have gotten it?"

"It's transmitted several ways, but I would imagine your son picked it up through the air. Someone's cough could have spread it. It's highly contagious."

"I've heard it's serious—" Reese blurted.

"It can be when left untreated. If I'm right, we'll put him in isolation and hydrate him with an IV to bring back his body's salt and fluid levels to normal. He should get through this just fine."

Should? She and Nick shared a panicked glance.

"Who's your pediatrician?"

"Dr. Hebert Wells."

"In a minute a team will come in to take a blood sample. When we know for sure what we're dealing with, we'll call him. If it's bacterial, your doctor will treat him with an antibiotic."

Reese hugged her arms to her waist in agitation.

"What more could we have done to have prevented this?"

The doctor eyed her with compassion. "As long as you're constantly washing your hands before and after you attend to your baby, that's pretty much all you can do." Jamie wasn't *her* baby, but she loved the sound of it.

"Reese has been very careful about that," Nick interjected. "I need to do it more often."

"Washing hands can prevent all kinds of illnesses."

Nick's lips tightened. "If an IV is called for, where will you insert it—he's so small?" He'd taken the question right out of her mouth.

"The IV team will decide, but probably in his foot. It hurts for a minute, but then it's over." Reese shared another worried glance with Nick.

"Go ahead and hold your baby until one of the staff shows you to the isolation area."

As the doctor left the cubicle, Nick reached for Jamie. Once he was back in his father's strong arms, he quieted down a little bit, but clearly he was miserable. Reese smoothed her hand over the back of his head. "You're all wiped out, aren't you, sweetheart."

"We're both here—" Nick talked to his son in a low, comforting tone "—and you're going to get feeling better soon."

Reese wanted to believe it, too, but she'd heard the underlying concern in his voice and was scared to death herself because the illness had robbed Jamie of his vitality.

In a minute someone came and took them through double doors to a restricted area where they were set up in a private room. Jamie cried some more. "I think he wants you, Reese." Nick handed the baby to her.

She hugged Jamie close and sang to him. The music kept him somewhat calm. When she lifted her eyes to Nick, she caught a look of such pain in his, it shattered her.

Something in his expression told Reese that Nick was thinking about his wife and how he'd lost her so quickly after they'd reached the hospital. In the two weeks she'd known Nick, he'd never talked about her except to explain how she'd died. Reese refused to consider the possibility that he was worrying his son would be taken from him, too, in so short a time.

"Nothing's going to happen to Jamie," she assured him with her heart in her throat. "You heard the doctor. Everyone's had Rotavirus in their lives. Even the two of us, and we're alive and healthy, right?" She flashed him a coaxing smile.

Reese wasn't destined to hear what he would have said back because two technicians came into the cubicle wearing masks. Jamie didn't like that and turned his head into her neck.

The taller one said, "If Mom and Dad will step outside the curtain, we'll get this over with quick." He reached for the baby Reese had to give up, but it killed her because Jamie cried out in protest.

"It's okay, sport," Nick assured him. "We'll be right outside." He reached for Reese's hand and led her beyond the curtain. She knew he wasn't thinking as he drew her along with him, but a sensation of warmth traveled up her arm into her body. He didn't let go the whole time Jamie cried. With both their emotions raw, the feel of his hand gripping hers gave her the strength to deal with this crisis.

The technician had called them Mom and Dad. Right now she couldn't imagine feeling any different if Jamie were her son. She loved that baby with every fiber of her being.

All these years she'd planned for a career, not realizing what it meant to love a child like she loved Jamie. The bond with him was so strong, it tore her apart to think of leaving him right now. When the day came that she had children of her own, how would she be able to leave them?

What if she *were* his mother and had to get back to her job of running a company? She couldn't see it, not when Jamie needed her and Nick so desperately.

Together they stood having to endure his frightened cries. "For the last two weeks he's only been with the two of *us,*" she whispered. "He's not used to anyone else."

In a minute the team left and another masked team showed up with their cart. "Stay where you are. This won't take us long."

Nick squeezed her hand gently before letting it go. She presumed their arrival made him realize he'd been holding on to hers all that time. Reese wished he wouldn't have relinquished it. Without that physical connection, she was snatched back from her fantasy about being Jamie's mother. Nick had been part of that fantasy, too. The three of them, a family. How was she ever going to say goodbye to them when the time came?

Deep in turmoil, she heard the baby let out a yelping cry like the one she'd heard through the monitor. They'd just jabbed him, she was sure of it, the poor darling. In reaction she smoothed her hands nervously over jean-clad hips.

It had been hours since she'd looked in a mirror. At least her hair was back in a ponytail and not messy. When they'd left for the hospital, she'd been in too alarmed a state to think about changing out of the jade-colored T-shirt she'd put on to study. But none of that mattered with Jamie lying there feverish and sick.

"They're taking a hell of a long time in there," Nick muttered.

Reese bit her lip. "It seems that way to me, too."

"At this rate he's going to think he's been abandoned."

"But he won't remember once it's over."

"I'm not so sure of that." Something in his tone told her that wasn't idle talk. She wanted to ask him what he meant, but one of the team came outside the curtain with the cart, preventing further conversation.

"You can go back in now. We've attached his foot to a pad for protection. You can hold him all you want, just be mindful of the tubing."

She and Nick hurried back inside to rescue his howling child, but were met by the other technician. "Wash your hands first, then put on the sterile gloves from the container on the wall. After you've done that, wear the masks we've left on the counter. Do this every time you leave the cubicle for any reason until the doctor tells you if your baby has Rotavirus or not. Dispose of everything in the bin inside the bathroom here. Leave through the other door that leads into the hallway."

"Thank you," they both said at the same time.

Once they were alone, Reese urged Nick to wash first. "Jamie needs you." Though everything in her screamed to pick up the baby, he wasn't her son and it wasn't her place.

The warning Reese's mother had given her about not getting too attached to the baby had gone by the wayside the first time she'd laid eyes on Jamie. The beautiful boy had caught at her heartstrings. After meeting his father, Reese knew why. Now—after loving and playing with him over the past two weeks—there were so many heartstrings being pulled by both Wainwrights, she realized she was in terrible trouble.

Once they were washed, gloved and masked, they spent the next hour taking turns holding him while they tried everything to settle him down. Finally he fell asleep and Nick lowered him to the crib.

"He's not in pain right now, Nick."

"We can be thankful for that small mercy at least."

"You look exhausted. This is going to be an all-night vigil. Why don't you slip out and grab a bite to eat in the cafeteria first. When you come back, I'll go get something. I'd rather it was you he woke up to later."

Nick's eyes looked fierce above the mask. "He wants you just as much." Her heart pounded dangerously, but it wasn't from hunger or fatigue. "I don't know what we'd do without you."

She knew the waiting was getting to him, but the more he kept telling her that, the more she wanted to believe it. "Hurry, before he wakes up looking for you."

"All right, but I won't be long." He disappeared into the bathroom and shut the door. Reese walked over to the crib and looked down at the dear little boy she'd been privileged to take care of so far.

When Reese had helped her mom with her baby sister, she'd only been fourteen. Though she'd loved Emma, she couldn't compare the feelings and emotions that filled Reese now. Jeremy had riddled her with accusations about being a cold woman who put a career above the feelings a *normal* woman possessed.

If he could see into her heart and soul right now, he would discover Reese was more than normal, and Jamie wasn't even her son!

After consuming a sandwich and a piece of pie in record time, Nick left the cafeteria and walked outside the hospital doors. He had a phone call to make, but cell phones weren't permitted inside. His father-in-law answered.

"Nick?"

"Sorry to call you this late, Walter, but I thought you should know I won't be able to bring Jamie to White Plains tomorrow."

There was a long silence. "Anne predicted right about you."

He took a fortifying breath. "Jamie's in the hospital with a bad flu bug of some kind. They'll be keeping him overnight. Depending on what's wrong after the tests come back, he might be here tomorrow night, as well. I'll keep you posted and we'll plan to bring him to White Plains next weekend instead."

"What kind of flu?" Anne demanded. She'd picked up on another house phone the minute Walter had told her who was calling.

"We don't know yet."

"This never happened when he was with us."

Nick was sorry she'd come on the line. This was exactly what he'd hoped to avoid. "Every child gets it, Anne. The point is, he's receiving excellent care. I have to go back to him now. Tomorrow I'll let you know how he's doing. Good night."

He hung up. It was automatic for him to check his voice messages. To his surprise there was one from his father. While his parents were traveling, they never called him. Out of curiosity more than filial duty, he clicked on.

"Nicholas? This is your father." Nick shook his head because that was the way he always started out any phone call to him. The distance between them continued to widen. "Your mother and I are back on Long Island. I came in the office and discovered you'd already gone home. Stan tells me you've got the boy with you at the penthouse. Why you would do that baffles me and could prove to be very unwise. We ran into the Ridgeways while we were vacationing in Cannes. They'll be back next week with their daughter Jennifer who's been staying with friends in England. She's a lovely young woman we want you to meet. Better not spring Jamie on her at first. You know what I mean. I expect a call from you before you go to bed."

Before I go to bed?

His father could say that when he never phoned for months at a time?

Nick clicked off. The pain he'd carried since he could first remember life kindled into white-hot anger. His parents could wait. Reese couldn't and neither could Jamie. He'd been gone too long as it was and hurried back to the E.R.

To his relief Jamie was still asleep. Reese's blue eyes, those mirrors of the soul, fastened on him with intensity. "The doctor still hasn't come back with the results."

"It's a busy night here. Why don't you go get something to eat now?"

"I will."

After she left through the bathroom, he washed his hands, then slipped on new gloves and a mask. Thankful his son was getting the rest he needed, Nick pulled up one of the chairs next to the crib to watch him.

He'd grown over the past couple of weeks. His father's question about why he would bring Jamie home to live could be answered by the baby lying right in front of him with an IV in his tiny foot.

This was why! There were changes going on every day of his son's life. Nick wanted to be in on all of them. No more chunks of time missing he could never get back.

Had his father or mother ever actually heard Nick say his first word or seen him take his first step? When Nick had gotten the flu as a baby, someone on the staff would have taken care of him. Nick's mother wouldn't have been able to tolerate being thrown up on. She would have left that to a nurse.

Reese on the other hand loved and kissed Jamie to death. That was her nature. Because of so much one-on-one attention, his son was blossoming. *You can't spoil a baby enough.* Those were her words. Nick believed in her philosophy. Every baby should be so showered.

Nick's parents didn't have a clue. They'd been raised by nannies and their parents before them. His father's mention of the Ridgeway's daughter, another woman who had to be made in the express image of the other women in Nick's life, sickened him.

"Mr. Wainright?" Dr. Marsh had come in.

Nick got to his feet. "What's the verdict?"

"Your son has Rotavirus. I've talked to your pediatrician. He'll be by in the morning on rounds unless the baby's temp spikes. In the meantime we'll continue to do what we're doing and will come in at intervals to check his vitals. Do you have any questions for me?"

"Not that I can think of right now."

"If you and your wife need a cot, they're in the closet behind you."

"I appreciate you telling me that."

"This part of the hospital has been redone for the comfort of the parents."

"Whoever planned it must have had a baby here at one time."

"No doubt."

"For your information, my wife has passed away. Reese is the nanny."

Nick had to give Dr. Marsh credit for not reacting the way he probably would have under other circumstances. "You're lucky to have found someone who has a strong mothering instinct. That's going to help your son."

"I agree."

Reese returned soon after the doctor had left and washed her hands. "Do you know anything yet?"

He told her what he'd learned. She finished tying the mask and walked over to the crib. "I should think sleep is the very best thing for him."

"We're going to need it, too. It's after eleven." He went to the closet and pulled out the made-up cots, placing them end to end. There was enough room for the staff to move back and forth changing the IV while they did vitals and programmed their notes into the computer.

He heard a sigh. "Bed sounds good. Thank you for setting them up." She removed her sandals and slipped under the covers with her head at the far end. Maybe she'd done it on purpose so their heads couldn't possibly be close to each other. He was sorry about that, but at least they'd be spending the night in the same room with Jamie.

Nick shut off the overhead light. After studying his son for another few minutes, he took off his shoes and lay down on top of the cot, putting his hand behind his head. From his vantage point he could see her lying there on her side toward Jamie.

"Reese? Are you asleep yet?"

He watched her shift in the cot. "No. I know you're worried about Jamie, but he's getting the best care possible."

"I believe that, too. I just wanted to say that the reason I was so long was that I had to let Jamie's grandparents know he wouldn't be coming to White Plains in the morning."

"I'm sure they were upset."

Reese didn't know the half of it.

"Don't be surprised if they show up tomorrow."

"That would only be normal. In my family if anyone were in the hospital, a whole crowd would descend."

Nick couldn't imagine what that would be like. "Too bad your parents are away and don't know he's ill."

"Actually they got back from Cannes today. I listened to my father's message on my voice mail."

"Are they coming over here tonight?"

"No. I didn't call him back."

A long silence ensued. "I see."

"You don't see at all, but you're so polite, you would never pry."

"Your personal life is none of my business."

"That's an excellent response."

"What do you mean?" She shot straight up in the cot. "I don't understand."

Just then one of the staff came in to check on Jamie. "How's he doing?" Nick asked as the nurse finished on the computer.

"His temp is up a little from before, but these things take time. Try to get some sleep while he's quiet."

Nick's stomach clenched. There was no way he could do that right now. He got up from the cot and walked over to the crib. At this point Reese joined him.

"He's *got* to be all right, Nick!" He heard tears in her voice.

Without conscious thought he put his arm around her shoulders and pulled her to his side. After dancing with her last week, he needed her warm, curvaceous body next to his. Though she'd told him no more repeats, the fact that she didn't fight him right now revealed her deep need for comfort, too.

"What you said earlier," she whispered. "If I—"

"Forget it," he broke in. "I'm afraid I'm not myself tonight. We may be employer and nanny, but sometimes the lines get blurred. We've lived under the same roof for two weeks now. I find myself wanting to ask you questions I have no right to ask."

"I know what you mean." The tremor in her voice made its way through to his insides.

"So you admit you're a little curious about me."

"Of course." He noticed her hands cling to the edge of the crib. "I wouldn't be human otherwise."

"Go ahead and ask me why I haven't told my parents about Jamie being sick."

She bowed her head. "Not if you don't want to talk about it."

"Actually I do. You recall our conversation about my family being blue bloods? Well, I made a vow that Jamie's life is going to be different. Yes, he's a Hirst and a Wainwright, but I won't let him grow up under a system where appearances count for everything. That kind of life might be desirable at first, but it ends up destroying you."

"You feel like that's what happened to you?" she asked quietly.

"Our whole families have been destroying themselves for generations to the point that they don't have that human quality of giving and receiving affection. They don't feel it."

She looked up at him with eyes that were suspiciously bright. "But you're nothing like that!"

The impulse to crush her in his arms was so strong, he forced himself to let go of her altogether. "I was on my way to being exactly like that until a client made a chance remark three weeks ago that opened my eyes."

"What did he say?"

"He'd been offering his condolences and said there was nothing like a child to help you get over your loss. He obviously assumed I was the typical new father having to get up with him in the night for his feedings. But he didn't realize he was talking to a Wainwright who'd come from a cloistered, upper-class aristocracy.

"You can't imagine how I felt at that moment knowing Jamie was at my in-laws' being taken care of by their staff and I'd let it happen. Worse, my own parents saw nothing wrong with it. But the real crime was the one I'd committed by letting him go home with them in the first place. By turning over my son's life to the hired help, I'd virtually abandoned him."

"But if you hated what your parents had done to you, then—"

"I know." He raked a hand through his hair. "It's complicated. At the time of Erica's death, everything was murky. But standing here now next to my son, I see things so clearly it terrifies me that I was once that other man.

"The truth is, I could have called my father back tonight and told my parents about Jamie, but they wouldn't have cared, and it wouldn't have occurred to them to come to the hospital. They've been emotionally absent from my life for thirty-four years. That's never going to change. My uncles, my cousins, they'll never change, either."

"Oh, Nick…I'm so sorry. I had no idea."

"How could you possibly know? You come from another world. A *real* world."

"At least Erica's parents have been there to support you."

"That's where you're wrong. They despise me."

"Because you hired me?"

"No, Reese. My problems with them stem back to a year ago when Erica agreed to a divorce."

"You divorced her?" She sounded shocked.

"Yes. We'd made one more stab at trying to patch up our two-year-old marriage, but it didn't work. It wasn't until after we separated that she told me she was pregnant. She moved back with her parents. I didn't see her again until I got a phone call that she was on her way to the hospital. You know the rest."

"So that's why there was no nursery at the penthouse."

"I let her have carte blanche decorating the apartment so she could entertain in style, but more often than not she stayed at White Plains. We lived apart much of the time, a situation that suited both of us. I know you can't comprehend that."

She kept her eyes averted. "It's just so sad."

"At the time it was simply the norm. When she died, I was devastated, but it was my guilt over our failed marriage that put me in a dark morass. I let them take the baby home. The problem is, Erica's parents believe that Jamie—and all the money that comes with him as my heir—belongs more to them than to me after I'd damaged the family pride. It was a case of 'it's just not done.'"

He heard a little moan come out of Reese.

"You sound horrified. A normal person would be. But in my world, I'd broken the code of our social mores by divorcing her and was viewed as a revolutionary. Letting her parents keep our son for a time would look good on the surface. My parents would prefer it if things stayed that way. Anything to preserve the image."

She shook her head. "How awful."

"I debated telling you all this. It's so messy and complicated and I'll understand if you don't want to involve yourself with it all. If you want to leave my employ, I'll give you a check for the full amount we agreed upon. But I would ask you not to leave until Jamie's on the mend."

Leave him and the baby?

If only Nick knew what Reese was really thinking.

Though the day would come when she would have to go, she would never be ready to give up him or the baby.

She sucked in her breath. "Don't be ridiculous. The arrangement we made was that I wouldn't go until the end of the summer. If you're still in agreement, then let's not talk about it again."

Relief flooded her system when she heard him say, "Then we won't."

"Good. Right now your son needs us focusing on him and nothing else."

No sooner had she delivered her words than Jamie woke up crying. Nick hurried around to the other side of the crib to pick him up.

"Does he still feel as hot to you?"

His dark eyes flew to hers. "Yes."

That one word filled Reese with fresh alarm. Jamie's temperature had been elevated for close to eighteen hours now. The IV was supposed to be doing its job.

They took turns holding him. The minutes passed. Another nurse came in to check on him. She left without saying anything to them. That really frightened her. This went on for another half hour. Then Dr. Wells walked in the room already masked and gloved.

He gave them a quick glance. "Sorry to hear your son's been sick, Mr. Wainwright. Let me take a look at him."

While Nick handed the baby over, Reese stood back to watch the pediatrician, thankful he'd come. In a minute he lifted his head.

"I'm going to have you start feeding him some formula. The nurse will bring it to you. Just an ounce at a time. He might throw it up at first, but you persevere and we'll see if it finally stays down. I'll be back later."

The next hour was nightmarish with Jamie spitting up ten minutes after every ounce. She didn't know how Nick was holding up. He'd taken over because of love for his child. That was the way it should be.

She folded the cots back up and put them away so there was room for the chairs. When she sat down next to him and the baby, the sun had come up. Though the blinds were closed, light illuminated the room.

Reese checked her watch. "Nick—do you realize he hasn't thrown up for twenty minutes?"

His head lifted. "That's definite progress." He sounded elated.

"It *is!*" she cried.

The nurse came in a little while later. "How's he doing?"

"It's been a half hour since he last threw up."

"Terrific." She took the baby's temperature. "It's down four-tenths. I'll call Dr. Wells and tell him. Let him sleep now." She hurried out of the room.

Nick stood up and lay the baby back down in the crib.

Reese followed him over. "The worst must be over."

They both heard the door open and Dr. Wells came back in to examine the baby. "He's going to be fine. For the rest of the day give him formula when he seems ready for it. We'll keep the IV going. This evening I'll come by on rounds. If all is well, he'll be able to sleep in his own crib tonight."

"That's wonderful!" Reese cried as he left the room. Luckily her mask muffled its full intensity.

Nick turned to her. His hands shot out to grasp her arms. "*You're* wonderful. I don't know what I would have done without you." Between his husky voice that sounded an octave deeper and those dark fringed eyes that were looking at her with such gratitude, she was overwhelmed by the feelings he engendered. But growing alongside her great happiness was a new fear clutching at her.

Last night he'd talked about the lines between nanny and employer getting blurred after living beneath the same roof. Try spending the whole night together in the same hospital room with the little baby they both adored.

This morning she couldn't find the lines anywhere.

CHAPTER SIX

"IS THE diaper bag packed?"

"All done."

"Don't forget your new bathing suit."

Reese blinked. "We're going swimming?"

"We might."

"In your in-laws' pool?"

"Maybe. They have several."

She'd been swimming in the pool on the terrace every afternoon while Jamie was napping. He'd had a slight cold since they'd brought him home from the hospital last Saturday night, but Dr. Wells said it was to be expected. A week later Jamie was well and beaming. Next week she'd be able to move him around on top of the water and see how he fared.

"Ready?" he called out.

"Just about."

While he was moving around in the apartment, she hurried back to her bedroom and stashed the new suit inside her purse. After breakfast she'd gotten dressed for the drive to White Plains. She'd chosen to wear a rose-colored sundress with a white, short-sleeved bolero jacket. It was a step up from jeans, more presentable for a nanny who was about to face the Hirsts again. A white ribbon for her ponytail to match her sandals, and she left the bedroom.

"Let's go!"

After putting the freeze pack with the milk into the diaper bag, Reese met him in the foyer. Nick had dressed in cargo pants and a tan crew neck shirt. Even though he'd shaved, there was that hint of dark shadow that gave him a slightly disreputable look, adding to his sensuality. The sight of him looking beyond handsome with his wavy black hair and the relaxed look on his face took her breath.

She quickly switched her gaze to his son strapped in his carryall. Nick had put him in his white outfit with the tiger on the front. The baby was three months and a week old now. He was bigger and looked so healthy you would never have guessed he'd been ill a week ago. Unable to resist, she kissed his cheek several times. His little mouth curved into a smile that reminded her of Nick. It turned her heart right over.

She tickled his tummy. "We're going on a trip in our favorite rocket ship." She sang the song one of her friend's four-year-old loved. Jamie loved it, too.

He laughed out loud, provoking a grin from Nick. His gaze found hers. "You sound happy."

"Who wouldn't be? When I think of last week…"

"Don't remind me."

They left the apartment. Soon they'd climbed in the limo and were headed out of the city under a semicloudy sky, but nothing could dim her elation at being able to spend the whole day with Nick and Jamie.

Since that night in the hospital when he'd told her about his background and failed marriage, she wasn't as nervous to meet Erica's parents. Forewarned helped her to be forearmed.

Nick's decision to break from tradition and bring on the condemnation of two families had been made because of his love and need of Jamie. It took an incredibly strong man of amazing character to do what he did. It couldn't have been easy and she didn't envy him having to deal with his in-laws today. For that reason Reese intended to be his support.

In some way things had been easier since the hospital. The bonding that had taken place with Jamie made everything they did seem more natural when the three of them were together. Nick had come home around four every afternoon. She understood his need to spend as much time as possible with his son.

Reese felt as if the penthouse had become a happy place for Nick. Nothing could mean more to her when she realized how much of his past had been marred by the weight of a painful childhood as well as a difficult marriage. Nick still hadn't told her all that had gone on between him and Erica to drive them apart, but then Reese was only the nanny. Every once in a while she had to remember that, but it was getting harder and harder.

On this trip she sat next to Jamie, who loved his pacifier and blue rattle. With Nick sitting straight across from the baby, he could talk to him and keep him entertained, but it was Jamie who entertained them. Every time he laughed, his pacifier fell out and Nick put it back in. Jamie thought it was a game and kept doing it. Maybe he was too little to realize what was going on, but it was hilarious and they laughed all the way to White Plains.

When they came in sight of the Hirst estate, Reese

understood even more the dividing line that separated people with lifestyles like Nick's and his former wife's from the rest of the world. They drove past a sign indicating public parking around the west side of the two-story mansion. Paul took the tree-lined driveway to the front entrance and helped Reese out with the diaper bag. Nick followed with Jamie and the three of them started up the steps. By the time they reached the front door, Walter Hirst had opened it. The older man couldn't hide his surprise at seeing Reese.

"We're in the dayroom."

If it had been Reese's father who'd opened the door, the first thing he would have said was something like, "There's my grandson! Come here and say hello to your old granddad." He would have reached for the baby and walked him through their house to show Grandma.

Reese had thought she was prepared for this, but even with the explanations Nick had given her, to see and feel the continued lack of personal warmth and affection coming from Erica's father disturbed her.

The interior of the mansion might be an architectural triumph of nineteenth-century elegance, but the only life Reese could see came from Jamie, whose head kept turning as they followed Mr. Hirst to a room with a surprising contemporary decor. His grandmother, wearing a stylish two-piece suit in lime-green, was just walking through the doors leading in from a beautiful flower garden Reese could see beyond her.

"We didn't expect you this early. I take it Jamie's better now."

"He's fine," Nick stated. "In fact you're perfect, aren't you, sport." He kissed his cheeks while he undid the straps and lifted him out. "You'll notice he's grown."

"Put him down in the carriage."

With no playpen or swing, Nick had little choice unless he wanted to plop Jamie in his grandmother's arms. But she gave no indication that she wanted to hold him. Reese knew there were many people in the world who couldn't show affection, no matter their social class. Still, this was Jamie's family and it just didn't seem natural.

Now that she thought about it, a hint of Nick's rebellion had come out when he'd shown them the nursery and deposited Jamie in her arms. Today he held back and abided Anne's wishes.

The trouble with a carriage was that it blocked part of the view for the baby, who started crying as soon as Nick moved out of his line of vision. Reese's first instinct was to take him right out. Like Nick, she, too, had to hold back from grabbing him.

"I brought this." Reese set the diaper bag down on one of the chairs. "It has enough bottles and diapers for today."

"We have everything he'll need. Walter? Will you tell the nurse they're here." Jamie was not happy and his cries were getting louder.

"I'll be back for him at six." Nick flicked Reese a glance. "Let's leave them alone, Ms. Chamberlain."

They walked out the mansion through the front door with Jamie's cries still following them. She assumed he meant they were going to explore the estate and go swimming later on. To her shock Nick headed for the limo and helped her inside.

She stared at him in puzzlement. "I thought our plan was to stay close by. What if Jamie needs you?"

"Then he'll cry his heart out until he falls asleep."

"Nick..."

His grim expression was too much. The past week had been so carefree, Reese could hardly bear to see his brooding expression come back. "I didn't have a choice, Reese, because I made them a promise. But after today, all promises are off."

He flicked on the intercom. "Paul? Drive us to the heliport."

"Where are we going?" she asked when he'd finished.

"Out on my sailboat."

Her heart thudded with sickening speed. "If we need a helicopter, it must be pretty far away."

"Don't worry. We're only going to Martha's Vineyard outside Edgartown. One of our summer homes is there."

A summer home there, an estate with horses on Long Island, a penthouse on Park Avenue, a villa in Cannes. Reese had an impression those possessions only constituted the tip of an enormous iceberg. If Jamie didn't have a daddy who'd decided to break the cycle of emotional neglect that went with so much luxury, he could be suffocated by it all the way Nick had been.

He studied her for a moment. "Have you ever been sailing?"

She knew it was his favorite sport. "No. One time our family went to Wisconsin and we crossed Lake Michigan on the ferry in choppy conditions. None of us did well. That's the sum total of my knowledge of being on water."

A light gleamed in his eyes. "As long as you can swim, that's all I need to know. When we get out beyond where the breeze fills the sail, you'll find out you're a wonderful sailor."

"That's wishful thinking. I only hope I won't be imitating Jamie's bout of last weekend."

He chuckled. "You don't have the flu."

Reese knew Nick wanted and needed this outing, if only to take his mind off leaving Jamie with his grandparents. *Please don't let me get seasick.* When she saw the helicopter, another prayer went up about not getting airsick. She'd never been on one of those, either.

In the end she needn't have worried because Nick's cell phone rang before they even exited the limo. After he picked up, his gaze sought hers. She tried to read his expression as he listened to the person on the other end. It went on for a minute. After he hung up, he told Paul to turn the limo around and go back.

Her brows lifted. "Jamie?"

"He won't settle down. Anne says the nurse can't do anything with him, so if she can't, that's it."

Reese bit her lip. "I was afraid of that. Jamie worships you." She bet Nick's mother-in-law told him it was the nanny's fault for spoiling him and probably decried Nick ever removing Jamie from their house in the first place.

"Nothing could please me more," he declared in a satisfied voice. "Now we can take him with us. I'll call ahead for a cooler of food and drinks to be packed for us."

The burst of elation exploding inside Reese only lasted until she remembered her mother's last question to her. *"You've got a terrific head on those shoulders and broke off with Jeremy for a reason. I don't have to worry about you losing sight of your career plans just yet, do I?"* Not for the first time, Reese had to remind herself that she was just the temporary nanny. But the pain she felt at the thought of leaving this little family was becoming too much.

When they reached the mansion, Reese could hear Jamie's heart-wrenching sobs from the foyer of the mansion. They hurried down the hall to the dayroom and found the nurse pacing the floor with him. His in-laws stood around looking upset.

"Hey, sport? What's going on?" Nick walked over to the distraught-looking woman and took the baby from her arms. Jamie caught sight of his daddy and lunged for him before bursting into another paroxysm of tears. Reese could almost hear him saying, 'Why did you leave me?'

When he burrowed his head into the side of Nick's neck, Nick must have felt it deep in his heart. In a few seconds peace reigned. While Jamie clung to him, everyone in the room looked infinitely relieved.

"I think there's been enough excitement for one day. Why don't you come to the penthouse next weekend and we'll try this again."

"We'll be in Salzburg. Don't you remember?" Anne sounded indignant. "You and Erica went with us two years ago."

"I'm sorry. This new job of parenting has taken over my life. Call me when you're back and we'll make arrangements. Have a safe trip."

Jamie refused to leave his arms, so Reese picked up the carryall and diaper bag before they headed for the limo waiting outside the mansion. Once Nick got in the backseat with him, Reese's eyes zeroed in on the baby.

"Your cute little face is all splotchy from crying. Here's your pacifier. Do you want your rattle, too?"

His fingers glommed right on to it. He didn't fight Nick as he strapped him in the infant car seat.

"Crisis averted," he said to Paul before the older man shut the door. In seconds they were off.

Her eyes flew to Nick's. "That wasn't a pleasant moment back there."

"No, and there's not going to be another one like it again."

She covered Jamie's face with kisses until she got a smile out of him. "You're so worn-out, you'll probably sleep all the way."

Reese didn't realize how prophetic her words would be. He slept through the fabulous helicopter flight that took them to the famous little island off Cape Cod. They were set down at Katama Airpark only a few miles from Edgartown.

Nick took them to one of the harbor restaurants where they ate a delicious shrimp lunch. Afterward they walked around the historic part of the town and visited some of the shops. It wasn't until they reached the boat dock on the Wainwright's property that the baby's eyes fluttered open. He'd missed everything.

Reese found it so funny, she started to laugh. Nick joined in. He was still smiling when he transferred his son from the ramp onto the end of the immaculate, twenty-three-foot sailboat called the *Aeolus*.

"What does it mean?" she asked him.

"In Greek mythology, Aeolus was the god of the winds."

"That's beautiful." The white keel had a blue stripe. She thought of the little boat she'd bought for Nick and couldn't wait for him to open his present, but she'd put it off until after they'd finished sailing.

Excitement mounted in Reese to see all the boats out on the water. This was a day out of time, one to treasure before they went back to the city. But having Jamie with them was the reminder she needed to remember she was his nanny, nothing else.

Nick brought out two adult life vests and an infant life jacket. While he went about getting the boat ready and undoing ropes, she laid Jamie down on one of the benches and changed his diaper. He loved being bare and kicked his strong legs as if he was doing exercises. She laughed with pure pleasure before putting a fresh diaper on him.

With him propped against her shoulder, she went down to the galley. There was a microwave so she could warm his bottle. By the time she climbed the stairs with him, Nick had everything ready to go. She put the bottle down. Together they helped put Jamie's infant vest on, but she was unbearably aware of Nick and his potent masculinity. Their hands brushed, sending rivulets of yearning through her.

He kissed his boy's tummy before snapping everything in place. "I know you don't like it, sport, but that's the rule." He fastened him back in his carryall. "You'll get used to it."

With a speed that took her breath, Nick's gaze unexpectedly flicked to hers. "Now it's *your* turn." The message in his dark brown eyes was unmistakable. They traveled over her features and down her body, melting her from the inside out. She got this heavy sensation in her legs. Her hands felt pains that traveled up her arms.

His male mouth was like a vortex drawing her in. Thrilled and terrified because her desire for him was so palpable he had to know it, she put out her hands to take the vest from him so he wouldn't touch her. Instead his hands closed over hers, pulling her against him, sending a paralyzing warmth through her body.

"I'm going to kiss you, and I very much hope that you won't fight me."

She couldn't have if she'd wanted to. From the moment she'd climbed in the back of the limo and had discovered a man who surpassed her every notion of the ultimate male, she'd wanted *him*. It was that simple, and that impossible, but right now she couldn't remember the reason why and didn't want to.

In the next breath he found her softly parted mouth. Incapable of doing anything else, she melted against him and let herself go, craving the taste of him as he took their kiss long and deep. Oh… She'd never felt sensations like this in her life. He drew her closer in a quick compulsive movement. The vest fell to her feet, but she was barely cognizant.

It came as a shock to realize his hunger matched hers, sending fire licking through her veins. Reese felt the low groan way down in his throat before it permeated her body. As it reached her inner core, her helpless cry drew a response of refined savagery from him.

"You couldn't possibly know how beautiful you are." A fever of ecstasy consumed her with each insistent caress of his lips on her face, her hair, her throat. "I want to take you below," he whispered against her lips, swollen from the passion they shared. "If I've shocked you, I've shocked myself more."

She took an unsteady breath and eased herself out of

arms that were slow to relinquish her. The slight rocking of the boat didn't help her equilibrium. "What's really shocking is that I'd like to go downstairs with you," she admitted because total gut honesty was required right now.

"But after I broke off with Jeremy, I made a promise I wouldn't let anything get in the way of my goals. A man can make you lose focus. Who knows what could happen to me after a glorious day on the ocean in your arms. I—I know it would be wonderful," she stammered, "because I've just had a taste of you and crave more."

Nick's eyes narrowed on her mouth. He might as well have started kissing her again. She had to look away or she'd fling herself back into his arms.

"Your honesty is another quality about you I admire." Out of the periphery she watched his hard body lounge against the side of the boat. "What happened between you and Jeremy?"

"Probably the kind of thing that went wrong with you and Erica." She'd reached the tipping point and needed distance from this man who'd caused her world to reel.

Jamie wasn't fussing yet, but she knew his hunger had been building. She pulled him out of his carryall, then sat down and settled him in her arms to feed him.

"You mean you allowed yourself to drift into your engagement?" he asked in a benign tone.

Her head flew back. "Is that what happened to you?" she asked before she realized how revealing that question must have sounded. All along she'd been thinking Erica had to have been his grand passion because he could have had any woman he wanted.

"Why don't we concentrate on you and Jeremy first."

"He's not in my life anymore."

"Humor me anyway," he insisted.

"Well, we met at the bank where my father does business. That was the summer before I started at Wharton. We fell in love and dated until I went away, then we relied on emails and phone calls until we could be together. I went home at every vacation opportunity. He came to see me twice.

"Last fall he asked me to marry him and gave me an engagement ring. He knew I didn't want to get married before graduation, but when I went home at Christmas, he wanted to be married right away. No more waiting.

"I told him I would, but that we'd have to live apart while I was still away at school. That's when he gave me an ultimatum. Either I marry him before the end of the month and stay in Lincoln, or we break up."

The baby had finished his bottle. She pulled a receiving blanket out of the diaper bag and put it over her shoulder to burp him.

"I thought I knew him, but I didn't. It finally came out that he didn't want a working wife. He made enough money and wanted me to stay home so we could start a family. I told him I wanted children one day, but my education and work came first.

"I was amazed that my scholarship to Wharton meant nothing to him. He had a finance degree and aspirations to rise to the top, but didn't take mine seriously. It's too bad he didn't realize I meant what I said. It would have saved us both a lot of pain. I gave him back his ring and told him goodbye."

"Have you seen him since?"

"No."

"He's probably still waiting for you to change your mind."

"Then he's waiting in vain."

In the silence that followed, Nick reached for his life vest and put it on. Clearly he considered this conversation over. She'd learn nothing more from him about his marriage because he'd come out here to sail.

After their brief, intimate interlude that could have ended in her making the most disastrous mistake of her life, he was ready to head out to sea, the rapture of the moment forgotten. She had the gut feeling that the invitation to join him below wouldn't happen again on this trip or any other trips he planned in the future.

If he thought she was still feeling needy after her broken engagement and that's why she'd been an ardent participant in what they'd just shared, then let him go on thinking it. She didn't want him knowing her guilty secret.

To have fallen in love with her employer went against all the rules of being a nanny, but that's what she'd done. She was madly in love with Nick Wainwright. Between him and his son, she would never be the same person again.

No one could tell her Erica Hirst hadn't been desperately in love with him, too. You couldn't be in his presence five minutes without wanting any love he was willing to give. If anyone had *drifted* into a permanent relationship—if that's what had really happened—it would have been Nick.

Erica must have been shattered when he'd asked her for a divorce. Reese wanted to believe that the knowledge she was pregnant with Nick's child had brought her some solace in spite of her grief. If Reese had been in her shoes, she knew she would have grieved over losing Nick.

How tragic that she'd died. Tears pricked her eyelids. She loved their beautiful boy with all her heart.

"Reese?" His voice had a deep, grating quality. "Are you all right? I didn't mean to dredge up your pain."

Maybe it was better he thought Jeremy was the source of her distress, but nothing could be further from the truth. She shook her head. "You didn't. I thought you and I were having a simple conversation. Naturally our pasts would come up." She put the baby back in his carryall. "I think your son is on the verge of falling asleep again. Where shall we put him while we're out sailing?"

"Keep him right next to you. I'll do all the work, but put on your life vest first." He handed it to her.

Back to square one, the place where she'd gotten too physically close to Nick and had given in to her longings. Not this time around!

She slipped it on and fastened the straps.

"Are you ready?"

Reese nodded.

He walked to the rear of the boat and started the motor at a wakeless speed. Slowly they headed toward the water beyond the buoys. Once past them, he cut the motor and raised the white sail. A light breeze filled it and then there was this incredible rush of sensation as the boat lifted and skimmed across the water. She found it wasn't unlike the feeling of Nick kissing her senseless.

When she was an old woman, all she would have to do was close her eyes and remember the sight of the gorgeous, powerfully built man at the helm with the wind disheveling his black hair. For a little while she would relive being crushed in his arms and invited to visit paradise with him. That kind of joy only came once.

She dreaded for the day to be over, but the time came when Nick had to take them back to the port. Twilight had fallen all around them. After they'd floated alongside the pier and he'd jumped out of the boat to tie the ropes, she rummaged in the big diaper bag for the gift-wrapped package.

While he was still down on his haunches, she handed it to him.

"What's this?"

"It'll be Father's Day in a few hours. Before Jamie fell asleep, he asked me to give this to you. He told me to tell you he had the most wonderful day of his life out here with his daddy."

A stillness surrounded Nick before he undid the paper and discovered the sailboat. In the semidarkness his white smile stood out. He turned it this way and that. "The *Flying NJ?*"

"Yes. A Nick and Jamie partnership. He thought you might like to put it on your desk at work."

"Reese..." He stepped back in the boat. With his hand still holding his gift, he cupped her chin with the other, lifting her face to his gaze. "No one ever gave me a present like this before."

"That's because it's your first Father's Day and your son isn't very old yet," she teased to cover the intensity of her emotions.

He brushed his mouth against hers, melting her bones. "Where did you come from, Ms. Chamberlain?"

"The East 59th Street Employment Agency."

"My secretary did good work picking you. I'm going to have to give her a bonus."

"I'm glad she picked me, too. Jamie's…precious." Her voice caught before she moved away from him. She was in danger of begging him to take her below. If that happened, then a whole night alone with him would never be enough.

CHAPTER SEVEN

Two weeks later Reese entered the apartment building with Jamie after an afternoon of walking and shopping. The concierge called to her. "You have mail, Ms. Chamberlain."

She saw a postcard from Rich Bonner, his fourth, forwarded from the post office in Philadelphia to her temporary address here. His persistence irritated her. There was also a letter from Wharton. The school was no doubt reminding her of the test coming up in two weeks. She'd registered for it and would be taking it online.

"Thank you, Albert."

Once she'd tucked the mail in the sack, she went on up to the penthouse. Before she read anything, she had something more important to do. Jamie would be four months old in another week, but she couldn't wait for his birthday.

Her sister had one of those fold-out colorful quilts with the ends of a mobile sewn in. When you opened it and set it on the floor, the mobile sprang open. The baby would lie there on his back entertained with all kinds and colors of small blocks and shapes and mirrors dangling above him. When she'd been walking through the toy store, she saw one like it and had to buy it.

"You're going to love this," she told Jamie as she wheeled him down the hall to her bedroom. As soon as she washed her hands, she pushed him through to the nursery and changed his diaper in his crib. She left him long enough to wash her hands again, then hurried back.

The little Tigger clock she'd bought for him last week said it was five after four. Nick would be home any minute. She lived for this time of the day when he walked through the front door and said he was home. Today was Friday, which meant he'd be home for the whole weekend.

He was always the perfect employer, but since their outing on the boat when she'd come so close to making love with him, he hadn't touched her and the deprivation was killing her.

"Come on, sweetheart." She picked up the baby, pouring out all her love on him. "You're getting heavier, do you know that?" With a kiss, she knelt down on the floor with him where she could place him under the mobile on his back.

"There." A red ladybug hung from a coil so you could pull on it. She put it in his hand. His fingers tried to crush it and it sprang away. Reese laughed and put it in his hand again, thus commencing a game that had them both laughing. She was so involved, she didn't realize Nick had come in the room until he'd gotten down on the floor with them.

"This looks so fun I think I'll try it myself." His hip brushed against hers as he put his head inside to kiss his son.

Jamie was overjoyed to see his father. In the excitement his hands knocked several objects so they swung.

Reese was so excited to feel Nick's body next to her, she almost forgot to breathe.

His deep laughter rumbled through her, enchanting her. When he backed out, he suddenly pulled Reese closer so she was half lying on top of him with her face over his.

"A man could get used to looking up when there's so much to entice him." He undid the ribbon on her ponytail and her hair cascaded around her face. "I've been wanting to do this for weeks."

It was his fingers twining in her hair that opened the floodgates. With no immunity against the intensity of his desire, Reese couldn't help but lower her mouth to his, aching for the assuagement only he could give.

With slow deliberation he began to devour her. His breath was so sweet, so familiar, her senses swam. They kissed as if obeying some primitive rhythm. His lips traveled to the scented hollow of her throat. "You smell divine, do you know that? You feel divine."

"So do you." She let out a small gasp because the pressure of his mouth had changed, becoming so exquisite and loving, she would have fainted from pleasure if she weren't already on the floor with him.

He rolled her over on her back and kissed her passionately again and again until she couldn't tell where one kiss left off and another one began. Caught up in a euphoria such as she'd never known, she had no idea what time it was or how much time had passed until Jamie started to make hungry noises. Good heavens, the baby—

"He can wait for his bottle one more minute, or two, or three," Nick said in a voice raw with emotion, pressing another hot kiss to her mouth, each one growing more urgent than the last.

Reese agreed as she gave in to the needs building inside her. His charisma had drawn her to him from the start, but now it was his sheer, potent male sensuality that had ensnared her. The slight rasp of his jaw brought out a wanton side in her she didn't know she possessed. His hunger, never satisfied, was making her feel immortal.

Only Jamie's cries becoming louder had the power to bring her back to earth. "Nick—"

His answering groan of protest meant he'd been brought back, too. She felt his hard-muscled body roll away. Reese caught a glimpse of dark eyes glazed with the heat of their passion before he got to his feet.

She looked around, surprised to see his suit jacket and tie on the floor. He had to have discarded them in a hurry after he'd walked in. Reese lowered her head. What had she done? What was she doing?

Nick left the room with Jamie to get him a bottle. By the time she got to her feet, her body couldn't stop throbbing. She was completely dazed by emotions and feelings that had overwhelmed her. In a way it really frightened her. Nick had the power to take away her heart, soul, mind, will, *everything*—without even trying.

But it was *her* fault, not his. There was no force involved with him. All he had to do was touch her or say something and she was incapable of denying him or walking away. To do that, she would have to break her contract. But giving up Jamie would break her heart and leave Nick in a crisis until he found another nanny.

You've gotten yourself in a terrible mess, Reese.

In a druggedlike stupor, she picked up the sack and

almost threw it away before she remembered the mail inside it. After pulling it out, she tossed the bag in the wastebasket and looked at the postcard first. Laguna Beach.

Hey, beautiful— Wish you were here surfing with me. There are some waves rolling in with your name on them. By any chance did you get a letter from Wharton?

Reese stared at the unopened envelope in her hand.

I got one the other day. Email me either way, okay? Hope you are ready for the exam! Ciao for now. Rich.

She had no intention of contacting him, but she did have to admit she was curious about his mention of a letter. He wouldn't have said anything if all that was in it was the reminder of the exam coming up.

Nick must have carried Jamie out to the terrace to feed him. Thankful he'd disappeared to give her time to gather her wits, she wasted no time opening the letter. It was from the dean of her department no less.

Dear Ms. Chamberlain:

Two students whose academic achievement has set them above the rest of their graduating class have been given coveted internships for the coming fall semester. It is my privilege to inform you that you are one of those two remarkable scholars.

Congratulations, Ms. Chamberlain, on your outstanding record. I am proud and pleased to tell you that you have been placed with Miroff and Hooplan located on Broadway in New York City, as an analyst. You'll do research and make books, but more detailed information will be forthcoming from my office shortly.

I wanted you to receive this letter in plenty of time to find living accommodations and plan your finances accordingly.

Again may I express my personal satisfaction over your stellar performance here at Wharton. Miroff and Hooplan will be fortunate to have you.

Best Regards.

Reese pressed the letter to her chest. Miroff and Hooplan was on the top-ten list of brokerage companies in the nation. She couldn't believe it. This truly was a dream come true.

Was it the dean Mrs. Tribe had talked to when she'd been checking on Reese's background?

As for Rich, his question meant he'd received the other internship. She wondered where he would be working. All she had to do was email him and she'd find out. Maybe it was uncharitable, but she hoped it wasn't next door or across the street from Miroff and Hooplan!

Though an internship meant being on call 24/7 as a grunt, she would be a grunt in an exclusive brokerage house. She felt a shiver of excitement run thorough her. She read the letter over again. Her parents needed to hear about this. They'd loved and supported her all these years so that she could realize her dream. She owed them for many things, but especially for their belief in her ability to succeed. Now would be a good time to reach her mother.

After moving the quilt mobile away from the crib, she left the nursery for her bedroom to make the call.

"Where are *you* going in such a hurry?" Reese had been moving so fast, she'd almost run into Nick in the hall. Jamie was resting against his broad shoulder. After the way she'd lost it in his arms, she could hardly look at him yet without blushing or feeling the strong passion between them again. "When I stopped for my mail, Albert told me you received some, too. By the rate of your speed leaving the nursery, it must be important."

Nothing got past Nick. Nothing.

"Something from Jeremy maybe?"

Jeremy—

After kissing Nick as if her very life depended on it, her ex-fiancé had been so far from her mind, she'd forgotten he existed. Reese struggled for breath. On a burst of inspiration, she handed him the letter. She needed to prove to herself as well as to him that no matter how attracted she was to him, she was still on the path to forging a place for herself in the business world.

She felt the full force of his penetrating gaze before he scanned the contents. As she watched him, his demeanor began to change. He'd been so certain this was about her ex-fiancé.

When he lifted his eyes, she saw an expression of incredulity stamped across his striking features. "I knew you were a student, but I had no idea you were the caliber of scholar to have earned this kind of entrée into Miroff's."

"The letter came as a complete surprise to me," she said in a quiet voice. "I was about to phone my parents with the news."

There was a pause before he said, "When you asked me about the stock market, I understand now that it was no idle question." He didn't sound accusing exactly, but he didn't sound himself, either. She couldn't decipher his reaction.

"It wasn't an in-depth question, either." Reese felt strange having to explain herself to him. Until now there'd never been this void between them. She didn't understand it.

"Jeremy really didn't know the real you, did he."

Jeremy again. Why did Nick sound so cold? That was the only word that came close to describing his response. Anger or rudeness she might have tolerated, but this aloof side of him was something new. If they could just get on a better footing.

"Can I do anything for you or Jamie?"

He shook his dark head. "Now that I'm home, you're free for the weekend."

To hear him say that in an almost wintry tone of voice was like being banished to the outer darkness. This was pain in a new dimension. For once she didn't dare kiss Jamie.

"Before I forget, your house phone rang this morning. I picked up so it wouldn't waken the baby. Someone named Greg called, but he didn't leave a message. About an hour later a man named Lew phoned wanting to speak to you. When he realized you weren't here, he said he'd catch up with you at the Yacht Club tonight. If you need me to watch Jamie, I—"

"I don't," he broke in, "but I appreciate the offer." He handed her back the letter. When she took it, the postcard fell out of her hand. Nick grabbed it up before she could. If he'd looked for Jeremy's name before returning it to her, then he would be disappointed.

Summoning all her strength, she picked herself up off the ground mentally and smiled. "If something should change, I'll be in my room studying."

"For what exactly?"

"The G7 and G65." He knew what they were. Once upon a time he'd had to study for them, too. "My exam is coming up before the end of the month."

"I have no doubt you'll crush it." Why was there that glitter in his eyes? Just a little while ago they'd been glazed with desire.

"We'll see."

The quilt mobile Reese had bought for Jamie was another hit out of the ballpark. Nick sat in the rocking chair and leaned forward, watching his son play beneath it. All the objects stimulated him so much, it took him a long time before he fell asleep. That suited Nick, who needed time to wind down before he exploded with emotions so foreign to him, he didn't know himself anymore. This was Leah's doing.

—I've found someone I believe will suit you and the baby.

—As long as she likes children and is a real motherly type and not some cardboard creation, I bow to your wisdom. Tell me more about her.

—You once told me you prefer to attack a new project without listening to any other voices first while you form your own opinion. I think that's a good philosophy, especially in this case.

This case meaning a young woman who played dual roles to perfection.

Nick bit down hard. Reese had wanted a job that only lasted three months and she'd meant it! Jeremy-whatever-his-name was a fool for not having realized he'd never been in the running for the long haul.

But now that Nick had taken the time to calm down, he realized his anger at Jeremy had been misplaced. The fault lay in himself for assuming he could talk Reese into staying on as his nanny longer than just the summer. When he thought of her leaving now, he couldn't handle it.

Filled with fresh panic, he pulled out his cell and called his secretary.

"Nick? I'm glad you phoned. Greg, Lew and your father have been trying to reach you. He told me to tell you the time for the Yacht Club party tonight has been changed from six-thirty to seven. I left the message on your voice mail."

"Thank you." He shot out of the rocking chair and wandered through the joining door to his bedroom. "Leah? How many women did you interview for the nanny position?"

"Four. Does this mean Ms. Chamberlain isn't working out?"

His hand almost crushed his phone. "She's working out very well, but I'm thinking of the future."

"What happened to the Cosgriffs' nanny?"

"Nothing that I know of, but I've decided I don't want her to come."

"Would you like me to start looking again?"

"Not quite yet, but I am curious. How many applied?"

"I believe Mr. Lloyd said they had five hundred and forty applications on hand."

Considering the state of the economy, he shouldn't have been surprised. "How did you tell him to screen them?"

"I asked him to pick out the ones with the highest education."

He rubbed the back of his neck in surprise. "That was it?"

"Yes. Those with undergraduate degrees or higher still wanting to take a nanny job for only three months would have something else going on in their brain. When he gave me the four names, I started making calls, checking references.

"One of Ms. Chamberlain's professors told me she had a spark of genius in her. That was a plus. She came from a family with five siblings and was the youngest applicant of the four, which I felt was another point in her favor. You have to be able to move quick and get down on the floor with a baby."

A wave of heat flooded Nick's system when he remembered what he'd been doing on the nursery floor with her less than two hours ago.

"What tipped the scales in her favor?"

"You mean you haven't found that out yet?"

Another layer of heat poured off him. Leah knew him too well. They had few secrets. One thing he could count on was her honesty.

"Did you know she was given an internship as an analyst at Miroff and Hooplan for the fall?"

"Well, I'll be damned. Good for her."

Nick had found out all he needed to know. "Talk to you later. And Leah—"

"Yes?"

"Thank you."

Before Jamie woke up, Nick needed to do damage control.

Reese had changed into white cargo pants and a khaki blouse. When she heard the knuckle rap, she was on her way out with no destination in mind. She'd lived through a tumult of emotions this afternoon and needed to walk until she dropped.

Grabbing her purse, she opened the door. Nick stood there without Jamie, his arm braced against the doorjamb. She braved his penitent gaze and felt her heart thud because the darkness she'd felt from him earlier seemed to have gone.

He studied her with relentless scrutiny, as if looking for some sign that he might be welcome. "To my shame I've overstepped my bounds twice now. You're a very attractive woman, but that's no excuse for my behavior every time I get within touching distance of you. I swear that as long as you're in my employ, you have nothing more to fear from me."

His words filled her with pain, but relief, too, because it meant no permanent damage had been done. She eyed him directly. "I was a willing participant, so it's obvious I haven't exactly been afraid of you, Nick."

"Nevertheless is there the possibility that you would forgive me and we could start over? Whatever else went on with me earlier has nothing to do with you. The thought that you might decide to leave me and Jamie before time terrifies the living daylights out of me."

A small smile broke the corners of her mouth. "It terrifies me, too, because I need the money you're paying me."

One dark brow dipped. "Do you need it enough to come with me this evening? We'll be taking Jamie to a party."

She folded her arms. "Why do I get the feeling this isn't just any party?"

"My parents expect me to marry again and have a woman picked out to become the next Mrs. Nicholas

Wainwright. Her name is Jennifer Ridgeway. I haven't seen her since her teens, but be assured her pedigree forms part of the framework of the upper crust. She'll be at the Yacht Club with her parents."

"I can see you're planning an all-out revolt."

"Yes." Reese could swear she saw fire in his eyes. "The sight of my son with his unsuitable nanny will dash every hope on all sides and make a statement that nothing else could do. It will be my virtual abdication from the family."

Whoa.

She felt Nick's conviction to her bones and knew tonight would change the course of his life and Jamie's forever. More than anything she wanted to be along to watch history being made.

"What should I wear?"

The lines darkening his face vanished. She saw his chest rise and fall due to the strength of his emotions. "How about that yellow outfit with a white ribbon around your ponytail?"

"I can do that. What about you?"

"No pedigreed member of the Yacht Club shows up in anything but formal dress. I'll wear a tux."

"And Jamie?"

A smile hovered around his compelling mouth. "His navy outfit with the Snoopy and his white high-tops. He'll be the first baby who ever made it inside the doors. If you're ready for Miroff and Hooplan, I know you'll be able to handle this crowd."

Her eyes suddenly moistened without her volition. That crowd included his parents, the two people responsible for bringing him into the world. She knew deep down somewhere he loved them because they *were* his parents. They'd bestowed every gift on him, given him every opportunity. There'd only been one thing lacking. She kept swallowing, trying to get rid of the thickness closing up her throat.

"How soon do you want to leave?"

"As soon as you can get Jamie and yourself ready. We'll be flying out to Long Island in the helicopter."

"I've had my shower. All I have to do is change clothes, then I'll take care of the baby and load his diaper bag."

He held her gaze. "One thing before we leave."

Adrenaline caused her heart to pound hard. "What is it?"

"I couldn't help but see the name of the person who sent you the postcard. Who's Rich?"

"My study partner at Wharton."

Nick cocked his head. "Does he measure up to your brilliance?"

Since emailing Rich a little while ago, Reese decided she'd better tell him now. "His full name is Richard Bonner."

His brows knit together. "That sounds familiar."

"It's because he just received word from the dean that he's been chosen to do an internship at Sherborne and Wainwright this fall."

He gave her an incredulous stare. "For years my uncle Lew has been in charge of choosing the interns. If they're not bright enough for him, he won't take one."

"Then there you go. Rich is the original whiz kid. He's apoplectic with joy about being chosen to work for the top company in New York. In case you're wondering, he has no idea you're my employer and I have no intention of ever telling him. Just imagine how crazy that would have been if you'd been stuck with me for a second round."

"Crazy doesn't begin to describe it," he ground out.

Two hours later the helicopter started to make its landing. Nick turned to her. "Welcome to The Sea Nook Yacht Club, listed on New York's Historical Register. Former home to the tall ships on Long Island's Gold Coast. Members only."

As it set down, Reese found the sight of the sprawling Tudor/Elizabethan estate overlooking the ocean surreal. Sailboats and yachts with pennants fluttering dotted the marina and beyond. To her, the world Nick had inhabited all these years was just as fantastic in its own way as Middle Earth or the Land of Oz.

Jamie reached for her after they climbed out of the helicopter. She held him as they walked next to Nick, who carried the baby's carryall and diaper bag across the grounds to the entrance. He looked adorable in his little navy suit. One day he would grow up to be as fantastic-looking as his gorgeous father, whose appearance in a black tux blew her away.

Nick had told her he wanted to arrive before anyone else. He preferred that his parents make the entrance with the Ridgeways instead of the other way around. The sight of Nick already installed with his nanny and child would set the ground rules in concrete for the future.

The club had its own concierge, a burly man complete with beard, dressed like a proper sea captain in a smashing blazer and slacks. He swept across the enormous foyer with a smile on his face. "Good evening, Mr. Wainwright."

"How are you, Max?"

"Very well indeed. It's been a long time since we last saw you here. May I take this opportunity to tell you how sorry I am about the loss of Mrs. Wainwright? It was a shock to everyone."

"Thank you."

"You're the first of your party to arrive. We've put you out in the conservatory. Your father wanted the best view and we were able to accommodate him."

"Thank you."

The man's gaze flicked to Reese. "On vacation are you, miss? I'm sorry, but only members of the Yacht Club are allowed inside. You're welcome to stroll about the grounds with your child, of course."

Nick's eyes caught hers for a moment. She saw a wicked gleam of amusement in their dark depths. He was enjoying this. "She's with me, Max. Ms. Chamberlain is my nanny and this is my son, Jamie. He's just out of the hospital and won't be separated from us yet."

Reese had to give the host points for his aplomb in an awkward situation he'd most likely never had to deal with before. She could hear him trying to decide how to handle this. He cleared his throat. "Of course. Go right on out."

"Thank you, Max."

Reese had to put up with unfriendly stares and lifted brows from the beautiful people decked out in formal attire. Nick appeared oblivious. He led her through some tall paneled doors to another section of the club, which had to have been someone's spectacular estate at one time.

They came to a private room with high paneled ceilings, all of it surrounded by floor-to-ceiling glass windows, a modern innovation. It was almost like being on the water. He pulled out a chair where he put Jamie's carryall, then fastened him in it.

Reese sat down next to the baby. "I believe if I were prone to it, I'd be seasick about now."

A heart-stopping smile broke the corner of his mouth. "It's been known to happen in this room."

"What's the history of this place?"

He took a rattle from the diaper bag and handed it to Jamie, who claimed it in a fist and put it directly in his mouth. They both laughed.

"My mother's ancestor, Martin Sherborne, was an English sea captain in the early 1600s who traded in all sorts of lucrative things that brought him wealth. When he bought up a lot of the land around Sea Nook and had this place built, the colonial governor of New York conferred the title of Lordship of Sherborne on him.

"Eventually his grandson donated this place to the Sea Nook Township and built Sherborne House where my mother grew up. It's located about ten miles from here. The estate borders Wainwright Meadows, known for its horses, where my father was born."

"How did they amass their wealth?"

"His ancestry developed tools for steam engines. Their manufacture proliferated beyond anyone's expectations. For those who live here, Sea Nook is known as Little England."

The sommelier approached, wanting to know their preference of wine. Nick turned to her. "Nothing for me," she responded.

"We'll both wait," Nick told him.

Reese leaned over to kiss the baby. "Did you hear all that your daddy said, Jamie? You could have been its newest prince," she teased, but she shouldn't have said anything because she saw Nick's jaw harden.

"*Could have* is exactly right. Don't look now but my cousin Greg has just arrived. It appears he's alone. He and his wife live at our property in the Hamptons. They're having difficulties right now."

Add one more property to the growing list. "Are you close to him?"

"No, but he works in the office and so far we've managed to get along."

"That's something at least."

When Nick smiled like that, she couldn't breathe. "At least," he drawled. "I'm afraid I've overloaded you with too much information."

"Not at all. It's like attending an on-site live college course covering the aspects of upper-class society in Colonial America. I wouldn't have missed it for the world."

"Greg!" Nick stood up and shook his cousin's hand. He was dark like Nick, a little shorter and heavier. "This is Reese Chamberlain from Lincoln, Nebraska. Reese, this is Greg Wainwright, one of the vice presidents of the brokerage."

"How do you do, Greg." She extended her hand, which he shook. Nick's cousin couldn't take his eyes off her. Nick didn't blame him. Anyone seeing Reese with that oval face and high cheekbones would call her a classic beauty. In the candlelight her light blue eyes let off an iridescent glow.

"Come around and say hi to Jamie."

His cousin's gaze shifted to the baby, but he didn't move from his stance. He flashed Nick one of those looks that said he needed to speak to him in private. *Not this time.* Nick had an idea what it was all about. In fact he'd been anticipating it.

"Won't you sit down? Or are you waiting for Uncle Lew?"

Greg shifted his weight, a sign that he was losing patience. "I need to talk to you alone for a minute. I tried to reach you earlier."

"I'm aware of that. You can say anything you want in front of Reese."

"Father sent me in here to talk sense to you."

"What sense is that?"

"This is a special dinner party." His brows lifted. "Max has let everyone know the…three of you are here," he said in a quieter voice.

Good. "Let's call a spade a spade. This was planned so the widower could meet wife number two, but my life has changed since Erica's death, Greg. No one owns me."

His face closed up. "Then I'm afraid you'll be dining in here alone."

"My parents should have thought of that before they tried to maneuver me into something that would hurt the Ridgeways. The fact is, no one consulted me. I intend to enjoy my dinner with my son and Ms. Chamberlain. You can tell that to Uncle Lew in private. What he tells father is up to him."

Greg studied him through new eyes. "What's happened to you?" It was a genuine question, requiring a genuine answer.

"The truth? I became a father, but I discovered I want to be a dad. Ms. Chamberlain is teaching me how."

His cousin seemed to have trouble articulating before he nodded to Reese and walked out of the room.

"Nick—"

The tremor in her voice was one of the most satisfying sounds he'd ever heard.

"The swordfish here is excellent by the way. If I order it for you, I promise you won't be disappointed."

CHAPTER EIGHT

For five solid days starting the next Monday, Reese took Jamie with her every morning and afternoon to hunt for an unfurnished studio apartment near Miroff's located on Broadway and Seventh. She needed one close enough to walk to her job.

By midafternoon she finally found it six blocks away above a small bookstore with signs saying that it was going out of business. You had to enter the store and walk to the back where there was a circular staircase leading to the studio. Both were owned by the bank.

She couldn't allow herself to think about where she was living right now. Moving from Nick's thirty-million-dollar penthouse to the tiny hole-in-the-wall that had no AC would be like going from the proverbial sublime to the proverbial ridiculous.

In order to hold it, she arranged for a six-month sub-lease starting now, even though the two guys living there wouldn't move out until the end of August. She would buy a futon and use it for a bed. Reese wouldn't need anything else since she'd be slaving day and night at the brokerage. If she was careful, the salary Nick paid her would cover the rent through January.

The small stipend she received from Miroff's would

have to be enough for her food and any other incidentals. But at least she'd taken care of her housing problem and could spend the next week studying for her exam coming up a week from today. With a sigh of relief she phoned Paul and asked him to drive her and Jamie to the park.

"This is more like it, huh." She gave him a bunch of kisses before carrying him over to the pond. "You like these sailboats?" In her mind's eye she could see the larger sleeker ones and yachts moored at Sea Nook. That night had marked another change in Nick. He seemed charged by a new energy.

Throwing off the yoke of his other self acted as some kind of catharsis. Twice this week he'd come home early, pulled on a pair of jeans with a T-shirt and made dinner. He put Jamie in the swing to watch him and held long conversations with him. When everything was ready, he'd invite her to eat on the terrace with them.

He cooked steaks and potatoes both times, reminding her of her father, who was a meat and potatoes man, too.

"Oh—my phone's ringing. Let's find out who it is." She pulled out her cell, but didn't recognize the name on the caller ID. After a slight hesitation she clicked on.

"Hello?"

"Ms. Chamberlain? This is Albert."

"Hi, Albert!"

"Sorry to disturb, but you have a visitor and I knew you'd gone out. He says it's urgent that he sees you. His name is Jeremy Young."

Reese closed her eyes tightly. She didn't blame her ex-fiancé for coming all this way without telling her. If their situations were reversed and she couldn't let him go without trying one more time, she would do the same thing. Her dad had probably told him about the internship and he'd made up his mind to talk to her again in the hope she wouldn't take it.

But it was no use. Their romance wasn't meant to be. Her plans for the future were set. She was so close now.

And then of course there was Nick. Every living moment with him meant falling deeper and deeper in love. She wouldn't be with him much longer, but it didn't matter. He'd colored her life forever. Nick and Jamie had her heart. All of it.

"I'm leaving for the apartment right now. Would you mind letting him in the penthouse? He's flown all the way from Nebraska and will appreciate freshening up before I get there."

"I'll be happy to."

"Thank you."

She hung up. "Let's go home, Jamie. We've got company."

When she pushed the stroller into the apartment a short time later, Jeremy stepped in the foyer from the living room.

"Reese—"

His was a dear face. Familiar, yet she couldn't conjure any feeling for him. Six months ago she couldn't have imagined not flying into his arms.

"It's good to see you, Jeremy." He was an attractive six-foot blond with dark blue eyes. He wore jeans and a button-down shirt with the hems out, his usual style when he wasn't in a business suit. But the wide smile that had been his trademark was missing. She saw pain in his eyes.

"You're not angry I just showed up?" he asked with an edge.

"No. How could I be? I'm only sad that you spent your time and hard-earned money for nothing."

"That's a matter of opinion. I've had some time to think since your dad told me you got that internship. I'd like to talk to you about it."

"Of course. Come out on the terrace with me and Jamie." She pushed the stroller through the apartment.

The second she opened the sliding door and they walked out, he let go with a long, low whistle. She watched him walk over to look out on the city. "My hell… I know there are people in the world who live like this, but to see it all up close makes me think I'm hallucinating."

"I've done a lot of that myself." She put Jamie on the lounger and changed him. Jeremy returned as she was snapping his suit.

"He's a cute baby. How old is he?"

"Four months."

"How much longer will you be here?"

"Until the end of August. That's when I start at Miroff's."

"Reese," he whispered. "I'll move to New York and get a bank job. If you're determined to be a career woman, then so be it. I don't want to lose you."

She hugged Jamie to herself, needing a minute to comprehend what he was saying. Reese could only imagine what it had taken for him to come to her like this. She needed to be so careful, but whatever she said, he was going to be hurt.

Taking a fortifying breath, she faced him. "I'll always love you, Jeremy, but I've had months to think about everything, too. Your instinct is to be the provider and come home to a wife who takes care of you and your children. A lot of men are like that. It's a wonderful instinct.

"What's wrong is that you met a woman like me who needs intellectual stimulation beyond mothering. I'd like to believe that in time I can do both. If we did get back together again, I'm sure it wouldn't be long before you'd start resenting me and I'd get upset with you because I would know I wasn't making you happy. It just wouldn't work."

"You're different than before," he said on a burst of anger.

She pressed her lips together. "I've had to put you away. It wasn't easy."

"But the point is, you *have* let me go."

"Yes," she answered honestly. This tearing each other apart was exactly what she didn't want to happen. "Jamie needs his bottle. I have to get it from the kitchen." Jeremy followed her. She took it out of the fridge and warmed it in the microwave.

"Has the baby's father made moves on you already?"

"Jeremy—please let's not do this."

"That's what you say when you want to avoid the issue."

She took the bottle out of the microwave. "I think you'd better go."

"No wonder you don't want to work anything out. There's nothing to stop you from staying on here permanently. You live in a virtual palace with New York at your feet. The money he's paying you is probably more than I make in a year at the bank."

Reese held the baby in her arms and fed him, praying Jeremy would see the futility in this and leave.

"Anyone home?"

Nick's deep male voice preceded him into the kitchen. She was sure Albert would have told him Jeremy was up here. Nick had announced himself in order to warn her he was on his way in.

The look on Jeremy's face reminded her of the Hirsts' expressions when they'd walked in the kitchen and had come face-to-face with Reese. Nick was a breed apart from other men. His polish and sophistication couldn't be denied. Besides his compelling physical attributes, there was something else you felt just being in his presence.

"Nick Wainwright?" She tried to keep her voice steady. "This is Jeremy Young."

Always the urbane host, Nick extended his hand. "It's nice to meet you, Jeremy."

"Likewise, Mr. Wainwright. You have a cute son."

"Thanks. I think so, too. Please excuse me for interrupting. I came to find him so we could play for a while." His eyes darted Reese an enigmatic glance before he lifted Jamie out of her arms. The baby was still drinking his bottle. "We're going out to the terrace, aren't we, sport."

Quiet reigned after his tall, hard-muscled body left the kitchen. Jeremy's eyes narrowed on Reese's upturned features. "Well…*that* just answered every question."

"Jeremy—" she called after him, but he was out of the kitchen and the penthouse like a shot.

He'd given her no choice by showing up without having called her first. How she hated hurting him. But if meeting Nick convinced him Reese was involved with her employer, then it had to be a good thing. Otherwise

Jeremy would go on hoping for something that could never happen.

She rubbed her arms, feeling at a totally loose end. She was too tired from walking so much to go out again, but if she stayed in, she knew she wouldn't be able to study. Nick needed his time with Jamie. That left TV. Maybe a good film was on.

In the end she didn't bother to turn it on. Instead she flopped across her bed in turmoil. Five more weeks to go, but Reese was in trouble. The ache for Nick was growing intolerable.

She flung herself over on her back. Somehow she would have to find a way to be around Nick every day and not let him know the kind of pain she was in.

An hour later hunger drove her to the kitchen where she found him making ham-and-cheese sandwiches. She felt his gaze scrutinize her. "Do you and Jeremy have plans later?"

She shook her head. "He'll probably be back in Lincoln by tomorrow."

"Did you know he was coming?"

"No. His arrival was a complete surprise. Albert called me while Jamie and I were at the park."

He pursed his lips. "Then let's eat. Grab us a couple of colas from the fridge and we'll go out on the terrace."

"That sounds good."

He reached for a bag of potato chips. Together they carried everything outside to the table. After they sat down, she opened her cola and drank almost half of it, not realizing how thirsty she was.

Nick relaxed in the chair, extending his long legs in front of him while he swallowed two sandwiches in succession. "Leah and I had a conversation the other day. When she chose you for the nanny, there were three other women who could have done the job. One of them is probably still available to work. But even if they've all found other employment, there'll be someone else."

A sharp, stabbing pain almost incapacitated her. "Why are you telling me this?"

"Because you need to be free to work things out with Jeremy. The man didn't fly all this way unless he were still terribly in love with you. I saw the look on his face. He couldn't say what he had to say with me walking in on him. If you go home now, it's possible you'll straighten out your differences and end up getting married."

Nick's last stab had dissected her heart. "You mean the way you and Erica straightened out yours?" Her pain had to find an outlet. He might just as well have been her patronizing uncle Chet patting her on the head and telling her she was too pretty to study so much. The guys would be intimidated.

He stopped eating and sat forward. "I was never in love with her."

The bald revelation was swallowed up in her pain because he wasn't in love with Reese, either. Not even close or he couldn't have suggested she abandon Jamie and follow Jeremy home.

In a rare display of sarcasm she said, "Well, that's an excellent explanation for why your marriage fell apart. Jeremy and I have irreconcilable problems *now,* and would never make it to the altar."

"Love is a rare thing," he came back in a mild mannered voice, the kind that set her teeth on edge. "You had that going for you once. He hasn't given up. It appears to me that anything's still possible."

"Not when he doesn't want a working wife."

"Would it be so terrible if you compromised in order for the two of you to be together?"

"Terrible?" she cried. "It would be disastrous."

"Why?"

"Because then neither of us would be happy." She shook her head. "You really don't understand. Let me ask you something. After you'd studied all those years to make your place at Wainwright's, what if Erica had said, 'You don't need to go to work now, Nick. Stay home with me. I have enough money to take care of both of us for a lifetime.'"

His lids drooped so the black lashes shuttered his eyes. "You can't use me or Erica for an example."

The first sparks of temper shot through her. "Why not? Blue bloods still make up part of our world, albeit a tiny percentage of the population."

She watched him squeeze his cola can till it dented. "Because for one thing, the kind of love that should bind a man and woman didn't define our relationship."

"Supposing it had?"

Nick didn't like being put on the spot. It only made her more determined to get her point across.

"What if you'd both been crazy about each other and she'd told you she wanted you to be home with her and the baby. Several babies maybe. What would you have said?"

His hand absently rubbed his chest. "It's an absurd question, Reese."

"Of course it's absurd to *you*. You're a man, right? And in the world you've come from, a man is better than a woman." She jumped to her feet, unable to keep still.

A white ring of anger had encircled his lips, but she couldn't stop now. "It would be purgatory for you if you couldn't get up every morning of life eager to match wits against your competitors.

"I heard your whole genealogy the other night at the Yacht Club. You come from an ancestry that made things happen. Like them you live to pull off another million deal today, and another one tomorrow, and all the tomorrows after that. It's what makes you, *you*."

He pushed himself away from the table and stood up. "And you're telling me you feel the exact same way?"

She let out a caustic laugh. "That's inconceivable to you, isn't it. *Moi?* A mere woman who has that same fire in her? Impossible. A woman who wants to make a difference? Unheard of, right?"

"Frankly, yes," he said in a voice of irony, "particularly when I see the way you are with Jamie. No one would ever guess you weren't his mother."

"You're not even listening to me because in your eyes a woman can't be both." She circled in front of him. "Let me tell you something about yourself, Nick. Though you've come a long way to rid yourself of the shackles imposed by thirty-four years of emotional neglect, you'll never be a man who could compromise on something so vital to your very existence as your work."

The glitter in those black depths should have warned her, but she was just getting warmed up.

"Yet you hand out advice to me and suggest I go home to patch things up with Jeremy as if my problem is nothing more than a bagatelle that can be swept under the rug. Be a good girl and do what girls are supposed to do, Reese. Let Jeremy take care of business so you can take care of his babies. Compromise for the sake of your love.

That's great advice, Mr. Wainwright, as long as *you're* not the one being forced to do the compromising."

"Are you finished?" he asked as if he'd grown tired of her tantrum. She couldn't bear his condescension.

"Not quite," she fired back. "One day I intend to open my own brokerage company right here in New York and be a *huge* success. In the meantime I'm contracted with you to take care of Jamie until I start my internship at Miroff's. For your information I never renege on my commitments, unlike you who would send me back to Nebraska on the next flight without a qualm."

She paused at the sliding door. "If you need me, I'll be in my bedroom studying."

Nick buzzed his secretary. "Leah? I'll be in Lew's office for a while." He'd done a little research and had requested this conference. "Hold my calls." If Reese needed him, she'd phone his cell. But she didn't need or want anything from him.

He still had the scars from their scalding conversation of three weeks ago. Nothing about their routine had altered since then, but the atmosphere had undergone a drastic change. When they talked about Jamie, everything was civil, but the gloom that had enveloped him after Erica had died couldn't compare to the darkness enveloping him now. A wall of ice had grown around his nanny. He couldn't find her anywhere. Her love and animation were reserved exclusively for his son.

Unable to take it, he'd gone off to Martha's Vineyard with Jamie every Friday afternoon. They'd sailed the whole weekend. Sunday nights he returned to the penthouse, always finding her bedroom door closed. He'd see the light beneath and know she was in there.

Today he knew she was taking her online exam. When he'd told her he would stay home to keep Jamie occupied, she'd told him it wouldn't be necessary. She'd handle both just fine, underscoring her assertions made during their heated exchange earlier.

On that black night Reese had delivered some salvos he'd never seen coming. Stunned by their impact, he'd barely functioned since then. This morning he'd found himself floundering in a dark sea and knew he couldn't go this way any longer.

The emotional temperature was distinctly cooler in his uncle's office. Lew sat at his desk, more or less squinting up at Nick as he walked in. Nick had committed the unpardonable at the club for which he'd been collectively shunned by the family.

That didn't bother him, but it had thrown Lew out of his comfort zone. The business Nick was about to conduct with him would dissolve what little relationship they had left. This meeting would supply the final punctuation mark.

"What was so important I had to tell my secretary to cancel my last two appointments for the day?"

Nick sat on the arm of one of the leather love seats. "I'm resigning from the company effective immediately and wanted you to be the first to know, besides Leah, of course."

"What?" Suddenly the mask of implacability fell from his face to reveal a vulnerability Nick had never seen before. "You haven't told Stan? Not even your father?"

"No. I'll leave that to you since you're closest to them."

"But you *can't* resign—this place would fall around our ears without you."

A genuine emotion for once. Who would have believed?

"I've named Greg as my replacement in the resignation letter I gave to Leah this morning. It's been dated and notarized. Your son has earned the right to head the firm. I've earned the right to do what's best for me."

He shook his head, clearly aghast. "What are your plans?"

"I'm keeping those to myself for the time being. This is my last day here. Except for a few personal items I'm taking with me, my office is ready for Greg to claim. My accounts are now his. Leah will stay on as his private secretary to make certain there's a smooth transition."

His uncle rose slowly to his feet. "Are you dying of a fatal disease?"

Nick made a sound in his throat. Illness was the only reason Lew could possibly imagine for one of the family to do something unprecedented and heretical.

"In a manner of speaking, but that's confidential. I'll be seeing you." He got up from the chair to shake his hand. His uncle's response reminded him of a person who'd just gone into shock.

On Nick's way out he stopped by Leah's office. "Is everything done?"

"It is."

"Did you get everything I needed?"

"It's all there in your briefcase. Paul's waiting out in front."

"You're the best friend a man ever had." The fact that it was a woman didn't escape him.

He slipped her an envelope with a check in it made

out to her, gave her a hug, then rode down the elevator and walked out of the building as if he had wings on his feet. A few minutes later he walked in the door of the penthouse feeling as if he'd been given his get-out-of-jail-free card.

"Reese?"

When she didn't answer, he headed for the terrace. The second he opened the sliding door he could hear her laughter. Over the hedge he could see her and Jamie in the pool. She'd pinned her ponytail on top of her head and was pulling him around on an inflated plastic duck. Evidently her exam was over and she'd decided to let off some excess energy. She was a knockout in that tangerine-colored bikini.

Since Reese hadn't seen him yet, he dashed back to his bedroom and changed into his swimming trunks. On his way out he grabbed a couple of bath towels and headed for the pool once more.

To his delight she and Jamie were still moving around in the water. She sprinkled his tummy several times, provoking little laughs from him. Would the day might come when she'd do that to Nick, but it would be more than laughter she'd get in return.

He dived in the deep end and swam underwater on purpose where he could feast his eyes on her long, gorgeous legs. They were an enticement he couldn't resist, but he *had* to.

A few feet from her, he surfaced and heaved himself up on the tile. She was all eyes when he came out of the water. *"Nick—"*

Yes, Nick. For a split second he could have sworn he saw longing in them before she turned to Jamie, who'd become her shield. "How was the exam?" His eyes were drawn to the small nerve throbbing at the base of her throat.

"Maybe I had a different battery than others who've taken it, but it wasn't as hard as I'd thought it would be."

"I'm sure you're glad it's over."

"Definitely." She twirled the duck around so Jamie could see him. "He's been waiting for you to come home."

What a sight! Her blue eyes were more dazzling than the water. He slid back in the pool and swam over to his son.

"Look at you having the time of your life out here." Jamie almost fell out of the floater trying to get to him. With a laugh, Nick caught him up to his shoulder and kissed him. While he was enjoying his son, Reese did a backflip and swam to the other end of the pool to get out. It was a good exit line, but he wasn't about to let her get away with it.

"Reese?" She looked back at him as she was about to walk off. "Whatever your plans are this evening, I need to talk to you first. Give me ten minutes and I'll meet you in the dining room."

"All right."

When she'd gone, he looked down at Jamie. "We've got to get out and dressed, sport. Tonight's kind of important." He swam over to the steps and climbed out. After wrapping him in a towel, he headed for the nursery and put him in a diaper and shirt.

Since he seemed content, Nick let him stay in the crib with his pacifier. Then he went to his bedroom to shower and change into trousers and a sport shirt.

Fifteen minutes later he gathered Jamie and the

swing. Reese was already waiting for them at the table in the dining room with her ponytail redone. The waiter had already brought their meal and had set everything up.

With Jamie ensconced in the swing, Nick was able to concentrate on Reese, who'd changed into a pale blue cotton top and denims. "Do you like lamb?" He lifted the covers off their plates.

"I love it."

"Then I think you'll enjoy Cesar's rack of lamb." So saying, he poured both of them water before starting to eat.

She followed suit. "Sounds like you're celebrating."

"I thought it sounded like a good idea. Your exam is over, and a Greek friend of mine named Andreas Simonides has invited me to spend some time with him and his wife, Gabi, on the island of Milos in the Aegean. We met a few years ago when we were both single and did some sailing together. He has stayed here at the penthouse on several occasions. He's married now with a three-month-old baby girl himself and is anxious to meet Jamie. So I told him I'd come."

"That sounds exciting." She was doing her best to act pleased for him, but she'd been with him and Jamie every day for weeks now. The thought of a separation caused such a great upheaval inside her, she could hardly breathe from the pain.

"I think so, too."

"When are you leaving?"

"Tomorrow morning."

That soon? "How long will you be gone?" She fought to keep her voice steady.

"Two weeks."

She didn't have time to hide her shock.

"Now that I've got Jamie, I feel like a long holiday. You'll be coming with us of course. His wife is an American, which will be nice for you."

Reese and Gabi sat in deck chairs on the patio surrounding the pool of the Simonides villa, watching the babies in their swings. Little Cristiana was as golden-blonde as Jamie was dark headed. They looked adorable together. Reese had never envied anyone until now, but she envied Gabi, who had Andreas's love and his baby.

Moaning inwardly, she looked all around her. The Simonides' family retreat was so gorgeous, it was beyond impossible to describe. A myriad of white, cubed-styled villas were clustered against the cliff abounding in flowers of every color and greenery all the way down to the water. There the white sand merged with an aquamarine ocean that took your breath.

This morning the men had gone fishing early, but they'd promised to be back by lunchtime. Reese's holiday would have been heaven on earth if she and Nick were lovers, but such wasn't the case. Nick had behaved like the perfect employer, albeit a kind, generous one. But he'd kept his distance and had given her plenty of time off so she could enjoy herself without having to tend Jamie every second.

Gabi was a sweetheart. She'd been the manager of an advertising agency back in Alexandria, Virginia, so they had a lot in common. The two of them had taken to each other at once and had flown to Athens several times to meet other members of the Simonides clan. They shopped and went to the opera, but for the most part, the time was spent on Andreas's fabulous gleaming white luxury cabin cruiser probably forty to forty-five feet long.

With the babies, the four of them visited all the wonders of the island. They walked through the little villages, ate local food, swam at the unique beaches and soaked up the Grecian sun in absolute luxury. But this idyllic time was fast coming to a close. Tomorrow they were due to fly back to New York.

True to their word, Nick came out on the patio with Andreas, both in shorts and nothing else, just as lunch was about to be served. The latter kissed his wife soundly before pulling Cristiana out of her swing to kiss her.

Writhing with unassuaged longings, Reese got up and slipped on her beach jacket while Nick grabbed Jamie and got into the pool with him. When they emerged and everyone was seated around the patio table eating, Nick glanced at her. "I've made arrangements for one of the maids to tend Jamie this afternoon so I can take you to a beach you haven't seen before."

"It's our favorite spot on Milos," Andreas said, covering his wife's hand.

"That sounds wonderful," Reese murmured, though something inside told her she'd be a fool to spend that much time alone with Nick. But she didn't want to argue in front of their hosts who'd been so fabulous to them, she'd never be able to repay them.

"Good. You're already in your bathing suit, so as soon as you've finished eating, we'll go."

Reese swallowed the last of her iced lemon drink and got up to give Jamie a goodbye kiss. "Be a good boy. We'll be back soon." The baby got all excited. His reaction warmed her heart.

"We'll go down this path." He started ahead of her. They zigzagged down to the private pier lined on both sides with various types of boats. Nick headed for a small jet boat they hadn't ridden in yet.

When he helped her to climb in, she felt fire shoot up her arm. This really wasn't a good idea, but she'd said she would go. Somehow she needed to turn off the hormones. To her chagrin she didn't know how.

Nick was so at home on the water, you would have thought he lived here year-round. After handing her a life jacket and telling her to put it on, he untied the ropes and they backed out into the blue bay. Once they got beyond the buoys, they sped through the glasslike water of the Aegean. Glorious.

When he turned his head and smiled at her, she was in such a euphoric state, she felt as if they were flying. "There's no beach in the world like the one you're going to see."

"I can't imagine anything more beautiful than the ones we've been to already."

"Papafragas is different. Have you had a good time so far? Feel like you've gotten away from all your studies and worries?"

Her lips curved into a full-bodied smile. "A good time?" she mocked. "That's like asking me if I've been having a good time in paradise."

"There are levels of excitement, even in paradise."

She averted her eyes. Yes. To be loved and make love with Nick would be the pinnacle, the only part of paradise she would never know.

They eventually drew close to another part of the island. Nick cut the motor and the momentum drove them toward a cave opening.

"I feel like a pirate."

He flashed her a penetrating glance. "Andreas tells me they used to roam these waters. We'll swim from here." Nick got out of his seat and lowered the anchor. "If you get tired, you've got your life jacket on to support you and I'll take us the rest of the way."

At the thought of him touching her one more time, adrenaline shot through her system, driving her to her feet. Without waiting for Nick, she leaped off the side and headed through the cave opening. Once beyond it she realized it was a long, natural, fjordlike swimming pool surrounded by walls of white rock.

"This is fantastic!"

"This is fantastic!" came the echo. She laughed in delight.

He caught up to her and they did the side stroke as they headed for the other end. His dark eyes held hers. "There are half a dozen caves in here. If we had more time, we could explore them."

Time. Her enemy.

Another fifty yards lay a strip of warm white sand from the sun finding its way down between the walls of rock. Nick reached it first and pulled her onto the sand. They both turned over to lie on their backs.

"You were right, Nick. This beach is incredible."

"Andreas said he used to come here with his brother Leon to play space aliens."

Her laughter rang out over and over because of the echo. "I love it here!" she cried. Again, her words reverberated, *Love it here, love it here, love it here.*

"You sound happy, Reese."

"Not happy. Something so much more, but there is no word in English for what I'm feeling right now."

"Then you admit you needed a vacation, too."

She let out an exasperated sound. "You know I did. I've been in school for so long, I almost forgot what it's like to play. Of course there's playing, and then there's the Wainwright-Simonides way of having fun."

This time Nick's deep, rich laughter resounded against the walls.

Reese smiled at him. "You sound like King Poseidon in here, coming up from the sea for a breather because he's happy, too."

"I am. When I think of the dark place I was before I hired you, I can't relate to it anymore. I have you to thank for that. There's no way in this world I'll be able to repay you for showing me how to be a dad to my son."

Her eyes filled with tears she fought to hold back. "You just have by giving me this trip. Andreas and Gabi are the nicest people I've ever known. It's been an experience I'll cherish all my life."

"I'm glad then," he said in a husky voice. Quick as lightning he rolled on his side, bringing him close to her. "Reese—" He put his hand on her arm, but she wasn't destined to succumb to her needs because four people had started down the rocks from the surface on their end of the beach and their voices were already making echoes.

She heard a groan of protest come out of Nick before he got up and pulled her to her feet. His eyes fused with hers. "A serpent has entered Eden. Let's go."

Much as she hated the intrusion, those swimmers had probably prevented her from confessing all to Nick and begging him to make love to her. She'd passed up her chance when they'd gone sailing at Martha's Vineyard.

This time she wouldn't have had the willpower to deny herself or him anything.

Other swimmers were pouring in at the other end of the cave entrance. Apparently it was a very popular place in the late afternoon. She and Nick had been lucky to have it to themselves for as long as they did.

On the other side of the rocks were two more boats with even more people jumping off to enter the cave. They asked questions of Nick in Greek. It gave her time to hurry around the end of their jet boat and climb the ladder before he could touch her. The unforgettable memories were storing up like mad.

During the trip back, Nick was unusually quiet. She was glad, because she was in no frame of mind to make small talk. It was good they were leaving in the morning. She couldn't take any more of this kind of togetherness, knowing it had no future.

As soon as they pulled up to the pier, she told him she was anxious to shower. After that she would relieve the maid of taking care of Jamie and would see him at dinner.

It turned out to be a big family affair with many of Andreas's family in attendance. So many children. So much love. All of them belonged to each other except for her and Nick.

Reese was actually glad when morning came and the three of them left in the helicopter for Athens. Once they were back in New York, they would return to their normal routine. Nick would go to work and Reese would continue to love the baby and take him everywhere with her until…

She couldn't think about *until*. The thought of moving to that tiny little room and starting her internship without them was anathema to her.

CHAPTER NINE

REESE had endured a terrible last night on Milos. She'd finally fallen asleep on a wet pillow. By the time they were in flight on Nick's private jet and she'd given Jamie a bottle, she was so tired, Nick took the baby from her and told her to go to sleep.

She didn't waken until the fasten-seat-belts sign flashed on. Jamie was strapped in his carrycot in the other club seat sound asleep. Reese looked at Nick.

"I'm sorry I slept so long."

"Evidently you needed it." He was staring at her rather strangely. She didn't understand.

"Is there something wrong?"

"Not at all."

Maybe it was her imagination. After leaving Greece, it was probably hard for him to come back to the penthouse, which was a huge reminder of the sadness he'd lived through during the past year.

The jet touched down and taxied to a stop in front of the private hangar. Out the window she saw Paul leave the limo and walk toward them. With Nick, everything ran like clockwork.

She undid her seat belt and stood up to stretch. Paul came on board and nodded to her before carrying Jamie off the jet. When she turned to Nick, he smiled. "You look rested."

"I am. How did Jamie do during the flight?"

"He was perfect."

"That's good." Why was he standing there, looking at her in such an odd way again?

"It's because of the expert care you've given him. He's thriving because of you. Now it's time for you to have a few weeks to yourself before you start your internship at Miroff's. My pilot has instructions to fly you to Lincoln as soon as I get off."

What? Her world started to reel.

"Andreas and I talked about it and thought it best that both you and Jamie have a clean break from each other. He's had maids and a housekeeper fussing over him while we were in Greece. Hopefully he'll adjust to the new nanny Leah has found for me. Since I don't have one complaint about you, I'm going to trust her judgment again."

He was sending her back to Nebraska, just like that?

"Please accept my gratitude for all you've done by accepting this last gift. As your employer, I have the right." So saying, he reached in his pocket for an envelope and handed it to her. "Inside this is an airline ticket for your flight when you come back to New York in two weeks."

Her mouth had gone dry to the point it was impossible to swallow. "I couldn't take it."

"If that's your decision, but I wish you'd reconsider." He took it and tossed it on the seat of the club car next to her. "The return date has been left open in case you didn't plan to arrive until the day you start at Miroff's.

Since I put your full salary for the three months specified into your account the day you came to work for me, I don't think I've left anything out."

No. Nothing. Absolutely nothing.

"I instructed Rita to pack the rest of your belongings. Paul brought them to the airport. They're being put on board right now. Since I'm sure your parents would want to know you're coming, why not phone them before the pilot's ready to take off?"

"I'll do that," she answered numbly.

"If you need anything, just ask the steward."

"I will. Give Jamie a goodbye kiss for me."

"Of course." He studied her for a moment longer. "Miroff's is going to be lucky to get you. Have a safe flight."

"I can't face the family tonight, Mom. Yesterday when I got home, I thought I could." Reese had been shucking the corn while her mom finished fixing the green salad for the barbecue. Her dad was outside getting the grill warmed up. The whole family would descend en masse in a little while.

"I know you're absolutely devastated, but that's the very reason why you need to."

Tears gushed down her tanned face. "You'll never know the pain I'm in. I honestly thought Nick had fallen in love with me, too. I'm such a little fool I can't believe it."

Her mom flashed her a commiserating look. "You know what you're going to have to do?" She sliced two rows of tomatoes and onions in perfect sections. "Put this experience behind you. I realize that's easy for me to say, but in a way he's done you a great favor. Another two weeks of togetherness would have made the parting nearly impossible. You have to think of Jamie."

"You're right." She wiped her wet cheeks with the back of her hands. "Nick could see how attached I've become to him. I love that little boy. He's so cute and darling, you have no idea."

"I'm sure he loves *you*. The hospital visit bonded you."

"I know," she said in a haunted whisper.

"Thanks to Nick's generosity, we have two weeks to talk this over without you having money worries or deadlines."

At any other time in her life Reese might have echoed her mom's feelings, but it was agony being away from Nick. Every time she thought about him and Jamie, she got this pain in her chest and could hardly breathe.

"Do you have pictures of them?"

"Yes. I had doubles made up for his baby book and kept some for me. I'll get them." She dashed through the house to her bedroom and grabbed the packet off her dresser. "These are the ones I took of them the day we put the nursery together. And here are some I took while we were on Milos."

Her mom wiped her hands and studied them. When she lifted her head, she took a long time before she spoke because her lovely gray-blue eyes said it all. "I think your pain is going to take a long time to go away. It's a good thing you'll be working so hard at Miroff's."

Her mom was right. She needed family around. Her sister Carrie would be here soon with her two children. The distraction would help, but then everyone would go home after the weekend was over and Reese would once more be a prisoner to her memories.

She didn't know how she was she going to make it through tonight, let alone the rest of her life without him and Jamie. But to her shock, she was still alive the next day and the day after that. Her dad put her to work at the lumberyard, which saved her life. She answered phones and did odd jobs for him.

On Friday of the second week her mom phoned the office. "I'm glad you answered it. An express-mail envelope just came for you. I had to sign for it." Reese's heart began to thud. Intellectually she knew it wasn't from Nick, but her heart was crying out otherwise. "Do you want me to open it?"

"Please. It could be my exam results, but I thought they'd just send my score online."

"Well, you *are* their top student."

Reese smiled to herself in spite of her pain. "I'm the luckiest girl in the world to have a cheering section like you, Mom. What's in it?"

"A letter from Miroff and Hooplan." Reese had been waiting for final instructions from them, but her disappointment was so acute that it wasn't from Nick, she sank down in the chair. "Do you want me to read it?"

"Yes. I need to know when to make my return flight."

"Let's see. It's very short. 'Dear Ms. Chamberlain, congratulations on your new appointment. Please report to our office on Monday, August 29, at 9:00 a.m. for an orientation that will last until 4:00 p.m.'"

"That's two days sooner than my studio apartment will be vacant—"

"Don't worry. Your father and I want to pay for a decent hotel for you to stay in until you're settled."

"You're wonderful. Thanks, Mom."

"It says, 'We look forward to working with you. Sincerest Regards, Gerald Soffe, Vice President of Internal Affairs.' Well, honey, that makes it official."

The taxi dropped Reese off in front of Miroff's on Broadway. She'd decided to dress in a summer two-piece suit in a melon color. Maybe she could get away with a ponytail later on, but today she wore her hair down. It fell from a side part and had a tendency to curl in the humidity.

She paid the driver and went inside carrying her briefcase that held her laptop. "I'm Reese Chamberlain. I was told to report to Mr. Soffe," she told the receptionist.

"Second door down the hall on your left. He's expecting you."

"Thank you." She started for her destination, realizing she didn't feel the excitement she should have. For the past two weeks she'd been in a depressed state. Coming back to New York had made it worse.

When she spotted his name and title on the door, she opened it and walked in to find another receptionist, who lifted her red head. "You must be Ms. Chamberlain."

"Yes."

"Go right on in."

"Thank you."

The second she entered the man's office, she saw a familiar figure seated behind the desk and let out a cry.

It was Nick!

He'd kept his dark tan since their return from Greece and his black hair had grown longer. In a dove-gray summer suit with a darker gray shirt and no tie, he was gorgeous beyond belief.

"Hello, Reese." His eyes played over her slowly, missing nothing from her head to her low heels. "Come all the way in and sit down."

He didn't need to tell her that. By the time she reached the nearest chair, she was out of breath and her legs no longer supported her. "H-how's Jamie?" she stammered like a fool.

"Other than missing you, he's perfect."

She'd started trembling and couldn't stop. "What's going on? Where's Mr. Soffe?"

"He's a professional friend of mine. I asked him to make himself scarce while I talked to you first."

Maybe she was hallucinating. "Why would you do that?"

"When my uncle Lew assigned Rich Bonner to be the fall intern, he made a mistake. You were the top candidate from Wharton's, but as you know, blue bloods don't consider women equal to men, so he chose Mr. Bonner, who'd been ranked second highest in his class."

Reese wanted to die. "You'll never forgive me for that, will you. Don't you know how sorry I am?" she cried out emotionally.

His eyes flashed dark fire. "You have nothing to feel guilty about. Why would you when it was the truth! I straightened things out with Gerald. He's been in contact with Mr. Bonner, who will be coming to work for Miroff's in a few days."

With those words, Reese felt as if she was in a strange dream where nothing was as it should be. "Don't think I don't appreciate what you've tried to do for me, Nick, but I don't want anything changed, because I have no intention of working for your corporation. Even though

I was a woman, Miroff's took me on. I plan to make them very happy with their choice."

He studied her for a tension-filled moment. "In that case you'll have to walk across the street with me while we visit with Greg, Uncle Lew's son. You met him the night we had dinner at the Yacht Club. You need to tell him what you just told me. Then he'll make it right with Gerald and your friend Rich."

Searing pain drove through her to think that in the future she'd be working across the street from Nick. She couldn't bear it.

He came around the desk and picked up her briefcase. "Shall we go?"

How many times had she heard him say that before in connection with Jamie. Like déjà vu she left the building with him. Whenever they walked together, she had to hurry to keep up with his long strides. They maneuvered the crowded crosswalk and eventually entered the tall doors of his family's firm.

Nick nodded to the foyer receptionist and continued to the elevator. "Greg's in his office waiting for us." They emerged on the third floor and entered a door marked Gregory Wainwright, President.

President? But *Nick* was the CEO.

Before she could ask what it meant, Leah Tribe was there to greet her. "We meet again, Ms. Chamberlain."

But Mrs. Tribe was *Nick's* secretary. What was going on? "How are you, Mrs. Tribe?"

"I couldn't be better. I hear you're going to be working for us. How do you feel about that?"

How did she feel? "I'm afraid there's been a mistake. I need to talk to Mr. Wainwright."

"Oh—" The secretary looked surprised. "Go right on in. He's expecting you."

Nick slanted her a glance she couldn't read. Still carrying her briefcase, he led her inside the inner door.

Reese remembered Nick's cousin, who got to his feet. He was a man in his thirties who bore a slight resemblance to Nick, though he was shorter and less fit looking.

"Greg? You were introduced to Ms. Chamberlain before. Apparently there's been a mistake. She intends to stay with Miroff's and you'll be getting Mr. Bonner as planned."

His cousin looked completely thrown, but before he could say anything there was a buzz, then Leah Tribe's voice came over the intercom. "I'm sorry to bother you, Mr. Wainwright, but Stan needs a minute of your time for something that can't wait."

"I'll be right there, Leah. Nick?" He turned to him. "If you'll keep Ms. Chamberlain occupied, I'll be back as soon as I can."

The door shut, enclosing the two of them in a silence so quiet, she was sure Nick could hear her heart hammering. He took his seat behind the desk. She found a wing chair opposite him and sat down.

"Did they let you go because of what happened at the Yacht Club?"

"No. It was my choice. In fact I stepped down before I left for Greece with you and Jamie."

"Why?" she asked in shock. "I don't understand."

He stared at her for a long time. "Because I wanted to be free. You see…I'm getting married right away. You could say I'm starting a new life."

Reese thought she would faint, but she wouldn't let

him know how his news had affected her. "Someone you've known for a long time?"

Nick cocked his head. "Do you remember the day you stepped into my limo for the first time?"

She frowned. "Surely you don't need an answer to that question."

"Surely you shouldn't have had to ask me that question at all," he fired back. "Who else would I marry but *you*."

Blood hammered in her ears. "Be serious, Nick," her voice trembled.

"I would never be anything else *but* with the woman who's about to become my wife and Jamie's legal mother. We took a vote while we were on Milos and decided it was you or no one. Andreas and Gabi seconded the motion."

Reese shook her head. "I'm so confused I must have missed something. I'm going to work at Miroff's. How could you think I would be your wife?"

"It's possible to be both. You convinced me of that a month ago during one of our more scintillating conversations. Here's my proposal. We get married in Nebraska and honeymoon there. I want to meet your family. Then we'll come back to the penthouse and you start work. I'll be a stay-at-home daddy during your internship."

She couldn't possibly be hearing him correctly.

"When you're through at Miroff's and graduate, we'll take care of Jamie together while you decide where and how you're going to start your own brokerage firm. You'll be doing it all on your own. When you're ready to take on a partner, I'm your man behind the scenes."

"Nick—"

"We'll get my office set up in the other bedroom

at the end of the hall like you wanted to do in the first place. I'll work for you at home. I'm counting on you being a huge success because you're going to be the one bringing in the money for both of us, starting with the stipend you'll make being an intern. You see, I've signed away my entire inheritance to the family."

Her gasp reverberated in the room.

"The money I earned myself allowed me to buy the penthouse. But it represents my old life with Erica. When your company gets off the ground, I want to sell it and buy us a house outside the city. Somewhere in a residential neighborhood where Jamie and another brother or sister can play with other children on the block and have a dog. The rest I'll invest for our children's future."

"Oh, darling—"

Reese flew out of the chair and around the desk. Her feet never touched the ground before she landed in his arms. She threw them around his neck, so deliriously happy she couldn't talk. Instead she started sobbing. "Nick— I love you and Jamie so terribly. You just don't know—"

"Tell me about it," he whispered into her hair, crushing her to death.

Neither of them was aware Mrs. Tribe had come in until they heard her voice. "I like what I see, you two. I like it very much."

Nick lifted his mouth from Reese's. "Thank heaven for you, Leah."

When the door closed, Reese urgently pressed her mouth to his again. She couldn't get enough and never would, but her euphoria was interrupted once more. This time she heard a baby crying, but it had lost its newborn sound.

"Jamie?"

"Who else? He's living for you to hug and kiss him, but this is one time he's going to have to get in line."

Miroff's closed down for Christmas on the eighteenth, which would be Reese's last working day as an intern. But when she approached Gerald a few days before and told him she had a special surprise for Nick that required the last day off, her boss was happy to give it to her.

In fact he handed her an enormous bonus for her outstanding work. Then he offered her a job with his company. She hadn't expected either offering and was overwhelmed.

After expressing her gratitude, she told him she couldn't accept the offer because she and Nick had other plans. But she thanked him with a big hug, which he reciprocated, and she gave him his Christmas present. It was a box of chocolate truffles from his favorite candy shop. She'd given the same gift to Leah.

On the seventeenth, she kissed her husband and son goodbye and pretended to leave for work. Paul was waiting for her out in front of the apartment building as always. When she climbed in the limo, she asked him to drive her to the studio apartment she'd leased in August. Unbeknownst to Nick, Paul had been bringing her here most every working day on her lunch break for the past four months.

When she got out of the limo into the freezing cold, she walked up to the window. He put it down. "This is for you. Merry Christmas." She handed him the gift she'd had engraved for him. It was a gold ring with a stunning black onyx stone. Inside it read, Ever Faithful.

"I don't know what Nick and I would do without you." She smiled. "Until later."

He winked. "I can't wait to see Nick's face when I pull up with him."

"I'm living for that, too."

When he drove off, she walked toward the entrance of the former bookshop with so much excitement, she could scarcely contain it. A large, classy-looking black-and-white-striped awning gave the storefront a whole new look and caught the eye of every passerby. Her eyes traced the formal gold lettering on the squeaky-clean glass door with a stunning holly wreath hanging above.

Chamberlain & Wainwright Brokerage.

For the rest of the day she wrapped presents and put them under the lighted Christmas tree in the center of the room. By two o'clock everything was ready upstairs and down.

With her pulse racing, she reached for her cell and phoned Nick.

"Reese?" She hadn't heard that tinge of anxiety in his voice for a long time.

"Hi, darling."

"Is anything wrong? You don't usually call me this time of day."

"Everything's fine. I'm just tired and feel like leaving early. Gerald gave me the time off. I thought if you and Jamie came and picked me up, we could have an early dinner at a cozy little place I've found."

Whenever Nick worried, he was always quiet before he responded. "We'll come right now. Are you sure you're all right? You've been working so hard you've knocked yourself out."

"No harder than you. How's our boy?"

"He's been trying to stand up, but keeps falling down."

"I have no doubts he'll be walking sooner than most children his age. Come soon? I miss you both horribly."

Convinced something was wrong, Nick phoned Paul and told him to bring the car out front. Getting up from his office chair, he rushed down the hall to the nursery. Jamie wasn't due to wake up from his afternoon nap for another half hour, but it couldn't be helped. It wasn't like Reese to call in the afternoon. That's when she was normally in conference with the staff.

"Sorry, sport." Jamie was still half-asleep while Nick changed his diaper and put him in his blue snowsuit with the white fake fur around the edge of the hood. He grabbed a couple of bottles of formula and put them in the diaper bag. Once he'd shrugged into his overcoat, they left the penthouse for the limo.

As far as he was concerned, this ought to be her last day at work. His wife was a dynamo and needed to slow down. They could go get a Christmas tree in a few days after she'd had a rest. Deep in thought, it surprised him to discover they'd turned off Broadway at Seventh. It had started snowing. What was going on?

He spoke into the intercom. "Paul? Did you have to make a detour?"

"No. Your wife phoned and asked me to drop you off at the restaurant to save time. It's only a few more blocks now."

Nick frowned. "Did she sound all right to you?"

"Perfectly."

He glanced out the window, not seeing anything

because Reese's call had disturbed him. Pretty soon they pulled to a stop in heavy traffic. Nick climbed out and lifted Jamie's carryall from the car seat. Paul came around and handed him the diaper bag.

When he looked around he said, "I don't see a place to eat anywhere. Are you sure you have the right address?"

"It's right there in front of you, Nick."

All he could see was a business of some kind. He brushed the flakes off his lashes. On the awning he saw the words *Chamberlain & Wainwright Brokerage.*

Suddenly he could feel the blood pounding in his ears.

His gaze darted to the front door with the same words done in gold lettering. Through the falling snow a Christmas tree with dozens of colored lights beckoned him from behind the glass.

"How long have you known about this?"

"About four months."

"You've been helping her?"

He nodded. "Driving her to and fro on her lunch hour. She gave me this." He held up his hand to show him the ring he was wearing. "There was an inscription." When he told Nick what it was, Nick felt this thickness in his throat. There was no one more exciting, more thoughtful, kind and full of surprises than his beloved wife!

"Thank you for helping her, Paul."

"It's been a pleasure. I'll be around when you need a ride home."

He started for the door.

Reese couldn't wait any longer and opened it. "Merry Christmas early, darling."

Nick came inside and shut the door, bringing the cold

in with him. She held her breath, waiting to hear what he would say and think. The first thing he did was put the carryall with Jamie in it on the floor and crush her in his arms. She got a face full of snowflakes, but she didn't care.

"I don't know how you did it," his deep voice grated, "but you *did* it."

"I hope you won't be upset I put your name on the door, too, but I am a Wainwright now."

"You most definitely are, my love. If you hadn't put it on there, I'd have been devastated."

"Oh, Nick—"

Their mouths fused in rapture. They clung for a long, long time.

"Mr. Soffe gave me a bonus," she explained when he let her come up for breath. "It was enough to buy all the office equipment and furniture."

"Where did you find this place? How did you manage it?"

"When I leased the upstairs part thinking I'd be living here while I worked at Miroff's, the place was going out of business. Mr. Harvey from the bank was one of the clients I've been working with at the brokerage.

"I told him my idea for my own plans and he was willing to give me a lease and a loan to refurbish the whole place without a cosigner. That's because of you, darling. But I have to make good this time next year to pay it back. Now I'm terrified!"

Nick laughed for joy and swung her around. "Of what? I'm convinced you can do anything! Trust my wife to pull all this together."

"I used part of the money you paid me to hire Toni to do the painting."

"The waiter? You're teasing me."

"I hope you're not upset about that. He paints houses and apartments on the side part of the week to earn money while he's at night school. He attached the awning for me, too. I think he did a wonderful job."

His dark eyes roved over her face before he covered it with kisses. "I think *you're* wonderful."

"Thank you for being there for me every step of the way. I've never known such happiness in my life. Now I want to make you happy. Take off your coat and follow me upstairs."

While he removed it, she undid Jamie from the carryall. "Don't you look so cute in your snowsuit? I could eat you up. Yes, I could." She kissed his neck while she took it off. He laughed over and over again as she kissed one cheek, then the other. "I love you, little guy."

She looked up to see the love light in Nick's eyes. "Come with me."

The three of them ascended the winding steps to the studio. Reese had bought a playpen, which she'd set up next to the double bed. She lay Jamie in it and handed him a ball just his size. "With the tiny kitchen to one side of the room, there's hardly any space left to maneuver."

"I like it when we're so close nothing comes between us," Nick whispered against her neck. He slid his arms around her hips and before she knew it, they'd fallen on the bed together. "I love this innovation, Mrs. Wainwright."

"I figure it will come in handy for small naps in the next seven and a half months."

"What are you talking about?" he murmured, burying his face in her neck.

She smiled secretly. "Why, Nick Wainwright—imagine the financial prince of Park Avenue having to ask a question like that."

He lifted his head to look down at her with fire in his dark eyes. "The *what?*"

"You heard me. That's my mom's secret name for you. You *are* known to have a computer brain that catapulted you to be the former CEO of Sherborne and Wainwright. No one would believe it if you couldn't calculate the significance of a simple number like 7.5."

His black brows furrowed.

"Maybe if we go downstairs and open a few presents, you'll understand."

"Give me a hint now." He claimed her mouth again in a deep kiss that went on and on.

"Even though we won't need it until July, I got it on sale now. It goes in the limo."

More silence, and then she heard his sharp intake of breath. He sat all the way up. If she'd been worried, she didn't have to be. On his handsome face she saw the eager, tremulous look of joy, making him appear younger.

"I've made you pregnant?" he cried. "But you went on the pill."

"No, I didn't. On our honeymoon there was a night when you told me you had this dream about giving Jamie a little brother or sister right away, so he wouldn't grow up alone the way you did. Of course you knew it wasn't possible you said and brushed it off as if it were nothing.

"After you went to sleep, I thought about it all night long and knew you were right. I grew up with siblings and can't imagine being an only child. I didn't want that for Jamie, either."

His hands cupped her face. "You've been to an ob-gyn?"

"Yes. He's one Leah recommended. I really like him. He said everything looks good."

"Reese—"

He lay back down and ran his hand over her stomach. "I can't believe you've got our baby in there."

"You're really happy about it?"

A sound escaped his throat. "What a question."

"I'm glad because I am, too. Ecstatic! We'll figure it all out."

"After taking care of Jamie, what's another one."

She laughed and rolled into him. "For the man who didn't know how to diaper a baby, you'd win the father-of-the-year award now. I sent for something special for you to celebrate. Why don't you go downstairs and get it. It's the carton with the red ribbon tied around the middle."

"I'll be right back." In a minute he'd returned.

She raised herself up on her elbow. "Go ahead and open it."

Like a little kid ripping at his Christmas present, he tore off the paper in no time. "What's this?" He lifted out the bottle. "Deer Springs Wine from Lincoln." His gaze flicked to hers. A smile lit up his face. "They produce wine in Nebraska?"

"It *is* pretty amazing. Pretty good, too. The label will tell you it comes from a hearty grape called the Edelveiss that can withstand the cold, the heat and the prairie winds."

His eyes glazed over. "That could be a description of

my Nebraska nanny who withstood everything thrown at her and is now a Seventh Avenue broker to be reckoned with." He walked to the kitchen and found a supply of paper cups she'd put out. After he removed the cork, he poured himself some.

Then he walked back to the bed and sat next to her. "*Salut*, my pregnant love," he spoke in a deep velvety voice. "May our partnership last forever."

"I'll drink to that one day. I love you, Nick. To *forever*."

ONLY ON HIS TERMS

ELIZABETH BEVARLY

For Wanda Ottewell.
With many, many thanks
and even more fond memories.

Prologue

Gracie Sumner came from a long line of waitresses. Her mother worked for a popular chain restaurant for three decades, and her grandmother manned the counter of a gleaming silver diner on the Great White Way. The tradition went all the way back to her great-great-great-grandmother, in fact, who welcomed westward-ho train passengers to a Denver saloon. Gracie may have brought a bit more prestige to the family trade by finding work in a four-star, Zagat-approved bistro, but the instinct and artistry of waitressing was pretty much encoded on her DNA, the same way her tawny hair and brown eyes were.

And that instinct was how she knew there was something more to the silver-haired gentleman seated at table fifteen of Seattle's Café Destiné than a desire to sample the pot-au-feu.

He had come in at the end of the lunch shift and asked specifically to be seated in her area, then engaged her in conversation in a way that made her feel as if he already knew her. But neither he nor the name on the credit card he placed atop his check—Bennett Tarrant—was familiar. That wasn't surprising, however, since judging by his bespoke suit and platinum card, he was clearly a man of means. Unlike Gracie, who was struggling to pay her way through college, and who, at twenty-six, still had three semesters left before earning her BA in early childhood education.

"Here you go, Mr. Tarrant," she said as she placed the server book back on the table. "I hope you'll visit Café Destiné again soon."

"Actually, Miss Sumner, there's a reason why I came here today."

Her gaze flew to his. Although she always introduced herself as Gracie to her customers, she never gave out her last name. Warily, she replied, "The pot-au-feu. Yes, it's the most popular item on our menu."

"And it was delicious," Mr. Tarrant assured her. "But I really came in to see you on behalf of a client. I inquired for you at your apartment first, and your landlady told me where you work."

Good old Mrs. Mancini. Gracie could always count on her to guard absolutely no one's privacy.

Mr. Tarrant withdrew a silver case from inside his suit jacket and handed her a business card. Tarrant, Fiver & Twigg, it read, and there was a New York City address. Bennett Tarrant's title was President and Senior Probate Researcher. Which told Gracie all of nothing.

She looked at him again. “I’m sorry, but I don’t understand. What’s a probate researcher?”

“I’m an attorney. My firm is one of several appointed by the State of New York when someone passes away without a will, or when a beneficiary named in someone’s will can’t be found. In such circumstances, we locate the rightful heirs.”

Gracie’s confusion deepened. “I still don’t understand. My mother died in Cincinnati, and her estate was settled years ago.”

Not that there had been much to settle. Marian Sumner had left Gracie just enough to cover four months’ rent and modestly furnish a one-bedroom apartment. Still, she had been grateful for even that.

“It’s not your mother’s estate my firm was appointed to research,” Mr. Tarrant said. “Did you know a man by the name of Harrison Sage?”

Gracie shook her head. “I’m afraid not.”

“How about Harry Sagalowsky?”

“Oh, sure, I knew Harry. His apartment was across from mine when I lived in Cincinnati. He was such a nice man.”

For a moment, she was overrun by warm memories. Harry had been living in the other apartment on the top floor of the renovated Victorian when Gracie moved in after her mother’s death. They had become instant friends—he filled the role of the grandfather she never had, and she was the granddaughter he never had. She introduced him to J. K. Rowling and Bruno Mars and taught him how to crush the competition in *Call of Duty*. He turned her on to Patricia Highsmith and Miles Davis and taught her how to fox-trot at the Moondrop Ballroom.

She sobered. "He died two years ago. Even though I haven't lived in Cincinnati for a while now, when I come home from work, I still halfway expect him to open his front door and tell me how he just got *The African Queen* from Netflix or how he made too much chili for one person." Her voice trailed off. "I just miss him. A lot."

Mr. Tarrant smiled gently. "Mr. Sagalowsky thought very highly of you, too. He remembered you in his will, which was just recently settled."

Gracie smiled at that. Although Harry's apartment had been crowded with stuff that was both eclectic and eccentric, nothing could have been worth much. After his death, she helped their landlord pack it all up, but no one ever came to claim it—Harry had never spoken of any family, so she'd had no idea whom to contact. Their landlord finally decided to toss it all, but Gracie offered to rent a storage unit for it instead. It had meant tightening her belt even more, but she hadn't been able to stand the thought of Harry's things rotting in a dump. She was still paying for the unit back in Cincinnati. She brightened. Maybe Mr. Tarrant could help her get it all into the hands of Harry's next of kin.

"I'm afraid it took me a while to find you," he continued.

She stiffened. "Yeah, I kind of left Cincinnati on a whim about a year and a half ago."

"Without leaving a forwarding address?"

"I, um, had a bad breakup with a guy. It seemed like a good time to start fresh. My mom and Harry were gone, and most of my friends from high school moved after graduation. I didn't really have many ties there anymore."

Mr. Tarrant nodded, but she got the feeling he wasn't too familiar with bad romance. "If you have some time today," he said, "we can discuss Mr. Sagalowsky's estate and the changes it will mean for you."

Gracie almost laughed at that. He made Harry sound like some batty Howard Hughes, squirreling away a fortune while he wore tissue boxes for shoes.

"There's a coffee shop up the street," she said. "Mimi's Mocha Java. I can meet you there in about twenty minutes."

"Perfect," Mr. Tarrant told her. "We have a lot to talk about."

One

As Gracie climbed out of Mr. Tarrant's Jaguar coupe in the driveway of the house Harry had abandoned fifteen years ago—the house that now belonged to her—she told herself not to worry, that the place couldn't possibly be as bad as it seemed. Why, the weathered clapboard was actually kind of quaint. And the scattered pea-gravel drive was kind of adorable. So what if the size of the place wasn't what she'd been expecting? So what if the, ah, overabundant landscaping was going to require a massive amount of work? The house was fine. Just fine. She had no reason to feel apprehensive about being its new owner. The place was…charming. Yeah, that was it. Absolutely…charming.

In a waterfront, Long Island, multi-multi-multi-million-dollar kind of way. Holy cow, Harry's old house could host the United Arab Emirates and still have room left over for Luxembourg.

In spite of the serene ocean that sparkled beyond the house and the salty June breeze that caressed her face, she felt herself growing light-headed again—a not unfamiliar sensation since meeting Mr. Tarrant last week. After all, their encounter at Mimi's Mocha Java had culminated in Gracie sitting with her head between her knees, breathing in and out of a paper bag with the phrase Coffee, Chocolate, Men—Some Things are Better Rich printed on it. To his credit, Mr. Tarrant hadn't batted an eye. He'd just patted her gently on the back and told her everything was going to be fine, and the fact that she'd just inherited fourteen billion—yes, *billion,* with a *b*—dollars was nothing to have a panic attack about.

Hah. Easy for him to say. He probably knew what to do with fourteen billion dollars. Other than have a panic attack over it.

Now that they were here, he seemed to sense her trepidation—probably because of the way her breathing was starting to turn into hyperventilation again—because he looped his arm gently through hers. "We shouldn't keep Mrs. Sage and her son and their attorneys—or Mr. Sage's colleagues and their attorneys—waiting. I'm sure they're all as anxious to get the formalities out of the way as you are."

Anxious. Right. That was one word for it, Gracie thought. Had the situation been reversed, had she been the one to discover that her long-estranged husband or father, a titan of twentieth-century commerce, had spent his final years posing as a retired TV repairman in the blue-collar Cincinnati neighborhood where he grew up, then befriended a stranger to whom he had left nearly everything, she supposed she'd be a tad anxious, too. She just hoped there weren't other words for what Vivian Sage and her son, Harrison III, might be. Like *furious*. Or *vindictive*. Or *homicidal*.

At least she was dressed for the occasion. Not homicide, of course, but for the formal reading of Harry's will. Even though Harry's will had already been read a few times, mostly in court, because it had been contested and appealed by just about everyone he'd known in life. This time would be the last, Mr. Tarrant had promised, and this time it was for Gracie. She looked her very best, if she did say so herself, wearing the nicest of the vintage outfits that she loved—a beige, sixties-era suit with pencil skirt and cropped jacket that would have looked right at home on Jackie Kennedy. She'd even taken care to put on some makeup and fix her hair, managing a fairly convincing French twist from which just a few errant strands had escaped.

She and Mr. Tarrant moved forward, toward a surprisingly modest front porch. As he rapped the worn knocker, Gracie could almost convince herself she was visiting any number of normal suburban homes. But the humbleness ended once the door was opened by a liveried butler, and she looked beyond him into the house. The entryway alone was larger than her apartment back in Seattle, and it was crowded with period antiques, authentic hand-knotted Persian rugs and original works of art.

She began to take a step backward, but Mr. Tarrant nudged her forward again. He announced their names to the butler, who led them through the foyer and down a hall to the left, then another hall to the right, until they were standing in the entryway of a cavernous library. Gracie knew it was a library because three walls were virtually covered by floor-to-ceiling bookcases filled with exquisite leather-bound collectors' editions. They matched nicely the exquisite leather-bound furnishings. And there were floor-to-ceiling windows that looked out onto the gleaming water. She might as well have fallen through the looking glass, so grand and foreign was this world to her.

Her breathing settled some when she realized the room was full of people, since that would make it easier for her to be invisible. Mr. Tarrant had cautioned her that there would be a veritable army of attorneys present, along with their clients—Harry's former business associates and family members. It had come as no small surprise to hear that Harry had left behind a widow and two ex-wives, along with three daughters by the exes and a solitary son by his last wife. Gracie had no idea how to tell one person from another, though, since everyone was dressed alike—the men in suits and the women in more suits and a couple of sedate dresses—and they represented a variety of age groups.

One of those suited men hailed Mr. Tarrant from the other side of the room, and after ensuring that Gracie would be all right for a few minutes without him, he strode in that direction. So she took a few steps into the fray, relieved to be able to do it on her own.

See? she said to herself. This wasn't so bad. It was just like working a wedding-rehearsal dinner at Café Destiné for some wealthy Seattle bride and groom. Except that she would be in the background at one of those events, not front and center, which would be happening here all too soon. Not to mention that, at a rehearsal dinner, she'd be sharing 18 percent of a final tab worth a couple of thousand dollars with two or three other waiters, and here, she would be receiving 100 percent of almost everything.

Fourteen billion—yes, *billion* with a *b*—dollars.

She felt her panic advancing again, until a gentle voice murmured from behind her, "How can you tell the difference between a bunch of high-powered suits and a pack of bloodthirsty jackals?"

She spun around to find herself gazing up—and up and up some more—into a pair of the most beautiful blue eyes she had ever seen. The rest of the man's face was every bit as appealing, with straight ebony brows, an aristocratic nose, a sculpted jaw and lips that were just this side of full. Not to mention a strand of black hair that tumbled rebelliously over his forehead in a way that made him look as if he'd just sauntered out of a fabulous forties film.

She took a quick inventory of the rest of him, pretending she didn't notice how he was doing the same to her. He had broad shoulders, a slim waist and the merest scent of something smoky and vaguely indecent. Gracie couldn't have identified a current fashion label if her life depended on it, but it was a safe bet that his charcoal pinstripes had been designed by whoever had the most expensive one. He looked like one of the high-powered suits in the riddle he'd just posed and nothing like a bloodthirsty jackal. She couldn't wait to hear the answer.

"I don't know," she said. "How can you tell the difference?"

He grinned, something that made him downright dazzling. Gracie did her best not to swoon.

In a voice tinted with merriment, he said, "You can't."

She chuckled, and the tension that had wrapped her so tightly for the last week began to ease for the first time. For that, more than anything, she was grateful to the man. Not that she didn't appreciate his other, ah, attributes, too. A lot.

"But you're one of those suits," she objected.

"Only because professional dictates say I have to be."

As if to illustrate his reluctance, he tugged his necktie loose enough to unbutton the top button of his shirt. In a way, he reminded her of Harry, someone who knew there was more to life than appearances, and there were better ways to spend time than currying the favor of others.

"Would you like some coffee?" he asked. "There's an urn in the corner. And some cookies or something, too, I think."

She shook her head. "No, thanks. I'm good." She didn't add that the addition of even a drop of caffeine or a grain of sugar to her system would turn her jitters into a seismic event. "But if you'd like some—" She started to tell him she'd be right back with a cup and a plate, so automatically did her waitress response come out.

But he offered no indication that he expected her to get it for him. "No, I've had my quota for the day, too."

The conversation seemed ready to stall, and Gracie was desperate to hold on to the only friend she was likely to make today. As a result, she blurted out the first thing that popped into her head. "So…this house. This room. This view. Is this place gorgeous or what?"

Her question seemed to stump him. He glanced

around the library as if he were seeing it for the first time, but he didn't seem nearly as impressed as she. "It's all right, I guess. The room's a little formal for my taste, and the view's a little boring, but..."

It was a rare individual who wouldn't covet a house as grand as this, Gracie thought. Although she had no intention of keeping it or much of anything else Harry had left her, since fourteen billion—yes, *billion* with a *b*—dollars was way too much money for a single individual to have, she still felt a keen appreciation for its beauty.

"Well, what kind of place do you call home?" she asked.

Without hesitation, he told her, "Bright lights, big city. I've lived in Manhattan since I started college, and I'm never leaving."

His enthusiasm for the fast-paced setting didn't seem to fit with how he'd reminded her of Harry earlier. But she tried to sound convincing when she said, "Oh. Okay."

She must not have done a very good job, though, because he said, "You sound surprised."

"I guess I am, kind of."

"Why?" He suddenly seemed a little defensive.

She shrugged. "Maybe because I was just thinking how you remind me of someone I used to know, and he wasn't a bright-lights, big-city kind of guy at all."

At least, he hadn't been when Gracie knew him. But Harry's life before that? Who knew? Nothing she'd discovered about him in the past week had seemed true to the man she'd called her friend for years.

Her new friend's wariness seemed to increase. "Old boyfriend?"

"Well, old, anyway," Gracie said with a smile. "More like a grandfather, though."

He relaxed visibly, but still looked sweetly abashed. "You know, the last thing a guy wants to hear when he's trying to impress a beautiful woman he's just met is how he reminds her of her grandfather."

He thought she was beautiful? Was he trying to impress her? And was he actually admitting it? Did he know how one of her turn-ons, coming in second after a bewitching smile, was men who spoke frankly and honestly? Especially because she'd known so few of them. Really, none other than Harry.

"I, uh…" she stammered. "I mean, um, ah…"

He seemed to take great pleasure in having rendered her speechless. Not arrogantly so, but as if he were simply delighted by his success. "So you're not a big-city type yourself?"

Grateful for the change of subject—and something she could respond to with actual words—she shook her head. "Not at all. I mean, I've lived in big cities all my life, but never in the city proper. I've always been a suburban girl."

Even though she'd never known her father and had lived in an apartment growing up, her life had been no different from her friends' who'd lived in houses with yards and a two-parents-and-siblings family unit. Her mother had been active at her school and the leader of her Brownie troop. And even with her meager income, Marian Sumner had somehow always had enough for summer vacations and piano and gymnastics lessons. As a girl, Gracie had spent summers playing in the park, autumns jumping into leaf piles, winters building snowmen and springs riding her bike. Completely unremarkable. Totally suburban.

Her new friend considered her again, but this time, he seemed to be taking in something other than her physical appearance. “At first, I was thinking you seem like the city type, too. The suit is a little retro, but you’d still be right at home in the East Village or Williamsburg. Now, though…”

His voice trailed off before he completed his analysis, and he studied Gracie in the most interesting—and interested—way. Heat pooled in her midsection, spiraling outward, until every cell she possessed felt as if it was going to catch fire. The entire room seemed to go silent for an interminable moment, as if everyone else had disappeared, and it was just the two of them alone in the universe. She’d never experienced anything like it before. It was…unsettling. But nice.

“Now?” she echoed, hoping to spur his response and end the curious spell. The word came out so quietly, however, and he still seemed so lost in thought, that she wondered if he’d even heard her.

He shook his head almost imperceptibly, as if he were trying to physically dispel the thoughts from his brain. “Now I think maybe you do seem like the wholesome girl next door.”

This time, it was Gracie’s turn to look abashed. “You know, the last thing a girl wants to hear when she’s trying to impress a beautiful man she’s just met is how she reminds him of a glass of milk.”

That, finally, seemed to break the weird enchantment. Both of them laughed lightly, but she suspected it was as much due to relief that the tension had evaporated as it was to finding humor in the remark.

"Do you have to go back to work after this thing?" he asked. "Or would you maybe be free for a late lunch?"

In spite of the banter they'd been sharing, the invitation came out of nowhere and caught Gracie off-guard. A million questions cartwheeled through her brain, and she had no idea how to respond to any of them. How had her morning gone from foreboding to flirtatious? Where had this guy come from? How could she like him so much after only knowing him a matter of moments? And how on earth was she supposed to accept an invitation to lunch with him when her entire life was about to explode in a way that was nothing short of atomic?

She tried to reply with something that made sense, but all that came out was "Lunch…? I…? Work…?"

He was clearly enjoying how much he continued to keep her off-kilter. "Yeah, lunch. Yeah, you. As for your work, which firm do you work for?" He glanced around the room. "Maybe I can pull some strings for you. I've known most of these people all my life. A couple of them owe me favors."

"Firm?" she echoed, the single word all she could manage in her growing confusion.

"Which law firm, representing which one of my father's interests?" For the first time since they began chatting, he sobered. "Not that they're my father's interests anymore. Not since that trashy, scheming, manipulative gold digger got her hooks into him. Not that my mother and I are going down without a fight."

It dawned on Gracie then—dawned like a two-by-four to the back of her head—that the man to whom she had been speaking so warmly wasn't one of the many attorneys who were here representing Harry's former colleagues. Nor was he one of those colleagues. It was Harry's son, Harrison Sage III. The man who had assumed he would, along with his mother, inherit the bulk of his father's fortune. The one whom Gracie had prevented from doing just that. The one she had earlier been thinking might be furious, vindictive and homicidal.

Then his other remark hit her. The part about the trashy, scheming, manipulative gold digger. That was what he thought she was? Her? The woman whose idea of stilettos was a kitten heel? The woman who preferred her hemlines below the knee? The woman who'd nearly blinded herself that morning with a mascara wand? The woman who intended to give away nearly every nickel of the fourteen billion—yes *billion* with a *b*—dollars with which Harry had entrusted her?

Because even without Mr. Tarrant's having told her about Harry's wish that she give away the bulk of his fortune to make the world a better place, Gracie would have done just that. She didn't want the responsibility that came with so much money. She didn't want the notoriety. She didn't want the pandemonium. She didn't want the terror.

Maybe she'd been struggling to make ends meet before last week, but she had been making them meet. And she'd been happy with her life in Seattle. She had fun friends. She had a cute apartment. She was gainfully employed. She was working toward her degree. She'd had hope for the future in general and a sunny outlook for any given day. Since finding out about her inheritance, however, she'd awoken every morning with a nervous stomach, and had only been able to sleep every night with a pill. In between those times, she'd been jumpy, withdrawn and scared.

Most people would probably think she was nuts, but Gracie didn't want to be a billionaire. She didn't even want to be a millionaire. She wanted to have enough so that she could make it through life without worrying, but not so much that she spent the rest of her life worrying. Did that make sense? To her, it did. To Harry's son, however…

She searched for words that would explain everything to Harrison Sage III quickly enough that he wouldn't have time to believe she was any of the things he'd just called her. But there was still so much of it she didn't understand herself. How could she explain it to him when even she couldn't make sense of it?

"I, um, that is…" she began. She inhaled a deep breath and released it, and then shifted her weight nervously from one foot to the other. She forced a smile she was sure looked as contrived as it felt and tried again. "Actually, I mean… The thing is…"

Gah. At this rate, she would be seeing Harry in the afterlife before she was able to make a complete sentence. *Just spit it out,* she told herself. But all she finally ended up saying was "Um, actually, I don't have to go back to work after this."

Well, it was a start. Not to mention the truth. *Go, Gracie!*

Immediately, Harrison Sage's expression cleared. "Excellent," he said. "Do you like Thai? Because there's this great place on West Forty-Sixth that just opened. You'll love it."

"I do like Thai," she said. Still being honest. *Forward, Gracie,* she told herself. *Move forward.*

"Excellent," he said, treating her again to that bewitching smile. "I'm Harrison, by the way," he added. "Harrison Sage. If you hadn't already figured that out."

Gracie bit back a strangled sound. "Yeah, I kinda did."

"And you are?"

It was all she could do not to reply, "I'm the trashy, scheming, manipulative gold digger. Nice to meet you."

"I'm—I'm Gracie," she said instead.

She was hoping the name was common enough that he wouldn't make the connection to the woman he probably hated with the burning passion of a thousand fiery suns. But she was pretty sure he did make the connection. She could tell by the way his expression went stony, by the way his eyes went flinty, by the way his jaw went clinchy…

And by the way the temperature in the room seemed to drop about fourteen billion—yes *billion* with a *b*—degrees.

Two

Harrison Sage told himself he must have misheard her. Maybe she hadn't said her name was Gracie. Maybe she'd said her name was Stacy. Or Tracy. Or even Maisey. Because Gracie was a nickname for Grace. And Grace was the name of the woman who had used her sexual wiles to seduce and manipulate a fragile old man into changing his will to leave her with nearly every nickel he had.

This was that woman? he thought, taking her in again. He'd been expecting a loudmouthed, garishly painted, platinum blonde in a short skirt, tight sweater and mile-high heels. One who had big hair, long legs and absolutely enormous—

Well. He just hadn't expected her to look like something out of a fairy tale. But that was exactly the impression he'd formed of this woman when she first walked into the room. That she was some fey, otherworldly sylph completely out of her element in this den of trolls. She was slight and wispy, and if she was wearing any makeup, he sure couldn't see it. Stray tendrils of hair, the color of a golden autumn sunset, had escaped their twist, as if all it would take was a breath of sorcery to make the entire mass tumble free.

And when had he become such a raging poet? he asked himself. Golden autumn sunset? Breath of sorcery? What the hell kind of thoughts were those to have about a woman who had robbed his family of their rightful legacy? What the hell kind of thoughts were those for a man to have, period? Where the hell had his testosterone got to?

On the other hand, he was beginning to see how his father had been taken in by her. Obviously, she was the kind of grifter who got better results as a vestal virgin than a blonde bombshell. Harrison had almost fallen into her trap himself.

It didn't matter *how* she'd conned his father. What mattered was that she'd swindled one of the last century's most savvy businessmen and convinced him to turn his back on everyone and everything he'd loved in life. Well, as far as his father *could* have loved anyone or anything—other than his fortune, his commercial holdings and his social standing. But then, what else was there to love? Money, power and position were the only things a person could count on. Or, at least, they had been, before everything went to hell, thanks to this, this…

Harrison took a step backward, and met Grace Sumner's gaze coolly. "*You're* the trashy, scheming, manipulative gold digger?" he asked. Then, because something in her expression looked genuinely wounded by the comment—wow, she really was good—he tempered it by adding, "I thought you'd be taller."

She mustered a smile he would have sworn was filled with anxiety if he hadn't known she was a woman who made her way in the world by conning people. "Well, I guess zero out of five isn't bad."

Harrison opened his mouth to say something else, but Bennett Tarrant—another thorn in the Sage family's side for the last two years—appeared next to Gracie, as if conjured by one of her magic spells.

"I see you've met Mr. Sage," he said unnecessarily.

"Yep," Grace said, her gaze never leaving Harrison's.

Tarrant turned to Harrison. "And I see you've met Miss Sumner."

"Yep," Harrison said, his gaze never leaving Grace's.

The silence that ensued was thick enough to hack with a meat cleaver. Until Tarrant said, "We should head for our seats. We'll be starting shortly."

Instead of doing as Tarrant instructed, Harrison found it impossible to move his feet—or remove his gaze from Grace Sumner. Damn. She really was some kind of enchantress.

In an effort to make himself move away, he reminded himself of everything he and his mother had been through since his father's disappearance fifteen years ago. And he reminded himself how his mother would be left with nothing, thanks to this woman who had, by sheer, dumb luck, stumbled onto an opportunity to bleed the last drop out of a rich, feeble-minded old man.

Fifteen years ago—half a lifetime—Harrison had

gone down to breakfast to find his parents seated, as they always were, at a dining-room table capable of seating twenty-two people. But instead of sitting side by side, they sat at each end, as far apart as possible. As usual, his father had had his nose buried in the *Wall Street Journal* while his mother had been flipping through the pages of a program for Milan Fashion Week. Or maybe Paris Fashion Week. Or London Fashion Week. Or, hell, Lickspittle, Idaho, Fashion Week for all he knew. So he'd taken his regular place at the table midway between them, ensuring that none of them was close enough to speak to the others. It was, after all, a Sage family tradition to not speak to each other.

They'd eaten in silence until their butler entered with his daily reminder that his father's car had arrived to take him to work, his mother's car had arrived to take her shopping and Harrison's car had arrived to take him to school. All three Sages had then risen and made their way to their destinations, none saying a word of farewell—just as they had every morning. Had Harrison realized then that that would be the last time he ever saw his father, he might have…

What? he asked himself. Told him to have a nice day? Given him a hug? Said, "I love you"? He wasn't sure he'd even known how to do any of those things when he was fifteen. He wasn't sure he knew how to do any of them now. But he might at least have told his father…something.

He tamped down a wave of irritation. He just wished he and his father had talked more. Or at all. But that was kind of hard to do when the father spent 90 percent of his time at work and the son spent 90 percent of his time in trouble. Because Harrison remembered something else about that day. The night before his father took off, Harrison had come home in the backseat of a squad car, because he'd been caught helping himself to a couple of porno magazines and a bottle of malt liquor at a midtown bodega.

Five months after his father's disappearance had come the news from one of the family's attorneys that he had been found, but that he had no intention of coming home just yet. Oh, he would stay in touch with one of his attorneys and a couple of business associates, to make sure the running of Sage Holdings, Inc. continued at its usual pace and to keep himself from being declared legally dead. But he wouldn't return to his work life—or his home life—anytime soon. To those few with whom he stayed in contact he paid a bundle to never reveal his whereabouts. He'd come back when he felt like it, he said. And then he never came back at all.

Harrison looked at Grace Sumner again, at the deceptively beautiful face and the limitless dark eyes. Maybe two judges had decided she was entitled to thc personal fortune his father had left behind. But there was no way Harrison was going down without a fight. He would prove once and for all, unequivocally, that she wasn't entitled to a cent. He'd been so sure the appeals court would side with the family that he hadn't felt it necessary to play his full hand. Until now. And now…

Soon everyone would know that the last thing Grace Sumner was was a fey, unearthly creature. In fact, she was right at home in this den of trolls.

Gracie wanted very much to say something to Harry's son before leaving with Mr. Tarrant. But his expression had gone so chilly, she feared anything she offered by way of an explanation or condolences would go unheard. Still, she couldn't just walk away. The man had lost his father—twice—and had no chance to make amends at this point. His family's life had been turned upside down because of Harry's last wishes and what he'd asked her to do with his fortune. She supposed she couldn't blame Harrison III for the cool reception.

Nevertheless, she braved a small smile and told him, "I doubt you'll believe me, but it *was* nice to meet you, Mr. Sage. I'm so sorry about your father. He was the kindest, most decent man I ever met."

Without giving him a chance to respond, she turned to follow Mr. Tarrant to the other side of the room, where chairs had been set up for everyone affected by Harry's will. They were arranged in two arcs that faced each other, with a big-screen TV on one side. She seated herself between Mr. Tarrant and two attorneys from his firm, almost as if the three of them were circling the wagons to protect her.

Gus Fiver, the second in command at Tarrant, Fiver & Twigg, looked to be in his midthirties and was as fair and amiable as Harrison Sage was dark and moody—though Gus's pinstripes looked to be every bit as expensive. Renny Twigg, whom Mr. Tarrant had introduced as one of their associates—her father was the Twigg in the company's name—was closer in age to Gracie's twenty-six. Renny was a petite brunette who didn't seem quite as comfortable in her own pinstripes. Even with her tidy chignon and perfectly manicured hands, she looked like the kind of woman who would be happier working outdoors, preferably at a job that involved wearing flannel.

Everyone else in the room was either connected to Harry in some way or an attorney representing someone's interests. Seated directly across from Gracie—naturally—were Harry's surviving family members and their attorneys. In addition to Harrison Sage III, there was his mother and Harry's widow, Vivian Sage, not to mention a veritable stable of ex-wives and mistresses and a half-dozen additional children—three of whom were even legitimate. As far as professional interests went, Harry had had conglomerates and corporations by the boatload. Add them together, and it totaled a financial legacy of epic proportion. Nearly all of what hadn't gone back to the businesses was now legally Gracie's. Harry had left a little to a handful of other people, but the rest of his fortune—every brick, byte and buck—had gone to her.

Oh, where was a paper bag for hyperventilating into when she needed it?

Once everyone was seated and silent, Bennett Tarrant rose to address the crowd. "Thank you all for coming. This meeting is just a formality, since Mr. Sage's estate has been settled by the court, and—"

"Settled doesn't mean the ruling can't be appealed," Harrison Sage interrupted, his voice booming enough to make Gracie flinch. "And we plan to file within the next two weeks."

"I can't imagine how that's necessary," Mr. Tarrant said. "An appeal has already supported the court's initial ruling in Miss Sumner's favor. Unless some new information comes to light, any additional appeal will only uphold those rulings."

Harrison opened his mouth to say more, but his attorney, a man of Mr. Tarrant's age and demeanor, placed a hand lightly on his arm to halt him. "New information will come to light," the man said.

Mr. Tarrant looked in no way concerned. "Mr. Landis, it has been twice determined that Harrison Sage, Jr., was of sound mind and body when he left the bulk of his personal estate to Grace Sumner. Another appeal would be—"

"Actually, we'll disprove that this time," Mr. Landis stated unequivocally. "And we will prove that not only did Grace Sumner exert undue influence over Mr. Sage of a sexual nature, but that—"

"What?" This time Gracie was the one to interrupt.

Mr. Landis ignored her, but she could practically feel the heat of Harrison Sage's gaze.

Mr. Landis continued, "We'll prove that not only did Grace Sumner exert undue influence over Mr. Sage of a sexual nature, but that he contracted a sexually transmitted disease from her which rendered him mentally incapacitated."

"What?" Gracie erupted even more loudly.

She started to rise from her chair, but Gus Fiver gently covered her shoulder with his hand, willing her to ignore the allegation. With much reluctance, Gracie made herself relax. But if looks could kill, the one she shot Harrison Sage would have rendered him a pile of ash.

Especially after his attorney concluded, "She used sex to seduce and further incapacitate an already fragile old man, and then took advantage of his diminished state to convince him to leave his money and assets to her. We're hiring a private investigator to gather the necessary evidence, since this is something that has only recently come to light."

"I see," Mr. Tarrant replied. "Or perhaps it's something you've pulled out of thin air in a vain last-ditch effort."

Unbelievable, Gracie thought. Even if she'd known Harry was worth a bundle, she never would have taken advantage of him. And she certainly wouldn't have used her alleged *sexual wiles*, since she didn't even have *a* sexual wile, never mind sexual *wiles*, plural. True friendship was worth way more than money and was a lot harder to find. And incapacitated? Diminished? Harry? Please. He'd been full of piss and vinegar until the minute that damned aneurysm brought him down.

Mr. Tarrant met the other attorney's gaze levelly. "Harrison Sage, Jr. changed his will in person, in the office of his attorneys, two of whom are seated in this room. And he presented to them not only a document from his physician stating his excellent health, both mental and physical, but his physician was also present to bear witness in that office. Your father's intent was crystal clear. He wished for Grace Sumner to inherit the bulk of his personal estate. Two judges have agreed. Therefore Miss Sumner *does* inherit the bulk of his personal estate.

"Now then," he continued, "on the day he amended his will for the last time, Mr. Sage also made a video at his attorneys' office that he wanted Miss Sumner and his family and associates, along with their representatives, to view. Renny, do you mind?"

Renny Twigg aimed a remote at the TV. A second later, Harry's face appeared on the screen, and Gracie's stomach dropped. He looked nothing like the Harry she remembered. He was wearing a suit and tie not unlike the other power suits in the room, a garment completely at odds with the wrinkled khakis and sweatshirts he'd always worn in Cincinnati. His normally untidy hair had been cut and styled by a pro. His expression was stern, and his eyes were flinty. He looked like a billionaire corporate mogul—humorless, ruthless and mean. Then he smiled his Santa Claus smile and winked, and she knew this was indeed the Harry she had known and loved. Suddenly, she felt much better.

"Hey there, Gracie," he said in the same playful voice with which he'd always greeted her. "I'm sorry we're meeting like this, kiddo, because it means I'm dead."

Unbidden tears pricked Gracie's eyes. She really did miss Harry. He was the best friend she'd ever had. Without thinking, she murmured, "Hi, Harry."

Every eye in the room fell upon her, but Gracie didn't care. Let them think she was a lunatic, talking to someone on a TV screen. In that moment, it felt as if Harry were right there with her. And it had been a long time since she'd been able to talk to him.

"And if you're watching this," he continued, "it also means you know the truth about who I really am, and that you're having to share a room with members of my original tribe. I know from experience what a pain in the ass that can be, so I'll keep this as brief as I can. Here's the deal, kiddo. I hope it didn't scare the hell out of you when you heard how much I left you. I'm sorry I never told you the truth about myself when I was alive. But by the time I met you, I was way more Harry Sagalowsky than I was Harrison Sage, so I wasn't really lying. You wouldn't have liked Harrison, anyway. He was a prick."

At this, Gracie laughed out loud. It was just such a Harry thing to say. When she felt eyes on her again, she bit her lip to stifle any further inappropriate outbursts. Inappropriate to those in the room, anyway. Harry wouldn't have minded her reaction at all.

He continued, "That's why I wanted to stop being Harrison. One day, I realized just how far I'd gotten from my roots, and how much of myself I'd lost along the way. People love rags-to-riches stories like mine, but those stories never mention all the sacrifices you have to make while you're clawing for those riches, and how a lot of those sacrifices are of your morals, your ethics and your character."

Gracie sobered at that. She'd never heard Harry sound so serious. He grew more so as he described how, by the time he'd left his old life, he'd become little more than a figurehead for his companies, and how unhappy his home life had become, and how all he'd wanted was to escape. So he left his work, his family and his "big-ass Long Island estate," returned to the surname his ancestors had changed generations ago and moved back to the blue-collar neighborhood in Cincinnati where he grew up.

At this, Gracie glanced across the room at Vivian and Harrison and saw them looking at the television with identical expressions—a mixture of annoyance, confusion and something else she couldn't identify. She tried to be sympathetic. She couldn't imagine what it must be like for them, being ignored by their husband and father for fifteen years, and then being disinherited by him. She supposed they were justified in some of their feelings toward Harry.

But maybe they should take a minute to wonder

why Harry had done this. He hadn't been the kind of man to turn his back on people, unless those people had given him a reason to do it.

Harry spoke from the video again, bringing Gracie's attention back around. "Vivian and Harrison, this part is for you. Billions of dollars is way too much for anyone to have. Gracie Sumner is the kind of person who will understand what an awesome responsibility that much money is, and she'll do the right thing by it. She won't keep it for herself. I know her. She'll get rid of it as quickly as she can, and she'll make sure it gets into the hands of people who need it."

At this, Gracie braved another look across the room. Vivian Sage, her hair silver, her suit gold, her fingers and wrists bedecked in gemstones of every color, looked like she wanted to cry. Harrison, however, was staring right at Gracie. But his expression was unreadable. He could have been wondering where to eat lunch later or pondering where to hide her body. She hadn't a clue.

Thankfully, Harry's mention of her name gave her a reason to look back at the TV. "Gracie, this part's for you. I could have given my money to worthy causes myself and saved you a lot of trouble. But being a better person than I am, you'll know better than I would what to do with all my filthy lucre. But listen, kiddo. This last part is really important. Keep some of the money for yourself. I mean it. Buy yourself one of those ridiculous little cars you like. Or a house on the water. Go to Spain like you said you wanted to. Something. You promise?"

Again, Gracie felt every gaze in the room arc toward her. She had no idea what to say. It just felt wrong to take Harry's money, even a modest sum. After that first meeting with Mr. Tarrant, Gracie had gone home and headed straight for Google. In every article she'd read about Harrison Sage, Jr., he'd been defined by his wealth. "Billionaire Harrison Sage, Jr.," he'd invariably been called. Even after his disappearance, when the word *recluse* had been added to his descriptions, it had still always been preceded by the word *billionaire*. In his old life, Harry had been, first and foremost, rich. Anything else had been incidental. Gracie didn't want to be one of the people who saw only dollar signs in conjunction with his name, and she didn't want to be one of the ones who took from him. Especially after he'd given so much to her.

"Promise me, Gracie," he said again from the big screen, obviously having known she would hesitate.

"Okay, Harry," she replied softly. "I promise."

"That's my girl," Harry said with another wink.

He said his farewells, and then the TV screen went dark. Again, Gracie felt tears threatening. Hastily, she fished a handkerchief out of her purse and pressed it first to one eye, then the other.

Across the room, Harrison Sage began a slow clap. "Oh, well done, Ms. Sumner," he said. "Definitely an award-worthy performance. I can see how my father was so taken in by you."

"Were I you, Mr. Sage," Bennett Tarrant interjected, "I would be careful what I said to the woman who owns the Long Island mansion my mother calls home."

It hit Gracie then, finally, just how much power she wielded at the moment. Legally, she could indeed toss Vivian Sage into the street and move into the Long Island house herself. That was what a trashy, scheming, manipulative gold digger who'd used her sexual wiles to take advantage of a fragile old man would do.

So she said, "Mr. Tarrant, what do I have to do to deed the Long Island house and everything in it to Mrs. Sage? This is her home. She should own it, not me."

Harrison Sage eyed Gracie warily at the comment, but he said nothing. Something in Vivian's expression, though, softened a bit.

"It's just a matter of drawing up the paperwork," Mr. Tarrant said. "Today being Wednesday, we could have everything ready by the end of next week. If you don't mind staying in the city for a little while longer."

Gracie expelled a soft sigh. Harry's Long Island estate had to be worth tens of millions of dollars, and its contents worth even more. Just shedding that small portion of his wealth made her feel better.

"I don't mind staying in the city awhile longer," Gracie said. "It'll be fun. I've never been to New York before. Could you recommend a hotel? One that's not too expensive? The one I'm in now is pretty steep, but I hadn't planned to stay more than a couple of nights."

"It's New York City, Gracie," Mr. Tarrant said with a smile. "There's no such thing as *not too expensive*."

"Oh, you don't want to stay in the city," Vivian said. "Darling, it's so crowded and noisy. Spend the time with us here in the Hamptons. It's beautiful in June. We've been having *such* lovely evenings."

Harrison looked at his mother as if she'd grown a second head. "You can't be serious."

Gracie, too, thought Vivian must be joking. A minute ago, she'd looked as if she wanted Gracie to spontaneously combust. Now she was inviting her to stay at the house? Why? So she could suffocate Gracie in her sleep?

"Of course I'm serious," Vivian said. "If Grace—you don't mind if I call you Grace, do you, darling?—is kind enough to give me the house, the least I can do is make her comfortable here instead of having her stay in a stuffy old hotel in the city. Don't you think so, Harrison?"

What Harrison was thinking, Gracie probably didn't want to know. Not if the look on his face was any indication.

"Please, Grace?" Vivian urged. "We've all gotten off on the wrong foot. This just came as such a shock, that's all. Let us make amends for behaving badly. You can tell us all about how you met my husband and what he was like in Cincinnati, and we can tell you about his life here before you met him."

Gracie wasn't sure how to respond. Was Vivian really being as nice as she seemed? Did she really want to mend fences? Or was there still some potential for the suffocation thing?

Gracie gave herself a good mental shake. She'd been a billionaire for barely a week, and already she was seeing the worst in people. This was exactly why she didn't want to be rich—she didn't want to be suspicious of everyone she met.

Of course Vivian was being nice. Of course she wanted to make amends. And it *would* be nice to hear about Harry's life before Gracie met him. She'd always thought the reason he didn't talk about himself was because he thought she'd be bored. His life must have been fascinating.

For some reason, that made Gracie look at Harrison

again. He was no longer glowering at her, and in that moment, she could see some resemblance between him and his father. They had the same blue eyes and square jaw, but Harrison was a good three inches taller and considerably broader in the shoulders than Harry had been. She wondered if he had other things in common with his father. Did he share Harry's love of baseball or his irreverent sense of humor? Did he prefer pie to cake, the way his father had? Could he cook chili and fox-trot with the best of them?

And why did she suddenly kind of want to find out?

"All right," she said before realizing she'd made the decision. "It's nice of you to open your home to me, Mrs. Sage. Thank you."

"Call me Vivian, darling," the older woman replied with a smile. "I'm sure we're all going to be very good friends before the week is through."

Gracie wasn't so sure about that. But Vivian seemed sincere. She, at least, might turn out to be a friend. But Harrison? Well. With Harrison, Gracie would just hope for the best.

And, of course, prepare for the worst.

Three

Gracie awoke her second day on Long Island feeling only marginally less uncomfortable than she had on her first. Dinner with Vivian last night—Harrison was, not surprisingly, absent—had been reasonably polite, if not particularly chatty on Gracie's part. But she still felt out of place this morning. Probably because she was out of place. The bedroom in which Vivian had settled her was practically the size of her entire apartment back in Seattle. Jeez, the bed was practically the size of her apartment back in Seattle. The ceiling was pale blue with wisps of white clouds painted on one side that gradually faded into a star-spattered twilight sky on the other. The satiny hardwood floor was scattered with fringed flowered rugs, and the furniture and curtains could have come from the Palace at Versailles.

How could Harry have lived in a house like this?

It was nothing like him. His apartment had been furnished with scarred castoffs, and the rugs had been threadbare. His walls had been decorated with Cincinnati Reds memorabilia, some vintage posters advertising jazz in Greenwich Village and a couple of paint-by-number cocker spaniels. And Harry had loved that apartment.

There had been no ocean whispers drifting through the windows in the old neighborhood. No warm, salt-laden breezes. No deserted beaches. No palatial homes. There had been tired, well-loved old houses crowded together. There had been broken sidewalks with violets growing out of the cracks. There had been rooms crammed with remnants of lives worked hard, but well spent, too. Life. That was what had been in her and Harry's old neighborhood. Real life. The sort of life she'd always lived. The sort of life she'd assumed Harry had lived, too.

Why had a man who could have had and done anything he wanted abandoned it all to live in a tiny apartment in a working-class neighborhood six hundred miles away? Harry Sagalowsky, alleged retired TV repairman, had turned out to be quite the mystery man.

For some reason, that thought segued to others about Harry's son. Harrison Sage was kind of a mystery, too. Was he the charming flirt she'd first met in the library yesterday? Or was he the angry young man who was convinced she had taken advantage of his father? And why was it so important that she convince him she wasn't like that at all?

Today would be better, she told herself as she padded to the guest bathroom to shower. Because today she and Harrison—and Vivian, too—would have a chance to get to know each other under better circumstances. They would get to know each other period. It was a new day. A day to start over. Surely, Harrison Sage would feel that way, too. Surely, he would give her a chance to prove she was nothing like the person he thought she was.

Surely, he would.

Harrison was deliberately late for breakfast, hoping that by the time he showed up, Grace Sumner would have left, miffed to be shown so little regard now that she was richer and more important than 99 percent of the world. Instead, when he ambled out to the patio, freshly showered and wearing a navy blue polo and khakis more suitable for playing golf than for being intimidating, he found her sitting poolside with his mother. Even worse, the two women were laughing the way women did when they realized they had some shared experience that had gone awry.

And damned if Grace Sumner didn't have a really nice laugh, genuine and uninhibited, as if she laughed a lot.

His mother sat on one side of the table, still in her pajamas and robe. Grace sat on the other, looking nothing like a gold digger and very much like a girl next door. At least, she looked like what Harrison figured a girl next door was supposed to look like. It was the way girls next door always looked in movies, all fresh and sweet and innocent. He'd never seen an actual girl next door who looked like that, since the girls he'd grown up with who lived next door—a half mile down the beach—had always looked…well, kind of like gold diggers, truth be told.

But not Grace Sumner. Her burnished hair was in a ponytail today, the breeze buffeting a few loose strands around her nape and temple in a way that made Harrison itch to tuck them back into place, just so he could watch the wind dance with them again. Her flawless face was bathed in late morning sunlight, making her skin rosy. The retro suit of the day before had been replaced by retro casual clothes today—a sleeveless white button-up shirt and those pants things that weren't actually pants, but weren't shorts, either, and came to about midcalf. Hers were spattered with big, round flowers in yellow and pink. Her only jewelry was a pink plastic bracelet that had probably set her back at least two dollars. Maybe as much as three.

Had he not known better, he could almost believe she was as innocent of conning his father as she claimed. He would have to stay on guard around her. Would that his father had been as cautious, none of this would be happening.

"Oh, Harrison, there you are!" his mother called out when she saw him. "Come join us. We saved you some caviar—mostly because Gracie doesn't like caviar. Can you imagine?"

No, Harrison couldn't imagine a woman who had just swindled herself billions of dollars not liking caviar. But it was an acquired taste for some people. She'd get the hang of it once she was firmly entrenched in the new life she'd buy with his family's money.

"And there's still some champagne, too," his mother continued. "Gracie doesn't like mimosas, either."

Neither did Harrison. Still, he would have expected someone like Grace to lap up champagne in any form from her stiletto. The thought made his gaze fall to her feet. She wore plain flat shoes—pink, to match the flowers on her pants.

Okay, that did it. No woman could be as adorable and unsullied as Grace Sumner portrayed herself. It just wasn't possible in a world as corrupt and tainted as this one. He stowed what little sentimentality he had—which, thankfully, wasn't much—and armed himself with the cynicism that was so much more comfortable.

Yeah. That felt better.

"Good morning," he said as he took his seat between the women.

"It *is* a good morning," his mother replied. "I slept so much better last night, thanks to Gracie."

Gracie, Harrison repeated to himself. His mother had tossed out the diminutive three times now. It was the sort of nickname any self-respecting girl next door would invite her new best friends to use. Great. His mother had fallen under her spell, too.

"You missed a wonderful dinner last night," she added. "Gracie is giving us the Park Avenue penthouse and everything in it, too. She's already called Mr. Tarrant about it. Isn't that nice of her?"

Harrison's gaze flew to Grace, who was gazing back at him uncomfortably.

"Really," he said flatly.

His tone must have illustrated his skepticism, because Grace dropped her gaze to the fingers she'd tangled nervously atop the table. The plate beside them held the remnants of a nearly untouched breakfast. In spite of her having looked like she was enjoying herself with his mother, she was clearly uneasy.

"It's the right thing to do," she said, still avoiding

his gaze. "Harry would have wanted his family to keep the places they call home."

"The right thing to do," Harrison told her, "would be to return everything my father left you to the family who should have inherited it in the first place."

That comment, finally, made Grace look up. "Harry wanted me to give his money to worthy causes," she said. "And that's what I'm going to do."

"When?" Harrison asked.

"As soon as I get back to Seattle. I want to meet with a financial consultant first. I have no idea what to do at this point."

Of course she wanted to meet with a financial consultant. She needed to find out how to bury that much money so deep in numbered and offshore accounts that no one would be able to find it after the new appeal ruled in the Sages' favor. Which reminded him…

Harrison turned to his mother. "I spoke with our attorney this morning. He's hired thc private detective we talked about, to explore this new…avenue."

Vivian said nothing, only lifted the coffeepot to pour Harrison a cup. Grace, however, did reply.

"You're wasting your money," she said. "Not only is this…new avenue…pointless, but I'll be happy to tell you anything you want to know about me."

He studied her again—the dark, candid eyes, the bloom of color on her cheeks, the softly parted lips. She looked the same way she had yesterday when she first caught his eye, the moment she walked into the library. He couldn't remember ever reacting to a woman with the immediacy and intensity he had when he'd met her. He had no idea why. There had just been…something…about her. Something that set her apart from everyone else in the room.

At the time, he'd told himself it was because she wasn't like anyone else in the room. His joke about the pack of bloodthirsty jackals hadn't really been much of a joke. That room had been filled with predators yesterday, which anyone who'd spent time with Park Avenue lawyers and socialites could attest to. And Grace Sumner had walked right into them like a dreamy-eyed gazelle who hadn't a clue how rapacious they could be. It was that trusting aspect that had gotten to him, he realized now. Something in that first moment he saw her had made him feel as if he could trust her, too.

And trust was something Harrison hadn't felt for a very long time. Maybe he never had. Yet there she had been, making him feel that way without ever saying a word. Now that he knew who she really was…

Well, that was where things got even weirder. Because even knowing who Grace Sumner really was, he still found himself wishing he could trust her.

He quickly reviewed what he'd discovered about her on his own by typing her name into a search engine. Although she had accounts at the usual social networking sites, she kept her settings on private. He'd been able to glean a few facts, though. That she lived in Seattle and had for a year and a half. That before that, she'd lived in Cincinnati, where she grew up. He knew she'd been working as a waitress for some time, that she was attending college with an early childhood education major—always good to have a fallback in case conning old men didn't work out—and that she never commented publicly or posted duck-face selfies.

It bothered him that her behavior, both online and

now in person, didn't jibe with any of his preconceived ideas about her. An opportunistic gold digger would be a braying attention-grabber, too, wouldn't she? Then he reminded himself she was a con artist. Right? Of course she was. Naturally, she would keep her true self under wraps. That way, she could turn herself into whatever she needed to be for any given mark. Like, say, a dreamy-eyed gazelle who made a mistrustful person feel as if he could trust her.

"All right then," he said, deciding to take her up on her offer. "Have you ever been married?"

"No," she said. But she didn't elaborate.

So he did. "Have you ever been engaged?"

"No," she replied. Again without elaboration.

"Do you have a boyfriend?"

"There's no one special in my life," she told him. Then, after a small, but telling, hesitation, she added, "There never has been."

Her reply was ripe for another question, this one way more invasive than she could have considered when telling him he could ask her anything. And had it not been for his mother's presence at the table, he might very well have asked it: *Does that mean you're a virgin?* It would have been perfect. If she replied no immediately after saying there had never been anyone special in her life, she would have sounded like a tramp. Had she answered yes, at her age, she would have sounded like a liar. Win-win as far as a court appeal was concerned.

Funny, though, how suddenly he wasn't asking because he wanted to use her status against her. He wanted to know about her status for entirely personal reasons. *Was* Grace Sumner a liar and a con artist? Or was she really as sweet and innocent as she seemed? And why was he kind of hoping it was the latter? Not only would it give him the upper hand if he *could* prove she was conning them all, but it would make her the kind of person he knew how to deal with. He knew nothing of sweetness and innocence. No one in his social or professional circles claimed either trait.

"Do you have any brothers or sisters?" he asked, trying a new tack.

She shook her head. "I'm an only child."

"Mother's maiden name?"

"Sumner."

The same as Grace's. Meaning… "No father?" he asked.

At this, she smiled. "Um, yeah, I had a father. Everyone does. Were you absent from health class that day?"

He refused to be charmed by her irreverence—or her smile. Instead, he asked, "What was your father's name?"

Her answer was matter-of-fact. "I don't know."

"You don't know who your father was?"

She shook her head, something that freed another tantalizing strand of gold from her ponytail. "My mother never told me. On my birth certificate, he's listed as unknown."

Okay, this was getting interesting. It wouldn't be surprising to anyone—like, say, a probate appeals judge—to discover that a young woman whose father had been absent when she was a child would, as an adult, turn to conning old men. Even if she hadn't set out to become a professional grifter when she was a little girl, should an opportunity for such present itself when she was older, it wasn't a stretch to see how a woman like that would take advantage of it.

Maybe she was right. Maybe he wouldn't need a private investigator after all.

"What about your grandparents?" he asked.

"I barely remember my grandmother," she said. "She died before I started school."

"And your grandfather?"

"He died when my mother was in high school. My grandmother never remarried."

Oh, this was getting too easy. A pattern had developed of male role models being completely absent from the life of little Gracie Sumner. It didn't take Freud to figure this one out.

Unable to help himself, he spoke his thoughts out loud. "So. Major daddy issues. Am I right?"

"Harrison!" his mother exclaimed.

Whether her reaction was due to anger at his invasive question or worry that it would make Grace change her mind about giving her back her homes, he couldn't have said. Still, he supposed maybe, possibly, perhaps, he had overstepped there.

"Sorry," he apologized. Almost genuinely, too. "That was out of line."

"Yeah, it was," Grace agreed.

Surprisingly, though, she didn't seem to take offense. Certainly not as much as Harrison would have, had he been asked the same question.

"No, Mr. Sage, I do not have daddy issues," she continued evenly. "I come from a long line of smart, independent women who didn't need the help of anyone—least of all a man—to get by."

He was surprised by the splinter of admiration that tried to wedge itself under his skin at her cool reply.

Until she added, "But you should probably talk to someone about your own issues."

He grinned at that. "What issues?"

"The one you have about strong, independent women."

"I don't have issues with women," he told her. "I have issues with *a* woman. A woman who took advantage of my father."

He could tell by her expression that there was more she wanted to say on that matter. Instead, she said, "If you'll both excuse me, I thought I'd take the train into New York today to do some sightseeing, since I may never have the chance again."

Harrison bit back a comment about the private jet and the yacht she owned, thanks to his father, and how she could go anywhere in the world she wanted, whenever she felt like it. Instead, he sipped his coffee in silence and tried not to notice the wisp of dark gold hair that was curling against her nape in a way that made him unwillingly envious. If she were any other woman, he would have reached over and coiled that strand of silk around his finger, then used it to gently pull her face toward his so he could—

So he could nothing, he told himself. Grace Sumner was the last woman he wanted to touch with affection. Or anything else. Even a ten-foot pole.

"That's a lovely idea," his mother said. "You should do some shopping, too. A young girl like you—" She smiled in a way that was kind of astonishing in light of the fact that she'd just encouraged a stranger to go out and spend money that should belong to her. "A young *rich* girl like you," she amended, "should have a closet full of beautiful things to wear. Beautiful *new* things."

The emphasis on the word *new* obviously didn't escape Grace's notice. She glanced down at her outfit, one that looked like something from a sixties flick titled *Beach Blanket Barbie.* Strangely, she didn't seem to think there was anything wrong with it. For a moment, she looked as if she wanted to explain her wardrobe choices, and then seemed to change her mind. Good call, Harrison thought. His mother never kept clothes past the season and year for which they'd been designed.

"Timmerman can drive you to the train," Vivian told her. "Just remember to be back by eight, because Eleanor is making something special for dinner tonight. In your honor."

Somehow, Harrison kept from rolling his eyes. His mother was becoming such a suck-up.

After Grace left, he finished his coffee, downed what was left of the bacon and toast and listened for the car to pull away from the house. Then he headed for his Maserati and made his way to the train station, too.

So Grace wanted to see the sights of New York City. Right. All along Fifth Avenue, he'd bet. Starting with Saks and ending with Tiffany, allowing just enough time for a late lunch at Le Bernardin. Luckily, he'd given himself the rest of the week off—he could do that, being the owner of his own company—to deal with The Sumner Problem, so he had no obligations today.

None except exposing a con artist who was so good at what she did, she could make a man long for things he knew he would never have.

* * *

It was some hours later that Harrison discovered how right he'd been in his suspicions—Grace Sumner did go shopping and treat herself to a late lunch. But only after seeing sights like the Empire State Building, Rockefeller Center and Times Square. And even though that last left her within walking distance of Fifth Avenue, she took the subway to go hopscotching all over Brooklyn. Specifically, through the thrift stores of Brooklyn. And instead of Le Bernardin, she bought her lunch from a Salvadoran food truck.

Grace Sumner was either a con artist of even greater sophistication than he'd thought, or she knew he was following her. And since he was confident he hadn't revealed himself, he was going for the former. Unless, of course, her intentions toward his father's money were exactly what she claimed, and she would be giving it all away, meaning she was on a major budget that prohibited things like Fifth Avenue shopping sprees.

Yeah, right. And maybe tonight, while he was sleeping, the Blue Fairy would fly into his room and turn him into a real boy.

What the hell kind of game was she playing? And how long was she going to play it? Even if—no, when—his detective discovered the truth about her, and an appeals court finally found in the Sages' favor, for now, his father's money legally belonged to her. It could be weeks, even months, before Harrison had the evidence he needed to win the return of his father's fortune. It would take even longer for another appeal in court. In the meantime, she was within her rights to spend every dime.

So why wasn't she doing that? And why was she

staying with his mother on Long Island, away from Bennett Tarrant and his colleagues, who were the only support she had? There was more going on here than a simple con. There had to be. Harrison just needed to figure out what it was. And he would have to do it within a week, since Grace would be leaving after the paperwork was complete to return the estate and the penthouse to his mother. Just who was Grace Sumner—wicked woman or good girl?

And the toughest question to answer of all—why was Harrison kind of hoping it was the latter?

Four

Until she saw it in action, Gracie never would have guessed how closely the New York Stock Exchange after the ringing of the bell resembled the kitchen of Café Destiné after the eighty-sixing of the béchamel sauce. Absolute mayhem. And she wasn't even *on* the floor. She was with Harrison in the gallery above it, looking down as millions of dollars' worth of commodities, futures and options—and, for all she knew, lunches, Pokémon cards and Neopets—were traded, bought and sold in a way she would never, ever understand. Not that Harrison hadn't tried to explain it to her. He'd used every minute of their drive from Long Island doing just that—probably because it kept him from having to talk to her about anything else.

It had been Vivian's idea that he should bring Gracie into the city again today, but for a different kind of sightseeing. Last night, over dinner, when Gracie and Harrison had been gazing suspiciously at each other across the table and responding to Vivian's attempts at repartee with little more than awkward mumbling, his mother had suggested the two of them should spend more time together so that each could get to know the other's version of the man they shared in common.

Gracie figured it was more likely, though, that Vivian was worried about the antagonism that could potentially mushroom between Gracie and Harrison, and how Vivian would then be left homeless.

So Gracie and Harrison had risen extra early to make it to Wall Street in time to hear the Friday opening bell. Early enough that Gracie only had time to consume a single cup of coffee. That had given her just enough presence of mind to at least pretend she understood all the stuff Harrison said about SEC, PLC and OTC—and the stuff about yearlings and bulls and bears, oh my—but it hadn't constituted much in the way of breakfast. Now her UGI was growling like a bear, her mood was fast depreciating and her brain was beginning to liquidate.

Hmm. Maybe she'd understood more of what he'd said than she thought. Despite the downturn of her current market…ah, she meant, body…she tried to focus on what he was saying now.

"My father had a real gift for trading," he told her.

Harrison fit in this world nicely with his dark slate suit and dove-gray dress shirt, but his necktie, with its multicolored dots, was a tad less conservative than the staid diagonal stripes and discreet tiny diamonds on the ties worn by the other men. Although Gracie had tried to dress for business, too, the best she'd been able to do was another vintage suit—the second of the only two she owned. This one was a dark ruby with pencil skirt and cinch-waisted jacket with a slight peplum. She'd thought she looked pretty great when she got dressed. Seeing the other women in their dark grays and blacks and neutrals, she now felt like a giant lollipop.

"His initial fortune," Harrison continued, "the one he used to buy and build his companies, was all earned in the stock market. He never went to college. Did you know that?"

There was something akin to pride in his voice when he spoke of Harry's lack of formal education. It surprised Gracie. She would have thought Harrison was the kind of man who wouldn't want anyone to know about his father's lack of education because it would be an embarrassment to the family name.

"I did know that, actually," she said. "But he told me it was because he couldn't afford to pay for college."

"He couldn't. Not after he graduated from high school, anyway."

"Harry never graduated from high school."

The moment the words were out of her mouth, Gracie regretted them. Not because she worried they would be an embarrassment to the Sage name, too, but because Harrison's expression made clear he hadn't known that. And now he was finding it out from someone he'd just met who had obviously known it for some time.

Nevertheless, he said, "Of course my father graduated from high school. Findlay High School in Cincinnati. Class of fifty-three."

"Harry never even made it to his junior year," Gracie told him. "He dropped out when he was fifteen to work in the Formica factory. He lied about his age to get the job and join the union."

Harrison gazed at her blankly. "Why would he do that?"

Oh, boy. There was obviously *a lot* he didn't know about his father's early life. And Gracie didn't want to be the one to let the cat out of the bag, which, in Harry's case, would be more like freeing a Siberian tiger from the Moscow Zoo.

Gently, she said, "Because by then, Harry's father was drinking so much, he couldn't hold down a job, and his mother was caring for his little brother, so she couldn't work, either. Harry had to be the one to support the family."

At the word *brother*, Harrison's eyes went wide, and Gracie's heart dropped to her stomach. Surely, he'd at least known his father had a brother.

"My father had a *brother*?"

Okay, maybe not. "Yeah. You didn't know?"

Although Harrison's gaze was fixed on hers, she could tell by the emptiness in those blue, blue eyes that his thoughts were a billion miles away. Or, at least, a few decades away. Or maybe he was just trying to decide whether or not to even believe her. But Gracie had seen photos of Harry's family. The old pictures were with his things in the storage unit.

Harrison shook his head lightly, honing his icy blue gaze—which somehow, suddenly, seemed a little less icy—on Gracie again. "But I always thought… I mean he told me… Well, okay he never really *told* me, but I always assumed…" When he realized he wasn't making sense, he inhaled a breath and released it. "I always thought he was an only child. By the time I was born, his parents were both dead, and he never mentioned any other family. Hell, he barely mentioned his parents."

Gracie tried to tread lightly as she told him, "Benjy—that was his little brother—had polio. He died when he was thirteen, and Harry was sixteen. It hit him pretty hard. His mother, too. She left home a year or so later, and Harry never saw her again. He took care of his dad for a couple more years, until he died, too, of cirrhosis. Then Harry left Cincinnati and didn't come back until after he retired from his job as a TV repairman.

"Well, that was what he told me, anyway," she quickly amended. "That he made his living in New York as a TV repairman. Obviously, that part wasn't true. But the rest of it was. When I packed up his things after his death, I found photos and some old diaries that belonged to his mother. I'll be sure everything is sent to you and Vivian once I get back to Seattle."

Harrison eyed her thoughtfully. A little too thoughtfully for Gracie's comfort. He was doing that thing again where he seemed to be trying to peer into her soul. And was succeeding. All he said, though, was "What else did my father tell you about his childhood?"

"He said that after his father died, he took what little money he'd saved and went to New York. TV was just starting to become popular, and he got a job in a little appliance shop and taught himself everything he could. After a while, he opened his own repair business in Queens and lived and worked there until he retired."

"He never mentioned getting married?" Harrison asked. "Three times, at that? Never mentioned having kids? Seven of us?"

She shook her head. "Never. I mean, I always wondered. He never said he *didn't* marry or have a family. But I didn't want to pry. He just told me that after he retired, he started missing Cincinnati, so he moved back to his old neighborhood."

Harrison said nothing in response to that, but he continued to look at Gracie in that way that made something hot and gooey eddy in her belly, melting bit by bit until it warmed her all over. How could he make her feel like that? He'd made no secret of the fact that he didn't trust her. He didn't even like her. Except for their initial meeting, the time the two of them had shared together had been combative at worst and uncomfortable at best. There should be no hot gooeyness in a situation like that.

But maybe that was the problem. Not the unpleasant times since the two of them met. But the handful of moments when the two of them had first encountered each other in the library. Something had definitely blossomed between them in those moments, and it had been anything but unpleasant. Those moments had been some of the sweetest Gracie had ever known. She'd never had a reaction to a man like she'd had to Harrison. Why couldn't the two of them hit Rewind and start over? Go back to that first second when her eyes met his, and she felt as if the pieces of her life that had been ripped apart in the days since meeting Mr. Tarrant had suddenly fallen back into place?

When Harrison still didn't respond to anything she'd told him, she asked softly, "You didn't know any of that stuff about his parents or brother, did you?"

He shook his head.

"What did your father tell you about his childhood?"

"Not much. That he grew up in Cincinnati. That his mother was a teacher and his father worked in a factory. That he used money he saved from a paper route to come to New York after high school."

His expression suddenly changed, moving from quietly preoccupied to fiercely keen. "After his arrival in New York, though, I heard all about that. Over and over again."

"Guess it didn't have anything to do with a TV repair shop, huh?"

He chuckled, but there was nothing happy in the sound. "No. It was all about how he found work as a runner for a brokerage in Manhattan and worked his way up, investing what he could where he could whenever he had a spare nickel. How he made his first million when he was twenty-five. How he bought his first business at twenty-seven. How, at thirty, he was worth tens of millions of dollars. At forty, hundreds of millions. Easy as pie. He had things fall into his lap and then was smart enough to exploit them for all they were worth. Hell, he berated me for not earning my keep when I was a kid. He may have gone into his office every day to keep an eye on things, but as far as actual work? He never worked a day in his life as an adult."

Gracie couldn't help the sound of disbelief that escaped her. "Oh, please. I never met anyone who worked harder than Harry Sagalowsky."

Harrison threw her another one of those dubious looks. "You said he was retired when you met him."

"Yeah, but he was active in his church, he volunteered at the veterans hospital, he served meals at a homeless shelter most weekends and he coached Little League."

She could tell Harrison stopped believing her with the first sentence—he even started shaking his head before she finished speaking. "My father never went to church, he was never in the military, he thought poverty was a scam and he hated kids."

"Your father sang in the choir," Gracie countered. "And he felt a debt to people in uniform because he grew up during a time when a lot of them never made it home from war. I'd think by now you'd realize how he feels about poverty, since he wants me to give away all his money to worthy causes. And I never saw him happier than he was when he was with his team. I bet you didn't even realize what a huge Reds fan he was, did you?"

Now Harrison was the one to utter an incredulous sound. "This just proves I can't trust anything you say. Nothing you've said about my father rings true. Nothing."

"And nothing you've said about him rings true for me, either."

She still couldn't understand how the Harry she'd known could have been a big-shot corporate mogul or abandoned a wife and son. There must have been a reason for it. He'd said in his video that his home life had become unhappy, but that should have made him determined to stay and fix whatever was wrong. Harry really was the finest man Gracie had ever met. So how could he have done things that weren't fine at all?

The tentative moment of…whatever it was she and Harrison had begun to share was gone. And really, did it matter how they felt about each other? Two judges had awarded Gracie Harry's fortune, and she was duty-bound to disburse it in a way that would honor his wishes. It didn't matter if Harrison Sage believed her. It didn't matter if he trusted her. It didn't matter if he liked her. And it didn't matter how he felt about his father, either, since it was too late for any attempts to make amends there. Harry's death had ensured that his son would never have a chance to understand the man beneath the high-powered pinstripes who had walked out on his family fifteen years before. There would be no resolution for that relationship. Ever.

Or would there?

Gracie studied Harrison again, remembering the way he'd been in the library, before their formal introductions. He had reminded her of Harry, she recalled. He had smiled like his father. He'd been as charming. As easy to talk to. He had the same blue eyes and, now that she paid more attention, the same straight nose and blunt jaw. Had circumstances been different, had Harry not been a titan of industry, had he spent more time with his family and given more freely of himself to them, things might have turned out differently for father and son. They might have recognized they had a lot in common. They might have even been friends.

"You didn't really know him, either, did you?" Gracie said softly.

Harrison deflated a little at the question. "The man I knew was nothing like you describe."

"Maybe while he was your father, he wasn't," she conceded. "And that's a shame."

Now Harrison stiffened. "Why is that a shame? My father was one of the most successful men of his time. How can there be anything shameful in that?"

"Because he could have been a successful father,

too," Gracie said. "I wish you'd known the man I did. The Harry I knew was a good guy, Harrison."

It was the first time she had called him by his first name, and it surprised her how easily it rolled off her tongue, and how good it felt to say it. Harrison seemed surprised, too. He opened his mouth to say something, then evidently changed his mind and glanced away. When he did, something—some odd trick of the light—shadowed his eyes, turning the anger to melancholy.

She tried again. "You know, there's a lot of your father in you. I recognized it right away, when you and I were talking in the library the other day."

He turned to look at her again, more thoughtfully this time. "That was who you meant when you told me I reminded you of someone."

She nodded.

"But he and I had nothing in common."

"You look like him."

"Not surprising, since we come from the same gene pool."

"You told me a joke, right off the bat. That was just like something Harry would do."

"That was just like something a lot of men would do if they were trying to impress a—" He halted abruptly, then said quickly, "That was just like something a lot of men would do."

"It still reminded me of Harry."

Harrison returned his attention to the trading floor. "He brought me here when I was a kid," he said quietly. "Once. I was six or seven. He wanted to show me how fortunes were made and lost. He said this—" he gestured down at the chaos below "—was what made the whole world work. He told me money was more important than anything, because it could buy anything. Not just material possessions, but *anything.* Adventure. Culture. Intelligence. It could buy friends. Allies. Even governments. Not to mention things like respect and dignity and love."

Gracie wanted to deny that Harry could have ever been that cynical or said anything that cold. Especially to a child. Especially to his own son. The man she'd known had thought money was what caused all the world's problems, not solved them. And he'd known it was a person's actions, not their income, that garnered respect and dignity and love.

"You can't buy love," she said softly.

Harrison looked at her. "No?"

She shook her head.

He glanced back down at the floor. "Maybe not. But you can buy something that feels like it."

"No, you can't," Gracie countered. "Maybe you can lie to yourself until you believe that, but..."

When he looked at her this time, she was the one to glance away.

"But what?" he asked.

She shook her head again. "Nothing."

He studied her so long without speaking that it began to feel as if he were trying to insert a little piece of himself inside her. What was weird was that a piece of him should feel like a pebble in her shoe. Instead, it felt more like more a ray of sunshine on her face.

"You must be hungry," he finally said.

There was a huskiness in his voice when he spoke that made something in her stomach catch fire. She didn't dare look at him for fear that those blue eyes would be burning, too. How did he do that? How did he make any given situation feel almost…sexual? He'd done it in the library that first morning, and again at breakfast yesterday. The man was just strangely potent.

"A little," she said, hoping her stomach didn't decide to punctuate the statement with the kind of growl that normally preceded a lunge to the jugular.

"My mother suggested I take you to my father's club for lunch," he said. "By the time we get there, they should be ready to serve."

"Lunch sounds great," she told him.

Even if lunch actually sounded like another opportunity for the two of them to find something to be at odds about. At least food would quiet the wild animal that seemed to have taken up residence in her belly.

Now if she could just figure out how to quiet the wild thoughts suddenly tumbling through her brain.

Harrison watched Grace from the other side of the table at the Cosmopolitan Club, doing his best to not notice how, in this place, surrounded by all its Art Deco splendor, she looked like some seductive film-noir siren. Her form-hugging suit, the color of forbidden fruit, was buttoned high enough to be acceptable in professional circles, but low enough to make a man—to make Harrison—want to reach across the table and start unbuttoning it. She'd worn her hair down today, parted on one side to swoop over her forehead, something that only added to her Veronica Lake, femme fatale appearance. All she needed to complete it was some raging red lipstick. As usual, though, she didn't seem to be wearing makeup at all. Meaning she was once again that combination of sexpot and girl next door that made him want to—

Okay, so it probably wasn't a good idea to think further about what her appearance made him want to do. Probably, it was better to look at the menu and figure out what he wanted. Besides Grace, he meant.

How could he want someone who had almost certainly taken advantage of his father and pocketed the family fortune? On the other hand, what did ethics and morality have to do with sex? It wasn't as if Harrison hadn't slept with other women who were ethically and morally challenged.

Wait a minute. Hang on. He replayed that last sentence in his brain. It wasn't as if he hadn't slept with *other* women like that? Meaning that somewhere in his subconscious, he was thinking about sleeping with Grace? When did that happen? Then again, why shouldn't he sleep with Grace? He might as well get something out of this arrangement.

"What's good here?" she asked, bringing his attention back to the matter at hand.

"If you like light, go with the brie salad. If you like sandwiches, try the club. It you want something more exotic, the curried shrimp."

"Oh, that does sound good," she said. She scanned the menu until she found a description, then uttered a flat "Oh."

"What?" Harrison asked.

"There aren't any prices listed on this menu."

He still couldn't decide whether or not she was pretending to be something she wasn't. If this was all an act, then she really did deserve an award. If it wasn't, then she was a pod person from outer space. No one could be this naive.

"You don't know what it means when prices aren't listed on a menu?" he asked skeptically.

"Of course I know what that means," she said. "No one's that naive."

"Then what's the problem?"

"I can't afford a place where the prices aren't listed. The money your father left me isn't mine."

"It is until you give it to someone else." And he still wasn't convinced she would do it.

"But—"

"Look, it's my treat," he interrupted. "I'm a member here, too."

"Oh," she said again. Only this time it wasn't a flat *oh*. This time it was a surprised *oh*. As in "Oh, you have your own money?"

"I do have a job, you know," he replied before she could ask.

"I didn't mean—"

"You thought I was just some lazy, entitled player who never worked a day in his life, didn't you?"

"No, I—"

"I actually have my own business," he said, hoping he didn't sound as smug about that as he felt, but figuring by her expression that he probably did. Oh, well. "Sage Assets," he continued. "We're consultants in financial risk management."

She clearly had no idea what he was talking about, a realization that nagged again at his conviction that she was driven only by money. "Which means what?" she asked.

"We advise businesses and investors on how not

to lose their shirts in times of financial crisis. Or any other time, for that matter. I started the company right after I graduated from Columbia, and it took off right away," he added modestly. Well, sort of modestly. Okay, not modestly at all. "That being a time of financial crisis. And my father wasn't the only one in the family with a gift for trading." Then, because he couldn't quite keep himself from saying it, he added, "I made my first million when I was twenty-three. I was worth tens of millions by the time I was twenty-seven."

Beating his father's timetable on those achievements by years. At the rate he was going, he'd be beating that hundreds-of-millions thing, too, by a good five years. Not that his father had ever realized—or would ever realize—any of those things. Not that that was the point. Not that Harrison cared. He didn't.

Grace didn't seem as impressed by his achievements as Harrison was. Then again, she had fourteen billion dollars. He was a lightweight compared to her.

"Well, for what it's worth," she said, "I didn't think you were a lazy, entitled player who never worked a day in your life."

"No?"

She shook her head. "I figured you had a job."

Only when she punctuated the statement with a smile did he realize she was making a joke. He refused to be charmed.

"Then you did think I was an entitled player."

Instead of answering, she glanced back down at her menu and said, "You know, I do like a good club sandwich..."

Their server came and took their orders, returning with their drinks. Grace reached for the sugar caddy and used the tongs to pluck out four cubes for her tea. After stirring, she took a sip, and then tonged in two more. As if Grace Sumner needed any more sweetness.

It didn't help that she kept glancing around the room as if she'd just fallen off the turnip truck. Of course, the place was pretty impressive. The Cosmopolitan had been built in the Roaring Twenties by a group of rich industrialists so they and all their equally wealthy friends would have a sumptuous sanctuary to escape the wretched refuse of New York. The furnishings were as rich, extravagant and bombastic as they'd been, all mahogany and velvet and crystal, and the current owners spared no expense to maintain that aura of a bygone era. He and Grace might as well have been lunching with Calvin Coolidge.

"I don't think I've ever been in a place like this before," she said. She grinned again before adding, "Unless you count the Haunted Mansion at Disney World."

Harrison smiled back, surprised to discover it felt genuine. Not sure why, he played along. "I wouldn't count that. They let in all kinds of riffraff at the Haunted Mansion, and the dress code is way too relaxed."

She gave the room another assessment and sighed. "I can't imagine Harry here. His favorite place for lunch was Golden Corral. And I never saw him in a suit."

"I don't think I ever saw him in anything but a suit," Harrison said. "When I was a kid, he was always already dressed for work when I got up, and he usually didn't get home until after I went to bed."

"What about on weekends?" she asked. "Or vacations? Or just relaxing around the house?"

"My father never relaxed. He worked most weekends. The only vacations I ever took were with my mother."

She shook her head. "Everything you tell me about Harry is just so not Harry. What happened to him, that he was so driven by work and money for so long, and then suddenly turned his back on all of it?"

Harrison wished he could answer that. Hell, he wished he could believe everything Grace had said about his father was true. But none of it sounded like him. Not the part about having a sick little brother, not the part about his dropping out of school and definitely not the part about coaching Little League or serving meals to the homeless. *Was* she a con artist? Or had she been as much a target of his father's caprice as the rest of them?

"If what you said about my father's childhood was true—"

"You don't think I was telling the truth about that, either?" she interjected, sounding—and looking—wounded.

"I don't know what to believe," he said honestly.

He still wasn't convinced she was as altruistic as she claimed. The return of his mother's house and the Manhattan penthouse were only drops in the ocean when it came to the totality of his father's wealth. She would still have billions of dollars after shedding those. And she hadn't committed any of those billions to any causes yet.

"But if what you said is true," he continued, "then it's obvious why he was driven by money. Anyone who grew up poor would naturally want to be rich."

"Why is that natural?" she asked.

He didn't understand the question. "What do you mean?"

"Why do you think the desire to be rich is natural?"

He was still confused. "Don't you think it is?"

"No. I mean, I can see how it might have motivated Harry, but not because it was natural. A lot of people are content with what they have, even if they aren't rich. There is such a thing as enough."

"I don't follow you."

At this, she leaned back in her chair and sighed with unmistakable disappointment. "Yeah, I know."

He was about to ask her what she meant by that, too, when their server returned to deliver their selections, taking a few moments to arrange everything on the table until it was feng shui-ed to his liking. After that, the moment with Grace was gone, and she was gushing about her club sandwich, so Harrison let her comment go. For now.

"So where else does Vivian want you to take me?" she asked.

"To one of my father's businesses and a prep school whose board of directors he sat on. And tonight one of his old colleagues is having a cocktail party. I was going to blow it off, but my mother is going and insists you and I come, too."

A flash of panic crossed her expression. "Cocktail party?"

"Is that a problem?"

"Kind of. I didn't bring anything to wear to a cocktail party."

"Fifth Avenue is right around the corner."

Her panic increased. "But Fifth Avenue is so—"

When she didn't finish, Harrison prompted, "So…?"

She looked left, then right, to make sure the diners on each side of them were engrossed in their own conversations. Then she leaned across the table and lowered her voice. "I can't afford Fifth Avenue."

Harrison leaned forward, too, lowering his voice to mimic hers. "You have fourteen billion dollars."

"I told you. That's not mine," she whispered back.

Seriously, she was going to insist she couldn't afford a dress? He leaned back in his chair, returning to his normal voice. "My father told you to take some of the money for yourself," he reminded her.

She sat back, too. "I refuse to pay Fifth Avenue prices for a dress when I can buy one for almost a hundred percent less in a thrift shop."

Harrison turned his attention to his plate, where a gorgeous swordfish steak was just begging to be enjoyed. "Yeah, well, I'm not traipsing all over Brooklyn again, so you can forget about going back there to shop."

The pause that followed his statement was so pregnant, it could have delivered an elephant. When he looked at Grace again, she had completely forgotten her own lunch and looked ready to stick her butter knife into him instead.

Very softly, she asked, "How did you know I went to Brooklyn yesterday?"

Crap. Busted.

He scrambled for a credible excuse, but figured it would be pointless. "I followed you."

"Why?"

Resigned to be honest, since she seemed like the kind of woman who would sniff out a lie a mile away, he said, "Because I wanted to see if you would go out and start blowing my father's money. On, say, Fifth Avenue."

"Why won't you believe me when I tell you I intend to give away your father's money the way he asked me to?"

"Because it's fourteen billion dollars. No one gives away fourteen billion dollars."

"I'm going to."

Yeah, well, that remained to be seen. Instead of continuing with their current topic, Harrison backpedaled to the one before it. "Don't worry about the dress. I'm sure we can find a store you like nearby. I'll ask the concierge on our way out."

Which would doubtlessly be the highlight of the concierge's month. Someone at the Cosmopolitan asking where the nearest thrift shop was. The club would be talking about that one for weeks.

Five

Gracie couldn't believe she was standing at the front door of an Upper East Side penthouse, about to ring the bell. How could she have insisted earlier that Harrison go ahead of her to the party so she could shop for something to wear? She was never going to be allowed into a place like this without him. She still couldn't believe the doorman for the building had opened the door for her in the first place—even tipping his hat as he did—or that the concierge hadn't tried to stop her when she headed for the elevator, or that the elevator operator had told her it wasn't necessary when she fumbled in her purse for the invitation Harrison had given her to prove she had been invited into this world. He'd just closed the doors and pushed the button that would rocket her straight to the top, as if that were exactly where she belonged.

This was the kind of place that wasn't supposed to allow in people like her. Normal people. Working people. People who hadn't even had the proper attire for this party until a couple of hours ago, and whose attire still probably wasn't all that proper, since she'd bought it at a secondhand shop.

She couldn't remember ever being this nervous. But then throwing herself into a situation where she had no idea how to behave or what to talk about, and didn't have a single advocate to cover her back, could do that to a person. Even if being thrown into situations like that had been Gracie's entire day.

After leaving the Cosmopolitan Club, she and Harrison had gone to the prep school where Harry had, once upon a time, sat on the board of directors. Interestingly, it was also the school Harrison had attended from kindergarten through twelfth grade, for a mere sixty-three thousand dollars a year—though he'd told her tuition was only forty-eight thousand when he started, so a big "whew!" on that. The kids had worn tidy navy blue uniforms, they'd walked silently and with great restraint through the halls, their lunches had consisted of fresh produce, lean meats and whole-grain breads trucked in from Connecticut and their curriculum had focused on science, mathematics and the classics. Art and music were extracurriculars that were discouraged in favor of Future Business Leaders of America and Junior Achievement.

It had been such a stark contrast to Gracie's public school education, where the dress code had been pretty much anything that wasn't indecent, the halls had been noisy and chaotic during class changes, the lunches had overwhelmingly been brown-bagged from home and filled with things factory-sealed in plastic and the curriculum had been as busy and inconsistent—in a good way—as the halls, with art and music as daily requirements.

So not only had Harry told his son that money was the most important thing in the world, but he'd also proved it by spending all his time making money and sending Harrison to a school more intent on turning its students into corporate drones than in guiding them into something constructive and fulfilling. What the hell had he been thinking?

The headquarters of Sage Holdings, Inc., where Harry had once been the man in charge, had been no better: all antiseptic and barren, in spite of being filled with workers. Workers who had spoken not a word to each other, because they'd all been confined to cubicles and hunched over computers, tap-tap-tapping on their keyboards with the diligent dedication of worker bees. How could Harry have made his employees work in such soul-deadening surroundings?

And would this party tonight reinforce her anti-Harry Sagalowsky feelings as much as the rest of today had?

Gracie inhaled a deep breath and released it, telling herself everything was going to be fine. She was fine. Her attire was fine. She'd been enchanted by the dress the moment she saw it, a pale mint confection of silk with a frothy crinoline underskirt, a ruched neckline and off-the-shoulder cap sleeves. She'd found accessories at the shop, too—plain pearly pumps and a clutch and a crystal necklace and earrings, along with a pair of white gloves that climbed midway between wrist and elbow. And she'd managed to twist her hair into a serviceable chignon and applied just enough blush and lipstick to keep herself from being as pale as… well, as pale as a woman who was about to enter a situation where she had no idea how to behave or what to talk about.

With one final, fortifying inhale-exhale—*for God's sake, Gracie, just breathe*—she pushed her index finger against the doorbell. Immediately, the door opened, and she was greeted by a smiling butler. Though his smile didn't look like a real smile. Probably, it was a smile he was being paid to smile.

Wow. Harry was right. Money really could buy anything.

No, it couldn't, she immediately reminded herself. Money hadn't been able to buy Gracie, after all. Not that Devon Braun and his father hadn't tried once upon a time.

Wow. Where had that memory come from? She hadn't given a thought to those two scumbags for a long time. And she wouldn't think about them tonight, either. This party would be nothing like the one that set those unfortunate events in motion.

She opened her purse to retrieve her invitation, since butlers were obviously way too smart to allow someone entry just because she was wearing a vintage Dior knockoff and a serviceable chignon. But even though the purse was roughly the size of a canapé, she couldn't find what she was looking for. Just her lipstick and compact in case she needed to refresh her makeup, her driver's license in case she got hit by a bus, and the paramedics needed to identify her body, and her debit card in case Harrison shoved her out of the car in a sketchy part of town and she needed to take a cab back to Long Island, which could happen, since he still didn't seem to believe her intentions toward Harry's fortune were honorable. But no invitation.

She must have dropped it in the elevator when she was fumbling to get it out of her purse the first time. She was about to turn back that way when the same dark, velvety voice that had rescued her from the crowd at the reading of Harry's will saved her again.

"It's all right, Ballantine," Harrison said from behind the butler. "She's with me."

She's with me. Somehow, Harrison made it sound as if she really was *with him*. In a romantic, intimate sense. A tingle of pleasure hummed through her.

Although Gracie had had boyfriends since she was old enough to want one, none had ever been especially serious. Well, okay, that wasn't entirely true. There had been one a while back who'd started to become serious. Devon Braun. A guy she'd met at a party she attended with a friend from school. A guy who'd taken her to a lot of parties like this one, since his family had been rich. But Devon had been sweeter and less obnoxious than most of the guys who came from that background. At least, Gracie had thought so then. For a couple of months, anyway.

But she wasn't going to think about that—about him—tonight. She'd done extremely well shoving him to the back of her brain since leaving Cincinnati, and she wasn't about to let him mess things up now. Tonight she was with Harrison. He'd just said so. And even if they went back to their wary dancing around each other tomorrow, she intended to avoid any missteps tonight.

Unfortunately, she was barely two steps past Ballantine the butler when she began to wonder if she'd been premature in her conviction. Because the minute Harrison got a good look at her, his smile fell. Somehow, Gracie was positive his thoughts just then were something along the lines of how he couldn't believe she'd shown up dressed the way she was.

When she looked past him into the room, she realized why. Although all the men were dressed as he was—in dark suits and ties—none of the women was dressed like her. Nearly all of them were wearing black, and although there were one or two bursts of taupe, there wasn't any clothing in the entire room that could have been called colorful. Or frothy. Or a confection. Except for a bubbly bit of pale mint silk on a woman who looked and felt—and was—completely out of place.

She forced her feet forward, manufacturing a smile for Ballantine as she passed him that was no more genuine than his, and made her way toward Harrison, whose gaze never left her as she approached.

Although she was pretty sure she already knew the answer to the question, she greeted him by asking, "Is there something wrong?"

He gave her a quick once-over, but didn't look quite as stunned this time. She decided to take it as a compliment.

"Why do you ask?" he replied.

She lifted one shoulder and let it drop. "You look like there's something wrong."

Instead of giving her the once-over this time, he simply studied her face. "You look..."

Here it comes, Gracie thought, bracing herself.

"...different," he said.

It wasn't the word she'd expected. Nor did she understand why he chose it. She hadn't done anything different today from what she'd done every other day he'd seen her. Maybe she'd put on a little more makeup and expended more effort on her hair, but what difference did that make?

"Good different or bad different?" she asked.

He hesitated, then slowly shook his head. "Just… different."

"Oh. Should I leave?"

At this, he looked genuinely surprised. "No. Of course not. Why would you even ask that?"

"Because you seem to think—"

"Gracie, darling!"

The exclamation from Vivian Sage came just in time, because Harrison looked like he wanted to say something else that was probably better left unsaid. Vivian looked smashing, her black dress a sleeveless, V-necked number that was elegant in its simplicity and sumptuous in its fabric. She carried a crystal-encrusted clutch in one hand and a cocktail in the other. She stopped in front of Gracie, leaning in to give her one of those Hollywood air kisses on her cheek before backing away again.

"Darling, you look absolutely adorable," she said. "You could be me when I was young. I think I had a dress just like that."

Of course she did. Except Vivian's would have had a genuine Dior tag sewn inside it, instead of one that *looked* like it said, Christian Dior Paris, but, upon close inspection, really said, Christina Diaz, Paramus. But Vivian had uttered the compliment sincerely, so maybe the evening wouldn't be so horrible, after all.

Then she had to go and ruin that possibility by turning to her son and saying, "Doesn't she look beautiful, Harrison?"

But he surprised Gracie by saying, "Uh, yeah. Beautiful."

Unfortunately, he dropped his gaze to the floor before saying it, thereby making it possible that he was talking about their host's carpet selection instead. Which, okay, was pretty beautiful, all lush and white, like the rest of the room.

This time, when Vivian leaned in, it was toward Harrison. "Then tell her, darling. A woman wants to be reassured that she's the most beautiful woman in the room, especially when she's at one of Bunny and Peter's parties." To Gracie, she added, "Bunny Dewitt is one of New York's biggest fashion icons. She's always being written up in the style section. Every woman here is worried that she's underdressed or overdressed or wearing something so five-minutes-ago."

Then Gracie had nothing to worry about. Her dress wasn't so five-minutes-ago. It was so five-decades-ago. She felt *so* much better now.

Harrison threw his mother a "thanks a lot, Mom" smile at her admonishment, but said, "You look beautiful, Grace."

He was looking right at her when he spoke, and for once, his expression wasn't inscrutable. In fact, it was totally, uh, scrutable. His blue eyes were fairly glowing with admiration, and his mouth was curled into the sort of half smile that overcame men when they were enjoying something sublime. Like a flawlessly executed Hail Mary pass. Or a perfectly grilled rib eye. Or a genuinely beautiful woman.

Then the *Grace* at the end of the sentiment hit her.

Nobody had ever called her Grace. Except for Devon, who'd told her she was too classy to be called Gracie—then turned out to be the most déclassé person on the planet. But she wasn't going to think about Devon tonight, so he didn't count.

And even if Harrison didn't think she was beautiful—or classy, for that matter—the fact that he was making an effort to…well, whatever he was making an effort to do…was a welcome development.

So she replied, "Thank you. And call me Gracie. No one calls me Grace." Well, except for the aforementioned—

Dammit, why did Devon keep popping into her head tonight? With no small effort, she pushed thoughts of the past to the back of her brain again, where they belonged. *And stay there.*

Harrison looked like he wanted to balk at calling her Gracie, but he dipped his head in acknowledgement that he had at least heard her.

"Ms. Sumner!"

Gracie was surprised—and delighted—to hear another familiar voice, and smiled when she turned to greet Gus Fiver, the second-in-command at Tarrant, Fiver & Twigg. He was dressed as conservatively as all the other suits at the party, but there was something about his blond good looks that made him seem far more relaxed. Instead of the briefcase she'd always seen him armed with before, this time he held a cut-crystal tumbler with what looked to Gracie's trained eye like two fingers of very good single-malt Scotch.

"Mr. Fiver," she greeted him. "What are you doing here?"

"Mr. and Mrs. Dewitt's son Elliot is one of my best

friends," he said. "Our families go way back. And please call me Gus."

Gracie turned to include Harrison and Vivian in the conversation, and then realized she had no idea how to do that. Although everyone in the small group knew each other already, it wasn't like the Sages and Tarrant, Fiver & Twigg were exactly best friends. "You, um, you remember the Sages, I'm sure."

Although there was a bit of a temperature drop not unlike the one she'd experienced in the Sages' library a few days ago, Harrison and Gus managed to exchange civil greetings. Vivian was a bit warmer, but she, too, was reserved. Gracie supposed it was the best any of them could manage, having been on opposite sides of a very contentious case for two years.

"I'm surprised to see you here," Gus said. Somehow, though, Gracie couldn't help thinking that the subtext of his sentence was something along the lines of "I thought by now one of the Sages would have suffocated you in your sleep." "I hope you've been enjoying your stay in the Hamptons."

"I have," she said, surprised to realize it was true. In spite of the weirdness of the situation and the wariness of the sort-of truce that seemed to have developed between her and Harrison—at least for now—her stay had been reasonably pleasant and abundantly enlightening. "Long Island is beautiful, and I'm learning all kinds of things about Harry I never knew before. Vivian and Harrison have been very accommodating."

"Vivian and Harrison." Gus echoed her use of their first names in the kind of speculative tone he might have used if he were conjecturing about the identity of Jack the Ripper. "I see."

Gracie supposed it was only natural that he would be skeptical. After all, the last time she'd seen him, Harrison had been accusing her of giving his father an STD and robbing him blind. Now that she thought about it, she, too, wondered why she wasn't still mad at Harrison.

In a word, hmm.

"I'm glad to hear it," Gus said. "And you'll be glad to know—as will you, Mrs. Sage—that the paperwork on the Long Island house and the Manhattan penthouse is in progress. We should be able to courier the papers to you in Amagansett Thursday or Friday, right on schedule."

"That is wonderful news," Vivian agreed. "Thank you again, Gracie."

"No thanks are necessary, Vivian. I'm sure Harry knew I would return the houses to you and that it's what he wanted."

"Yes, well, that makes one of us, darling. Oh, look, there's Bunny," Vivian said, lifting a hand in greeting to their hostess. "You'll all excuse me."

She hurried off without awaiting a reply, leaving Gracie to be the buffer between her son and the law firm that was her son's biggest antagonist.

"So, Gus," she said, grappling for some benign subject to jump-start the conversation. "How did you get into the long-lost-relative business?"

"Tarrant and Twigg recruited me when I was still at Georgetown law school. I was in my last year of probate law and wrote a paper on how to better employ the internet for heir hunting for one of my classes. My professor was a friend of Bennett's and thought he'd find it interesting so he passed it along to him. The next time Bennett was in DC, he and I met for lunch, and he offered me an associate position."

"So have you guys reunited lots of families?" she asked.

"Or split a lot of them up?" Harrison interjected.

Gracie threw him an irritated look, but Gus only chuckled.

"No, it's a fair question," he said. "Family estates can be very contentious, especially when they're large. Fortunately for us, we most often deal with single heirs to estates. Ones who are the last in a line, so there's no one to contest the terms."

"Well then," Harrison said, "aren't my mother and I lucky to be among the few, the proud, the contested."

Again, Gus smiled. "Well, we do seem to have had an unusual run lately of clients who could be wandering into some potential conflict. Once we find them, of course."

"And I'm sure you'll find them," Gracie said.

"We always do," Gus assured her. Then his expression changed. "Well, except for that once."

Gracie was about to ask him more about that, but someone hailed him from the other side of the room. So Gus bid her and Harrison a hasty farewell and made his way in that direction, leaving the two of them alone. And although they had been alone together pretty much all day with fairly little uneasiness, Gus's departure left Gracie feeling very uneasy indeed.

Harrison seemed to share her discomfort, because the moment his gaze met hers, he quickly glanced off to the right, and then turned his entire body in that direction. In response, Gracie turned away and shot her gaze in the opposite direction. Then both of them looked back at each other again, turning their bodies back a little, then a little more, until they were standing face-to-face again. For one long moment, they just stood that way, their gazes locked, their tongues tied. And then…

Then something really weird happened. It was as if some kind of gauzy curtain descended around them on all sides, separating them from everyone else in the room. Everyone else in the world. The clamor of the chattering people tapered to a purr of something faint and almost melodic. The gleam of the chandelier mellowed to a blush of pink. The chill of the air conditioning ebbed to a caress of awareness. And everything else seemed to recede until it was nothing but shadows and murmurs.

Gracie had no idea if Harrison felt it, too, but he stood as still and silent as she, as if he was just as transfixed and didn't want to move or speak for fear of ruining the moment, either. Time seemed to have stopped, too, as if nothing but that moment mattered. Then a woman somewhere in the room barked raucously with laughter, and the entire impression was gone.

Leaving Gracie—and possibly Harrison—feeling more awkward than ever.

"I'll go get us a drink," he said suddenly, sounding almost panicky. Yep, he felt the awkwardness, too. "What would you like?"

Like? she echoed to herself. How was she supposed to answer that? Her brain was so scrambled at the moment, she barely knew her own name, and he was asking her what she wanted? Well, okay, maybe she had an idea of what she, you know, *wanted* at the moment, but there was no way she was going to tell Harrison she wanted *that*. And how could she want *that* from him in the first place? Not only had she known him a mere matter of days, but she also wasn't even sure she liked him enough for *that*. And she was pretty sure he didn't like her, either, even if he was sharing weird, gauzy-curtain, shadow-and-murmur moments with her.

"Um, whatever you're having is fine," she said. "That will be fine. It's fine."

It was all Gracie could do not to slap a hand over her mouth to keep herself from further babbling. For one terrifying second, she honestly thought she was going to tell him that what she wanted was him. Then for another even more terrifying second she thought he was going to tell her that that was good, because he intended to have her. There was just something about the expression on his face just then that—

Thankfully, after one more panicky look, he bolted toward a bar in the far corner of the room, where a group of people had congregated, leaving Gracie alone to collect her thoughts. Unfortunately, her thoughts had wandered so far off that she was going to need an intergalactic mode of transportation to bring them all back.

By the time Harrison returned with their drinks, she had managed to gather herself together enough that her brain and other body parts were reasonably under control. At least until she went to remove her right glove so she could accept her cocktail, because that was when her fingers suddenly wanted to fumble all over the place. Possibly because he seemed unable to peel his gaze away from hers, and then seemed unable to peel it away from her fumbling fingers. After she finally wrestled off the glove, she made a tight fist to halt the trembling of her hand before accepting her drink. But it still trembled when she took the glass from him, enough that he cupped his hand over hers for a moment after transferring the drink to her, to make sure she didn't drop it.

And damned if that weird gauzy-curtain thing didn't happen again. This time, though, they were making contact when it did. She was able to feel how gently he was touching her, and how warm his hand was over hers, and how she wished more than anything he would never let her go. But he did let her go, finally, and up went the curtain again. Somehow, she was able to mumble her thanks, though whether her gratitude was for the drink, the way he touched her or the fact that the strange episode had come to an end, she couldn't have said.

Harrison's gaze met hers again, and he was smiling the same sort of smile he'd smiled when he'd told the butler she was with him. She lifted her drink for a sip and—

Wait. What? The import of that finally struck her. Harrison had been smiling when he told the butler "she's with me." Therefore something about her arrival at the party had made him happy. And something about telling Ballantine she was *with him* had made him happy, too.

Now he was smiling that same smile again, which must mean that he was viewing her less as an enemy. But that was good, right? It meant he was starting to believe Harry left his fortune to her for philanthropic reasons, not because she took advantage of him. So why did Gracie suddenly feel worried again, and for entirely different reasons?

For a moment, they only sipped their drinks in

silence—bourbon, not Gracie's favorite, but it was okay—and looked around the room. Then Harrison fixed his gaze—that blue, blue, good God, his eyes were blue gaze—on hers.

And very softly, he asked, "Earlier tonight, why did you ask if you should leave?"

It took her a moment to remember what he was talking about. Back when she first arrived at the party, when it was obvious he didn't like what she was wearing. "I thought you wanted me to leave because I was going to embarrass you and Vivian."

He looked surprised. "Why would you think that?"

She was surprised by his surprise. Wasn't it obvious why she would think that?

"Because I'm not…sophisticated," she said. "I'm not…elegant. I'm not…" Now she made an exasperated sound. "I don't know how to act around people like this, in situations like this. I don't *belong* here. Not that it ever mattered before, you know? I never needed to be sophisticated or elegant. I never wanted to be. But tonight…"

She trailed off without finishing, and Harrison looked as if he had no more idea what to say than she did. So Gracie sipped her drink again, finding the smoky flavor a little less disagreeable this time. See? People could learn to like things they didn't like before. They just had to give them a chance.

She looked at Harrison again. Harrison, who was so far out of her league, even intergalactic modes of transportation couldn't connect them. No way would he ever consider her sophisticated or elegant or think she belonged in a place like this. She wished she didn't care about that. She wished it didn't matter. She wished…

The irony of the situation was staggering, really. For the first time in her life, Gracie could—technically—afford anything she wanted. And the one thing she was beginning to think she might want was the only thing she would never be able to have.

Six

The morning after the Dewitts' party, Harrison lay in bed with barely four hours of sleep under his belt, staring at the ceiling and wondering why he couldn't stop thinking about Gracie, who for some reason now seemed exactly suited to that name. Mostly, he couldn't stop thinking about the moment he'd glanced past Ballantine to see her standing at the front door, looking like something that should have been under glass in a pastry shop.

He still didn't know what the hell had happened to him in that moment. He only knew that his stomach had pitched, his mouth had gone dry, his brain had fizzled and his…well, never mind what some of his other body parts had done.

And there had been nothing about her to warrant such a blatantly sexual reaction, which was all his reaction to her had been, he assured himself. Sexual. Even if it had felt like something different. Something more. It couldn't have been anything *but* sexual. She'd just looked so… She'd just seemed so… And he'd felt so… And he'd really wanted to…

He turned onto his side, toward the open window, and glanced at the chair draped with his discarded clothing of the night before. Ah, dammit. He didn't know what he'd wanted when he saw her standing there. Okay, yes, he did know that. What he didn't know was why. Okay, maybe he knew that, too. It had been a while since he'd acted on a sexual attraction. Probably because it had been a while since he'd felt a sexual attraction. All the women he knew were women he *knew*, and once he got to *know* a woman, he pretty much stopped being sexually attracted to her. There wasn't much point in continuing with something once you knew what it was like, and it stopped being challenging. Or interesting. So although Harrison knew *why* he found Gracie attractive, what he didn't know was why he found *Gracie* attractive.

Why her? He'd seen a million pretty girls in a million party dresses in his life. Hell, he'd helped a million pretty girls *out* of a million party dresses in his life. And Gracie wasn't even the kind of party girl he normally went for—the kind who wore lots of makeup and little clothing. What makeup she'd worn last night had whispered, not screamed, and there'd been nothing revealing about her dress. For God's sake, she'd even worn gloves.

Although, now that he thought about it—not for the first time since the night before—her collarbone had looked pretty damned lickable. As had the nape of her neck. And the line of her jaw. And her earlobes...

Really, all of her had looked pretty damned lickable.

He tossed to his other side, punched his pillow, closed his eyes and commanded his brain to grab another hour of sleep. Instead, his brain etched another vision of Gracie on the insides of his eyelids, this one of her looking dashed and asking him, "Should I leave?" He'd been stunned later when she told him she'd asked the question because she thought she was embarrassing him. Because she wasn't sophisticated or elegant and didn't belong in high society.

And all the while Harrison had been thinking how she was more elegant and sophisticated than any of them.

Just who was Gracie Sumner? *Was* she a con artist? Or was she something else?

Harrison bit back a groan. Why was he doubting her? Why was he doubting himself? She *couldn't* be anything other than what he'd suspected since he'd heard the particulars of his father's will. Okay, maybe she wasn't as predatory as he'd first thought, but his father had had too deep an appreciation for money—too deep an obsession with money—to give it all to a stranger and insist that she give it to even more strangers. Harrison Sage, Jr. had been the most calculating, close-fisted man Harrison III had ever known. Philanthropy was the last thing he'd thought about when he was alive. He wouldn't have felt any differently when thinking about his inevitable death. He would have made sure his fortune stayed with the family, where it would grow more obscene, even after he was gone. So what had happened to him to change that?

His father couldn't have been in his right mind when he put Gracie in charge of his personal estate. He had to have been mentally diminished, and she must have taken advantage of that. Maybe she'd convinced him to give his money to charity, and to put her in charge of the funds. And the moment the spotlight was off of her, she was going to take the money and run.

That had to be it. It was the only explanation that made sense.

He was through being enchanted by Gracie Sumner. *Grace* Sumner, he corrected himself. And he wouldn't be swayed by her again.

Gracie was the first to come downstairs the next morning, a not unexpected development, since Vivian had still been at the party last night when she and Harrison left, and Harrison had opted for a nightcap before he went to bed himself. No breakfast had been set up on the patio yet, so Gracie headed back into the house…mansion…palace…most gigantic residence she'd ever seen…to forage in the kitchen herself. She would at least start the coffee, since, as far as she was concerned, a day without caffeine was like a day without precious, life-giving oxygen. As she entered the hall she was pretty sure would lead to the kitchen, however, she crashed into the most gigantic man's chest she'd ever seen. *Oops.*

"Whoa," Harrison said as he wrapped his hands around her upper arms and moved her back a few steps. "What's the hurry? Are we planning to take advantage of everyone's absence to fill our pockets with anything that's not nailed down?"

Ignoring, for now, that neither her red-and-yellow

plaid pants nor her red short-sleeved blouse had pockets—and even if they did, no way could she stuff a Louis Quatorze buffet into one—Gracie frowned at Harrison. When they'd parted ways last night, they'd been on pretty good terms. In spite of some of the weirdness that had arced between them at the party, they'd eventually fallen into a reasonably comfortable fellowship that had lasted all the way through the ride home.

This morning, though, he seemed to want to return to the antagonism she'd thought had vanished. Or at least diminished to the point where he had stopped thinking of her as a thief. She took a step backward, removing herself from his grasp, and frowned harder. Not as easy to do as it should have been, because he looked even yummier than usual in casual dark-wash jeans and a white oxford shirt, the sleeves rolled to his elbows.

Instead of rising to the bait he was so clearly dangling in front of her, she said, "And good morning to you, too."

He deflated a little at her greeting. But he didn't wish her a good-morning in return. Instead, he told her, "The servants get the weekend off. Everyone's on their own for breakfast."

"Which isn't a problem," she said, "except that I don't know where the kitchen is."

He tilted his head in the direction she'd been headed. "You were on the right track. It's this way."

Gracie may have been on the right track, she thought as she followed him through a warren of rooms, but if he hadn't shown up when he did, they would have had to send a search-and-rescue team after her. It struck her again as she absorbed her grand surroundings just how rich Harry had been, just how much he'd turned his back on when he ran away to Cincinnati and just how out-of-place the man she'd known would have been in these surroundings.

Even the kitchen reeked of excess, massive as it was with state-of-the-art appliances—some of them things Gracie didn't recognize even with her restaurant experience.

"Coffee," she said, hoping the word sounded more like a desire than a demand, thinking it came off more as a decree. "Um, I mean, if you'll tell me where it is, I'll make it."

"I set it up last night. Just push the button."

She looked around for a Mr. Coffee, and then reminded herself she was in the home of a billionaire, so switched gears for a Bonavita or Bunn. But she didn't see one of those, either. When Harrison noted her confusion, he pointed behind her. She turned, but all she saw was something that looked like a giant chrome insect. She looked at him again, her expression puzzled.

"The Kees van der Westen?" he said helpfully.

Well, *he* probably thought it was helpful. To Gracie, a Kees van der Westen sounded like something that should be hanging in the Metropolitan Museum of Art. When she continued to gaze at him in stumped silence, he moved past her to the big metal bug, placed a coffee cup beneath one of its limbs, and pushed a button. Immediately, the machine began to hum, and a beautiful stream of fragrant mahogany brew began to stream into the cup.

"Wow," she said. "That's more impressive than the espresso machine we have at Café Destiné." Then, because she hadn't had her coffee yet so couldn't be held responsible for her indiscretion, she asked, "How much did that set you back?"

Harrison didn't seem to think the question odd, however. He just shrugged and said. "I don't know. Six or seven thousand, I think."

She couldn't help how her mouth dropped open at that. "Seven thousand dollars? For a coffeemaker?"

"Well, it does espresso and cappuccino, too," he said. "Besides, you get what you pay for."

"You know what else you can get for seven thousand dollars?" she asked, telling herself it was still because she hadn't had her coffee, but knowing more that it was because she wanted to prove a point.

He thought for a minute. "Not a lot, really."

"There are some cities where seven thousand dollars will pay for two years of community college," she said. "What you think of as a coffeemaker is a higher education for some people."

His expression went inscrutable again. "Imagine that."

"I don't have to imagine it," she said. "I've done a lot of research. Do you have any idea how many lives your father's fourteen billion dollars will change? Any concept at all? Do you even know what *one* billion dollars could buy?"

Instead of waiting for him to answer, she continued, "One billion dollars can send more than twenty-five thousand kids to a public university for four years. Twenty-five thousand! A billion dollars can put two million laptops in public schools. A billion dollars can buy decent housing for six thousand families in some places. A billion dollars can run seven thousand shelters for battered women for a year. You add up how many lives would be improved. And that's only the first four billion."

Harrison's expression remained fixed, but something flickered in his eyes that made her think she was getting through to him.

So she added, "Your father's money can bring libraries to communities that don't have one. It can put musical instruments in schools that can't afford them. It can build playgrounds in neighborhoods that are covered with asphalt. It can send kids to camp. It can build health clinics. It can fill food banks. Maybe that was why Harry changed his mind late in life about what he wanted to do with his money. So he'd be remembered for changing the world, one human life at a time."

At this, Harrison's expression finally changed. Though not exactly for the better. "And what about his family?" he asked. "Did my father have to completely shut us out? You keep talking about him as if he were this paragon of altruism in Cincinnati, conveniently forgetting about how he turned his back on his family here. Not just me and my mother, but my half sisters and their mothers, too. My father spent his life here taking whatever he wanted whenever he wanted it, often from people he claimed to love. Now he wants to give it all back to strangers? Where's the logic in that? Where's the commitment? Where's the obligation? Where's the… Dammit, where's the love?"

His eruption stunned Gracie into silence. Not because of the eruption itself, but because she realized he was right. She'd been thinking of Harry's fortune as an all-or-nothing behemoth, something that either went to charity or to the Sages, and neither the twain should meet. But Harry could have left something to his family. Not just to Harrison and Vivian, but to his ex-wives and other children, too. So why hadn't he?

"I'm sorry," Gracie said, knowing the words were inadequate, but having no idea what else to say. She didn't know why Harry had excluded his family from his will. Maybe he'd figured Harrison would be fine on his own and capable of taking care of Vivian. Maybe he'd assumed his divorce settlements with his exes were enough for all of them and his other children to have good lives. And probably, that was true. But he still could have left each of them *some*thing. Something to show them he remembered them, to let them know he had loved them, even if he hadn't done that in life.

Because one thing Gracie did know. As rough-around-the-edges and irascible as Harry could be, he *had* been able to love. She'd seen him express it every day. Maybe not in his words, but in his actions. He'd loved his parents and little brother once upon a time, too. And if he'd been able to love a family as fractured as his had been when he was a boy, then he *must* have loved Harrison and Vivian, too, even if he'd never been any good at showing it. Maybe if Harrison had known him the way Gracie did, he would be able to see that, too.

If only she could take Harrison back in time a few years and introduce him to the version of his father she knew. If only he could see Harry in his flannel bathrobe, shuffling around his apartment in his old-man slippers and Reds cap, watering his plants, his favorite team on TV in the background, his four-alarm chili bubbling on the stove. If only he could see Harry's patience when he taught her to fox-trot or his compassion when he filled trays at the shelter or his gentleness showing some kid how to hold a bat.

And that was when it hit her. There was a way she *could* show Harrison those things. Harry wouldn't be there physically, of course, but he'd be there in spirit. Harrison had shown her his version of his father in New York yesterday. So why couldn't Gracie show him her version of Harry in Cincinnati? They could fly there tomorrow and spend a couple of days. She could take Harrison to the storage unit to go through his father's things. They could watch the Little League team Harry coached. She could show Harrison the hospital and shelter where Harry volunteered and introduce him to some of the people who knew him. She could even take him dancing at the Moondrop Ballroom.

Harrison had never known that side of his father. Maybe if they went to Cincinnati, he'd see that Harry wasn't the cold, rapacious man he remembered. And maybe, between the two of them, they could figure Harry out, once and for all.

"Harrison," she said decisively, "we need to go to Cincinnati."

His expression would have been the same if she had just smacked him with a big, wet fish. "Why do we need to go to Cincinnati?"

"So you can meet Harry."

"You've already told me all about him."

"And you don't seem to believe any of it."

He said nothing in response to that. What could he say? He *didn't* believe anything she'd told him about Harry. Not really. He was the kind of person who needed to see stuff with his own eyes to be convinced.

"I have to go back to work next week," he said,

lamely enough that Gracie knew that wasn't the reason he was balking.

"You can give yourself a couple more days off," she said. "You're the boss."

He said nothing again, but that only encouraged her. "Look, you took me on the Harrison Sage, Jr. tour of New York City. So now let me take you on the Harry Sagalowsky tour of Cincinnati."

"And did the Harrison Sage, Jr. tour change your mind about your friend Harry?" he asked.

Gracie hesitated before replying. "Not really," she admitted. But she quickly declared, "But it's given me a lot to think about. It's added a lot to my picture of Harry, and even if the things I learned don't paint him in the greatest light, I'm still glad to have learned them. I want to do the same for your picture of Harrison, Jr.," she added more gently. "So you'll have more to think about, too."

This time, Harrison was the one to hesitate. Finally, he told her, "It won't make any difference in the way I feel. About my father or you."

Something in the way he said it, though, made Gracie think he was at least willing to give it a chance. Where his father was concerned, anyway. Although maybe he meant—

"It doesn't matter how you feel about me," she said before her thoughts could go any further, wishing that were true. Wondering why it wasn't. She really shouldn't care about how Harrison felt about her. Her only goal at the moment was to help him move past his resentment toward his father. But she couldn't quite forget those few moments the night before when things had seemed…different between them. And she couldn't forget the way he'd looked when she told him all the things he hadn't known about his father's past. Like a hurt little kid who was just trying to make sense of things and couldn't.

Let me help you make sense of it, Gracie silently bid him. *Of your father and of me. And let me try to make sense of you, too.* Because somehow, it was beginning to feel just as important for her and Harrison to understand each other as it was for them to understand Harry.

Harrison hesitated again. Long enough this time that Gracie feared he would decline once and for all. Finally, reluctantly, he told her, "Okay. I'll go."

She expelled a breath she hadn't been aware of holding. "Great. How long will it take you to pack?"

Seven

Gracie couldn't have ordered a better day for a baseball game. June was the kindest of the summer months in the Ohio Valley, the skies blue and perfect and the breezes warm and playful. The park where Harry's Little League team, the Woodhaven Rockets, played had four baseball diamonds and every one of them was filled. She and Harrison had arrived early enough to find a bleacher seat in the shade, up on the very top bench, where they could see all the action. She'd instructed him to wear the team colors, so he'd complied with gray cargo shorts and a pale blue polo that made his blue, blue eyes even bluer. She'd opted for white capris and a powder-blue sleeveless shirt for herself.

They'd arrived in Cincinnati the evening before, late enough that there hadn't been time to do much more than say good-night and turn in. Harrison had wanted to have lunch before the game today, but Gracie told him that until she presented the league with a check from Harry's estate, concessions were where they made most of their money for uniforms and equipment, so the least she and Harrison could do was plunk down a few bucks for a couple of hot dogs and sodas. Not to mention if Dylan Mendelson was still on the team, there might be some of his mom's red velvet cupcakes.

The Rockets were leading in the seventh inning four to zip, their pitcher barreling ball after ball over home plate without a single crack of the bat. If this kept up, it was going to be a no-hitter.

"Way to go, Roxanne!" Gracie shouted to the pitcher at the end of the inning as the teams were switching places. "Keep it up, girlfriend!"

When she sat back down, Harrison said, "That's a *girl* pitching?"

"Damn straight. Don't sound so surprised. Girls are great ballplayers."

"No, it's not that. It's that she must not have been on the team when my father coached it."

"Your father was the first one to recognize what a good arm she has. Making her the Rockets' pitcher was one of the last things he did before he died." She brightened. "Now there's a legacy for you. Thanks to Harry, Roxanne Bailey might be the first woman to play in the Majors."

Judging by his expression, Harrison was doubtful. Or maybe it was his father's actions he was doubting.

"What?" she asked.

He hesitated, as if he were looking for the right words. "My father never…cared much…for women."

He seemed to realize Gracie was about to object, so he held up a hand and hurried on. "Oh, he liked women. A lot. My mother would tell you he liked them too much. But he only hired them for clerical positions and never promoted any to executive. He just didn't think women could do anything more than be pretty and type."

"Wow," Gracie said. "That is so *not* the Harry I knew. He put up with a lot of crap from some of the dads for making Roxanne the pitcher, but he didn't back down. And I never saw him speak to a woman any differently than he spoke to a man."

Harrison looked out at the field, but his expression suggested he was seeing something other than a bunch of kids playing baseball.

"Gracie?" a woman called out from behind the bleachers. "Gracie Sumner, is that you?"

She turned to see Sarah Denham, the mother of the Rockets' catcher, standing below them. She, too, was dressed in the team colors, a Rockets ball cap perched backward on her head, hot dogs in each hand.

"Hi, Sarah!" Gracie greeted her, happy to see a familiar face.

"I thought that was you," Sarah said. With a smile, she added, "It's strange to see you without Harry. What are you doing back in town?"

At the mention of Harry's name, Harrison turned around, too, clearly interested in meeting someone else who knew his father in this world. So Gracie introduced the two of them.

"I am so sorry for your loss," Sarah told him. "Your father was one of the nicest men I ever met. He was so great with these kids."

Harrison was clearly surprised by the statement, in spite of Gracie having already told him the same thing.

Sarah continued with a smile, “And his jokes! He kept these kids in stitches.”

“My father told jokes?” Harrison asked, startled.

“Oh, my gosh, yes,” Sarah said. “What did one mushroom say to the other mushroom?”

Harrison smiled. “I don’t know.”

Sarah smiled back. “You’re a fun guy. Get it? Fungi?”

Harrison groaned. “That’s a terrible joke.”

“I know,” Sarah agreed with a laugh. “They were all like that. The kids loved them.” She turned to Gracie. “So where are you living now?”

Gracie’s back went up almost literally at the question. Her own past in Cincinnati was the last thing she wanted to revisit, especially in front of Harrison. “Seattle,” she said, hoping Sarah left it at that.

But of course, she didn’t. “So far away? I mean, I knew things with Devon got bad—”

At this, Harrison snapped his attention to Gracie.

“—but I didn’t know you went all the way across the country,” Sarah said.

“That’s all in the past,” Gracie said. Then she rushed to change the subject. “Hey, did Trudy bring any of her red velvet cupcakes?”

“She did,” Sarah said. “But they’re going fast.”

The perfect excuse to escape. “You want a cupcake?” she asked Harrison as she stood. “My treat. I’ll be right back.”

Before he could reply, she was trundling down the bleachers toward the concession stand. And just as she tried to do whenever Devon Braun intruded into her life, she didn’t look back once.

* * *

Gracie hadn't visited the self-storage unit with Harry's things since snapping on the padlock two years ago, so she braced herself for the discovery that everything might be a little musty. And dusty. And rusty. Fortunately, both she and Harrison were dressed for such a development: he in a pair of khaki cargo shorts and a black, V-neck T-shirt, she in a pair of baggy plaid shorts and an even baggier white T-shirt. Each was armed with a box cutter, and they'd brought additional boxes in which to pack anything Harrison might want to ship back to New York right away.

She had deliberately saved the storage shed for the last day of their trip, because it held what was left of the heart and soul of Harry Sagalowsky. After yesterday's game, they'd visited the shelter and hospital where Harry had volunteered, and where many of the people remembered both him and Gracie. Then she and Harrison had had dinner at her and Harry's favorite hole-in-the-wall barbecue joint, where the owner-chef had come out to regale Harrison with stories about how he and Harry had always argued good-naturedly over whose sauce was best. The chef had finally admitted—but only to the two of them—that there was something about Harry's chili he had never been able to duplicate and he was pretty sure it had something to do with the cumin.

Gracie and Harrison had ended the day by retiring to his hotel room with a rented DVD of *The African Queen*, Harry's favorite movie, something that also surprised Harrison because, even though it was kind of a war movie, it had a romance in it, too, and his father had thought the idea of romance was foolish.

Gracie wondered if Harrison thought that, too. For the most part, he didn't seem any more of a romantic than he claimed his father had been, but there had been times over the last couple of days—and times when they'd been in New York, too—when she'd caught him looking at her in a way that was… Or else he'd said something in a way that was… Or the air around the two of them had just seemed kind of… Well. Gracie wasn't sure if the right word for those occasions was *romantic*. Then again, she wasn't sure it was the wrong word, either. Because something about those occasions, especially over the last couple of days, sure had felt kind of…romantic.

That wasn't likely to change tonight, since the last leg of their tour would be at the Moondrop Ballroom, the epitome of old Hollywood romance, where Gracie would try to teach Harrison to dance the way Harry had once taught her.

If, after all that, Harrison still saw his father as a coldhearted, cold-blooded cold fish who hadn't cared about anything but money, then he was a lost cause, and Gracie didn't know what to do. Of course, she still hadn't accepted the coldhearted, cold-blooded cold fish who'd only cared about money that Harrison kept insisting Harry was, so maybe she was a lost cause, too. At least they could be lost causes together.

She had to wrestle with the storage-unit padlock for a few seconds until it finally gave. Then it took both Harrison and her to haul up the big, garage-type metal door. It groaned like a dying mammoth when they did, and the storage unit belched an odor that was a mix of old books, old socks and old man. Gracie gazed into the belly of the beast, a cinderblock room about twenty feet wide by twenty feet deep, wondering where to begin.

"I probably should have tried to find Harry's family as soon as he passed away," she said when she realized how musty, dusty and rusty everything was. "But I truly didn't think he had anyone."

"Was no one at his funeral?" Harrison asked, the question touched with something almost melancholy.

Maybe there was part of him that still had the capacity to forgive, and even love, his father—or, at least, think fondly of him from time to time. Although he might never fully grieve the loss of a man he hadn't seen in half a lifetime, and hadn't really ever known, maybe he was beginning to entertain the possibility that his father wasn't the villain he'd thought him to be.

In spite of his somber tone, Gracie couldn't help but smile at the question. "There were lots of people. His visitation was three days long so that everyone could have a chance to pay their respects. Even after that, there were still hundreds of people who attended the funeral."

"But no one from his family," Harrison said, still sounding pensive. "Not from any of his families."

"In a way, he had family here," Gracie said, hoping Harrison wouldn't take it the wrong way. She didn't want to diminish his and Vivian's ties to Harry. She just wanted to comfort him, and make him realize his father hadn't been without loved ones when he died.

But Harrison didn't seem to take offense. "That's not the same," he said. "Someone from his real family should have been here."

Gracie extended a hand to touch him, waffled for a moment and then placed her palm gently against his shoulder. Harrison looked over at the contact, his gaze falling first on her hand, then on her face, but he didn't move away.

"Your father touched a lot of lives, Harrison," she said softly. "He made a difference for a lot of people when he lived here. And he'll make a difference for a lot more when his fortune is given away."

Harrison inhaled a breath and released it. Then, not even seeming to realize he was doing it, he covered her hand with his. "I just don't understand why he felt like he could only do that for strangers."

Gracie didn't understand that, either. There had to be a reason. But they might never know what it was. She looked into the storage unit again. Maybe they could start looking for an explanation here.

She had taken care to organize Harry's things when she stowed them. Furniture on the left, boxes on the right, clothes and miscellaneous in the middle, with two narrow aisles separating everything to enable access. Nearly half the boxes held books and his record collection, mostly jazz and big band. Many of the rest held his accumulation of Cincinnati Reds memorabilia. It was the boxes in front, though, that Gracie wanted to open first. They were the ones that contained Harry's personal items, including the photographs Harrison needed to see.

She strode to the one closest to the front, pressed her blade to the packing tape seam and slid it along the length of the box with a quick *z-z-zip.* Harrison took a few steps into the unit as Gracie finished opening the box and removed a couple of layers of cedar-scented tissue paper. The first thing she encountered underneath was a beer stein from the last Oktoberfest she and Harry attended. She smiled as she lifted it up for Harrison to see.

"Zee?" she said, affecting her best German accent—which, okay, wasn't all that good. "Your papa luffed hiss *Schwarzbier und leberwurst*. He *vas* a real *Feinschmecker*."

Harrison chuckled at that. He even took a few more steps toward her. But all he said was, "Um, *Feinschmecker*?"

"Ja," Gracie replied. Then, returning to her normal voice, she said, "I wanted to slap him the first time he called me that. German isn't the easiest language to figure out."

"So what's a *Feinschmecker*?"

"A connoisseur of fine foods. Okay, maybe beer and liverwurst don't qualify as such. Suffice to say he enjoyed good *Hausmannskost*."

Harrison nodded. And came a few steps closer. "I never knew my father spoke German."

"Very well, in fact," she said. "He grew up in one of the German neighborhoods here."

Gracie held out the beer stein for Harrison to take. It was stoneware and decorated with a dachshund wearing lederhosen and playing an accordion. Gingerly, he closed the last few feet between them and took it from her.

"Harry was good at the chicken dance, too," she said as she released it.

"No," Harrison said adamantly, finally meeting her gaze. He set the beer stein on top of another still-closed box. "You will never convince me my father did the chicken dance."

Gracie picked through some of the other items in

the box. "If you're ever in Seattle, look me up. I have photographic evidence. Oh, look!" she cried as she picked up something else, cutting Harrison off from commenting on the "if you're ever in Seattle" thing. What was she thinking to say something like that? "I gave Harry this for Christmas!"

She withdrew a plastic electronic device the size of a toothbrush that, when its buttons were pushed, lit up, made funny noises and was generally annoying. She handed it to Harrison.

"What is it?" he asked.

"A sonic screwdriver like the one Doctor Who uses."

"But Doctor Who is science fiction. My father hated science fiction."

"Your father loved science fiction." She gestured toward the boxes in back. "There's a ton of Ray Bradbury, Isaac Asimov and Harlan Ellison books in those. You'll see."

Harrison began pushing the buttons on the sonic screwdriver one by one, the same way Harry had on Christmas morning after unwrapping it. Then he grinned. In exactly the same way his father had.

"Okay, here's what I've been looking for," she said when she uncovered the shoebox with Harry's photographs. She began sorting through them, and then was surprised when Harrison reached in, too, and pulled out a handful to look through himself.

"Here," she said, pausing on one. "This is what I wanted to show you. It's your dad and his brother, Benjy, when they were kids."

She handed the black-and-white photo to Harrison. The edges were frayed, the corners bent, and it was creased down the middle, creating a fine white line between the two boys. They were on the front stoop of the brownstone where the family had rented an apartment. Benjy was sitting on a square box nearly as big as he was. Harry had his arm around his brother, and both were grinning mischievously.

"Your dad is on the left," Gracie said. "He was six in the photo. Benjy was three. The box Benjy's sitting on is where the milkman left the weekly milk deliveries. Harry said the reason they're smiling like that is because they just put the neighbor's cat in the box without telling anyone, and with Benjy sitting on it, the poor thing couldn't get out."

Harrison nodded. "Now *that* sounds more like my father."

"He assured me they let it go right after their neighbor snapped the photo, and he promised it wasn't hurt."

She watched as Harrison studied the photo, but his expression revealed nothing of what he might be thinking or feeling. Finally, he said, "That's my dad, all right." After a moment, he added, "And I guess that's my uncle. Or would have been, had he lived."

Gracie sifted through the photos until she found another one. "And here are your grandparents."

Harrison took it from her, studying it with the same scrutiny he'd given the first photo.

"You look just like your grandfather," she said. "He couldn't have been much older in that picture than you are now."

He considered the photo for another moment. "I can't believe my father never told me about any of this. About where he came from, or his little brother, or what his parents were like." Now he looked at Gracie. "But then, I never asked him about any of it when I had the chance, did I? I never took an interest in where he came from when I was a kid. It never occurred to me that his history was mine, too. I know everything about my mother's family. But they're Park Avenue fixtures. They've been rich since New York was New Amsterdam. My father marrying her was the biggest social coup of his life."

"Maybe that was why he never talked about his past," Gracie said. "Maybe he didn't think it could stand up to Vivian's. Maybe he thought you would be ashamed of an alcoholic grandfather and a grandmother who abandoned her only surviving child."

"The same way he abandoned his family," Harrison said softly.

Gracie sighed. "Yeah. I guess so."

He shook his head. "I wouldn't have been ashamed of any of that. I would have felt bad for him. If I'd known how much he lost when he was a kid… How hard he worked to try to keep his family together… How poor they were all along…"

"What?" she asked when he didn't finish.

"I don't know. Maybe it just would have helped me understand him better or something."

Harrison continued sifting through the photos of his father's family—of his family—lost in thoughts Gracie figured she would probably never be able to understand. Thoughts he would never share with her, anyway, she was sure. Funny, though, how there was a quickly growing part of her that really wished he would.

Sunlight was slanting into the storage unit in a long beam of late-afternoon gold when Harrison finally closed the lid on the box of things he wanted to take back to New York with him. The rest could wait for him to have it moved professionally. There was plenty of room in his mother's attic to store everything. Not that he had any idea why he wanted to store it all. There was nothing of value among his father's things. The furniture was old and scarred. The clothes were old and worn out. The knickknacks were old and kitschy. Even the books and records were run-of-the-mill titles that could be found in a million places. For some reason, though, Harrison didn't want to let go of any of them.

So everything Gracie had said was true. Neither she nor his father had made up any of it. Harrison Sage, Jr. really had had a little brother. He'd really dropped out of school to go to work—one of the things they'd found was his first union card, issued when he would have been fifteen. And he really had lost his parents in terrible ways—they'd also found diaries written by his grandmother describing it all. Harrison had scanned a couple of them, but he wanted to read them all in depth when he got back to New York.

As he gazed upon the boxes and bags that held all his father's worldly possessions—or, at least, all the worldly possessions he had wanted to surround himself with as his life drew to a close—Harrison tried to understand how and why his father had lived his life the way he had. How and why a man who'd had *everything* in New York had preferred to spend his last years in a place where he had had nothing.

Gracie's words echoed through Harrison's head. *There were hundreds of people who attended the funeral.* A lot of them were people Harrison had met yesterday. Kids who loved terrible jokes. A World War

Two veteran whose only visitor most weeks had been Harry Sagalowsky, who brought him a magazine and a cup of coffee, then stayed to talk baseball. A homeless mother he'd helped get a job at a local factory, who was then able to move herself and her kids into their own place and start life anew.

Big damn deal.

There would have been *thousands* of people at his father's funeral if he'd died in New York. And they would have *really* known him. They would have known how much he was worth and recognized his accomplishments in the business and financial worlds. They would have known what companies he'd acquired, which ones he had shed and which ones he had his eye on. They would have known which of his latest ventures had been most profitable. They would have known his favorite drink, his favorite restaurant, the name of his tailor. Hell, they would have known who his current mistresses were and where he was keeping them.

But here? What was the value in delivering a magazine or helping in a job hunt or making kids laugh? What difference did it make if Harry Sagalowsky had shared part of his day with others, supplying simple pleasures and favors to people who needed them? Who cared if one person took time to acknowledge another person's existence in the world and share a little bit of himself in the process? What was so great about making a connection with other people to let them know they were important? Who needed to be remembered as a normal, everyday person who made other normal, everyday people happy when he could be remembered as a titan of commerce who'd made billions of dollars for himself instead?

Thankfully, Harrison's spiel was in his head. Because if he'd said those things out loud, Gracie would have read him the riot act. And he probably wouldn't have blamed her. Okay, maybe he was starting to see why his father had wanted to spend his final years here. Because here, with people who didn't know him as Billionaire Harrison Sage, Jr., he could live a life free of that image and be…well, some guy named Harry who did nice things for other people. Things that maybe didn't change the world, but things that made a difference on a smaller scale. Things that would maybe make up for some of the stuff Billionaire Harrison Sage, Jr. did during his lifetime, like putting money ahead of everything else.

Like turning his back on his family.

Not that Harrison thought what his father had done here in Cincinnati would ever make up for that. But he could see where his father might think it would.

"Did you get everything you want?" Gracie asked.

Her question registered on some level, but Harrison didn't know how to answer it. No, he didn't get everything he wanted. There were still answers to some questions about his father. There was still his father's estate. There was still fifteen years of his life that his father could have been a part of but wasn't. And the other fifteen years when his father was around, but not really part of his life, either. And then there was still the most maddening thing of all that he wanted.

There was still Gracie Sumner.

The trip to Cincinnati had been as eye-opening for him where she was concerned as it had been where his father was concerned. A lot of the kids on the baseball team had responded to her with genuine affection, even begging her to do an impression of a rival coach they must have seen a dozen times before, but still left them rolling with laughter. She'd stopped for five dozen doughnuts before they'd hit the veterans' hospital, and the staff had received them with thanks in a way that indicated it was something she'd done all the time when she lived here. At the homeless shelter, she'd shared fist bumps with a half-dozen men and asked them how things were going. More to the point, she'd listened to each of them when they replied.

And tonight, she wanted to take Harrison to a place called the Moondrop Ballroom. Somehow, he was certain she would know people there, too. And that they would love her the same way everyone else in this city seemed to.

All of these things made him wonder again about this Devon person whose name had come up more than once today—never in a good way. And every time, Gracie's reply had been the same before she'd changed the subject: *that's all in the past*. But how could it be in the past when everyone kept bringing it up?

"Harrison?" she asked.

Only then did he realize he hadn't answered her question about having everything he wanted from the storage unit. "For now," he said. "I'll get the rest of it as soon as I can."

He turned around in time to see her struggling to lift a box that was too wide for her to carry. When she began to pitch backward with it, Harrison lurched toward her, grabbing the box from the side nearest him. For a moment, they grappled to stabilize it, and then, as one, they set it down where she had been aiming. That, however, left the two of them standing literally shoulder-to-shoulder, something that each seemed to notice at once, and something that left them both speechless. They were also unable to make eye contact, since every time their gazes met, they glanced away from each other.

Where before the air in the storage unit had just been uncomfortably warm, it suddenly felt like a sauna. It was a really bad analogy, Harrison decided, since it also brought to mind naked, sweaty bodies wrapped in towels. Towels that could be removed with the simple flick of a wrist, thereby allowing lots of other, infinitely more interesting ways for naked bodies to get sweaty.

"Well, that was close," he said. Not that he was talking about the box they'd just saved, but Gracie didn't have to know that.

"Yeah," she said breathlessly.

A little too breathlessly. Maybe she wasn't talking about the box, either. Maybe she'd been having some sauna ideas, too. As if triggered by such a possibility, a single drop of perspiration materialized from behind her ear, rolled along her jaw, then down the front of her neck, before finally pooling in the delectable divot at the base of her throat. Harrison watched its journey with the same single-minded fascination a cheetah might show toward a wildebeest, wanting to pounce the moment the time was right. Like right now, for instance. But Gracie lifted a hand to swipe the drop away before he had the chance. Dammit.

But when his gaze met hers again, he saw that the reason for her reaction wasn't because she'd felt the perspiration running down her neck. It was because she had noticed his preoccupation with it. Their gazes locked for a minute more, and the temperature ratcheted higher. A single strand of damp blond hair clung to her temple, and it was all he could do not to reach for it and skim it back, and then follow his fingers and brush his lips over her damp skin.

"We, uh, we should get going," she said roughly, the words seeming to echo into his very soul. "We have to…to get cleaned up before going to the Moondrop. And we need to have, um…" She hesitated just a tiny, telling moment before finally concluding, "Dinner. We need to have dinner."

Dinner, he echoed to himself. Yes, they would definitely have that before going to the Moondrop. But maybe later, if the stars were aligned—and if they were both still having sauna thoughts—they could have something else, too.

After all, dancing could really work up a sweat.

Eight

Having known the Moondrop Ballroom was one of the places where she would take Harrison, Gracie had packed the dress and accessories she'd bought for the Dewitts' party and instructed Harrison to bring a suit. So it was a surprise when she answered his knock on her hotel room door to find him on the other side wearing a tuxedo. He even had a white silk scarf draped around his neck. She battled the wave of heat that wound through her at the sight of him, so dashing and Hollywood handsome, and the feeling was not unlike the one she'd experienced in the storage unit that afternoon.

And what the hell had that been about? One minute, she'd been about to drop a box on her toe, and the next, Harrison had been staring at her neck as if he wanted to devour her. His damp T-shirt had been clinging to him like a second skin, delineating every bump of muscle on his torso. His dark hair had been falling rakishly over his forehead, his blue eyes had been hot with wanting, and…and… And, well, suddenly, she'd kind of wanted to devour him, too.

"You look…nice," she finally said.

He smiled. "You look beautiful."

"Thanks," she replied, the heat in her belly nearly swamping her.

"So what time does this thing start?"

When Harry was alive, he and Gracie had been regulars at the Moondrop for Fox-trot Fridays, with an occasional appearance for Samba Saturdays and Waltz Wednesdays. Her favorite nights, however, had been Tango Tuesdays, which, as luck would have it, was tonight.

"There's a beginner's hour at seven," she said, "which is where the instructors give some basic lessons for people who've never been dancing before. The main event is at eight. If you want to go early for the first hour, though, we can," she added, thinking Harrison might not be comfortable jumping in with both feet, especially with the tango, since that was probably the hardest dance to know where to put both feet.

"You know what you're doing, right?" he asked. "I mean you said you and my father did this sort of thing on a regular basis."

"Yeah, but Tango Tuesdays tend to be tricky."

He smiled at her unintended alliteration. "But aren't you trained in tango? A tip-top tango teacher I can trust?"

Gracie smiled back. "Totally top-notch."

His eyes twinkled. "Terrific."

Another moment passed where they did nothing but smile and twinkle at each other. Then Harrison, at least, seemed to recall that they had something to do.

"So…do we have time for dinner?"

"Sure."

She gathered her purse and exited, pulling the door closed behind them. When Harrison proffered his arm with all the elegance of Cary Grant, it somehow felt totally natural to tuck her hand into the crook of his elbow. The warmth in her midsection sparked hotter, simmering parts of her that had no business simmering this early in the evening.

Or ever, she hastened to correct herself. At least where Harrison was concerned. That way lay madness.

Maybe this part of his Harry tour hadn't been such a good idea. If this was the way her body reacted when it was just hand-to-elbow contact, what was going to happen when they got into dance mode? Sure, ballroom dancing in its purest form allowed for space between the bodies, but there were still a lot of parts touching. Not just hands and elbows, but shoulders and backs. Waists. Hips.

Yikes.

Then she remembered this was tango Tuesday. Uh-oh. That meant leg contact. Torso contact. Damn. Why hadn't they been in town for open dance night instead, where she could have insisted they do the bunny hop or something? And now she'd gone and told him she would be his top-notch tango teacher. Tsk, tsk.

Note to self, Gracie, she thought as they waited for the elevator—and her stomach did a little cha cha cha. *It's a treacherous tactic, teaching tango to a tempting, um, guy.*

* * *

Stepping into the Moondrop Ballroom was like stepping back in time. Not just because it had been beautifully preserved in all its postwar elegance since opening in the 1940s, but because the people who came here did their best to dress as if they'd been preserved from that period, too. Most of the regulars were elderly, people who remembered coming here or to ballrooms like it when they were young. That was why Harry had liked the Moondrop so much. But many were Gracie's age or younger, newcomers to ballroom dancing who loved the period and wanted to experience the manners and styles of the time, if for just one evening. Even the orchestra dressed the part. The ceiling was painted the colors of twilight with twinkling white lights that looked like stars. Each wall had a silhouette of the 1940s Cincinnati skyline, topped with more stars. Between the décor and the music—the band never played anything written after 1955—it was easy to forget there was another world beyond the front doors.

"Wow, this place is like something out of a movie," Harrison said when they entered, clearly having fallen under the spell of the ballroom as quickly as Gracie had the first time she was here.

"Isn't it wonderful? It's exactly like I remember."

"How long has it been since you were in town?"

She stiffened at his question, even though it was one she'd fielded in one way or another ever since her arrival. "I left six months after Harry's funeral," she told him. "I haven't been back since."

"But you have so many friends here," he said. "I mean, all those people yesterday obviously knew you pretty well. But it sounded like you haven't stayed in touch with any of them."

"That's because I haven't."

"Why not?"

He didn't seem to be asking out of idle curiosity. But she told herself she was imagining things. She was just hypersensitive because of all the questions she'd fielded about Devon since she'd come back.

All she said was "It's complicated, Harrison."

He looked as if he might let it go, but then said, "Because of Devon."

For some reason, hearing that name spoken in Harrison's voice was far worse than hearing it in anyone else's.

"Yes," she said. "Because of him."

"Do you want to talk about it?"

She shook her head. And she told Harrison what she'd told everyone else, what she told herself whenever Devon invaded her thoughts. "That's all in the past."

Harrison looked like he was going to say more, but the band saved her, striking up the first notes of "La cumparsita."

"Well, aren't you lucky?" she said. "You're going to wet your tango feet with the mother of all tango tunes."

He listened for a moment. "I recognize this song. This is in *Some Like It Hot* when Jack Lemmon is tangoing with Joe E. Brown."

And when Tony Curtis was making out with Marilyn Monroe, she thought, but hopefully neither of them would mention that part. Judging by Harrison's expression, though, he was definitely thinking about it. And also judging by his expression, he knew she was thinking about it, too. Damn.

"Shall we?" he asked, tilting his head toward the dance floor, where a number of people were already in full tango mode.

She smiled in a way she hoped was flirtatious. Not that she was flirting with him or anything. She was just keeping in the spirit of the Moondrop Ballroom, that was all. "If you think you're ready for it."

He smiled back in a way that went way beyond flirtatious and zoomed right into bewitching. "I'm ready for anything."

As if to prove it, he extended his left hand, palm up. The moment she placed her right hand against it, he closed his fingers over hers, drew her close and lifted their hands to chin height—his chin, not hers—so her arm was higher. Then he pressed his other hand to the small of her back and drew her body, very firmly, against his. There was nothing tentative in his hold. His confidence was absolute. Her own body's response was just as fierce. In every single place they touched, little explosions detonated under her skin, rushing heat to every other part of her body.

The moment she was in his arms, he assumed a flawless tango stance, placing his right leg between hers and his left alongside her right. Then he began to guide her forward. Well, for her it was backward, since—obviously—he intended to lead. His first step was with his left foot, all fine and good—except for how Gracie's insides were turning to steaming lava—and his next was with his right, which would have also been fine if Gracie had reacted the way she was supposed to and stepped backward.

But thanks to the little-explosions-of-heat thing, not to mention the steaming-lava thing, she wasn't exactly on her game. So his step forward pressed his thigh into the juncture of her legs, and *wow*, talk about an explosion of heat *and* steaming lava. Her entire torso seemed to catch fire and melt into his. Even though she was pretty good at the tango, she stumbled those first few steps, something that made Harrison splay his fingers wide on her back and pull her closer still, and— *Oh. My. God. She was going to spontaneously combust!* After that, it was all Gracie could do to just try and keep up with him.

He led her deeper into the crowd of other dancers with a few perfectly executed *barridas*, sweeping his feet along the floor in a way that made hers move that way, too. Then he spun them in a perfect *boleo*, punctuating the move with a beautiful *gancho*, wrapping his leg briefly around hers before turning her again. Then he threw in a *lápiz,* tracing a circle on the floor with his free foot—he was just showing off now—and followed with a *parada*, where he suddenly stopped, literally toe-to-toe with her, to perform a really delicious *caricia.* He drew his leg slowly up along hers, then pushed it slowly back down again, generating a luscious friction. She wished he would do it again, and he did. Then he did it again. And again. And—holy mother of mackerel—again.

By now Gracie's heart was hammering hard inside her chest, even though they'd only been dancing a matter of minutes, and he'd been doing most of the work. Harrison had to feel the pounding of her pulse, too—their bodies were so close, in so many places—but he didn't say a word. He only held her gaze tight with his and began to dance again, with all the grace and style of a *vaquero.* As the final notes of the song came to a close, he pulled her close one last time, and then—of course—he tilted her back until her head was nearly touching the floor, in a dip that was nothing short of spectacular.

At that point, they were both breathing heavily, a combination of both the dance and their heightened awareness of each other. They'd also earned an audience, Gracie realized, when she heard applause. Or maybe that was just in her own brain, acknowledging his skill at…oh, so many things, because she honestly wasn't even conscious of anyone in that moment but him.

Still poised in the dip, her free arm looped around his neck, she said breathlessly, "You've been holding out on me."

He grinned. But he didn't let her up. Instead he only roped his arm more possessively around her waist and pulled her closer to him. He, too, was out of breath, his voice quiet when he spoke. "My mother made me take cotillion classes when I was in middle school. I hated it until I realized how many points knowing how to dance earned me with girls. Knowing the tango multiplied those points by about a thousand."

"I can see how that would work in a guy's favor."

Still, he didn't let her up, and still, Gracie didn't care. For one interminable moment, it almost seemed as if he were bending his head closer to hers, as if his mouth were hovering over hers, as if he actually intended to—

She closed her eyes, and for the merest, faintest, most exquisite millisecond, she thought she felt the brush of his lips over hers. But when she opened her eyes, he was levering her to a standing position, so she told herself she'd only imagined it.

The crowd had dispersed, caught up in another song, another dance, another moment. But Gracie couldn't quite let this moment go. Their fingers were still curled together, her other hand still curved around his nape while his was still pressing into the small of her back. Although they'd stopped moving, she couldn't seem to catch her breath. And in spite of the music that still swirled around them, she couldn't seem to make herself move.

But neither, did it seem, could he. His breathing was as erratic as hers, and he wasn't any more inclined to move than she was. And that maybe-imaginary, maybe-not kiss still had her brain so muddled, she wasn't sure what to do. Even when he began to lower his head toward hers—there was no mistaking his intention this time—she didn't know how to react. Not until his mouth covered hers completely. After that, she knew exactly what to do.

She kissed him back.

The feel of his mouth on hers was extraordinary, at once entreating and demanding, tender and rough, soft and firm. He kissed her as if he had done it a million times and never before, confident of his effect on her and tentative in his reception. Gracie kept her hand cupped over his nape, and with the other, threaded her fingers into his hair. It had been so long since she had been this close to a man, so long since she had allowed herself to get lost in the sensation of two bodies struggling to become one. She didn't want it to stop. She wanted to stay here in this spot, with this man, forever.

By the time he pulled back, her brain was so rattled,

her body so incited, her senses so aroused, all she could do was say the first thing that popped into her head. "I thought you didn't like me."

He nuzzled the curve where her neck joined her shoulder. "Oh, I like you very much."

"You think I took advantage of your father."

He nipped her earlobe. Gracie tried not to swoon. "I don't think that at all."

"Since when?" she asked, her voice barely audible.

Instead of answering, he skimmed his lips lightly along her throat, her jaw, her temple. But just when she thought she would melt into a puddle of ruined womanhood at his feet, he straightened. And then he began to lead her in the tango again, as if nothing had happened.

Well, nothing except a major tilt of the earth's axis that had just changed *every*thing for Gracie.

It was that damned dress.

That was what Harrison told himself as he and Gracie sat on opposite sides of a cab as it sped down Hamilton Avenue, back toward their hotel. Someone somewhere had put a spell on that dress that made men's brains turn to pudding whenever they got within fifteen feet of it. And when it was on someone like Gracie, with creamy skin and silky hair and eyes dark enough for a man to lose himself in for days, well… It was amazing all he'd done on that dance floor was kiss her.

But he had kissed her. And he'd told her he liked her. Very much. But he hadn't been able to answer her question about "since when." Probably because he didn't know "since when."

When had that happened? Today at the storage unit?

Yesterday at the baseball game? That morning at the stock exchange? He honestly didn't know. He only knew he had been wrong about her. She really had been his father's friend and nothing more. She really was a decent person. She really was a girl next door.

Now he just had to figure out what to do. Almost since the moment they met, he'd been suspicious of her. But he'd also been attracted to her. He'd wanted to expose her as a fraud, but he'd also wanted to have sex with her. He'd been sure every word she said about his father was untrue, but he'd learned things about his father from her that he'd never known before.

Hell, no wonder he didn't know what to do.

Bottom line, he told himself. That was what everything came down to in life. What was the bottom line?

The bottom line was he liked Gracie. The bottom line was he wanted her. The bottom line was she'd kissed him back on that dance floor. The bottom line was she wanted him, too.

So why not do what he always did when he was attracted to a woman, and she was attracted to him? Once they got back to the hotel, they could have a nightcap and then hop into bed and enjoy themselves. No harm, no foul, a good time had by all. There was nothing in this encounter that was any different from any other encounter he'd had with a woman. Maybe the circumstances of their meeting were a little weirder, but the essentials were the same. Man, woman. Hormones, pheromones. Foreplay, play, replay. He'd done it a million times, a million ways, with a million women. So what was the problem?

He looked at Gracie again. She was staring out the window, the passing streetlights throwing her beautiful face into light, then dark, then light, then dark. Maybe that was the problem. All this time, he'd been trying to focus on her dark side. Now he was seeing the light. And he… Hell, there were times when he wondered if he even had a light side.

What would happen if his dark side mingled with Gracie's light side? Would it leave them both more balanced? Or would it just turn everything gray?

As if he'd uttered the question out loud, she turned to look at him. She really was beautiful, whether in light or dark. And he really did want her. He just wished he knew what the fallout of having her would be. And that thought was strange, because he'd never worried about fallout before.

Clearly, girls next door were a lot more dangerous than con artists.

When they arrived back at Gracie's hotel room and she turned to tell Harrison good-night, she could see he was no more ready to say the words than she was. In fact, the way he was looking at her now was a lot like the way he'd looked just before he'd kissed her at the Moondrop Ballroom. So it really didn't come as a surprise when he took a step closer and dipped his head to hers. Nor was it surprising when she took a step forward and tilted her head back to meet him.

The kiss was even better this time. Maybe because Gracie played an equal part in it from the beginning, or maybe because she had time to enjoy it from the very start. Something about the feel of Harrison's mouth on hers felt like coming home. But to a home where she didn't have to live all by herself.

Reluctantly, she ended the kiss. "Do you… Um, do you want to come inside?"

He met her gaze intently. "Yeah. Are you sure you want me to?"

She nodded.

"Because if I come inside, Gracie, I won't leave until morning."

Actually, she was kind of hoping he wouldn't want to leave at all. But morning was good for a start. "That's okay," she told him. "I don't want you to leave." There. Let him make of that what he would.

He dipped his head forward in silent acknowledgment. Then he followed her into the room and closed the door behind them, taking care to tuck the Do Not Disturb notice into the key slot as he did.

She started to ask him if he wanted to order something from room service, a snack or a bottle of wine or a game of Jenga or anything that might slow this thing down. But he obviously didn't want to slow down, because he pulled her close, looped his arms around her waist and kissed her again. He brushed his lips lightly over hers, and then skimmed them along her jaw, her cheek, her temple. With each new caress, her pulse leaped higher. When she splayed her fingers open on his chest, she felt his heart thumping against her palm, every bit as ragged and rapid as her own. When his lips found hers again, he deepened the kiss, and she opened her mouth to invite him in.

As he kissed her, he scooted one hand from her waist to the top of her dress. He pulled the zipper down down down, until it stopped at the base of her fanny, and the dress fell completely open. Then she felt his warm hand on her naked skin, his fingers pressing into her, pushing her more closely against him. He traced the outline of her mouth with the tip of his tongue, and then darted it inside to explore more thoroughly. His fingers went exploring, too, down to the waistband of her panties, dipping lower until his palms were pressing into the tender flesh beneath.

Gracie tore her mouth from his at the contact, gasping for breath, wondering again if this was such a good idea. But when her gaze met his, when she saw how dark his eyes were with wanting, how ruddy his cheeks were with his desire, how damp his mouth was from her own, she moved her fingers to his shirt, carefully slipping the buttons from their fastenings, one by one.

Harrison watched, his own breath shallow and warm against her temple, his hands still where he'd left them, curving over her bare bottom. Her fingers began to tremble after the third button, but she managed to undo them all. He released her long enough to shrug out of his shirt and jacket at once, leaving him bare above the waist, an absolute feast for her eyes.

His torso was long and lean, his shoulders wide and rugged, all of him corded with muscle. Her hands were on him before she even made the decision to touch him, her palms flattening against his smooth flesh, her fingertips raking gentle lines along each salient ridge until she reached his shoulders. Then she ran her hands down over the bumps of biceps, triceps and everything that came after.

When she reached his wrists, he turned his hands so they were grasping hers, and then urged her arms down to her sides. With one deft move, he hooked his fingers in the sleeves of her dress and nudged them over her shoulders, tugging on the garment until it pooled in a heap of frothy mint at her feet. Beneath it, she wore only white lace panties and a strapless bra. His gaze flew to the latter, followed by his hands. Without hesitation, he cupped one over each breast, making his claim to her absolute. Gracie fairly purred at the contact, and then lifted her hands to his torso again, touching him just as intimately. After squeezing her breasts gently, he moved his hands to her back, unhooking her bra to let it fall to the floor before pulling her body flush against his.

The sensation of finally touching him, flesh to flesh, heat to heat, was breathtaking…literally. Gracie's breath caught in her throat at the contact. He lowered his head and kissed her again, driving a hand between their bodies to grasp her breast once more. He moved his thumb over her nipple several times, before cradling her fully in his hand. She felt him swell to life against her, getting harder with each touch, until he was straining against his zipper. When she lowered her hand to his fly, he began backing her toward the bed. The action moved her hand more intimately against him, making him harder still.

By the time they reached the bed, his pants were open, and she was stroking him over the silk of his boxers. He growled something unintelligible against her mouth, and then sat down on the edge of the mattress, bringing her down on his lap to face him, her legs straddling his. For a moment, he only held her there with a hand on each hip, kissing her and kissing her and kissing her. Then he moved his mouth to her breast and kissed her there, too. First one, then the other, licking her, sucking her, driving her mad. Gracie twined her fingers in his hair and held him there, relishing each new touch of his tongue. Then she felt his hand between her legs, pressing into her over her panties, gently rubbing her with one finger, then two, creating a delicious friction that nearly drove her mad.

And then he was pulling the fabric aside, pushing his fingers into the damp folds of her flesh, slipping one finger easily, deeply into her. Gracie cried out at the contact and instinctively tried to close her legs. But Harrison pushed his own wider, opening her more, making her even more accessible to him. For a long time, he fingered her, until she thought she would explode with wanting him. Only when her entire body shuddered with her orgasm did he slow his movements. And only when her body relaxed in her release did he let her rest.

For all of a minute.

Then he was rolling her onto her back on the bed and pulling down her panties, until she lay blissfully and wantonly naked. She sighed with much contentment and threw her arms above her head, dissolving into a pool of something sweet and hot. The sensation doubled when she opened her eyes and saw Harrison shedding his trousers, his cock fully erect and ready for…oh, anything.

When he lay down beside her, she closed her hand over him, dragging her fingers slowly down his heavy length and up again, palming the damp head before repeating her actions. He closed his eyes as she caressed him for long moments, his breathing deep and ragged, his body hard and tense. When she sensed he was close to coming, he grabbed her hand and stilled her motions, and then opened his eyes.

"Not yet," he murmured.

She started to object—she certainly hadn't stopped him—but he sat up and rolled on a condom. Then he pulled her up beside him, grabbed her by the waist and set her astride him again. As she draped her arms over his shoulders, he rubbed his cock against the wet flesh between her legs until he was as damp as she. Then he pushed himself inside her—deep, *deep* inside her. So deep, she wasn't sure where his body ended and hers began. Still gripping her hips, he pushed her up until he almost withdrew, and then urged her back downward. Over and over he entered her, seeming to go deeper with each stroke. Then he withdrew and levered both their bodies onto the mattress until Gracie was on her knees with her shoulders pressed to the mattress, and he was entering her again from behind.

She clutched the sheet in both hands, hanging on for dear life, knowing they were both close to coming now. Harrison rose up on his knees and held her hips, pulling her back toward him as he thrust forward, until finally, finally, both of them came.

For one long, lingering moment, it seemed as if neither of them would ever move again. Then he rolled onto his back beside her, and she straightened until her belly and breasts were flat against the bed. She felt his hand on her bottom, gently stroking her sensitive skin, and she somehow managed to move her own hand to his chest. The skin she encountered was hot and wet, his chest rising and falling with his patchy respiration. She turned her head to look at him, only to find him staring intently at her.

Neither of them said a word. For Gracie, that was because she had no idea what to say. Never, ever had it been like this with a man. No one had made her feel so desirable and so desired. She'd never felt the things Harrison made her feel and would never feel them with anyone else. She didn't know how she knew that, but she did. There was something between them, right here, right now, that was different from anything she'd ever known before. Anything she would ever know again. And she just wasn't sure how she felt about that.

Until he smiled. And she knew he felt it, too.

Only then could Gracie close her eyes and let sleep take her. For a little while, anyway. Because she knew she hadn't had nearly enough of Harrison. Not tonight. Not forever. She only hoped he felt that part, too.

Nine

Harrison awoke to a buzzing sound, and wasn't sure at first what it was. A hum of satisfaction after a night of unbelievably good sex? The fizzing of his brain when he recalled some of the finer moments of that sex? The thrum of his heart at the sight of Gracie, naked and rosy beside him?

She lay on her stomach, the sheet dipped low enough to reveal the expanse of her tantalizing back and the soft indention of the two perfect dimples over her ass. He stirred to life at the sight of them, and it was all he could do not to run his tongue down the length of her spine. He wanted to hear her make that sound again, that little gasp of delight when he moved his hand between her legs and dragged his little finger higher, inserting it softly and gently fingering the more sensitive, sultry part of her.

He bit back a groan at the memory and did his best to stifle the response of his erection. *Later*, he promised himself. After she was awake. They could both probably use a little more sleep. Even if he knew his body and brain both were done sleeping for a while.

He couldn't remember a morning after with a woman when he didn't want to race out of her bed or chase her out of his. Normally, at a moment like this, he was considering the scenario in the same way a jewel thief plans a heist, tracing his route from leaving the bed without waking his companion to completing his escape without setting off an alarm. At this point, he probably could be a jewel thief, so expert had he become at vanishing without detection.

But he didn't want to vanish this morning. And he kinda did want to wake his companion. And not just so they could have another round of riotous lovemaking, either. He was actually looking forward to having breakfast with her. Just the two of them, sharing coffee and toast and quiet conversation. And that, probably, was the weirdest thing of all. That he wanted more from Gracie than sex. He never wanted anything from a woman but sex. And once he'd had sex he seldom wanted a woman again. And breakfast? Conversation? Ah, no.

It finally dawned on him that the buzzing that had awoken him had come from his phone, lying on the nightstand beside him. He palmed it and held it up where he could see it. A text from a number he didn't recognize, one with a New York City area code. He thumbed the prompt and found a message from the private investigator his attorney had hired after the reading of his father's will. The one who was supposed to prove Gracie was the gold-digging con artist they'd all been so sure she was.

Damn, what a waste of money that turned out to be.

The text was short and to the point: Check your email.

In spite of Harrison's certainty that his original opinion about Gracie was wrong, something pinched in his chest when he read the message. He told himself that a terse direction to check his email meant nothing. The PI's initial report probably said something like "You're an idiot, Sage. The woman you hired me to expose as a predator is actually one of the nicest, most decent people in the world."

So why the pang in his chest? Why did he suddenly want to check his email? Why did he want to see a report if he already knew what it said?

He looked at Gracie again. She was still asleep. So, with all the stealth of a jewel thief, he eased himself out of bed, slipped on the hotel bathrobe he had shed a couple of hours ago and retreated to the other side of the room. He cracked the curtains enough to allow in a slice of morning sunlight, and then thumbed the email icon on his phone and waited. There were a lot of new messages, since he hadn't checked his mail since yesterday morning. Even so, his gaze flew immediately to the one from the PI. With a subject head of Re: Grace Sumner, the body of the email read, As per agreement, initial report attached. Information gathered to date. Harrison skittered the cursor over the link to the attachment. But something made him hesitate before clicking on it.

Would opening this file after last night constitute a violation of trust? He supposed it depended on what last night was. If it was just sex, then no, this wasn't a violation of trust, since no trust had been established. Sex and trust didn't go hand in hand unless the people having the sex had some kind of agreement. If they were married, for instance. Or if they had made a commitment or developed feelings for each other. Feelings of love, say.

None of those things applied to him and Gracie. Did they? They certainly weren't in love. They'd only known each other a week. And they really hadn't made a commitment to each other. Last night was just…

Well, he still wasn't sure what last night was. But even if he did feel different this morning from the way he usually felt after spending the night with a woman, there was no reason for him to hesitate. And hell, the PI's report probably just confirmed that she was on the up-and-up.

Before he could second-guess himself again, Harrison clicked on the attachment. Immediately, a document opened on his screen. And he began to read.

Gracie awoke slowly and squinted at the bedside clock, startled to discover it was after ten-thirty. She never slept this late. Of course, she'd never spent the night the way she spent last night, either. Harrison Sage was certainly a thorough lover. She stretched languidly and smiled at the pleasant stiffness in her muscles, marveling again at how quickly things between them had changed. Not that she was complaining—she liked this new direction. A lot.

Blame it on the ballroom, she thought with a happy sigh. Or on Harrison's sweet, wistful expression as he sorted through his father's things yesterday. Or on his cheering for Roxanne at the top of the ninth inning and his genuine delight when the Rockets won their game. Or on their intimate conversation at the stock exchange, or even those minutes in the library that first morning, when he'd charmed her out of her anxiety. Those blue, blue eyes. That luscious smile. That wounded soul. How could she not fall for a guy like that?

Any rancor Harrison had shown since meeting her had been the result of hurt and grief. Any chilliness had come from his fear that she was taking advantage of his family. Had the situation been reversed, had Gracie been the one who'd lost her father and felt as if Harrison were threatening her family, she would have behaved the same way. They'd just needed to get to know each other, to understand and trust each other. Anything that had happened before last night didn't matter now. Because all of that had changed. They never could have been as good together as they were last night if they didn't know, understand and trust each other now. If they didn't care about each other.

And Gracie did care about Harrison. She cared about him a lot.

She shrugged into the remaining hotel robe and crossed the room to where he sat with his back to her, reading something on his phone.

"Good morning," she said as she approached him.

He jumped up from the chair and spun around so quickly, she might as well have fired off a shotgun. And when she saw his face, something cool and distressing settled in her belly. Because he didn't look as though he thought it was a good morning at all.

"What's wrong?" she asked.

For a moment, he only stared at her, as if he were

searching for the words he wanted to say but had no idea where to find them. Or maybe he was searching for something else, something just as nebulous and elusive.

Finally, he pulled himself up until he was ramrod-straight and crossed his arms over his midsection as if trying to keep himself that way. "Two words," he said. "Wilson Braun."

Gracie's heart dropped at the mention of Devon's father. How on earth had Harrison heard about him? More to the point, *what* had Harrison heard about him?

"He's Devon's father," she said. "And like I said, anything that happened between me and Devon is in the past. You seemed to be okay with that. What does Wilson have to do with anything?"

Harrison studied her more intently, as if he'd been expecting a different reaction from her. "I was okay with the past when I thought Devon Braun was just an old boyfriend."

"He is just an old boyfriend." Among other things. Things Gracie preferred not to think—or talk—about.

"An old boyfriend you tried to extort a lot of money from."

The accusation washed over Gracie like a wave of polluted water. She closed her eyes in an effort to block it out, but that only made it worse. So that was what he'd heard about Wilson. The same thing a lot of other people had heard. Exactly what Wilson had wanted them to hear.

She opened her eyes again and met Harrison's gaze levelly. "That isn't true," she said, surprised by how calmly the words came out.

"My PI says it is," Harrison told her.

The PI, she remembered. The one his attorney had hired to prove Gracie was a predator who'd seduced an old man and stolen his fortune. The PI she'd been so certain wouldn't be a threat because her life was an open book. She should have realized he would eventually get to the chapter about Devon and his family. The problem was, he'd undoubtedly read a heavily edited version of the story—since Wilson Braun had made sure no one would ever hear the real one—and that was what he'd relayed to Harrison.

She sighed. "And of course you always trust people to tell the truth right off the bat, don't you?" The way he had with Gracie. Hah.

The charge had the desired effect. His brows arrowed downward and he looked less sure of himself. "He has no reason to lie."

"Maybe he's not lying. Maybe he's just misinformed." Hey, Gracie would give the PI the benefit of the doubt. She didn't like to jump to conclusions the way a lot of people obviously did. Even if there was a good chance the PI had been paid a pile of money by Wilson Braun to bury the truth like so many others.

Harrison's expression fell a bit more, as if it hadn't occurred to him that the PI could be wrong. Nevertheless, he said, "This guy doesn't make mistakes. He's one of the best in the business."

Yeah, so was Wilson Braun. At least, when it came to the business of silencing other people or smearing their reputations.

"What did your PI tell you?" she asked.

Harrison hesitated again before replying, "He spoke at length to Wilson Braun about your relationship with his son, and he sent me copies of emails from Wilson to you that indicate you tried to blackmail the family for six figures in exchange for your silence on the matter of an alleged assault Devon committed—a story that you manufactured in the hope of profiting from it."

The first part of Harrison's statement didn't surprise her. Devon's father had always made sure his emails were worded in such a way that they never quite sounded like what he was actually trying to do—bribe Gracie in exchange for recanting what she'd witnessed so the charges against his son would be dropped. It was money Gracie had refused to take. It was the second part of Harrison's statement, the part about him believing she would lie about something like that in order to pocket a pile of cash, that did surprise her. If after everything the two of them had shared, and after the way they had been together last night, he could go back to thinking the worst of her this easily and this quickly…

Very quietly, very evenly, she said, "The story wasn't manufactured. Devon tried to rape a friend of mine at a party. Thankfully, I walked in on it before it became an actual rape, otherwise that's what Devon would have been charged with, and that would have been the story his father would have been trying to suppress."

She paused, letting that sink in. Judging by the way Harrison's expression changed, it did. Some. So Gracie told him the rest of it.

"But Devon had beat her up pretty bad, so I took her to the hospital, and she filed a police report and told the cops what happened. I corroborated her story. Then Wilson Braun tried to bribe both of us to shut up and pretend it never happened. Did your PI find his emails to my friend, too?"

Harrison shook his head, still looking a little torn. "No. He was only interested in information on you."

"Then do you have copies of *my* emails in response to Devon's father?" she asked, already knowing the answer. If he'd read those, they wouldn't be having this conversation, because he'd already know the whole story.

He sounded even more uncertain when he responded, "He's working on it. Your old service provider won't release them without a warrant. Wilson Braun volunteered his."

"Yeah, I bet he did. He was super careful about what he said to me and my friend in his emails. Too bad neither of us was wearing a wire when he spoke to us in person. And he did everything he could to discredit us."

It was why the case had never gone anywhere and the charges were ultimately dismissed. Because the Brauns were one of Cincinnati's oldest and most revered families. They had more money and power than an entire Mount Olympus full of gods. People like that thought the world was at their disposal. They couldn't be bothered with things like the truth if it meant their perspective had to be changed or defended.

And Harrison was just like them, she realized. He'd decided a long time ago that Gracie was someone who couldn't be trusted and only cared about herself. And in spite of everything the two of them had shared, he'd gone right back to thinking that the minute he was given a chance. If his feelings for her were even a fraction of what hers were for him, he would never—could never—suspect her of doing what he was accusing her of now. He would trust her because he knew what kind of person she really was. Instead, when another member of his tribe said Gracie Sumner was a liar, then by all means, she must be a liar.

"You don't believe me, do you?" she asked anyway.

His expression revealed nothing of what he was thinking or feeling. Which probably told Gracie everything she needed to know. If he couldn't trust that she was telling him the truth… If the past few days hadn't changed the opinion he'd originally held of her… If last night had meant nothing to him…

"I don't know what to believe," he said softly.

Yep. That was everything Gracie needed to know.

"You'd rather put your faith in a private investigator who doesn't even have all the facts than in me. You'd rather believe Wilson Braun, a man you've never even met, than me."

"I didn't say that," he said.

She inhaled a deep breath and released it slowly. "Yeah, you did."

How could she have been thinking he had changed? How could she have been thinking she was falling in love with him? Someone who couldn't be trusted and only cared about himself.

"I think you should go," she said.

"But—"

"Now, Harrison."

Reluctantly, he gathered his clothes from the night before and went into the bathroom to change. When he came out again, his white tuxedo shirt hung unbuttoned over his black trousers, and the rest of his clothes were wadded in his hands. Gracie still stood where she'd been before, her arms roped across her chest, feeling colder than she'd ever felt in her life. When Harrison stopped near her on his way to the door, looking as though he wanted to say more, she only pointed toward it silently and turned her back. But when she heard the click of the latch, she called out to him over her shoulder one last time.

"Harrison."

He turned slowly, but said nothing.

"I'll have Mr. Tarrant send the documents to transfer ownership of the houses to Vivian to me in Seattle and return them to him as soon as possible. And I'll ask Vivian to ship anything I left at her house to me at home. There's no reason for me to go back to New York. Or to stay here in Cincinnati."

He paused for another moment, and then closed the door behind himself. Only then did Gracie allow herself to collapse into the chair he'd vacated. And only then did she allow her heart to break.

Harrison felt flummoxed when he got back to his own room, wondering if he'd just screwed up the best thing that ever happened to him.

No, he immediately told himself. There had been nothing to screw up. All he and Gracie had had was a single night of spectacular sex. And lots of good things had happened to him in his life. He had money and professional success. What could be better than those?

Now his PI had information that might just prove Gracie was the financial predator Harrison had suspected her of being from the outset, something that increased his chances of winning back his father's estate. And that was really good.

So why didn't any of that make him feel good? Why did he feel so bad?

The answer came to him immediately, but he didn't

much care for it. Maybe because, on some level, he actually wasn't convinced that Gracie was a financial predator. Maybe he'd been too quick to come to the conclusions he had.

He tossed his wadded-up clothing onto the still-made bed and fell onto the mattress. Then he pulled up his web browser on his phone and typed the name *Devon Braun* in quotations, along with the word *Cincinnati.*

The first hits that came up were for his Twitter and Facebook accounts. Harrison saw photographs of an innocuous-looking guy of above-average appearance who talked mostly about sports and a band Harrison hated. No red flags. Just some guy whose family happened to have a lot of money.

Scrolling down, he saw a link to a blog that covered Cincinnati crime called "Word on the Street." It was written by a local resident unaffiliated with law enforcement and clearly stated that it reported gossip, rumor and innuendo. Not exactly something that instilled great confidence.

But still interesting.

The piece was more than a year old and described a rape charge filed against the member of a prominent local family, indicating that it came after sexual assault and battery charges against him in another incident were dismissed. Neither of the victims was named. Nor was the perpetrator. So why had this item come up in a search for Devon Braun?

Maybe because the author of the piece had hidden his name on the site somewhere so that it would still appear in searches for Devon but avoid the wrath of Wilson Braun?

If that was the case, if Devon Braun had committed these crimes and the charges against him had been buried, then there was still a criminal on the loose in Cincinnati, which was a scary enough thought in itself. But somehow even scarier was the thought that maybe Gracie had been telling the truth all along and really was the best thing that had ever happened to him.

And scariest of all was the thought that Harrison had screwed that up. Bad.

The feeling only grew stronger when he was back in his Flatiron District high-rise with the boxes from the storage shed he'd brought with him. The cartons were dented and misshapen from the trip, and each bore numerous Sharpie markings, in different colors and handwriting—his father's, Gracie's and his own.

They looked completely out of place in Harrison's bedroom, with its wall of windows offering spectacular views of the nighttime skyline, its sleek, tailored furnishings and monochromatic taupe decor. They didn't look anything like Harrison or the man he remembered as his father. They looked a lot like Gracie, actually, offbeat and colorful and full of character. They looked as if they belonged to someone who had spent their life, well, living. Yet they were set against the backdrop of a room that looked as if it belonged to someone who hadn't lived at all.

Was that how he seemed? Like someone who had never lived? Sure, he spent the majority of his days—and sometimes his evenings—in his office or someone else's. And okay, most of his socializing had something to do with work. But that was what a person had to do to build a successful life. All Harrison had required of his home was that it look like it belonged to a successful, wealthy man, because those were the adjectives he'd wanted attached to himself. His place had always reinforced that desire.

So why did he suddenly feel kind of useless and needy?

The boxes, he decided, could wait. Unfortunately, he couldn't find enough space in any of his closets to stow them. So he shoved them into the corner of his bedroom, where they'd be—mostly—out of view. Funny, though, how his gaze kept straying to them all the same.

Work, he reminded himself. He had a ton of it to catch up on before he went back to the office tomorrow.

He started a pot of coffee, headed to his office and pulled up his email. Then he scrolled to the one he'd received from his PI this morning. Then he hit Reply and started typing. But he didn't ask for more information about Gracie. Instead, Harrison asked for more information about Devon and Wilson Braun. And he made sure, before he hit Send, that he tagged it "highest priority."

It was nearly two weeks before he received a reply—at 8:13 on a Tuesday night, thirteen days, eight hours and thirty-seven minutes after calling Gracie Sumner a liar in Cincinnati.

Not that he was counting or anything.

And not that he hadn't replayed nearly every minute the two of them spent together during that time—like Gracie's shy smile that first day in the library, and how the wind played with her hair during breakfast, and her chirpy "batter, batter, batter, suh-wing, batter" support of the Rockets, and their chaste but mind-scrambling kiss in the Moondrop Ballroom. And not that, with each passing day, he'd become more convinced that he'd had something with her he would never find again and had completely, irrevocably screwed it up.

Because even before emailing his PI, on some primal level, Harrison had known he was wrong about Gracie and should never have accused her of lying. Especially after the night they'd spent together. He'd just been so stunned—and, okay, kind of terrified—by the speed and intensity of his response to her. So he'd looked for the quickest, easiest way to escape. The PI's report had offered the perfect excuse to put Gracie at arm's length again. Hell, arm's length? He'd sent her to the other side of the planet.

And then he began to worry that there was nothing he could say or do to repair things. That even if he did, Gracie might not forgive him or take him back. That he'd spend the rest of his life thinking about how happy they could have been together. How happy *he* could have been. If only he hadn't jumped to some stupid conclusion that ruined everything.

In spite of all that, Harrison clicked on the file from his PI. And immediately realized that yep, he was a first-class, numero-uno, see-exhibit-A jerk. Because Gracie had indeed told him the truth about Devon Braun. All of it. The assault on her friend, the police report, Wilson Braun's bribes to suppress it. And Gracie Sumner's refusal of the money he'd offered her.

Harrison grabbed a sharp knife from the kitchen and headed for his bedroom. He pushed a chair into the corner where he'd stacked the boxes from Cincinnati, and stabbed the packing tape seam of one to open it. He wasn't sure why he suddenly wanted—needed—to go through his father's things. Maybe because they were the only link he had to Gracie, and he just wanted to touch something she had touched herself.

His grandmother's five journals sat on top. She'd written the first entry the day his grandfather proposed to her and the last the day she abandoned her family in Cincinnati. Harrison had skimmed the first two diaries that day in the storage unit, so he picked up the third, opening it and riffling through the pages to check the dates at the top of each. Toward the end, he found an envelope shoved between two pages.

There was no writing on the outside, and the flap wasn't sealed. Inside was a letter written in his father's hand, dated two years before his death. It started off "Dear Vivian…"

Harrison stopped reading there, telling himself he should give it to his mother. But he wasn't sure his mother would even want to read it. Still, he should probably let her decide. Then again, maybe he should read a little of it first, to make sure its contents wouldn't make her feel even worse about his father's behavior than she already did.

Dear Vivian, I hope you and Harrison are doing well.

Oh, sure, he thought. His father had been out of their lives for more than a decade, and they'd had no idea what made him leave or if they'd ever see him again. Why wouldn't they be doing well? He made himself read more.

I suppose that was a ridiculous sentiment, wasn't it? How could you and Harrison be doing well in the situation I created for you? Please, first, let me apologize for that. Then let me try to explain.

Harrison had never heard his father apologize for anything. Whenever he was wrong about something, Harrison Sage, Jr. had only made excuses. And he'd never felt the need to justify anything, either. Harrison kept reading.

And, wow, did he learn a lot.

The letter was long, chronicling everything his father had done since leaving New York and his reasons for doing so in the first place. How he'd begun to feel as if he didn't know himself anymore. How there was nothing left in him of the boy who had hoped to become a major-league baseball player. How his intention when he came to New York as a teenager was to make enough money to support himself and the family he hoped to have someday but how, once he'd started making money, he'd fallen under its spell, and had wanted to make more. And then more. And then more. How it had become something of an addiction that motivated every decision he made and eclipsed everything else in his life.

He'd thought the only way to break the addiction was to remove himself from its temptation. He hadn't meant to stay away from New York—or his family—for as long as he had. But with each passing week, then month, then year, it became harder for him to figure out how he could ever apologize and atone for his behavior. Eventually, he had come to the conclusion that it was too late to even try, and his wife and son would never take him back. He knew by then that Harrison had built a successful business and was outearning his father, so he'd be able to care for himself and his mother. They couldn't possibly need—or want—Harrison, Jr. after all this time.

That was why he had decided to leave his money to Gracie. Because he'd known that Vivian and Harrison wouldn't want anything he'd earned after he shunted them aside. He'd known Gracie would disperse the funds charitably, but, even more importantly, she would also give a sizable chunk of it to Vivian and Harrison. That was the only way he'd been sure they would accept any of his wealth. If it came from someone else. Someone like Gracie, who was the kindest, fairest, most generous person he'd ever met. In fact—

The letter ended there, midsentence, suggesting his father had wanted to say more. Why hadn't he finished the letter? More to the point, why hadn't he mailed it?

The answer to both questions was right there in the letter. His father had been convinced Harrison and his mother wanted nothing to do with him. He'd convinced himself that he couldn't make up for what he'd done, so there was no point in even trying.

And that kind of thinking was crazy. Harrison and his mother would have absolutely welcomed him back into their lives. It would have taken time—and, possibly, professional counseling—to put things back to rights, but hell, his father could have at least tried. It was never too late to ask for—or obtain—forgiveness or make amends. It was never too late to start over.

Harrison halted when he realized that so much of what his father had said in his letter mirrored what he himself had begun to fear about Gracie. His father had been sure he'd irreparably botched his relationship with the people he loved, so he hadn't even tried to fix it and lived the rest of his life alone.

Gracie was right. There really was a lot of his father in Harrison. The question was, did he want to end up the same way?

Ten

"That should do it," Gracie said as she lifted her pen from the last of a dozen checks she had signed in a row. "For today, anyway."

Cassandra Nelson, the financial advisor Gracie had hired to help her distribute Harry's money, smiled. She reminded Gracie of Vivian Sage, with her always perfect silver hair and chic suits. Gracie was wearing a suit, too, a new one—well, new to her, anyway. It was a lavender Givenchy from the 1950s. A real Givenchy, not a knockoff, one of the few things she'd let herself purchase with some of the money Harry had insisted she spend on herself.

It had been nearly a month since she'd returned to Seattle, and she hadn't heard a word from Harrison. Vivian had written to thank Gracie for transferring the deeds to the Sage homes along with a sizable share of

Harry's estate, closing with her hope that Gracie would "come and visit us when you're in New York again." *Us*, not *me*, clearly including Harrison in the invitation.

Not that Harrison had had any part in doing the inviting, Gracie was certain. Vivian was just being polite. She clearly didn't know that her son still clung to the idea that Gracie was a crook even after she'd given away so much of Harry's money. It was only natural Vivian would include Harrison in an invitation to visit. And it was only natural for Gracie to decline.

Even if she still thought about him every day. Even if—she might as well admit it—she still cared for him.

"Philanthropy isn't for sissies," Cassandra said, jarring Gracie out of her thoughts. "People think all you do is throw around money. But there's a lot of work and paperwork that goes into it. Especially with an estate as large as Mr. Sage's."

"So I'm learning," Gracie replied.

Boy, was she learning. Not just about money and how to use it, but about how people reacted to you when you had access to that money. She'd received enough invitations to functions over the last few weeks to keep an army of billionaires busy. Already, she'd put three of Harry's billions to good use, for everything from endowing university chairs to bailing out failing mom-and-pop businesses.

"Now then," Cassandra said, "do you want to talk about your own future? Please?"

Ever since Gracie's first visit to the office, Cassandra had been badgering her about how much of Harry's money she was going to put aside for herself, to make sure she was covered for the rest of her life. But Gracie always stalled. Naturally, she did want to be covered for life, but she wasn't sure Cassandra's idea of what that meant mirrored her own.

Cassandra's focus would be on Gracie's financial needs, where Gracie was more concerned about intangible needs. Personal needs. Emotional needs. No amount of money could guarantee those. Harry's money hadn't exactly brought her any happiness so far. On the contrary. Not that she wouldn't keep some—Harry had insisted, after all—but tallying a specific amount wasn't something she wanted to think about. Not yet.

Before Harry's fortune, all Gracie had ever wanted was a job she enjoyed, friends to have her back, a decent place to live and a man who would love her till the end of time, the same way she would love him. Seriously, what more could anyone want or need beyond that?

But now, when she looked down the road to the future, there was only a curve around which she could see nothing. She told herself she must still have a destination, but she just didn't know what it was anymore. Or who it was with. If anyone.

Gracie bit back a sigh. "Cassandra, I promise I'll get to it before all this is done, okay?"

They made an appointment for their next meeting, and then Gracie left, to go…somewhere. She had no idea where. She'd quit her job at Café Destiné since Harry's generosity meant she could return to school full-time in the fall and earn her degree by December. So job hunting could wait until then. In the meantime, there was still most of summer to get through, and little to fill the weeks.

Her days since returning to Seattle had mostly been

filled with internet searches for places to donate Harry's money, reading and discovering British TV shows on Netflix. Maybe she should get a cat…

Finally, she decided to return to her apartment. Maybe she could check out the next episode of *Call the Midwife* or something. She was sorting through her mail when she topped the last stair to her floor, so she wasn't looking where she was going as she ambled forward. That was why she didn't notice the guy waiting by her front door until he'd placed his hands on her shoulders to prevent her from running into him. She leaped backward at the contact, her entire body on alert. Just as quickly, Harrison lifted his hands in surrender mode and apologized.

"I'm sorry," he said. But the expression on his face seemed to suggest he was sorry for a lot more than just startling her.

It was as if he'd been conjured by all the thinking she'd been doing about him, as if he were here because she'd somehow wished for it strongly enough. In spite of how things had ended between them, she'd found it impossible to stay angry with him. Harrison Sage III was a product of the world in which he'd grown up, one of deep wealth and shallow feeling, where people viewed each other as opportunities and commodities instead of human beings. Mostly, she was just sad. Not only about how things had turned out between them, but also about how he had to live in that world and didn't seem to know how to leave it.

"What are you doing here?" she asked.

He said nothing at first, only scanned her up and down, as if refreshing his memory of her. Then he said, "You cut your hair."

Her fingers flew to her slightly shorter tresses. "Just a trim."

"I like it."

"Thanks."

She studied him in return and realized he'd changed some, too. Not his expensive, tailored, dark-wash jeans or his crisp, white oxford shirt. But the fatigue in his eyes that hadn't been there before, and the shadow of uncertainty in his expression. Harrison Sage had been many things since Gracie had met him—from antagonistic and suspicious to adorable and sweet—but he'd never been uncertain. To see him that way now made her feel…

Well, actually, seeing him looking uncertain made her feel a little more sure of herself.

"So…what are you doing here?" she asked again.

He hesitated, then replied, "I finally had all of my father's things shipped to New York from Cincinnati."

That was good, Gracie thought. But she wasn't sure why he'd had to come all the way to Seattle to tell her that.

"And as I was unpacking everything in my mother's attic," he continued, "I realized there might be something in there that you wanted to keep for yourself. I mean, you never asked for anything—"

It was nice to hear him finally say what he should have known all along. Gracie really had never asked for anything. Not from the storage unit. Not from Harry's estate. Not from Harrison. Even though it would have been nice if Harrison had given her a little something—like his trust or his appreciation or…or his love.

"But I thought you might want a keepsake," he continued. "Something that would remind you of him. Of your time with him."

"Thanks, but I don't need any reminders," she said. She pointed to her forehead. "Everything I need to remember Harry is right here."

"Wow. You really didn't want anything from him, did you?"

"Only his friendship," she said. "Thanks for finally noticing."

He said nothing in response to that.

So Gracie asked again, a little more wearily this time, "What are you doing here, Harrison?"

He studied her again. "I came for you. If you'll have me."

She felt the same tingle of pleasure that wound through her that night at the Dewitts' party, when he told the butler that she was with him. Because this time, he said it in a way that was even more romantic and intimate. She said nothing in response, however. She wasn't *with him* now any more than she had been that night.

When she remained silent, he began to look even more fatigued and uncertain. And more panicky. "Gracie, I am so sorry about what happened in Cincinnati."

The apology surprised her. Even with him standing here, having traveled more than two thousand miles to offer it, she was amazed he didn't try to stall or use a "sorry, not sorry" euphemism. Then again, maybe he wasn't apologizing for their last conversation. An awful lot had happened when they were in Cincinnati. Maybe he was sorry the two of them had shared that delicious tango. Maybe he was sorry the two of them had made love. Maybe he was sorry for those three red velvet cupcakes at the Rockets game.

"I'm sorry I ever doubted you," he went on.

Oh. Okay. Well, that was a start.

"I'm sorry I thought… I'm sorry I made you feel like a—a…"

"A trashy, scheming, manipulative gold digger?" she supplied helpfully, harkening back to their first meeting.

"Yeah," he said sheepishly. "Like that. I'm sorry I was such a colossal jerk."

Better. But he wasn't quite done yet.

"I'm sorry I jumped to conclusions after reading the PI's report," he continued. "I never should have read the damned thing to begin with. Not after we—"

He halted before finishing. Not that she needed him to finish, since she knew perfectly well what he was referring to now. He shouldn't have read the report after the night the two of them spent together. After everything they'd experienced together. He should have trusted her instead. He was right about that and everything else. But the fact remained that he did do all those things, and that he didn't trust her. It was nice of him to apologize for that now, but…

"But you did doubt me," she said. "Even after—" Gracie couldn't quite put that night into words, either. So she hurriedly said, "And you did jump to—and cling to—conclusions. And you were a colossal jerk."

"I know. I'm sorry."

She didn't want to make him grovel—well, okay, she *did*, but she wouldn't, because that was the kind of thing people did in his world, not hers—so she told him, "Okay. I appreciate the apologies. Thank you."

He looked even more surprised by her capitulation than she'd been by his apology. "So you forgive me?"

She inhaled deeply and released the breath slowly. That was a tricky one. *Did* she forgive him? In spite of all of her thinking about him over the last month, the idea of forgiving him had never come up. Then she realized the reason for that. It was because she already had forgiven him. She wasn't sure when or why. Maybe she just hadn't wanted to be the kind of person who held a grudge. Nobody was perfect. Imperfection was part of being human.

"Yeah," she said. "I forgive you."

It didn't mean that everything was okay between them. It just meant that she was willing to listen to what he had to say.

So she asked one more time, "Why are you here, Harrison? If all you wanted to do was apologize, you could have texted me from New York and saved yourself a lot of money on plane fare. I know how important money is to you, after all."

He winced. "Gracie, that's not… It's just… I mean…" He expelled a frustrated sound. "Look, can we talk? Can I come in?"

She would have told herself there was no point in either of them saying anything else, but he had gone to some trouble and expense to get here. The least she could do was hear him out.

"Okay," she said. "We can talk."

She unlocked the door and entered her apartment, and then swept a hand toward the interior to silently invite Harrison in, too. He entered quickly, as if he feared she might slam the door in his face, and she told him to sit wherever he wanted.

She was reminded again of the day they met on Long Island and thought about how different things were here in her world. The view beyond her window wasn't of the ocean, but of another building across the street. Where the Sages' library had been filled with expensive collector's editions of books, her shelves were crammed with well-thumbed paperbacks. Instead of leather furniture, her sofa and lone chair were upholstered in a chintz floral long past being fashionable, and her coffee table was an old steamer trunk placed horizontally. Instead of lush, jewel-toned Aubussons, her hardwood floor sported a rubber-backed polyester area rug.

Harrison seated himself on the sofa, close enough to one side that it was clear he was making room for her on the other. Deliberately, Gracie chose the chair. His expression indicated he understood her decision and was resigned to it—for now. Even though he was the one who had asked if they could talk, the moment they were both seated, he fell silent.

So Gracie said, "What did you want to talk about?"

He threw her a look that indicated she should already know. And, of course, she did. But just because she didn't want to make him grovel didn't mean she was going to make this easy for him.

"Oh, I don't know," he said. "Maybe about developments in the Middle East? Or why we have to learn trigonometry in high school when we never actually use it in real life? Or how the music these kids listen to today is nothing but crap?"

Dammit, he was trying to be funny and charming like he was that first day in the library. She had to stop him before she started falling for him the way she did then.

"I choose trigonometry," she said. Because there was nothing funny or charming about math.

"Okay," he agreed. "But first, I want to talk about me and you."

Again he'd opted not to stall. How was she supposed to stay cool when he kept trying to get to the heart of things? To the heart of her?

"There is no me and you," she told him.

"There was," he retorted. "Before I screwed it all up."

She still wasn't prepared for him to go there so swiftly and candidly. She said nothing in response to his statement, but met his gaze levelly in a silent bid to go on.

"A couple of things," he began. "First, when I got back to New York, I had my PI look into Devon and Wilson Braun."

"Because you still didn't believe me," she said.

He shook his head. "That was what I told myself in Cincinnati, but I knew I was wrong to have mistrusted you before I even left your hotel room. I was just too stubborn and too stupid to admit it—to you or to myself. But we'll get to that. The reason I had my PI look into the Brauns was because I just wanted to make sure those guys got what was coming to them. And they will. My PI collected enough info on both Brauns—they're even worse than you thought—to cause them a lot of trouble for a long time. With the law, with their friends, with their jobs, you name it. Those guys are going to spend the rest of their lives in disgrace and dishonor, and, more than likely, prison. I told my guy to get all the info to whomever he could trust will do the right thing with it."

"Wow," she said. "Thank you, Harrison."

"Now then," he said. "About that morning in Cincinnati."

She couldn't quite stop herself, and replied, "The morning you called me a liar."

He started to deny it, and then seemed to realize it would be pointless. "There's something you have to understand about me, Gracie."

"What?"

He didn't hesitate at all this time. "I've never met anyone like you before."

That comment, too, surprised her. "But I'm a totally normal person. There are millions of people like me."

"Number one, no, there aren't. There's no one like you. And number two," he continued before she had a chance to say anything, "until you came along, I thought everyone in the world was like me. Because everyone I met *was* like me. Selfish, greedy takers who looked at every new opportunity, experience and acquaintance with the same question—what's in it for me? There was no reason for me to think you weren't like that, too. It never occurred to me that there were people in the world who wanted to help other people and make a difference. People like you and my father. Selflessness was an alien concept to me. To me, it made more sense that you would steal from my father than it did that he or you would give money to people who needed it."

She remembered how his father had taught him when he was still a child that money was more important than anything else. She remembered how he'd gone to a school for thirteen years that stressed financial success over any other kind of success. Lessons learned in childhood went deep, she knew. People could talk all they wanted about how when adults made stupid choices, they had to live with the consequences, never taking into account that those adult choices were based on childhood experiences. If someone was taught early on to choose money over happiness, then no one should be surprised when, as an adult, that person chose money over happiness.

"So when you told me you were going to give away my father's money," Harrison continued, "I didn't believe you. That didn't make sense to me. At least, it didn't until you took me to Cincinnati, and I saw how much my father meant to so many people. That's when I started to understand why he would want to give something back."

Dammit, he was doing it again. Being that sweet guy who made her fall in lo— Who had made her fall for him.

"That morning in Cincinnati, after we…" He hesitated again, but his gaze locked with hers. "I'd never felt the way I felt that morning, Gracie. Ever. Always before with women, I wanted to be gone before they woke up. But with you…" He smiled halfheartedly. "With you, I realized I never wanted to be with anyone else again."

There went the happy humming in her blood again. It was nice, having that back.

He continued, "And I guess I kind of panicked, when I understood what that meant. That I…had feelings for you…that I'd never had for anyone before.

That I wanted to see you again. Probably forever. That scared the hell out of me."

The humming thrummed louder. Faster.

"When I got the PI's report, and I read the lopsided version of what happened, it was easy for me to jump to the conclusion I did, because it meant I had an excuse for not wanting to wake up next to you every morning. It meant I didn't have to be in… It meant I didn't have to…care for you…the way I did. It gave me an excuse for going back to being the guy I was before. The one who didn't have to feel things. Life's a lot easier when you don't have to feel. Feeling is hard. And exhausting. And scary."

Oh, Harrison...

"But even after you were gone, I kept feeling. Every day. Every night. I couldn't stop thinking about you. But I didn't know what to say or do that would make up for what I did. I was afraid you'd never want to see me again after that. And I didn't blame you. I worried it would be pointless to apologize or to try to make up for it, figured you wouldn't talk to me if I tried. I started envisioning a horrible life without you. Then I found this."

He reached into his back pocket and withdrew an envelope. "It's a letter from my father I found in one of my grandmother's diaries. He wrote it to my mother two years before he died but never mailed it. You should read it, too."

Gracie balked. "But if it was meant for Vivian…"

"Mom's read it and doesn't mind my sharing it with you. It's important, Gracie."

Gingerly, she took the letter and read it in its entirety. When she looked up at Harrison again, it was with a heavy heart. "I can't believe he didn't think you and Vivian would forgive him."

"I can," Harrison said. "Because I thought you'd be the same way."

"But that's crazy."

"I know that now. But, clearly, I had a lot to learn about people. I still do. I just hope it's not too late. Because I don't want to end up like my father." He smiled. "Except for the part about where he got to spend the rest of his life with you."

Okay, that did it. Her heart was fully melted. Harrison must have realized that, because he smiled and scooted down to the other side of the couch. Close to Gracie, where his knee could gently touch hers. And even that tiny little contact made her feel better than she had in weeks. Four weeks, in fact. Four weeks, one day, three hours and twenty-seven minutes.

Not that she was counting or anything.

He lifted a hand and, after only a moment's hesitation, cupped it over her jaw. Unable to help herself, Gracie turned her head until his fingers were threaded in her hair, and then moved her hand to his cheek, too, loving the warmth under her palm. Her heart hammered faster when she remembered what happened the last time she touched him this way. His pupils expanded, his lips parted, his breath stilled. But he didn't move an inch.

So Gracie did.

She stood and took his hand in hers, and then led him to her bedroom. It was all the encouragement Harrison needed, because the moment she turned to look at him, he pulled her into his arms and covered her mouth with his. He kissed her lovingly, deeply, and for a very long time, cupping her jaws in both hands. Gracie splayed her fingers open on his chest, loving the feel of his heart racing against her hand, as rapidly as her own. After a moment, she moved her hands to the buttons of his shirt and began to unfasten them, her fingers sure and steady this time. He, in turn, dropped one of his hands to the single, oversized button on her jacket, freeing it and spreading the lapels open. He looked surprised to discover she wore only a bra beneath.

He was also more than a little aroused to discover that. Because he immediately freed his mouth from hers and skimmed the jacket over her shoulders to look at her. To help him in that respect, she reached behind herself to unzip her skirt, and let that, too, fall to the floor. The pale lavender lace bra and panties she wore were nearly transparent, leaving nothing to the imagination. When Harrison saw her effectively naked, he sucked in a deep breath and released it slowly.

"Is this the kind of thing you always have on under your clothes?"

He obviously remembered the lacy ensemble she'd been wearing in Cincinnati, and it was actually one of her more conservative sets. She nodded.

"This is the kind of thing you were wearing all those times I was with you in New York and Cincinnati?"

"Yeah," she said. "Except sometimes a little more revealing than this."

His eyes went wide at that. "You're not really much of a girl next door, are you?"

The question confused Gracie. "What do you mean?"

He only smiled and shook his head. "Nothing. Just..."

But he didn't finish. At least, not with words. Instead, he went back to unbuttoning his shirt and shrugged out of it, and then pulled Gracie close again… in a perfect tango hold, which meant really close, really intimate and really, really arousing. He danced her the few steps to her bed, and then spun her and dipped her deeply. As he nuzzled the place where her neck met her shoulder, he dragged a hand down the outside of her bare leg, lighting little fires all along the way. When he reached her calf, he moved his hand to the inside of her leg and drew it upward again, halting scant inches away from the hot, damp core of her.

Although Gracie caught her breath in anticipation of his touch there, she still gasped at the contact, so sure and steady were his fingers over the sheer fabric. Slowly, carefully, he righted them both to standing again, but he caressed her though her panties the entire time, and she was in no way steady on her feet. So he maneuvered their bodies until they were lying on the bed facing each other. He kissed her as he continued to stroke her, this time dipping his hand inside her panties, but Gracie somehow found the presence of mind to unfasten his belt and zipper. Then she tucked her hand inside his jeans and boxers to grasp him in her hand, rubbing him slowly up and down, too.

For long moments, they kissed and pleasured each other manually, their tongues darting in much the same way as their fingers. But when Gracie felt herself nearing an orgasm, she circled his wrist and withdrew his hand in an effort to slow the pace. He seemed to understand and used the opportunity to rise and shed what was left of his clothing. Gracie did likewise, and then bent over the bed to turn it down. Harrison was behind her naked body in a heartbeat, covering her breasts with his hands and moving his cock, already sheathed in a condom, between her legs to wreak havoc where his fingers had been before. She sighed as he caressed her breasts and thumbed her ripe nipples, guiding his hips forward and back to create a delicious friction for their bodies. When she bent forward more, he gripped her hips and entered her from behind, slow and slick and deep, again and again and again. But once more, he stopped before Gracie or he could climax, urging both of their bodies onto the bed.

When he turned to lie on his back, she sat astride him and began to move backward so that he could enter her again. But he halted her and instead pushed her body forward, more and more, until the heated core of her was poised above his head. Just as she realized his intent—and before she could prepare herself—he lowered her onto his mouth, pressing his tongue to the damp folds of flesh he had already incited to riot. Gracie was washed away to a place where her thoughts evaporated, and she could do nothing but feel...exquisitely, outrageously euphorically.

As his tongue lapped at her, he moved his hands to her bottom, curling his fingers into the cleft that bisected it, stroking her sensitive skin up and down, circling the delicate aureole at its base before darting away again. The sensations that rocked her every time he came close wound the hot coil inside her ever tighter. When he finally slipped a finger inside her there, moving his tongue inside her at the same time, she cried out. Never had she felt such a rush of heat or exhilaration. But as the cataclysms began to slow, Harrison tasted her again, deeper this time, and penetrated her again, deeper this time, and set off the waves of pleasure a second time.

She cried out again at the sensations rocking her. Harrison rolled her onto her back, gripping her ankles to spread her legs wide and drape them over his shoulders. Then he lifted her from the bed to drive himself deep inside her once more.

A third wave began to build inside Gracie as he bucked against her, climbing higher and higher, hotter and hotter, until she was crashing to the ground, and Harrison was right there with her. As they lay beside each other afterward, panting for breath and groping for coherent thought, she wondered if it would always be this way with them. If there would ever come a time when their lovemaking wasn't explosive and fierce, when they didn't feel so urgent and intense.

But all the thought did was make her smile. Somehow, she knew they would have lots of time together to discover each other. They would have lots of lovemaking. Lots of feelings. Lots of chances.

She looked at Harrison, lying beside her with his eyes closed, his hair damp, his chest rising and falling raggedly. A chance was all she'd wanted from him. And it was all she'd needed to give him in return.

"I love you, Harrison Sage," she said softly.

He opened his eyes and smiled. "I love you, Gracie Sumner."

Okay, maybe there was one other thing she'd wanted from him. Now she had that, too. And when it came to love, not even fourteen billion—yes, *billion* with a *b*—dollars stood a chance.

Epilogue

It was snowing on Roosevelt Avenue in the borough of Queens. The fat, frilly flakes danced to and fro around Gracie as she stood at the edge of a vacant lot that would soon be a pediatric clinic. Although it was early April, and the snow wasn't supposed to last for more than a day—a good thing in light of this afternoon's ground-breaking ceremony—Gracie liked seeing it. There was something promising about snow. Something clean. Something genuine. Something hopeful. Something that said everything was going to be just fine.

And everything was fine. The clinic was the last recipient of Harry Sagalowsky's billions. In the last ten months, she had spent his money on hundreds of projects and thousands of institutions that would affect millions of people. She'd traveled all over the country to participate in not only ground-breaking ceremonies, but also ribbon-cutting ceremonies. She'd visited preschools, elementary schools, high schools and colleges, attended meetings in churches and synagogues, temples and mosques. She'd even been invited to a couple of weddings and a barn-raising that had been facilitated by Harry's estate.

She had seen firsthand the good things money could do when it was placed in the right hands. Harry had been wrong about money causing the world's problems. Greed did that. Money properly spent could create a utopia. She hoped Harry was resting easily now, wherever he was.

"Not the best weather for a ground-breaking," Bennett Tarrant said from his position on her left.

He was elegantly bundled in an exquisitely tailored camel-hair overcoat, a paisley silk scarf tucked beneath the lapels. Gus Fiver was a mirror image of him, his own coat a few shades lighter, and Renny Twigg almost epitomized Gracie's initial impression of her as someone who should be working outdoors in flannel, wrapped as she was in a red-and-black-checked wool coat that was belted at the waist.

Gracie would have felt bland beside her in her own creamy Dior-style coat, circa 1950, if it hadn't been for the luscious way Harrison was looking at her—the same way he'd been looking at her since she'd come out of his bathroom wrapped in a towel this morning. And that was a weird thought, since she'd come out of his bathroom wrapped in a towel lots of times. So why was today any different?

He was another reason the last ten months had been so fine—and so hectic. Bicoastal relationships weren't the easiest thing to maintain. But she'd wanted to finish her degree in Seattle, and his business was in New York, so one of them had flown across the country almost every weekend. Or he'd flown to whatever event she was attending with Harry's money to join her. She sent up another silent thank-you to Harry for making that possible. Yes, he'd wanted her to buy a house on the water or go to Spain with some of his money, but using it to see a man who had become more important to her than anything had given Gracie a lot more happiness.

But she'd had her degree for more than two months and still didn't have a job. Of course, that could be because her work with Harry's money had intensified once her classes concluded. It could also be because her search for work in Seattle had been kind of halfhearted. Then again, her search for work anywhere had been kind of halfhearted. There were probably more positions in a big city like New York—and, truth be told, she'd applied for as many jobs here as she had in Seattle. But as good as things had been between her and Harrison—and as big a pain as it was living thousands of miles apart—neither had brought up the subject of taking things to the next level. Like living in the same city.

"I like the snow," Gracie said in response to Mr. Tarrant. "It's very pretty."

"I like it, too," Renny Twigg said from his other side. "It looks like wrapping paper on this big, beautiful gift that Harrison Sage is giving to the neighborhood."

Gee, Renny Twigg had something of a whimsical streak, Gracie thought. Maybe she really should be doing something besides working for a probate firm.

"I think they're about to begin," Bennett Tarrant said. "Shall we?"

The ground-breaking ceremony went off without a hitch. Gracie and Harrison laughed as they jabbed their shovels into the ground, fighting to get them deeper than a couple of inches into the frozen sod. Gracie even stepped up onto the top of the blade of her own shovel in an effort to drive it deeper. But all that did was send her teetering backward. Thankfully, Harrison was there to catch her. He set her on the ground beside him before returning both their shovels to the community leaders in charge.

Once all the thanks had been made and the farewells uttered, Tarrant, Fiver & Twigg returned to the big black Town Car that had brought them, and Gracie and Harrison headed for his. As they strode across the vacant lot, the snow began to fall harder around them, blurring the rest of the urban landscape, making her feel as if there were no one in the world but them. Harrison seemed to sense it, too, because he entwined his gloved fingers with hers.

"I heard you applied for a teaching position at my old school," he said. "Kindergarten. Starting this fall."

Dang. Busted.

"Well, the listing came up on LinkedIn," she said, "so I thought, what the hey. I mean, I've applied at schools all over the place," she added, fudging the truth a bit, since she hadn't applied for positions in, say, Nauru or Abu Dhabi—or anywhere else that wasn't Seattle or New York. "I probably won't get it, though, since I'm sure they want someone seasoned who feels the same way about education that they do."

She couldn't help adding, not quite under her breath, "More's the pity."

Harrison grinned. "I've spoken to the director about you. Seeing as I'm sitting on the board now and all, I have some pull there."

Gracie grinned back. "So then I guess I really can kiss that position goodbye, since you know the first thing I'd do is rally for art and music classes to be mandatory and for the uniforms to be eighty-sixed."

Harrison's grin grew broader. "You should be getting a call this week, actually. You could really shake things up there. Get 'em while they're young and teach them about the stuff that's really important. Not that I told the director that part. I just told her you're exactly the kind of teacher that place needs. And hey, you'll have an ally on the board."

Gracie chuckled. "Thanks, Harrison." Then she sobered. "Of course, that means I'll be moving to New York. Will that be a problem? For us, I mean?"

Now his expression turned confused. "How could that possibly be a problem for us? We'd finally both be in the same place at the same time for more than a few days."

She shrugged. "I know, but we haven't—"

"Of course, apartments are crazy expensive in Manhattan," he interjected. "Living there on a teacher's salary would be impossible."

Ah. So. Evidently, that "taking things to the next level" discussion was still on hold for a while, since anything she would be able to afford in New York was probably still going to land her in another state like Connecticut or New Jersey. Still, they'd at least be closer.

"Yeah, crazy expensive," he reiterated. "So it would probably be better if you move in with me."

Oh. Okay. So maybe they *were* going to talk about it?

"Or we could look for a new place together," he continued.

Wow. *Really* going to talk about it. At least, they would be, if Gracie wanted to jump in. At the moment, though, she wasn't sure what to say. Harrison clearly was, though.

"But you know," he said, "the school where you'll be working is pretty traditional. For now, anyway. They might frown on one of their kindergarten teachers living in sin."

So then maybe they *weren't* going to talk about it. Or take it to the next level. Never mind.

Harrison sighed with resignation. "So it might be best if you just marry me."

Before Gracie could say a word—he'd just skipped every level there was!—he withdrew a small velvet box from inside his coat and opened it. Nestled inside was a diamond ring. An old diamond ring. A modest diamond ring. An absolutely beautiful diamond ring. It was probably about a third of a carat, mounted on a white gold, filigreed setting, and it was dazzling amid the falling snow.

"It was my grandmother's," he said. "I found it in one of the shoe boxes where my dad stowed stuff. The minute I saw it, I thought of you. If anyone could make this represent happy memories instead of sad ones, it's you."

That, finally, made Gracie break her silence. "You

told me you finished going through your dad's things back in October."

"Yeah, I did."

"So you've been thinking about giving me this since then?"

"No, I found this in August. But you were so busy with school and my dad's estate, I didn't want to overwhelm you."

Overwhelm her? He'd overwhelmed her the minute she saw him.

He smiled again, a little less certainly this time. "So what do you say, Gracie? Will you marry me? Or should I have asked you sooner?"

Well, he could have asked her sooner, she supposed. But it was never too late for something like this. Then again, with Harry's money no longer a strain on her time, and with her starting a new job in a few months, and with Harrison just looking so gorgeous and being so wonderful…

"Your timing is perfect," she said.

Just like you, she thought.

"Just like you," he said.

"Just like us," she amended.

He smiled at that. As he removed the ring from the box, Gracie tugged the glove off her left hand. And when he slipped it over her third finger, it was… Well, it was perfect, too.

"I love you, Gracie Sumner," he said softly, pressing his forehead against hers.

"I love you, Harrison Sage," she replied.

As the snow continued to swirl around them, and as he covered her mouth with his, Gracie couldn't help thinking she'd been wrong about the clinic for which they'd just broken ground. It wasn't the last recipient of all that Harry left behind. Because she'd just received the last—and best—part of that herself.

* * * * *

A COWBOY IN MANHATTAN

BARBARA DUNLOP

For my husband

One

As the pickup truck rocked to a halt in front of her family's Colorado cattle-ranch house, Katrina Jacobs started a mental countdown for her return to New York City. In the driver's seat, her brother Travis set the park brake and killed the engine. Katrina pulled up on the silver door handle, releasing the latch and watching the heavy passenger door yawn wide-open. Then she slid gingerly down onto the gravel driveway, catching most of her weight on her right foot to protect her injured left ankle.

A week, she calculated. Two weeks, max. By then she would have done her duty as a daughter and a sibling. Her ankle would be in shape. And she could get back to her ballet company in Manhattan.

Katrina hated Colorado.

Travis retrieved her small suitcase from the truck box. From experience, she knew it would be covered in stubborn grit, just like everything else in Lyndon Valley. She could vacuum it as much as she liked, but the dust would remain.

She wrenched the stiff door shut and started to pick her way across the uneven ground. She'd worn a pair of navy suede Gallean ankle boots, with narrow toes, low heels and kicky little copper chains at the ankles. They topped a pair of skinny black slacks and a shiny silver blouse.

She probably should have gone with sneakers, blue jeans and a cotton shirt, but she couldn't bring herself to traverse both JFK and Denver International looking like a hick. She wasn't often recognized in public, but when she was, people inevitably snapped a picture. Between cell phones and digital cameras, everyone in the world was potential paparazzi.

In his faded blue jeans, soft flannel shirt and scuffed cowboy boots, Travis fell into step beside her. "You want to take Mom and Dad's room?"

"No," she responded a little too quickly. "I'll bunk with Mandy."

Katrina hadn't lived at home full-time since she was ten years old. That summer, with the support of her rather eccentric aunt, she'd enrolled in New York's Upper Cavendar Dramatic Arts Academy, a performing-arts boarding school for girls. Maybe it was because she'd left home so young, but to this day, she was intimidated by her stern, forceful father. His booming voice made her stomach jump, and she was constantly on edge whenever he was around, worried that he'd ask an embarrassing question, mock her career or make note of the fact that she was an all-around inadequate ranch hand.

Her father was away from the ranch right now, having just moved to a rehab center in Houston with a leading-edge stroke recovery program. There he was impressing the staff with his rapid improvement from his recent stroke. Still, the last thing Katrina needed was to be surrounded by his possessions.

"He loves you," said Travis, his voice gentle but his confusion evident. "We all love you."

"And I love you back," she returned breezily, as she took the stairs to the front porch, passing through the door into the cool, dim interior of her childhood home. It was large by ranch house standards, with a big, rather utilitarian entryway. It opened up into a large living room, with banks of bright windows overlooking the river, a redbrick fireplace and enough comfy furniture to hold the family of five children and often guests. The kitchen was spacious and modern, with a giant pantry and a big deck that led down to a rolling lawn. And upstairs, there were six bedrooms, though one had been converted into an office after Katrina had left for good.

She knew love was compulsory. But the truth was, she had nothing in common with the rest of her family. They saw her as some spoiled, fragile princess who couldn't even ride a horse, never mind toss a hay bale or swing an ax straight.

For all that she was a principal dancer in a ballet company that regularly sold out New York City's Emperor's Theater, and that she'd made the cover of *Dance America* and the *Paris Arts Review,* in Colorado she'd never be anything but the girl who couldn't make it as a ranch hand.

"Hey there, Kitty-Kat."

Before she could respond to his greeting, her oldest brother, Seth, swooped her up in his strong arms.

"Hi, Seth." Her hug was slightly less enthusiastic. She was embarrassed by the childhood nickname her two brothers had bestowed upon her.

He let her go, and she stepped aside with a determined smile on her face. The smile faltered when she caught sight of a third man behind him. A taller, broader man, with penetrating gray eyes, a grim mouth and what she knew would be callused hands that could probably lift a taxi cab right off the asphalt. Though it had been a few years since she'd seen him, there was no mistaking their neighbor Reed Terrell.

He gave her the slightest of nods. "Katrina."

"Reed," she nodded in return, a fuzzy hitch coursing through her chest. It was trepidation, she told herself, a visceral reaction based mostly on his size and strength and overall rugged appearance.

Just then her sister Mandy burst down the stairs. "Katrina!" she cried, elbowing Seth out of the way and pulling Katrina into her arms.

Katrina hugged her sister tight in return. The next youngest after Katrina, Mandy was the one who had always tried to understand Katrina's passion for dance.

Mandy released her, scanning Katrina from head to toe. "You look *gorgeous.*"

Katrina knew it was a compliment. But when her family called her *pretty,* she couldn't seem to help hearing *useless. Pretty* didn't get you anywhere in Lyndon Valley.

"Thank you," she told her sister, self-consciously smoothing back the wisps of blond hair that had escaped from the twisted knot at the back of her head. Maybe she should have gone with sneakers and blue jeans after all, or perhaps skipped her makeup this morning. She could feel her family sizing her up and finding her frivolous.

"You remember Reed?" Mandy gestured to the big man standing silently in the background.

"Certainly," said Katrina.

Her gaze involuntarily met his again, and a shiver ran through her body, momentarily making her knees go weak. For a woman with a dancer's balance, it was a ridiculous reaction. What was the matter with her?

She tried to drag her gaze from his, but for some reason, it stuck like glue.

"I can't wait for you to meet Caleb again," Mandy rattled on in an excited voice. "You probably don't remember much about him, since he left Lyndon ten years ago."

"I know he's Reed's twin brother," said Katrina.

Reed's nostrils seemed to flare when she uttered his name. The men were fraternal twins, not identical. She remembered Caleb as a smaller, less intimidating version of his brother.

Good thing.

For Mandy's sake.

Katrina caught her sister's expression, and saw that her eyes were sparkling with unadulterated joy.

"Congratulations," she put in belatedly, giving Mandy another tight hug.

"We're thinking of a late-fall wedding. You know, after Dad is up and around again. You'll be a bridesmaid, of course."

"Of course," Katrina forced out a laugh. She wasn't wild about family togetherness. But Mandy loved it, and Katrina wouldn't do anything to mar her sister's big day.

"You'll look so beautiful in a bridesmaid dress."

"It's what I do best," Katrina joked, keeping the smile pasted on her face. For some reason, she darted a look at Reed and saw his eye-roll.

He obviously thought she was being conceited. Fine. Easy for him to judge. She was willing to bet not a single person in his entire life had ever called him useless. Around here, he'd be revered for his strength and his hard work. He didn't have to live with being pretty.

Not that he wasn't attractive. In fact, there was an appealing dignity to his craggy features. His chin might be overly square, and his nose slightly crooked, but his eyes were an intriguing, silver-flecked gray, and his full lips were—

Wait a minute. She gave herself an abrupt mental shake. What on earth was the matter with her? Reed was a tough, hulking, strong-willed cowboy. He could out-macho anyone in Lyndon Valley, and there was nothing even remotely appealing about that.

Since Reed Terrell was alive, conscious and male all at the same time, he had the hots for Mandy's sister Katrina. It didn't mean he had to act on it, and it sure didn't mean he'd succeed even if he tried. Everything about the woman said she was out of his league, from the wispy updo of her wheat-blond hair to her sexy boots, the clingy slacks and shimmering blouse in between.

When he'd met her earlier at the Jacobs ranch, her earrings had been dangling strands of gold, silver and diamonds, while a matching necklace glimmered against her dainty cleavage. She should have looked comically out of place on the ranch, but she didn't. She looked like a princess inspecting the commoners, someone to be revered and admired, then left untouched. Which was exactly what Reed intended to do.

Now he entered the foyer of his own family's ranch house,

shutting the door against the gathering dusk, another long day of work behind him. For years, Reed had lived in the spacious, two-story house with his exacting father. Though his father was dead, out of habit, Reed placed his hat on the third hook from the left and straightened the mat beneath his feet. There was a place for everything, and everything was always in its place in the Terrell household. His father had prized practicality, but also quality, so the hardwood floors were clear maple, the furniture was custom-made and the kitchen appliances were top-of-the-line, replaced every ten years.

The outbuildings that housed the cowboys and staff necessary to run the big ranch were also kept in tip-top shape, from the cookhouse to the bunkhouses to the barns and sheds. The line shacks were all getting older, but they were still kept clean and in good repair.

“Danielle wants to talk to you,” his brother Caleb announced as he walked down the hallway from the kitchen at the back of the house, phone in hand.

“I don’t have anything more to add.”

Caleb frowned. “You can’t let fifteen million dollars just sit in a bank account.”

“You can always take it back,” Reed responded, squaring his shoulders. He still thought it was ridiculous that his brother had paid him for half the family’s ranch.

“Would you let me hand you half of Active Equipment for free?” Caleb referred to the company he’d spent the past ten years building in the Chicago area.

“Don’t be ridiculous.”

“Same difference.” Caleb held out the phone. “Talk to her. She has some ideas.”

Danielle Marin was Caleb’s lawyer. Following the debacle of their late father’s will, she’d drafted the papers that switched ownership of the Terrell ranch from Caleb to Reed. Then she’d worked out the financial transaction where Caleb bought half of it back.

Reed wasn’t exactly grateful to her for helping to put him in his current financial position, but he had to admit, the woman seemed to know what she was doing.

He took the phone. “Hello?”

As usual, Danielle’s tone was crisp, no-nonsense. “Hi, Reed. I was wondering if you’d had a chance to look over the package I emailed to you yesterday?” Then her voice became muffled as she obviously spoke to someone at her end of the line in Chicago.

“Not yet,” he answered. He only opened his email about once a week. He didn’t have a lot of technically inclined friends. Most of the people he knew still called on a landline or simply stopped by the ranch when they had something to say.

She sighed into the receiver. “You’re losing both income and investment potential every day you wait.”

“You’ve pointed that out.”

“Can you give me some general parameters? Do you want to keep your investments in the country? Go international? Blue chips? Emerging markets?”

“I was thinking about buying a sports car,” he drawled, impatient with having to worry about the damn money. There were real problems requiring real solutions right here on the ranch.

Her voice instantly perked up. “So, you’re saying I should keep some ready cash for luxury purchases?”

“I was joking, Danielle. We don’t have paved roads in Lyndon Valley.”

“You could always drive it on the highway. What appeals to you? Lamborghini? Ferrari?”

“It was a *joke.*”

“Stop joking.”

It was Reed’s turn to sigh. “Fine. Keep the money in the country.” He at least knew he wanted that much.

“Right. So, maybe some blue chips? Or do you want to look at a percentage of a start-up? I can make some recommendations on sectors and states.”

Reed didn’t want to think about this right now. Quite frankly, all he wanted to do was to strip off his dusty clothes, take a hot shower, grill up a steak, and then picture Katrina's deep blue eyes for a while before he drifted off to sleep.

"I'll let you know," he told Danielle.

"Soon?"

"Yeah. Sure. Soon. See you." He handed the phone back to his brother.

"You're a pain in the ass, you know that?" Caleb pointed out as he put the phone back to his ear. Then his expression faltered. "No, not you, Danielle."

Reed chuckled at his brother's embarrassment, feeling better already.

He crossed through the living room, took the staircase to the second floor, took off his clothes and tossed them into the hamper before stepping into a steaming shower. As he rubbed in the spice-scented shampoo, he realized his hair was getting too long. He supposed he could find a few more reasons to make the drive into Lyndon and get it cut while he was there, or he could buzz it short with his razor again. Though the last time he'd done that, Mandy had laughed at him for days.

Thoughts of Mandy took him to thoughts of Katrina. He switched the water to cold, finishing off with a brisk rinse before stepping out of the deep tub.

He changed into clean jeans and pulled a worn gray T-shirt over his head, running his fingers through his damp hair. He left his feet bare, padding down to the kitchen. The barbecue was out back on the deck, overlooking a bend in the Lyndon River. But it was a warm May day, and shoes were definitely not necessary.

He smelled steaks grilling and knew his brother had a head start on dinner. He'd learned that steaks were the only thing Caleb knew how to cook. Thinking about his brother's ineptitude in the kitchen made something warm settle deep into Reed's chest.

It had only been a few weeks since he'd reconciled with his fraternal twin brother. They'd been estranged and angry with each other since their mother had passed away ten years ago. They'd both blamed their cruel, domineering father for her death from untreated pneumonia. But their reactions had been poles apart. Caleb had left home in anger. Reed had stayed behind to protect his mother's ranch heritage.

Reed heard a female voice through the screen door.

Mandy, obviously.

When Caleb had come home to settle problems with the will, the two had reconnected and fallen deeply in love. Reed smiled. He'd always thought of Mandy as a sister. It would be nice to have her officially become part of the family.

He grabbed himself a cold bottle of beer from the fridge, flipped the cap into the trash can and headed outside. There, he stopped short, seeing Katrina sitting at the table. Hearing his footsteps, she turned toward him.

A glass of red wine dangled between delicate fingers tipped with sculpted nails. And she was laughing at something Mandy had said. Her jewel-blue eyes were alight in the evening sunshine. The slanting rays glinted off her shimmering blouse where it clung to softly rounded breasts. As a professional dancer, her body had a perfect shape and symmetry that kick-started his libido.

As she took in his expression, her smile faltered, and the glow left her blue eyes. "Hello, Reed." She paused. "Something wrong?"

He realized he was scowling. She was Mandy's sister. He shouldn't be secretly fantasizing about her. She might not spend much time in Lyndon Valley, but he was going to have to make this work.

"Nothing's wrong," he insisted, striding forward. "I'm hungry." He forced himself to focus on Caleb who was wielding a spatula over the grill.

"About ten minutes," Caleb offered.

Since dishes, salads and bread were already set out on the rectangular table, Reed chose one of the low-slung wooden Adirondack chairs, parked his body and took a swig of his beer.

Mandy moved to the barbecue beside Caleb, placing her hand lightly on his shoulder, their backs to Reed and Katrina.

"Did you have a nice flight in?" Reed asked Katrina, keeping his tone polite and even.

"It was good." She nodded, her tone even in return. "Very comfortable." She swiveled to perch herself backward on the bench seat at the table, fully facing him.

In his peripheral vision, he saw Mandy playfully kiss his brother's cheek and whisper something in his ear.

"First class?" he asked Katrina.

"Why?"

He caught the narrowing of her eyes. "No reason."

"You think I'm a princess?"

"I'll take that as a yes." Truth was, he was thinking that nobody had a "very comfortable" flight in coach. He was also thinking that first-class seating was a waste on somebody as petite as her.

Their gazes clashed for several seconds.

"Staying long?" he tried, wondering if she'd turn that into an insult, as well.

But her expression faltered, and she didn't answer for a moment. "A week. Maybe two."

"Still dancing?" He didn't know anything about her life in New York City, except that she was some kind of important ballerina, and Mandy was anxious to go see her perform.

"Still dancing," she confirmed, with a quirk of a smile. "You're still ranching?"

"Still ranching." He nodded. "You must be here on vacation?"

"Yes," she replied, the barest hint of sarcasm in her tone.

"What?" he probed.

"What?" she responded, concentrating on taking a sip of her wine.

"It's not a vacation?" he guessed.

She glanced sideways at her sister for a split second. Then she shrugged. "No pool deck or palm trees. But I guess you could call it a vacation."

"Princess," he muttered through a smile.

"A girl's got to keep up her tan."

He gave a pointed glance to his deeply browned forearms. “Not a problem around these parts.”

“I bet you’ve got those farmer-tan lines at the short-sleeve mark.”

He couldn’t seem to stop his smirk. “I bet you’ve got those princess tan lines at the bikini mark.”

She didn’t miss a beat. “Much more attractive.”

To that, he gave her a mock toast. “No argument from me.”

Then, to his surprise, she leaned forward and lowered her voice. “Truth is, I twisted my ankle.”

He leaned forward to meet her, lowering his own voice to match. “Is that a secret?”

She shook her head. Then she shrugged her slim shoulders. “Not exactly, I just…” Her red lips pursed together, and he couldn’t help thinking about kissing her.

Her cheeks flushed a light rose.

Was she thinking about kissing him back?

As quickly as it formed, he banished the thought. It was a ridiculous assumption.

“Are you embarrassed about hurting yourself?” He settled on a much more likely explanation.

“It was a silly accident,” she confessed. “I’m usually really careful about my shoes, but—”

“Rare, medium or well?” Mandy called to them.

Reed didn’t take his gaze off Katrina. “Rare.”

“Medium,” she put in. “And nothing too big, please.”

Reed felt a smile grow. “You’re not up for a cowboy twelve-ouncer?”

Her hand moved to rest on her flat stomach. “My dance partner has to be able to lift me.”

“Maybe you need a stronger partner.”

“What I need is to lose two pounds.”

“You look perfect to me.” The soft words were out before he could censor them.

A slow blink camouflaged her reaction. Then she brought her teeth down on her bottom lip and determinedly turned her attention to Caleb, who was carrying the platter of steaks to the table.

Reed had said something wrong. He wasn't sure what it was, but she'd abruptly shut him out.

Katrina didn't know why she'd told Reed about her ankle last night. It was a foolish slip of her tongue. It compromised her ongoing efforts to keep her two worlds apart, and this morning she vowed to do better.

In the years since her father's sister, her generous Aunt Coco, had taken her under her wing and convinced her parents to let her move to New York City with her, she'd been living two separate lives. In New York, enrolled in the ballet program at the Academy, she felt vibrant and alive. She was a part of the cultural mosaic Auntie Coco, a renowned contemporary painter, had been so careful to expose her to while she was growing up. She fitted in. She was normal, accepted, even respected. In Colorado, she was out of step. An anomaly who could never show weakness.

She often wondered why her aunt had decided to rescue her from the ranching world, what it was she'd recognized as a kindred spirit in a ten-year-old child. She'd always meant to ask. But Coco had died of a sudden aneurism two years ago before Katrina had had the chance.

Now, she came to the bottom of the stairs of the Jacobs' house and took a bracing breath. Her two brothers and two sisters were already dressed for the day's work, sitting at the breakfast table eating pancakes, bacon and scrambled eggs. It never ceased to amaze her that Mandy and Abigail could consume so many calories and keep such trim figures.

As she pivoted around the end of the staircase, she was careful not to limp. Then again, Reed would probably tell Caleb, and Caleb would tell Mandy, and once again she'd be the pathetic, weak branch on the robust Jacobs family tree.

She approached the breakfast table to a chorus of good mornings, taking the empty place next to Mandy, searching the table for fruit, or maybe a whole-grain muffin. But a platter of fluffy pancakes was handed her way, followed by maple syrup and a mounded serving tray of eggs.

"Thanks." She nodded to Abigail, setting the heavy platter down in an empty spot in front of her plate. "Is there maybe an apple or something in the fridge?"

Everything seemed to still for a moment as four sets of eyes turned her way.

"I'm not a huge breakfast eater," she explained, ignoring the tantalizing scents of melting butter and warming syrup.

Abigail started to stand.

"No, no." Katrina quickly waved her off, coming to her feet. Pain tripped in her ankle from the sudden movement, but she schooled her features. "I'll get it." She quickly headed for the kitchen.

"Abigail and I can stay on the ranch for a few more days," Seth said, his conversational voice coming through the big, open pass-through between the kitchen and dining room. "But then they'll need us in Lyndon to help with my campaign."

Katrina spotted the family cook, Henrietta, in the pantry off the kitchen, restocking the shelves from a cardboard box. She smiled a greeting to the familiar woman as she pulled open one side of the big stainless-steel refrigerator.

In the pocket of her slacks, her cell phone vibrated. She retrieved it to see an unfamiliar New York City number.

"Hello?" she inquired, moving to a far corner of the kitchen, where a solid wall blocked the noise from her siblings' conversation.

"Hello, Katrina."

Her teeth clenched at the sound of Quentin Foster's voice. A member of the Liberty Ballet Board of Directors, the last time they'd spoken, he'd been hitting on her.

"I wanted to see how you were feeling," he continued, tone solicitous.

"Fine," she told him evenly, wondering how she could diplomatically end the call. He was an important man in the organization, but his flirtatious manner had gotten entirely out of hand.

"We're all very worried about you."

"I'm fine. I'll be back soon."

"Back?" His tone slipped. "Have you left the city?"

"I'm visiting family. I really need to go. Thanks for calling."

"Katrina, wait."

She braced herself. "Yes?"

"Have you had another chance to think about what I said?"

About becoming his lover? "I haven't changed my mind."

In her peripheral vision, she caught her brother Seth's curious gaze on her. "I do have to go. Thank you for your concern." She quickly hit the off button then shut down her phone, turning her attention back to her family.

"Mandy's riding up to take a look at the Blue Lake herd today," said Travis. "And I'll check to see how many have moved through the canyon."

Katrina knew there was a science to herd distribution across their vast rangelands, taking in the seasons, weather reports and rainfall, but she had no idea how it worked. More than once, she'd privately mused that if she'd lived in the 1800s, she'd probably have died young of stupidity or been killed off by her outraged community because of her ineptitude.

"What time is the vet due in?" asked Abigail, refilling her coffee cup.

"He said around eleven," Mandy offered. "But you know how those things go."

"I have to touch base with the campaign office before I do anything else," said Abigail, reminding Katrina of her oldest brother's upcoming campaign for the mayor's seat in Lyndon.

Katrina selected a smooth, deep-green Granny Smith apple from the crisper drawer, rinsing it under the tap before returning to the table.

"What about you?" Travis asked her as she sat back down.

"Me?" she responded, confused by his question. Were they still talking about the mayoralty campaign?

"You want to ride up to the lake with me today?" asked Mandy.

Katrina hesitated, glancing at the expressions around the

table. She couldn't believe they'd forgotten. She'd never mastered riding a horse. The animals still frightened her. The thought of sitting on top of one for six hours made her cringe.

"I have a pretty rigorous rehearsal and training routine," she told everyone.

Seth waved a dismissive hand. "Take a day off."

"I—"

"The fresh air will be good for you," Travis declared.

Only Mandy was looking at her curiously.

"I wish I could," Katrina lied with a shake of her head. "But I need to stay in shape."

"Horseback-riding is good exercise," said Travis.

"Is there a bicycle anywhere around here?" She tried to change the subject. Jogging would be the simplest exercise, since she didn't have access to a gym. But the jarring would be too hard on her healing ankle, especially over uneven ground.

Her siblings glanced at each other.

"A bicycle?" Seth repeated the question.

"I like to bike," said Katrina. "It's good for my quads."

Travis snorted. "A little productive work would be good for your quads too."

"Travis," Abigail warned.

"There might be an old bike in the blue shed," said Mandy. "We can look after breakfast." She glanced at the apple in Katrina's hand. "You sure you don't want something hot?"

Katrina shook her head. "I'm good." She took a big bite of the apple, mumbling her appreciation of the tart flavor.

After a drawn-out moment, everyone's attention went back to their own meals.

After a few minutes, Mandy rose to take her dishes into the kitchen then returned to the dining room and slid back into her chair. "We'll go whenever you're ready," she said to Katrina.

"I'm ready now." Katrina rose. She'd rather eat her apple on the run than sit here on edge, waiting for more uncomfortable questions and opinions.

She'd worn blue jeans and a simple white blouse this morning, and she popped her feet into a pair of sneakers.

Mandy stuck a battered Stetson onto her head. Her boot heels clunked on the wooden porch, while Katrina followed silently on rubber soles. She wished she'd thought to bring along a hat. She had a white baseball cap from the Met that she could easily have tucked into her suitcase.

It took about five minutes to walk the path to the blue shed, called that because of its blue door. There was also the green shed, the yellow shed and the view shed, which had a red door. Katrina had never figured out why her family wasn't consistent with the names. But she'd stopped asking questions like that a long time ago.

Mandy pushed open the door and made her way into the crowded storage building. "You haven't told me what you thought of Caleb."

"He seems like a nice guy," Katrina answered honestly as she followed inside. Caleb had been friendly, polite and funny last night.

Mandy turned to stare, her tone turning incredulous. "'A nice guy'? That's all you've got for my fiancé? He's an *amazing* guy."

"I only just met him again."

Caleb was six years older than Katrina, and she barely remembered him from when she was a child.

"Well, sure. But it's pretty obvious, don't you think?"

Katrina couldn't help but grin at her sister's mock outrage. "I'm sure he's amazing. And it's pretty obvious he's got it bad for you."

"Yes, he does," Mandy answered with conviction, wrinkling her nose and sticking it primly in the air. She turned sideways to slip between a set of shelves and an ATV.

Katrina followed, tone playfully placating. "And who could blame him? You're a great catch."

Even in the dim light, Mandy's eyes sparkled as she moved some plastic bins out of the way. "What about you?"

"I'm not a particularly good catch." What could Katrina bring to a relationship? An extensive designer wardrobe? An ability to make small talk at cocktail parties? A demanding and precarious career?

"I meant are you seeing anyone?"

"Oh."

Mandy moved a tarp as she made her way farther into the shed. "But of course you're a great catch. You're like some kind of dream trophy wife."

Katrina didn't want to be a trophy wife. "I'm not seeing anyone."

"Really? What about all those debonair rich guys who go to the same parties as you?"

"None of them have asked me out."

"They have so," Mandy contradicted.

"Okay, some of them have. But nobody lately." Unless you counted Quentin Foster. Katrina shuddered at the mere thought of the offensive man. He hadn't asked her for a date. His had been a bald proposition, followed by an unsettling threat.

"New York men don't know a good woman when they see one," Mandy put in staunchly. "Aha. Here we go."

Katrina banished thoughts of Quentin, coming up on her toes to peer over a wooden crate. Sure enough, there was a sturdy-looking mountain bike propped up against a workbench. She normally rode a stationary one at the gym a few blocks from her apartment, but she was willing to adapt.

"Will we be able to get it out of there?" she asked Mandy.

"Easy." Mandy hoisted it in the air, over the clutter and outside. There she pumped up the flat tires at the compressor.

Katrina was more than a bit in awe of her older sister. "I can't believe you did all that."

"All what?"

"Pumped up the tires. You actually know how to run a compressor."

"You actually know how to stand up in toe shoes. So, what's the plan? How far do you want to ride?"

Katrina shrugged. "Fifteen, twenty miles." Then she'd limber up, work on her arms a bit, and see how her ankle was holding up.

"I'm going up to Caleb's later," said Mandy.

"That's nice."

Mandy glanced at her watch. "If you wait until afternoon to leave and take the river trail, I can meet you at the Terrells' and drive you home after dinner."

Katrina hesitated. She wasn't wild about spending more time with Reed. The man made her jumpy and self-conscious. But Mandy was the closest thing she had to a buffer against her other siblings. If Mandy wasn't around, she feared her brothers would try to railroad her into something uncomfortable, like riding a horse.

"Sure," she found herself saying. "I'll meet you up at Terrells'."

Two

Reed couldn't seem to get his father's voice out of his head. As he had when Wilton Terrell was alive, he got up every morning focused on an ambitious list of jobs around the ranch. Then he worked as hard as he could until the end of the day. And if something went wrong, if he made a mistake, did less than one hundred percent, he'd reflexively brace himself for Wilton's anger.

Obviously he knew he'd never have to deal with his father's anger again, but his emotions were taking a while to catch up. He couldn't say he was sorry the obstinate old man had died, though he was beginning to recognize what a powerful impact Wilton had had on his life.

His brother Caleb told him it was crazy to keep up the breakneck pace. Caleb was searching for a full-time ranch manager to add to the foreman and ranch hands that helped with the day-to-day work. But Reed couldn't switch gears that easily.

Now, he returned the cleaning supplies to the tack room, hung up his saddle and emptied the combs and brushes he'd used on his horse, replacing them in their respective drawers and closing the cabinet before shutting off the light and exiting the room.

The sun was hitting the horizon in an orange ball, decorated by pink clouds above the snowy peaks of the distant Rockies. He crossed the wide driveway turnaround, heading for the house. A truck pulled up, and he caught sight of the Jacobs' ranch logo on the door. Before he could stop it, a hitch of excitement shot through him. But then he saw that only Mandy was inside the cab. No Katrina.

He lengthened his stride, coming up to the driver's door and pulling it open for her. "Hey, Mandy."

She smiled a greeting as she slid out of the cab, reaching back inside for a baking tin sitting in the center of the bench seat.

"Brownies," she offered, waving it in front of his nose.

"Sounds great. Caleb's probably inside."

"With Katrina?"

Reed felt another small shot of adrenaline. "Katrina's here?"

"I sure hope so. Mom left her a box of things to sort through in the attic, then she was coming up here."

"I've been in the barn for a while." He might have missed Katrina's arrival. Then again, he didn't see another Jacobs' pickup anywhere, so perhaps Mandy was mistaken.

"Hmm." Mandy's gaze searched the yard.

"What?"

"She rode up here on a bike."

"You mean a horse?"

Mandy gave an eye-roll as she started for the front door. "Yeah, because I usually mix those two things up."

Reed automatically fell into step and lifted the tin from her hands. "Katrina rides a motorcycle?" He simply couldn't picture it.

"A bicycle. She wanted to get some exercise."

Okay. Weird, but okay. They mounted the stairs, and Reed pushed the door open, waiting for Mandy to go inside.

"I don't see how they could possibly make it any more complicated," Caleb was saying into the phone as he paced from the living room into the entry hall. He lifted his chin in a greeting to them both. "I don't think Danielle wants to fly all the way down to Brazil." He paused. "In person? Really?" He braced his hand against the end of the archway and gave a disgusted shake of his head.

Mandy moved down the hall to the kitchen, glanced inside, then came back.

"Katrina here?" she stage-whispered to Caleb.

He narrowed his eyes in confusion.

"Is Katrina here?" she repeated.

He gave her a shrug of incomprehension. "Tell her to take the jet," he said into the phone. "We're going to have to give that woman a huge bonus."

Mandy turned to Rccd, her forehead wrinkling in worry. "She was going to ride up the river trail. She should have been here by now."

"On it," said Reed, moving immediately back to the door and heading outside.

Katrina was probably stuck somewhere along the trail. Or maybe she'd grown tired and was resting. There was a slim chance she gotten herself into real trouble. But the river trail was well-marked and relatively smooth and safe. The odds were definitely on the side of a delay rather than a catastrophe.

He strode back across the driveway, hopping onto an ATV that was parked next to the barn. He turned the key and the machine roared to life beneath him. He glanced at the sky, judging he had at least an hour before dark. It should be plenty of time, but he wasn't going to waste any of it.

He drove about four miles down the trail before he spotted her. The bike was tipped at the edge of the trail, and Katrina was crouched over it, looking small and forlorn in the midst of an aspen grove. She stood as he approached, and her shoulders relaxed as she obviously recognized that it was him. He saw the chain was off the bike, and her small hands were black with oil.

He'd give her an A for effort, but a failing grade for actual accomplishment. He knew six-year-olds who could reattach a bicycle chain. He brought the ATV to a stop and killed the engine as he dismounted.

"Looks like you've got a problem," he opened, struggling not to smile at her rather adorable helplessness.

She gestured to the bike. "I came around the corner, hit a bump, and the chain fell off."

His smile broke through as he checked out her blackened hands. "Any luck putting it back on?"

"Are you mocking me?"

He moved on to inspect the broken-down bicycle. "I'm making small talk, Katrina. Quit being so sensitive."

"I'm not being—"

"You've got a chip a mile wide on those skinny little shoulders."

"I'm not an auto mechanic," she harrumphed.

"And I'm not a ballerina."

She didn't seem to have a response to that.

"There's no point in getting my hands dirty fixing it here," he noted, lifting the bike by the frame and carrying it to the ATV. "Unless you're set on riding it the rest of the way."

"In the dark?"

"I wouldn't recommend it." He balanced the bike on the wide front rack, uncoiling a bungee cord to fasten it down. "But it's up to you."

"No," she responded tartly. "I don't want to ride a bike the rest of the way."

"You okay?" he asked belatedly, wrapping the cord around the bike frame and hooking the end to the rack. She didn't appear hurt, but he supposed that should have been the first question out of his mouth. That was a miss.

"I'm fine," she huffed.

He glanced up, taking a more detailed look at her. "You didn't fall or anything?"

She shook her head. "The chain came off." She held up her hands. "I stopped and I tried to put it back on."

"I can see that."

"I didn't just sit down and wait for a knight in shining armor."

"That's a relief. Because you got me instead."

She blinked sheepishly, seeming to remember her own manners. "Thank you," she offered.

He couldn't help but grin at her discomfort. "That wasn't what I was fishing for. But you're welcome." The sight of her looking so vulnerable in the vastness of the landscape tightened his chest. "Anytime."

"I guess these things come in threes."

"Threes?" He glanced around, wondering if he'd missed something.

"I had that ballet shoe come apart on me," she offered ruefully, glancing at her ankle. "And I almost took a tumble over some cables near the stage because they were partially hidden by a curtain."

He sure didn't like that mental picture. But he kept his tone easy. "You do seem to be accident-prone."

"Ironic." She sighed. "Because this time I was purposely attempting to stay *out* of trouble."

"Admirable," he acknowledged.

"Mandy wanted me to go horseback riding," she continued. "And my brothers wouldn't let me say no, and I knew I'd just slow the whole process down. And I thought..." She gestured to the disabled bike. "Bike-riding is one of my favorite exercises."

Surely she didn't ride a bike in the bumper-to-bumper traffic of New York City. "Through Central Park?" he hoped.

"In my gym," she admitted. "A stationary bike."

He wanted to tease her about that. But the truth was, he was glad to hear it. Better to be inside a building than fighting for road space with delivery vans, buses and taxis.

"I can set this one up as a stationary for you," he found himself offering. "In the barn. On a stand. It wouldn't be high-tech, but I can add a little resistance, and you'll stay safe and sound." Even as the words poured out of this mouth, he asked himself what the hell he thought he was doing? He had a million more pressing jobs that needed his attention.

She moved toward the ATV. "Wouldn't my brothers have a laugh at that."

He watched her grow close, transfixed by her beautiful face, the depths of her eyes, the motion of her deep pink mouth.

"We can keep it our secret," he offered.

She hesitated, watching him closely. "I'd jog, but I can't because of my ankle. And I have to do something." She drew a deep sigh. "I spent all day yesterday sitting on airplanes. I was going to warm up on this ride, and then get in some stretching. But now, my muscles are cold."

"You're cold?"

"Too cold to stretch."

He quickly unbuttoned his shirt.

"What are you—"

He stepped in and draped it over her shoulders. "Put it on," he said gruffly. It was going to get even colder once they got up to speed on the trail and the wind hit them.

"I don't need—" Her gaze caught and held on his bare chest. She blinked twice, then looked away, wordlessly slipping her arms into the sleeves. They hung about six inches past her fingertips, so she rolled them up to a thick band around her forearms.

She fastened the shirt buttons, and her cute black tights and pink T-shirt disappeared beneath the voluminous cotton.

She glanced down at herself. "Lovely."

He cocked his head to one side. "I think it's the spring tent collection from Dior."

"You know Dior?"

"How do you mean?"

"It's a fashion-design house."

"No kidding," he drawled.

"It's just—"

"We do have satellite television out here."

"And you use it to watch fashion shows?"

"Hardly," he scoffed. "But they make the occasional pop-culture reference during professional bull-riding."

"Did I insult you?" she asked, looking genuinely regretful.

"I'm not living under a rock, Katrina."

"I never thought you were."

He swung his leg over the wide seat of the ATV. He wasn't insulted. He couldn't care less what she thought of his television-watching habits.

Truth was, he didn't know why she'd struck a nerve. Maybe it was because she pointed out the vast differences between them, and how far she was out of his league. Not that it mattered, he ruthlessly reminded himself. No matter how sexy Miss Katrina Jacobs might appear, he was keeping his hands and his thoughts to himself. His life was complicated enough.

"Hop on," he told her gruffly, sliding forward to give her room on the seat behind.

She approached the ATV with caution, obviously sizing it up.

"You need some help?"

"No," she flashed.

"Hand on my shoulder," he instructed.

After a long hesitation, she touched him tentatively.

"Other hand."

"Sorry."

"Left foot on that peg."

"Okay."

He captured her forearm to steady her. "Step up and swing your leg over the seat. Grab my other shoulder if you need to."

She did. Her slight weight rocked the ATV, and her butt came down on the seat, her breasts brushing his back and her thighs coming up against his.

She sucked in a breath.

"You're going to have to hang on to me," he warned.

"I know."

He turned the key, and the ATV rumbled to life.

"Katrina?" he intoned, waiting for her to follow his instructions.

"My hands are filthy."

"I can take it." He reached back and grasped each of her wrists, wrapping her slim arms around his waist and anchoring her hands to his bare stomach.

Her breasts pressed tighter against his back, her cheek rested between his shoulder blades, while her inner thighs cradled his hips. Raw, painful desire rocketed through him, and he wondered how long he could reasonably take to drive back to the house. He wanted her to stay wrapped around his body for hours and hours.

In the shower on the second floor of the Terrells' house, Katrina's skin still tingled where she'd been pressed up against Reed's body—which was pretty much everywhere, from the inside of her knees to the hairline above her temple. The ATV had rumbled between her legs, while the heat from Reed's bare back had seeped its way through his shirt, her T-shirt and right through her bra.

Mandy had brought along a change of clothes for Katrina. In fact, she'd brought along Katrina's entire suitcase. She'd drawn Katrina aside and confessed she was plotting to have them spend the night at the Terrells', so she could be with Caleb. Katrina had easily agreed to stay. Away from her family's ranch was good for her state of mind. And it was less emotionally draining to be here with Mandy than interacting with all of her siblings. Caleb had been warmly receptive to the plan. Reed was best described as neutral.

Now, Katrina pulled back the blue-and-green-striped shower curtain and carefully climbed out of the deep tub. The bathroom was neat but compact, with little counter room around the sink and only a couple of spots for hanging clothes and towels on the back of the door. While she dried off and wrapped a white towel around her wet hair, she realized the error in her planning.

Her sweaty clothes were in a heap on top of the hamper, while her fresh clothes were still folded in her suitcase in the guest room. She was going to have to cross the hallway wrapped in nothing but a towel. There wasn't even a robe she could borrow hanging anywhere in the bathroom.

Resigned, she wrapped the biggest towel firmly around her body, tucking in the ends between her breasts. She rubbed a spot in the steamed mirror, turning and coming up on her toes to make sure the towel covered the necessities, just in case she met someone on the way. Then she gathered her wrinkled exercise outfit and her underwear, rolling them into a neat ball before cracking the bathroom door to make sure the hallway was all clear.

She listened carefully but couldn't hear a sound. The guestroom door was about ten feet down the hallway in the opposite direction of the stairs. It was open, and it would only take her about five seconds to make it there.

She took a breath, opened the bathroom door wide, listened one last time, then scampered across the hardwood floor, scooting safely into the guest room, quickly closing the door behind her. She closed her eyes with a heartfelt sigh, and leaned solidly up against the door.

"Katrina?" Reed's voice made her eyes fly open.

She gave a little shriek. The towel slipped, revealing her breasts for a brief moment until she grasped the corners, struggling to form a coherent word. "Wha—"

"Sorry." He quickly averted his gaze. "Mandy asked me to bring you some fresh sheets."

"I…" She could feel her face flush hot. The rest of her body flushed, too. Desire zipped from one extremity to the other, settling in a slow burn at the base of her abdomen.

She swallowed. She had to say something. But she couldn't for the life of her figure out what that might be.

Reed moved toward her, keeping his gaze studiously on the floor in front of him. "I'll get out of your way."

She told herself to move, unblock the door so the man could leave already. But her feet were glued to the floor, her heart pumping deep and slow inside her chest.

He came closer and closer, and all she could do was stare.

A knock on the door behind her nearly made her jump out of her skin.

"Katrina?" Mandy called. "You in there?"

The absurdity of the situation suddenly hit her. And Katrina recovered her sense of humor. What was she expecting Reed to do here? Make a move with Mandy and Caleb downstairs? Ridiculous. She quickly found her voice.

"I'm naked in here," she called out to Mandy. "And Reed's remaking the bed."

There was a stunned silence on the other side of the door.

"You shouldn't have done that," Reed intoned. "Get out of the way."

Mandy stammered from outside. "I'm… Uh…"

Reed snagged Katrina's bare shoulder, moving her off to one side. His warm, callused palm left a distinct tingle in its wake. He quickly swung the door open.

"Mix-up," he told Mandy. "Your sister thinks she's funny."

"He was lying in wait for me," Katrina countered, still feeling breathless.

"I thought you'd take longer in the shower," Reed protested.

"Why? Because I'm from New York City?"

"Because you're a girl."

"I'm a woman."

Mandy's attention was flying back and forth between the two.

Reed's nostrils flared as he sucked in a deep breath. "And now you have fresh sheets."

"Thank you," Katrina returned breezily.

She was scrambling to tamp down her powerful sexual reaction to him. It was strange and more than a little unsettling to have her hormones run amok like this.

Maybe it was brought on by the stress of the afternoon. He had rescued her, after all. He'd lent her his shirt and brought her back here to where she was safe and warm. Had his white-knight behavior tripped some anthropological hormonal switch, making him seem like mate material? She sure hoped it was temporary.

"Caleb's pouring the wine," Mandy offered, watching her closely.

"Then I'll get dressed," said Katrina, pasting on an unconcerned smile.

These things were obviously mind over matter, and she was a very disciplined person. Reed was just a man. And a stubborn cowboy at that. She preferred her men more urbane and refined, a guy who could pull off a tux and discuss literature, fine cuisine and world events.

Mandy stepped backward into the hall, obviously intending to wait there until Reed joined her.

"It was an *accident,*" Reed told Mandy with firm conviction.

"I know." She nodded. "Could have happened to anyone."

Reed set his jaw in annoyance and moved through the doorway.

Once in the hall, he turned back to glare his annoyance at Katrina.

"You're not funny," he admonished. But a split second later, his frank, heated gaze slid from her towel-covered hair to her bare feet and back again.

Her toes curled into the soft carpet, and her stomach rolled anxiously. Hoo boy.

Katrina woke up in the Terrells' guest room in the early, dark hours of the morning and couldn't seem to get back to sleep. Bothered by the time-zone change, her nagging ankle, and the fact that Reed was sleeping on the other side of the thin bedroom wall, her brain couldn't seem to relax.

Since Mandy had brought all of Katrina's sister's clothes to the Terrells' house, she had options. She changed into a simple black-and-white leotard, then searched her way through the house for a suitable space to exercise. She found a big rec room in the basement that was perfect. It had a smooth Berber carpet, a big open space in the middle and a ledge that ran the length of the room at a height where she could brace her hand for balance.

She plugged in her earbuds, turned on her player and made her way through a low-impact aerobic workout, getting the blood flowing and warming up her muscles. Then she ran through a familiar stretching routine, easing down into the splits, bending sideways first, then forward at the waist, stretching out her arms.

After a few minutes, she paused, sensing someone watching.

She turned toward the door to find Reed leaning laconically against the doorjamb.

"I saw the lights." He straightened and ambled into the room, dressed in jeans and a white T-shirt, hair tousled, muscles bulging everywhere.

She pulled her legs beneath her and rolled to her feet. "I couldn't sleep. Time-zone change."

"Yeah, me, too. Not the time-zone thing. But I couldn't sleep." He pointed above his head. "I'm cooking sausage and eggs. You hungry?"

She shook her head. "I'm not much of a breakfast eater."

Reluctant to stop while her muscles were warmed up, she crossed to the edge of the room, bracing her hand on the ledge. Facing Reed, she raised one leg behind her, gently gripped her toes and stretched out her quad.

"You don't seem to be much of an eater at all," he observed.

"Weight's an issue in my profession." Not only was a sleek form vital to her look on stage, but she had her partners to think about.

"How much do you weigh?"

She shot him a look of disbelief. "Do you really expect me to answer that?"

He shrugged and moved farther into the room. "Why not? I must weigh two, three times what you do."

"Reed, you don't ask a lady her weight."

"Say that again."

"You don't ask a lady her weight?"

"No, the Reed part."

She gave him a frown. What was that? Was he flirting? Why would he flirt?

He stared back in silence for a long moment. Then he said, "I made you something."

Though the words took her by surprise, she rolled with it, telling herself it was better to move on. If Reed started flirting with her, she'd have to decide how to react. She knew how she was supposed to react, but it was completely different from the way she wanted to react.

She pulled her feet together and bent forward, putting her hands flat on the floor. "What did you make me?"

"It's a surprise."

"You want me to guess?" She stood again and raised her leg to the ledge, stretching her body along its length.

"No, I…" He paused. "How do you *do* that?"

"Do what?"

"Go all pretzel-like."

"Practice." She'd started when she was ten years old, when everything about her body had been extraordinarily flexible. "Is it something to eat?" she asked him. "If it is, you should know I like fruit and whole grains."

"Is that why you skipped the brownies last night?"

"I noticed you ate mine."

"Always happy to help a lady in distress."

She couldn't help laughing at that. "Ever the gentleman."

"Yes, I am."

She straightened. "Okay, I'll admit, you've got me curious."

His eyes warmed. "You want to come and see?"

"Depends. Where are we going?"

"The barn." His gaze scanned her body. "You'll have to put on something warmer than that. And remember, the hands are working out there."

She glanced down at her simple leotard set. "You know I go up on stage in less than this."

"Not in Colorado, you don't."

"Fine." She started for the door, passing by him and calling over her shoulder. "You got any more of those cotton shirts? That'll cover up everything that counts."

"What's mine is yours." He started in behind her. "In fact, I've got a nice set of pajamas you might like. Red-and-gray plaid, very boxy. You take the tops."

And he'd take the bottoms.

Oh, he was definitely flirting. She stopped abruptly in the doorway and he almost barreled into her.

He raised a hand and braced himself on the doorjamb. "What?"

She turned. "You shouldn't do that."

"Do what?"

"Talk about sharing pajamas."

His lips curled up in the barest of smirks. "Is that what you thought I meant?"

"You know you did."

There was a silent pause.

"Okay," he admitted.

He stared down at her, and a pulse pounded in her temple, while heat coiled in the center of her body.

He leaned almost imperceptibly in, and his voice went husky. "You should get dressed."

"I know."

He blinked. "Now," he muttered.

He was absolutely right. They'd taken this as far as they dared. She quickly turned and mounted the staircase.

She felt him behind her as far as the main floor. Then, she noted thankfully, he broke off to return to the kitchen.

Back in the guest room, she forced the sexy exchange from her mind, firmly telling herself to get it under control. She changed to some casual clothes and went back downstairs.

Together, they crossed to the main barn, traversing its length to a quiet corner behind a half wall. There she stared in astonishment at the contraption he'd made out of the bicycle.

"How did you do this?" she asked him. "*When* did you do this?"

The mountain bike was propped up on a rack, with the front wheel removed and rollers pressing against the back wheel. The rollers were attached to a long bolt with a butterfly screw that could be used to change the tension.

"This morning," he answered. "I told you, I couldn't sleep."

"I didn't think you were serious."

"About not sleeping?"

"About—" She gestured. "About disabling my bike."

"It's what you wanted."

"It's not what I wanted. It's what you offered." She didn't know why she was annoyed. Maybe because he hadn't given her a choice. Maybe she was touchy today when it came to men telling her what to do. Or maybe anger was just the easiest emotion for her to deal with right now when it came to Reed.

"It's too dangerous for you to be cycling around the ranch," he informed her.

"In your opinion."

"In everybody's opinion."

"So you decided to stop me?"

He nodded sharply. "I did."

"Don't you think that might be a little high-handed?"

"What? Keeping you safe?"

"I'm a grown woman, Reed."

"And?"

"And it's not up to you to decide how to keep me safe."

He gave a grunt of disbelief. "I'm the one who has to come rescue you."

"Nobody asked you to rescue me."

"Mandy did."

"Well, I didn't."

"So, I should have left you there?"

"You should have asked me before disabling my bicycle."

She wasn't sure why she was drawing this out. Truth was, it was going to be a whole lot easier to bike in here where it was smoother on her ankle and she didn't have to watch for obstacles and worry about breakdowns.

"Do you want me to take it apart?"

She caught a glimpse of hurt in his tightening expression and instantly regretted her reaction. "No. No, I don't."

"Good enough, then." His tone was sharp. He turned on his heel, leaving Katrina alone.

Three

No good deed ever went unpunished. Reed banged a frying pan against the stovetop, wondering if he was just too stupid to remember that fact.

He was up to *here* with being criticized and having his efforts go unappreciated. It was one of his father's favorite head games, pretending to want one thing, then changing the rules at the last minute and acting as though Reed had misunderstood the instructions.

He turned the sausages in the big skillet and cracked a couple of more eggs into a glass bowl.

"Smells good," came Caleb's voice as he entered the room, making a show of sniffing the air. "I can't believe you're such a good cook."

"I can't believe you're such a hopeless cook," Reed returned.

His brother had spent the past ten years building up his business, Active Equipment, while living in downtown Chicago. If it weren't for restaurants and take-out food Caleb would have starved to death years ago.

"I thought you'd be out working by now." Caleb crossed to

the coffeemaker, snagged a cup from the lowest shelf and poured himself some coffee.

"Guess I'm just lazy."

"Whoa," Caleb drew back at the tone of Reed's voice. "What's up?"

"Nothin'." Reed took a fork and beat the dozen eggs into a scramble, adding onions, peppers and a dollop of milk.

Caleb settled back against the countertop. "It's just you and me here, bro. He's gone."

Reed drew a breath and forced his features to neutral. "I know he's gone. Corby says the parts are in for the irrigation system on the oat field. Thought I'd start up there."

"Get one of the hands to do it."

"No need." Reed wasn't about to become an armchair rancher. The irrigation system needed fixing, and he knew how to fix it.

Caleb took a long sip of the black coffee. "Did you get a chance to look at the ranch manager résumés?"

"Not yet."

"Are you ever going to look at the ranch manager résumés?"

"Said I would." Reed dumped the egg mixture into a sizzling pan. Caleb was the one who wanted to hire a full-time manager. Reed didn't have a problem running the ranch himself.

"Who put the burr under your butt this morning?"

"Morning, Caleb," came Katrina's voice. Her soft footsteps sounded in the pass-through as she entered the kitchen from the living room.

Reed reached for a spatula, stirring the eggs without turning around. He could feel his brother's gaze linger on him a moment longer.

"Morning, Katrina," Caleb offered cheerfully. "Sleep well?"

"I did. Thank you." Her voice was sweet, melodious, without a trace of upset. Obviously, she'd moved on. Well, he would, too.

He turned to face her. "Eggs?"

Puzzlement flicked through her blue eyes. "No, thank you."

He knew he'd asked her that once already this morning. But what did she expect? That he'd own up to having spent the past hour with her? That he'd give Caleb the details of their argument?

Offering her some eggs was a perfectly ordinary thing to do in this circumstance.

"Fruit?" he continued, not quite masking the edge to his tone.

"Love some," she responded, lips compressing ever so slightly.

"There are oranges on the table, grapes and plums in the fridge. Help yourself."

Caleb moved into action. "Let me—"

"I'm sure she's capable of opening a refrigerator door," Reed told his brother.

"What is your *problem?*" Caleb demanded.

"It's fine," Katrina cut in, heading for the fridge. "He's worried that I'm nothing but decorative."

"She's our guest," Caleb exclaimed.

"Who's a guest?" asked Mandy, breezing into the kitchen. "Me?" She beelined for Caleb, planting a kiss on his cheek. Her hair was damp, her face free of makeup, and she wore a cotton shirt with the sleeves rolled up to midforearm, a faded pair of jeans and no-nonsense boots. She was the kind of woman to whom Reed ought to be attracted.

"Me," corrected Katrina, from behind the open fridge door. By contrast, she now wore a clingy pair of hunter-green slacks with rhinestones decorating the pockets and the hems. Her butter-yellow tank top was cropped, showing off smooth arms, a strip of skin above her waistband, her navel winking sexily every time she moved. Her earrings sparkled with tiny green stones while a silver medallion dangled above the scooped neckline of her top.

She was on a cattle ranch for goodness' sake, not at a nightclub.

"Okay…" Mandy drawled, obviously waiting to be brought up to speed on the discussion.

Katrina straightened, a deep purple plum in her hand. "I was about to offer to do the dishes." She pasted Reed with a challenging expression, then took a slurping bite of the plum.

He nearly dropped the spatula.

"Don't be ridiculous," Mandy quickly put in.

It took Reed's lungs a moment to start functioning again. "If you gals need to head home right away…"

Caleb's arm snaked out around Mandy. "I'm not letting this one go yet."

"I have work to do at home," Mandy admonished.

"Hire another hand. I'll pay for it. You're my fiancée, and I have dibs."

Katrina's gaze rested on Reed, making him feel guilty for his snarky attitude. But he'd done her a favor this morning, and she'd treated him like something nasty on the bottom of her shoe. She might get away with that back in New York City, but it wasn't cutting it out here.

"Exactly how long do you expect me to stay?" Mandy teased Caleb.

His voice went deep, communicating more emotion than a single word. "Forever."

Realizing he'd nearly burned the eggs, Reed twisted the burner control to the off position and moved them to one side.

"Cute." Mandy patted Caleb's cheek, seeming completely unaffected by his staunch declaration.

"Well, *I* should get back," said Katrina.

"Oh, no." Mandy walked forward toward Katrina before coming up against the tether of Caleb's hand in hers. "Stay."

Katrina turned to her sister. "Why would I stay?"

Stay and ride your bicycle, Reed found himself fuming. The least she could do was give it a try.

"You might as well be here as down there," said Mandy. "We haven't had a chance to talk." She tugged playfully at Caleb's hand, while he held her fast. "And I don't think this one's going to let me leave."

Out of the corner of his eye, Reed saw Katrina glance his way.

"Reed's not going to care," said Mandy.

"I don't want to get in the way."

Reed turned to face her full-on. "This isn't a country club."

Her head jerked back, eyes going wide, as if he'd wounded her, and he immediately felt like a heel.

"Reed!" Caleb admonished. "What the hell?"

"It's okay," said Katrina, setting down the half-eaten plum. "Obviously, I should—"

"No, you *shouldn't.*" Mandy shot Reed an annoyed glare. "He's in a bad mood, that's all. Terrell men get that way."

"Excuse me?" Caleb was obviously affronted at being lumped in unfavorably with his brother.

Katrina seemed to be at a loss. She suddenly struck Reed as a fragile, frightened bird. And he had to struggle against an overpowering urge to reach out and reassure her. He wanted to draw her into his arms and apologize for anything he'd ever done, thought of doing or might do in the future to hurt her.

But the rational side of him knew that would be ridiculous. She'd trounced all over his best intentions this morning, and now she was using those big, gorgeous blue eyes to bring the world onto her side.

Well, he wasn't falling for it.

"You're more than welcome to stay," Caleb told her staunchly.

Katrina looked to Reed, and he felt his defenses melting like spring snow. He fought against it, but stubborn as he was, she won the battle without lifting a finger.

"You're welcome to stay," he echoed his brother's invitation.

Then he determinedly turned his attention back to breakfast. The sausages were overdone, as were the eggs. He'd forgotten to push down the toast, and he couldn't seem to remember what the hell he'd done with the strawberry jam.

Katrina felt as though she was ten years old again, trailing along behind Mandy through the Terrell barn, feeling out of place, her nose wrinkling at the smell, making sure she steered clear of anything with hooves and teeth.

"There's a gorgeous meadow up by Flash Lake," Mandy was saying. She stopped beside a stall to scratch the nose of a chestnut mare. "It's really not that far to ride. The fireweed's up, and the lilies and columbine. You should see something more than the ranch yard while you're here."

"You don't remember, do you?" Katrina asked.

"Remember what?"

"That I don't know how to ride."

Mandy turned. "That's ridiculous."

"No, it's not."

"Of course you know how to ride."

Katrina shook her head, then tucked her loose hair behind her ears. "You guys used to put me up on a horse a lot. But I could barely hold on. I sure couldn't control it." If her horses hadn't willingly followed her sisters' and brothers' animals back home, she'd have been permanently lost in the wilderness.

"I can teach you," Mandy broke in.

Katrina laughed at that, deciding it was time to come clean. It had to be better than riding. "I'm afraid of horses, Mandy."

Her sister's forehead wrinkled. "What are you talking about?"

"They scare me half to death."

"Why?"

"Because they're big. They're strong. They're unpredictable, and one of them bit me once."

Mandy shook her head. "You can't put up with that. You have to show them who's boss."

"Does that sound like me?"

Mandy crossed her arms over her chest, leaning back against a stall fence and lifting one heel to brace it on the bottom rail, while the mare nudged at her ear. "I guess not," Mandy allowed, firmly pushing the horse's head away.

Katrina gave a self-deprecating grimace. "I can't even boss around five-foot-two male ballet dancers."

Mandy laughed at that. "I really could teach you."

"To boss my ballet partners around?"

"To ride horses."

Katrina took an involuntary step backward. "I don't think so."

"It's easy."

"Maybe so, but I don't want to learn how."

"But—"

"I'm only going to be here for a week, and there aren't a lot of horses in New York City."

Mandy's eyes narrowed. "But you'll come back, though, especially once Dad's home."

Katrina felt a familiar knot form in her stomach. Maybe it was because she'd left home so young and she didn't really know her father. Or maybe it was because she'd always sensed his disappointment in her. But the thought of being in the same room, of coming under his scrutiny, of dealing with the walking-on-eggshells feeling she got whenever he looked her way, made her want to turn and run.

"Katrina?" Mandy prompted.

"My schedule's pretty busy."

"But you do get time off."

"I do. But there are rehearsals. I'm doing a little teaching now." Katrina turned and started walking, not wanting to face her sister while she stretched the truth.

Mandy followed her lead. "You really do hate it here, don't you?"

"It's…" Katrina struggled for the right words. "Intimidating."

"I don't see why." Mandy urged Katrina down a side aisle.

"Of course you don't. You're like Ms. Super-Rancher."

Mandy laughed while she pushed open a door, and the sunlight flooded through. "You make a bigger deal about everything than it has to be. You always have."

"I do not." Katrina stopped short, unease shooting through her.

They'd walked outside into a large, green field, fences in the far distance. It was dotted with horses, in ones and twos, heads down, grazing.

"I won't let them get you," Mandy assured her.

"I'm not in the mood for an intervention." At her mother's insistence, Katrina was here to touch base with her family. But she wasn't here to conquer her fears and become a better human being.

"We're just walking. It's nicer out here than it is in the barn."

"In the barn, they're all behind fences."

"If they attack, I'll throw myself in front of you."

"Funny." Mandy might be taller and heavier than Katrina, but it was still a hundred-odd pounds against two-thousand. If a horse went rogue, Mandy wouldn't be able to save her.

Mandy turned so they were headed along the fence line, and Katrina felt a little better. At least there was a handy escape route if they needed one.

"So, what's the deal with you and Reed?"

Katrina stumbled on a clump of grass. "Huh?"

"Everything was fine last night."

"Everything was fine this morning, too."

Mandy crammed her hands into the front pockets of her jeans. "I know Reed very well. We were like brother and sister for the ten years Caleb was away. He's mad at you, and I'd like to know why."

Katrina shrugged. "You'll have to ask him."

"He won't answer."

"Then I guess we'll never know."

Mandy shook her head. "What makes you think you can start lying to me now?"

"Practice."

"Katrina. Seriously. Sometimes I feel like I don't even know you."

Katrina counted to ten inside her head. She knew she should say something innocuous and noncommittal, brushing off the comment and moving on. But some obstinate corner of her brain compelled her to speak up. "Maybe it's because you don't."

Mandy stopped dead. "What?"

Katrina knew it was past time to shut up. Unfortunately, her mouth didn't seem to get the message. "Travis says you all love me."

"We do."

"You don't even know me. You don't know I'm afraid of horses. You don't know I'm afraid of chickens. You don't know I'm afraid of Dad."

Mandy drew back in obvious shock. "Dad?"

Katrina's mouth seemed to be on autopilot. "And you have absolutely no idea that I'm afraid my ankle won't heal properly and that my dancing career will be over."

Mandy immediately reached for Katrina's hands, drawing her close, searching her expression. "Sweetheart, what's going on? What's wrong with your ankle?"

"It's nothing," said Katrina.

"What is it?" Mandy insisted.

Katrina waved a dismissive hand. "I had one of my pointe shoes give out, and I twisted my ankle."

"Are you okay?"

"I'm fine. I'd rather you didn't tell anyone."

"They'll want to know you're hurt," Mandy insisted. "They'll want to help."

"There's nothing they can do. I just need some rest, to let it heal."

"It was your shoe? Does this kind of thing happen often?"

"Hardly ever. Thank goodness." Katrina was having an unlucky streak, and she was going to get past it. Her ankle would heal. She should never have admitted out loud that she was worried. She wasn't. Not really.

She drew a bracing breath. "Mandy, I'm sorry. I didn't mean to say anything. I don't know what I was thinking—"

"I'm not the least bit sorry." Mandy tugged firmly on her sister's hands. "I want to know you, Katrina. No matter what's going on inside that crazy head of yours, we all *do* love you."

"I'm not crazy." Just because she didn't like ranching, didn't make her insane.

"Bad choice of words."

Suddenly, Katrina felt dead-tired. She didn't want to have this debate. It was bad enough that Quentin was out to get her and that her career might be hanging in the balance; she didn't need to add her childhood baggage to the mix.

"Do you think someone could drive me back to our place?" She'd make an excuse to catch a flight in the morning.

Mandy gave her head a vigorous shake. "Not a chance. Now

that we've broken the ice, we are going to talk, young lady." She tucked Katrina's hand into the crook of her arm and began walking again.

Katrina scoffed out an exclamation of disbelief. "I don't think so." It was a momentary lapse, not the breaking of an emotional dam ten years in the making.

"So, what happened with Reed?" Mandy repeated.

"Nothing."

"I think he likes you."

"I think he hates me."

"Yeah? Well, you're afraid of chickens, so I'm not much for trusting your judgment."

"I really want to go home." Katrina sighed.

"If by home, you mean Caleb and Reed's house for margaritas, then that's exactly where we're going."

"I can't drink margaritas. I'll get fat."

"Oh, yes, you can. We'll burn off the calories somehow. But you, my darling, are in serious need of a stiff drink and a big sister."

"Your sister claims I've upset you." Reed's voice interrupted Katrina in what she guessed was her thirteenth mile on the makeshift stationary bike, burning off the four giant golden margaritas from this afternoon. She and Mandy hadn't exactly had a full-on heart-to-heart, but they'd definitely broken the ice.

The sun was going down now, but Katrina was still feeling a little tipsy. The barn had grown quiet while she rode, with only the occasional whinny punctuating the steady whirr of her bike wheel.

"I'm not upset." She reached for the plastic water bottle in the wire holder on the bike frame, popping the top and squirting some of the tepid liquid into her mouth.

"Good to know." He crossed his arms over his broad chest, leaning sideways against a rough wood post.

Katrina snapped the cap back into place and slid the bottle back into its holder. She braced her hands on the handlebars and upped her speed.

A few moments went by in silence. Lights flicked off in the far reaches of the barn, and doors banged shut behind ranch hands packing it in for the night.

"Gone far?" asked Reed.

"Fourteen miles or so, I think." She swiped the back of her hand across her damp forehead. She was dressed in lightweight black tights and a baggy white tank top, but the air in the barn was still warm and close around her.

He went silent again, gazing dispassionately at her while she rode.

After about five minutes she cracked, straightening on the bike seat to look at him. "What are you doing?"

"Waiting."

"For what?"

"Mandy says you're worried about your ankle."

"Mandy needs to stop discussing my private business with everybody in the valley."

"I already knew about your ankle."

"She didn't know that."

"She does now."

Katrina stopped riding and huffed her frustration. "Are you going to get to your point?"

"I already did. Your ankle."

"What about it?"

He shifted away from the post, moving closer to her. "Will you let me look at it?"

Though she'd stopped riding, she was still growing hotter. "Are you a doctor?"

"No."

"A physiotherapist?"

"Nope."

"Guy with an ankle fetish?"

Reed cracked a grin. "No. But I've worked on a lot of horses with strained tendons."

She coughed out a laugh. "Good for you."

He braced a hand between hers on the handlebars. "I know how to make a herbal wrap that will increase circulation."

She crooked her head to look up at him. "Is this a joke? Did Mandy put you up to this?"

"I'm completely serious."

"I'm not a horse."

His gaze flicked down for a split second. "In fact, you are not. But the principle's the same." He motioned for her to lift her foot.

She ignored the gesture. "I thought you were mad at me."

"I am."

"So, why do you want to help?"

"Because you need it."

"And because Mandy asked you?"

"Mmm-hmm."

Katrina considered his expression seriously. "Were you ever in love with my sister?"

"No." He reached down and lifted her ankle, crouching and resting her leg across his denim-covered knee.

She didn't fight him. "Are you lying to me?"

"No."

"So, there's nothing between you and Mandy?"

"She's marrying my brother. That's what's between us." He tugged at the bow and loosened the laces of Katrina's sneaker.

"I don't even know how to interpret that." Did he mean Caleb had come between him and Mandy?

Reed gently removed Katrina's shoe and set it on the worn, dusty floor. "There's nothing to interpret."

"You're being deliberately oblique."

Reed shook his head, slipping off her sock. "What makes you think I had a thing for Mandy?"

"Because you're doing her a favor. By helping me. What other reason would there—"

His large warm hands wrapped around her ankle, and she jumped at the electric sensation.

"It's not Mandy." He rotated her ankle. "Does this hurt?"

Katrina sucked in a breath and tried to tug her foot out of his grasp.

"Hold still."

"It hurts."

"Sorry." His thumb pressed on the inside of her foot below her ankle bone. "This?"

"Yes," she hissed.

He tried the opposite side of her foot and glanced up.

She shook her head in an answer.

"Point your toe?"

She did.

"Other way."

She flexed. "Ouch."

"Yeah," he commiserated, moving back toward the sorest spot. He made small circles with the pad of his thumb, massaging in a way that hurt, but the pain wasn't too sharp.

She steeled herself to keep still.

"Relax," he instructed. His attention moved farther up her calf.

Okay, that didn't hurt at all. In fact, it felt very nice. Very, very nice. She closed her eyes.

His deep voice was low and soothing as it rumbled in the cavernous space. "I'm going to move you."

"Hmm?"

"You lean over any farther and you're going to fall off the bike seat." His hands left her leg, and suddenly he was scooping her from the bicycle, lifting her, carrying her.

"What—"

"Over here." He nodded to a small stack of hay bales against a half wall.

He set her down, and the stalks of hay prickled through her tights.

She shifted. "Ouch."

"Ouch?"

"It prickles."

Reed shook his head in disgust, coming to his feet, striding away, his boot heels clomping on the floor.

Katrina straightened. But just as she was debating whether to hop her way back to her discarded sock and sneaker or get her bare foot dirty, Reed returned with a dark green horse blanket over one arm.

He spread it across the hay bales, then unceremoniously lifted her to place her on the thick blanket.

"Better?" he asked, tone flat.

"I only have thin tights on," she protested, gesturing to the contrast of his sturdy jeans. "The hay pokes right through them."

"Did I say anything?"

"You think I'm a princess," she huffed.

"You are a princess." He crouched down in front of her, lifting her foot to his knee again.

"I have delicate skin and thin clothing."

His strong thumb began to massage again, working its way in circles up the tight muscles of her calf. "Am I hurting you now?"

"No."

"Good. Lean back. Try to relax. We'll talk about your clothes later."

She leaned back against the hay. "They're nice clothes."

"For Manhattan."

"For anywhere."

"Shut up," he said gently.

She did. Not because he'd told her to, but because his hands were doing incredible things to her calf. She found herself marveling that such an intense, powerful, no-nonsense man could have such a sensitive touch.

He took his time, releasing the tension from her muscles, gently working his way toward the injured tendon. By the time he got there, the surrounding muscles were so relaxed that it felt merely sore, not the burning pain she'd been experiencing for the past two weeks.

He moved away from her ankle, back up her calf, leaving bliss in his wake. Then, to her surprise, he started on the sole of her foot. She wanted to protest, but it felt too good as his fingers dug into the ball of her foot and the base of her heel. And when he switched to the other foot, she was beyond speech. Her sympathetic nervous system fully engaged, and her brain went to autopilot.

"Katrina?" Reed's deep voice was suddenly next to her ear.

She blinked against the fuzziness inside her brain, realizing that he'd leaned down on the hay bales beside her. Her eyelids felt heavy, and her mouth couldn't seem to form any words.

"Do I have to kiss the princess to wake her up?" he joked.

"Am I sleeping?"

"I hope so. You were snoring."

"I was not." She brought him into focus and saw that he was grinning. She couldn't believe she'd fallen asleep during a foot massage. "Do you have magic hands?"

"I do," he intoned.

The barn was quiet, the light dim all around them. They were alone and his eyes were pewter-dark, molten, watchful. His face was hard-wrought, all planes and angles, beard-shadowed, with that little bump on his nose that seemed to telegraph danger.

She had a sudden urge to smooth away that imperfection, to run her fingertips across his whisker-roughened chin and feel the heat of his skin. He'd said something about kissing her. Was he thinking about it now? Would he do it?

Her gaze shifted to his full lips, imagining their softness against her own.

"Katrina." His voice was strained.

She wanted him to kiss her, desperately wanted to feel those hot lips come down on hers, his hard body press her back into the hay, his magic hands wrap around her waist, along her back, over her buttocks, down her thighs. She just knew he would take her to paradise.

"The herbal wrap," he said.

She blinked. "Huh?"

He eased away from her. "I should put it on your ankle now, while your muscles are warmed up."

"But…" No. That wasn't how this was supposed to end.

"It'll help," he assured her.

"Reed?"

He straightened, no longer looking at her, his voice growing more distant. "I know you're not a horse. But trust me. The principle really is the same."

She didn't doubt it was. But that wasn't her problem. Her problem was that she was powerfully, ridiculously, sexually attracted to Reed Terrell, and it didn't look like it was going away anytime soon.

Four

Reed swung the eight-pound sledgehammer over his head, bringing it down on the wooden stake with a satisfying thump. He drove it halfway into the meadow grass, then hit it once more, anchoring it firmly into the ground. He took a step back and set down the hammer. Then he consulted his house plans, lined up the electronic transit to position the next stake before repeating the process.

An hour later, as the sun climbed across the morning sky, he stripped down to his T-shirt, tossed it aside and shaded his eyes to gaze across the flat meadow that overlooked Flash Lake into the foothills and far across to the Rockies.

He'd known for years that this would be the perfect spot. Milestone Brook babbled fifty feet from where he'd build his deck. He already knew he'd put in a footbridge, teach his sons to fish for rainbow trout and build a picnic table on the opposite side of the bridge so his family could spend Saturday afternoons eating hamburgers, playing horseshoes or badminton.

He could picture the living room. He could picture the view. He could picture six kids racing around in the yard. He could even picture his future wife chasing down a toddler. She'd be beautiful in blue jeans and boots, a cotton shirt and a Stetson.

In his mind's eye, she turned and smiled. And he realized it was Katrina.

Reed felt as if he'd been sucker-punched.

He shook his head to clear it. That wasn't right. It wasn't right at all. He'd come up here today to get away from Katrina. His burgeoning attraction to her reminded him that it was past time to get going on the rest of his life. And the rest of his life sure didn't include a tiny, blond-haired, blue-eyed ballerina.

"Reed?" Her voice startled him, and he spun around to see her crossing the meadow toward him.

She moved steadily closer. Her hair was pulled up in a ponytail. She wore tiny diamond earrings that sparkled in the sunshine. Designer jeans clung to her hips, while a deep purple cap-sleeved T-shirt molded to her breasts, nipping in at her waist, ending just above her low waistband. Even without makeup, her lashes were thick and dark, her lips deep red, and her cheeks soft pink.

"What are you doing?" she asked him, glancing around at his work.

"What are *you* doing?"

"Walking." She came to a halt a few feet away. "It's a low-impact exercise."

"I thought you were biking for that."

"Variety," she answered, tipping her head to one side.

He fought an urge to take a single step forward, cup her face, and drink in a deep kiss. But somehow, it seemed sacrilegious, as if he was cheating on his future wife.

She peered pointedly around. "A building site?"

"I'm staking out the foundation," he admitted. "For my house."

"Seriously?" She shaded her eyes to scan his work. "You're building a house up here?"

"No. I'm building a secret military installation, with a formal dining room and a view of the lake."

She gave an eye-roll and paced her way toward the pattern of stakes. "It's big."

He found himself following behind. "Four bedrooms."

"Where's the front door?"

"You're standing on the porch."

She pointed. "So, here?"

"Go on in."

She glanced back at him to grin. "Thank you."

"Dining room on the right," he told her, oddly pleased to share his plans with someone. He'd designed them himself, keeping them secret from his father and everyone else. "Straight ahead takes you into the great room and the kitchen."

"On the left?"

"Media room, then utility room. You can cut through there to the garage."

She walked straight through the future great room toward the back of the house.

"That'll be a breakfast nook," he described. "There'll be French doors here that go out onto the deck."

"Great view," she put in.

"Isn't it? Master suite will have the same view."

She gazed out at the river. "But I don't understand."

He stopped next to her in the position he planned for the deck railing, resting his hands in his front pockets. "I like a nice view of the lake."

"I don't understand the new house. What's wrong with the old one?"

He'd made plans to build the new one before his father had died. But he saw no reason to change the plans now. "Caleb and Mandy can live there."

"But they're only going to be here part-time, right?"

"Probably. But they'll want their own space. And I'll want mine. So will my wife."

She turned to stare at him, and her eyes went round, her tone became incredulous. "You're getting married?"

"Yes, I am."

"Do you have a secret fiancée?"

"Not yet."

"Who?" she asked.

"I told you, not yet."

"But who is she?"

"I don't know."

Katrina canted a hip to one side, while her face screwed up in puzzlement. "You're building a house for a fiancée you haven't yet met?"

"You got a problem with that?"

She paused. "Truthfully, I think it's kind of sweet."

"I was going for practical."

"Well, you got sweet."

He scoffed out a laugh. "I'm not sweet."

She lifted her left ankle and twisted it in the air. "Your wrap helped."

"Yeah?"

"I'm positive it did," she confirmed, while his mind wandered back to their near kiss last night in the barn.

A rumble sounded in the distance, and Katrina braced her feet to the ground, turning sharply toward it.

"What's that?" she asked.

"Horses." He listened for a moment. "Small herd."

"Where?" She took a sideways step in his direction, her gaze darting around.

"Over the rise. Coming this way."

They were definitely at a gallop, and Reed wondered what might have startled them. Could have been anything.

"But there's a fence, right?" Katrina asked.

"What do you mean?"

"Between us and them?"

"Nope."

She paled. "Nope?"

He shook his head to confirm, and she moved so close she was touching him.

The sound grew louder.

"They're headed for the lake," Reed reassured her.

"Are we going to be trampled?" She turned her face into his chest.

He struggled not to laugh, placing a reassuring arm around her shoulders. "No, we're not going to be trampled. They'll head straight downhill."

"You can't know that."

"Even if they don't, they'll see us. They'll go around us."

"Are you lying? Are we about to die?"

He grasped her upper arms, putting her away from him, staring down into her eyes. "Seriously, Katrina. Calm down."

Her eyes were wide, ice-blue with fear. "What if they're angry?"

"They're thirsty," he assured her.

The herd appeared on the rise, their hooves thundering, the ground shaking. Katrina squealed and threw herself against his chest.

"See? They're turning," he told her.

Exactly as he'd expected, they curved around the knoll, taking the downhill route toward the lake. The dozen sleek brown, black and white bodies moved off into the distance. The sound diminished, and the ground vibrations disappeared.

Reed noticed Katrina was shaking.

"Hey." He smoothed back her hair. "Big-city princess, there's nothing to worry about."

"I'm sorry," she mumbled.

"Nothing to be sorry about."

"Then I'm embarrassed."

"Okay, that's a valid emotion."

She socked him in the bicep with the flat of her fist. "I'm not used to horses."

"No kidding."

Now that she'd calmed down, he allowed himself to focus on the feel of her in his arms. She was softly curved, perfectly proportioned. The top of her head only came to his chin, but she was looking up, and if he dipped his head, tipped it on an angle, his lips would be on hers.

His hand convulsed against the small of her back. Her hips

pressed against the V of his thighs. Her hands were warm where they rested against his back. And a surge of desire crested in his veins.

His gaze met hers, opaque and darkened to midnight-blue. The world stilled and paused for breath around them, the birds going silent, the wind going still; even the sound of the brook was muffled in the thickening air. His free hand rose to cup her cheek, sliding into her hairline as he dipped his head. Her sweet breath mingled with his.

"Tell me no," he rasped. Nothing short of her genuine protest would stop him this time.

But she stayed silent, stayed pressed against him, her lips slightly parted.

He cursed under his breath and crossed those final inches that brought his lips flush against hers. The burst of passion was instantaneous, igniting every fiber of his body to a roaring need. Her lips were full, tender and hot, and they tasted like summer nectar.

He urged them apart, delving deep with his tongue, his fingers tangling in her hair, his other arm wrapping fully around her waist, pressing her tight against his intense desire.

His kiss was too hard. His hold was too tight. He lifted her easily off the ground, even as a small speck of sanity that was struggling deep inside his brain ordered him to slow it down, to let her go, to back off.

But she moaned against his mouth, the vibration setting off another chain reaction of passion. Her hands fisted into his sweat-dampened shirt, while the softness of her breasts burned an imprint into his chest.

A horse whinnied in the distance, and the sound of the brook flowed into his ears. Birds came back to life, while the breeze picked up, cooling his overheated skin.

With steely determination, he forced himself to break the kiss. "I'm sorry," he breathed, still drinking in the feel of her soft curves.

"I'm not," she gasped.

His body convulsed. "Don't say that."

"Okay." A pause. "I won't."

He sucked in a couple of deep, deep breaths, forcing his hand to fall away from her cheek. Then he regretfully touched his forehead to hers. "I was out of line."

"Why are you blaming yourself?" Her breathing was as deep as his. "There are two of us here."

"I'm trying to be a gentleman."

She drew slowly back. Wisps of blond hair had worked free from her ponytail. Her lips were swollen red, cheeks flushed, eyes bedroom-soft with a sensual message. "In some circumstances, being a gentlemen is overrated."

Reed groaned his frustration. "You're killing me, Katrina."

"Not exactly what I was going for."

"You want me to kiss you again?" he demanded, knowing he couldn't take much more of her flirtatious teasing.

"You want to kiss me again, cowboy?"

"More than I've ever wanted anything in my life."

They stared at each other in charged silence.

"But I won't," he determined, gritting his teeth.

He wouldn't, because if he kissed her again, he knew he wouldn't stop. It wouldn't matter that the bedroom of his future house was nothing but a few stakes in the ground—he'd make passionate love to her, right here in the thick grass of the meadow. And then he'd have to build a different house, in a different location, because she'd be all he ever remembered here.

Katrina wasn't completely without experience when it came to men.

Okay, so she was mostly without experience when it came to men. But it wasn't her fault. She'd gone to an all-girls school until she was eighteen, graduating straight into the Liberty Ballet company. Until graduation, she'd been surrounded by girls and the few male dancers who'd participated in performances. The male dancers were nice guys, many of them fun and funny, but none of them interested her romantically.

She'd dated a little in the past year, mostly men she'd met

at fundraisers or parties connected to the dance company, but nothing had ever turned into a relationship.

And then there was Quentin. But she sure wasn't counting that. Reed's kiss, on the other hand, she would definitely count. Quentin was a member of Liberty Ballet's board of directors. Close to twenty years older than Katrina, he'd been dogging her since she'd become a principal dancer. Frustrated by her lack of uptake on his intense flirting, he'd finally cornered her in his office two weeks ago, forced a slobbery kiss on her mouth and baldly propositioned her. When she'd broken away, firmly telling him she wasn't interested, he'd grown angry and threatened to destroy her career.

She didn't know how or if he'd be able to make good on that threat. But he certainly knew the movers and shakers of the ballet world.

She ran a brush through her wet hair, gazing into the dresser mirror in the Terrells' guest room. Odd, the differences between Quentin and Reed. Quentin was urbane, educated, fastidious and debonair. Reed was raw, passionate, assertive and unruly. But there was no contest over who she'd trust.

Her fingertips went reflexively to her lips. She could swear they were still tingling from Reed's kiss this afternoon. He'd been the one to call a halt. He'd broken away and given them both a moment of sanity. If he hadn't done that, she was sure she would have lost her virginity to a rugged cowboy right there in the middle of a Lyndon Valley meadow.

She shook her head, even as her smile and the warm glow remained. Like any woman, she'd fantasized about her first time making love. It had always involved a posh hotel suite, and a man who'd laid his bow tie and tux over a French provincial armchair before joining her in a lacy, canopied bed. Lyndon Valley, blue jeans, an imperfect nose and a beard-rough chin weren't even on her radar.

"Katrina?" Mandy rapped lightly on the door.

"Come in," Katrina called, determinedly banishing thoughts of Reed and tightening the sash of her satin robe.

The door opened. Like Katrina, Mandy had showered recently. Her damp chestnut hair was combed back in a ponytail, and she'd pulled on a hunter-green T-shirt over a pair of beige cargo pants.

"How're you doing?" Mandy opened, letting the door swing closed behind her, getting comfortable on the corner of the bed and curling her bare feet beneath her. "Ankle holding up?"

"I'm fine," Katrina answered. "It's doing okay."

She really was fine, she realized. Quentin was far away and suddenly easy to push from her thoughts. He'd been obliterated by Reed. She felt buoyant and upbeat from all that fresh air. Her ankle had survived the walk with surprising strength. It felt a whole lot better than it had yesterday.

"Seth called," said Mandy.

"Is he ordering us back home?" Katrina crossed to her suitcase, open on a low table in the corner of the room. She'd been wondering how long her other three siblings would let her and Mandy hide out at the Terrell ranch.

"Sort of. He wants us to go to Lyndon with him tomorrow. The Lyndon Hospital is hosting a charity ball, and he thinks it'll be good for the campaign to have a strong Jacobs contingent by his side."

Katrina glanced over her shoulder. "He wants us to campaign for him?"

"Nah. All we have to do is show up, dance and smile for the cameras. Cakewalk for you."

Katrina retrieved a simple black knit skirt and a filmy copper cap-sleeved blouse. "Are we talking ballgowns and the whole nine yards?"

Mandy nodded. "It'll be formal."

"Then I'll have to go shopping." Which was a waste, since Katrina had a dozen perfectly appropriate ballgowns hanging in her closet in New York City. "And maybe do something with my hair. And I don't know what I've got for shoes."

If she could be positive any photos taken at the event would only be used locally for Seth's campaign, she wouldn't worry. But she and her fellow dancers at Liberty Ballet were under strict orders from the publicity department that every single public appearance, every picture, every interview, had to comply with company policy.

From the top of her head to the tips of her toes, she had to be esthetically perfect.

"Lyndon does have stores," said Mandy.

"And I'm going to need them," Katrina joked, stepping into the skirt.

"You'll probably have a lot more fun this trip. You're dressing up and dancing instead of slogging through the barns and worrying about horses."

Katrina paused, sensing a conspiracy. "You didn't tell Seth what I said?"

"No, no." Mandy determinedly shook her head. "It's a coincidence, I promise." She paused. "But there are some nice things about Colorado, you know."

Katrina fastened the skirt at her waist. "There are some nice things about New York City, too."

"You mean like traffic and muggings?"

"I mean like Central Park and the Met."

"Lyndon has an arts center, an orchestra and a museum."

Katrina slipped off the robe and put on the blouse over her lacy bra, fastening the tiny buttons up the front. "You really love it here, don't you?" She padded across the bedroom and joined her sister on the opposite corner of the bed.

"I really do," Mandy agreed.

"Won't you and Caleb mostly live in Chicago after the wedding?"

"We think it'll be about fifty-fifty. I'll put up with Chicago for him, and he'll put up with Lyndon Valley for me."

"So, one of you will always be unhappy?" Katrina didn't want to question the wisdom of her sister's marriage plans, but theirs didn't sound like a particularly smart arrangement.

Mandy's voice went soft. "Caleb hated his father. He didn't hate Lyndon Valley. And now that Wilton is gone, he'll remember all the things he loved about the ranch."

"You sure?"

"I'm positive."

Katrina plucked at the quilt. "Well, I'll never leave New York City."

"Not even for the right man?"

"The right man is already there."

Mandy straightened, her expression perking up. "I thought you said you didn't have a boyfriend."

"No boyfriend." Katrina was taking a page from Reed's logic. "I haven't met him yet. But I know he's out there, picking out an impressionist painting for his penthouse, balancing his stock portfolio and dry-cleaning his tux."

Mandy laughed, even as Katrina's thoughts flicked back to Reed.

"Did you know Reed was building a house?" she found herself asking her sister.

"What do you mean?"

"He showed me the building site today. Up in one of the top meadows beside Flash Lake. He's got it all staked out. I didn't see the drawings, but he talked like it was all planned. He says he's going to find himself a wife and start a family. You and Caleb get to keep this house."

"Really?" Mandy drew the word out in obvious contemplation.

"So this is something new?" Katrina confirmed.

"He told Caleb he was planning to raise a family here on the ranch. But, as far as I know, he didn't say anything about building a new house." Mandy shifted on the mattress. "I take it you're not fighting anymore?"

Katrina felt her cheeks heat and struggled to control the reaction. "We were never fighting." She glanced away. "It was… He just… He's helping me with my ankle."

Good grief. Why was she having trouble with such a simple explanation? It wasn't as though she was lying. Everything she was saying was true.

Mandy blinked. "Katrina?"

"Hmm?"

"What's going on?"

"What do you mean?"

"Are you attracted to Reed?"

Katrina formulated an answer. "Reed is Colorado."

If ever there was a man who was a perfect metaphor for a place, he was it.

"And you hate Colorado."

"I'm intimidated by it."

Mandy's gaze was probing. "So you're intimidated by Reed?"

"Why does this conversation feel like a chess game?"

"Because you're being evasive."

"I like my men in tuxedos," Katrina answered honestly.

Mandy grinned and chuckled. "Then tomorrow night at the ball ought to be very interesting."

"Why?"

"Because Reed will be in a tux."

"Not a problem," Katrina answered with conviction. It was one thing to dress a man up, but the grit of Colorado tended to stick.

The elevator door opened into the lobby of the Sunburst Hotel in downtown Lyndon, and Katrina nearly stumbled on her high-heeled silver sandals. Reed didn't look remotely gritty. Quite the contrary, he looked fantastic in a tuxedo.

Next to a marble pillar and an oversize leather furniture grouping, he was joking with Caleb, Travis and Seth. He was the tallest of the three, broad-shouldered, clean-shaven, with his hair freshly trimmed and his dark eyes zeroing in on her.

"Wow." The word whooshed out beneath her breath. She had to remind herself to keep walking between Mandy and Abigail.

"You mean Caleb?" Mandy asked, a thread of amusement in her tone.

"Right," Katrina returned without missing a beat. "Caleb." Her gaze stayed glued to Reed.

"Seth's tie is crooked," Abigail put in, quickening her pace, clearly hoping to get to Seth and correct the problem before anyone else noticed.

"Liar," Mandy muttered to Katrina.

"Who? Abigail?"

"Admit it, you're attracted to Reed."

"Not at all," Katrina lied.

"You haven't taken your eyes off him."

"I was thinking he's too tall." Among other things. He was also too strong, too determined, too attractive and far too good a kisser for a Colorado cowboy.

"He looks great in a tux," Mandy singsonged.

"All men look great in a tux." Though few men looked *that* great in a tux.

As they drew closer, Caleb gave a low whistle of appreciation, his gaze warm on Mandy in an off-the-shoulder, full-skirted, full-length gown in shimmering silver.

"I love it when you dress up like a girl," he told her, putting an arm around her bare shoulders, placing a gentle kiss on her temple.

Abigail finished with Seth's tie, chatting to him about the attendees at the ball, enumerating those he should seek out. Travis joined in their conversation, joking about who could make the biggest financial contribution to Seth's campaign, as the three started toward the hotel exit. Mandy took Caleb's arm and they fell into step behind, leaving Katrina and Reed to bring up the rear.

"You look very nice," Reed offered to Katrina, taking in her slim-fitting, butter-yellow satin gown. The V-necked bodice was crisscrossed with tiny strands of crystals that also ran the length of the spaghetti straps accenting her bare shoulders. The back dipped low, while the hem flared out. The skirt was snug at her hips, but loose enough along the length of her legs to allow for dancing.

She'd bought some inexpensive but fun dangling crystal earrings that now hung below her simple updo. She'd paired them with an elaborate necklace of crystals interspersed with yellow topaz snug against her throat. Her makeup was to Liberty Ballet standards, a little heavier than Katrina preferred, but nobody in the ballet company would have a complaint if her photo ended up in a national magazine.

"Thank you," she answered Reed, still drinking in his appearance.

He'd skipped the bow tie, going instead for a classic Windsor knot of taupe silk with a matching pocket square in the black coat, all over a crisp white shirt. The tux fitted him extremely well, and she wondered if it was possible that he owned it.

His strong, weathered hands and his slightly imperfect nose were the only things that stopped him from being equally urbane as any man she'd met in New York City. The realization was both disconcerting and exhilarating.

He held out his arm. She automatically slipped her hand into the crook of his elbow, the strength of his ropy muscles evident through the supple fabric.

"You look very nice, too," she returned the compliment.

"I feel like a penguin," he grumbled. "Do you have any idea how hard it is to move in one of these things?"

Katrina gestured to her slim-fitting dress. "As opposed to moving in this?"

"Nobody expects you to hop out of the car and change a tire."

"You're planning to change a tire tonight?"

"You never know what might happen."

She couldn't help but laugh at that.

He took her hand and pressed it to his jacket pocket.

She felt a hard, rectangular lump against his hip. "What on earth?"

"Multitool," he told her. "Knife, screwdriver, file, pliers."

"You're armed with a tool set?"

"Yes, ma'am."

"We'll be in a ballroom," she pointed out. "I expect there's a maintenance crew. And the worst thing likely to happen tonight is a broken shoe buckle."

They passed through the hotel exit to the sidewalk, where a lineup of shiny black SUVs waited for guests. She glanced around but didn't spot her sisters and brothers.

"I can fix a broken shoe buckle," said Reed. "I can also repair a harness, remove a splinter, whittle some kindling and fix an outboard motor."

"I can't do any of those things, with or without a multitool. Well, maybe remove a splinter," she allowed. Then she glanced ruefully at the tiny clutch purse that contained nothing but the bare necessities. "But not with anything I brought along tonight."

Reed opened the back door to one of the vehicles. "That's the beauty of the system," he told her, cupping his palm over her elbow to help her into the seat.

She glanced up questioningly.

He gave her a grin and a waggle of his brows. "You brought me. You don't need anything else."

"You're a living, breathing multitool?" she guessed.

His eyes darkened ever so slightly, and his tone went low. "That I am."

Had he just turned shoe-buckle repairs into a flirtation?

Before she could decide, he gently shut the door behind her, rounding the back of the vehicle to climb in the other side.

"To the Hospital Ball?" the driver asked Reed.

"Yes, please," he answered, stretching his arm across the back of the seat.

The driver nodded and pulled the vehicle into traffic.

Reed angled his body so that he was gazing at Katrina. He didn't say anything, just watched her while they made their way along Seventh Street toward Main.

She gazed back, meeting his eyes, strangely not feeling the need to break the silence. The moment stretched on, and she found herself remembering their kiss, his touch, his taste, the sound of his voice rumbling next to her ear and the woodsy scent of his skin.

"You going to be able to dance?" he asked gruffly, with a nod toward her left ankle.

"I think I can make it through a waltz or two," she answered.

Progress was slow on her ankle. Then again, at least she was making progress. For the few days before she'd come back to Colorado, the healing had seemed to stall. She'd been terrified it would never get better, or it would take so long to get better that she'd lose her position with the ballet company.

A shiver ran through her at the unsettling thought.

"Save a dance for me?" Reed asked quietly, his eyes glinting silver.

"I will." Katrina realized once again how safe she felt with Reed. There was nothing to worry about right now. Nothing was going to cause her any trouble tonight. Not even a flat tire.

As Reed would have expected, Katrina was the belle of the ball. Dinner had ended, but the dancing was not yet underway. So far, it had taken her nearly twenty minutes to make it halfway across the ballroom toward the ladies' room. Men stopped her, clustered around her, asking questions, obviously offering compliments, lingering when they shook her hand, making excuses to touch her.

Reed downed a swallow of champagne, wishing he had something stronger to quench his thirst.

Travis Jacobs took the chair next to him, nudged his elbow, and offered him a single malt, neat, in a heavy crystal glass.

Reed gratefully accepted. "Thanks."

Travis slouched back, propping his elbow on the opposite chair, his voice a drawl. "I see the way you're looking at my sister."

Reed took a swallow of the Scotch. "Same way every other guy in the room is looking at your sister. You don't like it? Don't let her dress like that."

"You Terrells need to keep your hands off the Jacobs women."

Reed gave a snort of derision. "Caleb's marrying one of them, and I haven't touched any of them."

Kissing Katrina didn't count. It was a well-accepted fact that *touching* in this context meant something considerably more than kissing.

Just then the orchestra came up and the lights went down. Reed and Travis both watched as yet another man approached Katrina. His gaze scanned her thoroughly from head to toe, then he stood far too close, his expression animated, his hand too familiar on her arm. Katrina took a step back, but the guy didn't let her go.

Reed firmly set down his Scotch glass and came to his feet. "I assume dancing is acceptable," he said to Travis, even as he moved away from the table.

"If it gets her out of that jerk's clutches, go for it."

Reed nodded in response, already pacing his way toward Katrina.

Once there, he snaked a proprietary arm around her slim waist. "Sweetheart," he drawled, his hard glare causing the jerk to pull back as if he'd been scalded.

"Are you ready for that dance?" he continued, turning his attention fully onto Katrina, dismissing the other man with a cold shoulder.

The man withdrew, muttering something unintelligible.

A beat went past.

"Did you just rescue me?" Katrina asked in obvious amusement.

"Story of my life."

"I was fine."

"You didn't look fine." Reed knew he should remove his hand from her waist, but he left it there anyway.

"He was a little too friendly," she admitted. "But I could have handled it."

"You didn't need to handle it. That's why you brought me along, remember?"

She pivoted to look at him. "I thought you were only planning to fix shoe buckles and remove splinters."

He couldn't help but smile at her joke. "I also dance."

"The two-step?"

"If that's what you want."

She cocked her head. "This is a waltz."

Reed removed his arm from her waist, tucking her hand into the crook of his arm. "Then let's waltz."

He steered her toward the dance floor where the ensemble was playing a classic ballad. There, he drew her into his arms, and his entire body seemed to sigh in satisfaction as she settled against him.

She was fluid and graceful, light on her feet, sensitive to his slightest nuance. He tucked her more closely to his body, his hand coming in contact with the bare skin revealed by the plunging V at the back of her dress. Her soft skin was so distracting that he struggled for something coherent to say.

"You're a very good dancer," he opened.

There was a smile in her voice when she answered. "Thank you. I've had a few lessons."

He gave a sheepish grin in return. "I guess you have."

"But it was nice of you to notice," she continued with what sounded like sincerity. "And you're not so bad yourself."

"High-school gym class," he admitted. It wasn't something he'd done frequently since then, but when he did, he always enjoyed it.

The lights dimmed further, and the band switched songs to another famous fifties cover tune. Reed saw no reason to let her go, so he let one song blend into the next, keeping her snugly in his arms.

They silently wound their way toward a set of doors that were open to a wide veranda. It was darker at this end of the ballroom, the music was lower and a cool breeze wafted in from the riverbank. She molded closer against him.

"Cold?" he whispered, gathering her tight, even as he turned so that his body was blocking the breeze.

"I'm fine," she answered into his chest.

Reed was fine, too. In fact, he was a whole lot better than fine. He wished that time would stop, that the world would fall away and leave him here alone with Katrina.

But then he caught sight of Travis far across the room, closely watching their every move. And he knew the world wasn't going anywhere anytime soon. Not that Reed blamed Katrina's brother for worrying. Reed definitely shouldn't be trusted with her.

"You go to things like this in New York City?" he found himself asking, curious and wondering how safe she'd be with neither of her brothers around to run interference.

Did she dress this provocatively for functions in New York? It was obvious she wasn't wearing a bra, and he couldn't help but wonder what exactly she had on underneath the clingy satin dress.

"Things like what?" she asked, voice slightly dreamy.

"Dances, charity functions."

"Yes." She nodded. "We're contractually obligated to make public appearances. It's good for contributions to have recognizable performers attend Liberty Ballet fundraisers."

Reed didn't like the sound of that. "It's compulsory? What if you don't want to go?"

She tipped her chin to look up at him. "It's my job."

Reed's spine stiffened. "It's your job to dance with random men?"

"Random men with a lot of money to contribute."

"I don't like it."

"Really?" she drawled. "And your opinion counts why?"

Reed didn't have a good answer for that. "What about your brothers?"

"What about them?"

Reed's glance darted to Travis again, finding him absorbed in a conversation with two other men. "Do they know?"

"You mean, do they know…" she made a show of glancing surreptitiously around the dance floor then lowered her voice to a stage whisper "…about my wicked little ballroom-dancing secret?"

A surge of jealousy hit Reed at the thought of her other dance partners. Giving into impulse, he stepped through the patio door, spinning her outside, away from the crowd.

"Hey," she protested.

But instead of stopping, he let their momentum carry them along the fieldstone wall. He came to a halt beside a square stone pillar, his forearm tightening across the small of her back, the darkness closing around them to give privacy.

She gasped in a breath, lips parting, eyes wide.

He gave her half a second to say no, then swooped in for a kiss. He came down harder than he'd intended, openmouthed, tongue invading, greedily savoring the sweet, moist heat of her mouth.

After a startled second, she tipped her head back, welcoming him, her tongue tangling with his. Her spine arched, and her hips pressed against the steel of his thighs. Her arms twined around his neck, and his free hand closed over her rear, the thin fabric of her dress all but disappearing in his imagination.

"Are you naked under this?" he rasped, kissing her neck, her shoulder, brushing a spaghetti strap out of the way to taste her tender skin.

"Are you naked under that?" she asked in return, tone teasing, her hands slipping beneath his jacket to wrap around him, branding him through the cotton of his shirt.

"Yes," he hissed, then resumed the kiss that went on and on, pushing want and need into every fiber of his body. His world contracted to Katrina, her taste, her feel, her scent. His hands roamed, while his lips savored, and her lithe body imprinted itself on his skin.

A woman's laughter penetrated his consciousness, as a group of people wandered onto the deck.

Reed forced himself to let go, fisted his hands and gritted his teeth, struggling hard to bring himself back under control.

When he found his voice, it was a mere rasp. "What are we doing?" What was *he* doing? What on earth had gotten into him?

Her hands were still braced on his chest, and her lips curved into a secret smile. "I believe it's called kissing."

It was so tempting to fall back into the moment. But he couldn't allow it. This chemistry between them flew out of control the instant he let his guard down.

"What is the *matter* with *me?*" he ground out.

Why couldn't he leave her alone? She was a family friend and a neighbor, soon to be an in-law. She wasn't some temporary pickup in a honky-tonk.

She eased away, straightening the strap of her dress. "Are you saying 'not here'?"

He wished it were that simple. "I'm saying not ever."

Her smile faltered, and he immediately felt like a cad. Bad

enough he'd accosted her. Now he'd insulted her. He hadn't meant it the way it sounded. He raked a hand through his short hair, putting more space between them. "I'm sorry."

She pressed her lips together. "No problem." She made to move around him.

He reached out. "Katrina."

But she brushed his hand away. "No need for an explanation."

He snagged her wrist, stopping her. "It's not that I don't want—"

"You're embarrassing me, Reed." Her tone was brittle; her crackling blue gaze staring straight ahead.

He leaned down, lips close to her ear, attempting to make it better. "Listen to me."

"No." She tried to free her wrist.

"I want you, Katrina," he confessed. "I want you very, very badly."

"I can tell."

He mustered his strength. "Give me a break. Your sister is marrying my brother."

She pinned him with a glare. "Is this some archaic chivalry thing?"

"Yes." For want of a better term, it was.

She leaned into him, the tip of her breast brushing his arm. "Well, you might want to get over that."

"Katrina," he warned on a growl.

"Because I want you, too, Reed. Very, very badly."

His hand went lax at her frank admission. It gave her a moment to escape, and she took it.

Five

Katrina couldn't believe the way she'd taunted Reed. She'd never said anything remotely that bold to a man.

She made beeline back to the Jacobs' table, her emotions vacillating between rattled, embarrassed and just plain annoyed.

She was a grown woman. Where did he get off protecting her from herself? As though she wasn't capable of making up her own mind? She knew her sister was marrying his brother. So what? She and Reed were adults.

From the empty round table she caught a glimpse of him far across the ballroom. His gaze scanned the cavernous room, stopped on her and he immediately headed her way. She took a bracing sip of her champagne.

Annoyed. She was definitely going with annoyed.

Her brother Travis dropped down in the chair beside her. "What's this I hear about you being afraid of horses?" he asked.

"What's this I hear about you riding bulls again?"

"Who told you that?"

"Mandy said you did the rodeo down in Pine Lake."

"At least I'm not afraid of them."

"You ought to be. You're not eighteen anymore."

"Nice deflection," Mandy put in as she took the chair on the opposite side of Katrina. Caleb pulled out the one next to her.

"Music's nice," Katrina observed, turning her attention to Mandy.

"I could teach you to ride in under a week," said Travis.

"A nice eclectic mix of songs," Katrina noted to no one in particular. "That's my preference for an evening like this."

"Excuse me?" an unfamiliar male voice sounded just behind her.

Katrina turned to see a rather handsome man in his mid-thirties, his hand held out to her, palm up.

"Would you care to—" The man's gaze abruptly flicked upward. "Never mind," he muttered, dropping his hand. "I'm sorry." Then he turned away.

Katrina watched his retreat in puzzlement. Not that she wanted to dance. Her ankle was starting to ache. But it was very strange behavior.

"Thing is," Travis carried on in a firm voice. "There's absolutely no reason for you to be afraid of them."

Katrina turned back, knowing she wasn't going to be able to avoid the topic forever. But as she turned, she met Reed's hard gaze. He'd planted himself on the chair directly across from her, his face twisted into a tight frown. She guessed that explained the would-be dance partner's abrupt departure.

"You're in pretty good shape," Travis continued talking to Katrina. "And you must have decent balance."

"Decent," Katrina agreed, still watching Reed. The meddler.

"You might want to tackle that chicken fear, too," said Mandy, a gentle teasing note in her tone.

Katrina took a long swallow of her champagne. It was her third glass tonight, and she noted the alcohol was putting a pleasant lethargy in her limbs. Reed's expression began to look faintly amusing, and the company of her siblings didn't seem quite as intimidating as usual.

Abigail arrived and took the chair next to Reed. "What are we talking about?" She glanced to the faces around the table.

Travis spoke up. "Katrina's irrational fear of Colorado."

"It's not a fear," she defended. "More…" She paused to find the right word. "A distaste."

"That's silly," said Abigail. "What's not to love around here? The mountains, the trees, the clear air, the clean water."

"The dust," said Katrina, polishing off her champagne. She glanced around for a waiter. Hang the calories. She wanted to maintain this buzz.

"You get used to the dust," said Mandy.

"You're missing my point." Katrina's tone was sharp enough that her siblings sat back in surprise. A little voice inside her told her to shut up, but just then a waiter came by, offering her a fresh glass of champagne, and she knew this was the day to go for it.

She accepted a fourth glass.

"Then what is your point?" Travis demanded.

In her peripheral vision, she saw Reed direct his frown at her brother.

"I don't want to change for Colorado," she carried blithely on. "I want Colorado to change for me."

"Now *that's* what I call a diva," said Travis.

"Travis," Mandy objected.

"Is that what you all think of me?" Katrina knew they did, but this was the first time she'd brought it out into the open.

Travis opened his mouth to speak, but Caleb intoned in a low warning. "Travis."

Katrina's champagne glass was suddenly removed from her hand. Startled, she glanced down and realized Reed had leaned across the table to take it from her. He set it down out of her reach.

"Hey," she protested.

"Excuse me while I put on the kid gloves," Travis drawled.

"She's your sister," said Caleb.

"And that means I get to have an honest conversation with her."

"Not tonight, it doesn't," said Reed. Somehow, he had appeared by her side.

Katrina glared at Travis. "I am not a diva." She knew divas, and Travis had obviously never met one. "Just because I don't happen to like horses or Holsteins or cowboys."

"Your family is full of cowboys," Travis pointed out.

"But you all clean up nice," chirped Mandy in an obvious attempt to lighten the mood.

Caleb backed up her effort, making a show of raising his glass. "Let's hear it for clean cowboys."

Abigail and Mandy immediately played along. "Clean cowboys."

Travis grimaced, but Caleb stared him down until he gave in and raised his glass.

Katrina quickly stretched out to snag her own. "Too bad they don't stay that way long."

Everyone groaned, but it quickly turned to good-natured laughter.

She took a big swallow.

Reed muttered darkly in her ear. "You about done?"

"Done what?" she asked tartly, reminding herself that she was angry with him. It hadn't been very gentlemanly of him to break off their kisses. Then again, he'd kind of stood up for her against Travis just now.

"Abigail," said Reed. "I think Katrina's ready for bed."

A saucy comeback was on the tip of Katrina's tongue. But when she swiveled to deliver it, she caught Reed's thunderous expression. And she wasn't quite brave enough to embarrass him.

"Are you going to wrap my ankle?" she asked him instead.

"No."

"But it's sore."

"You've had too much champagne.

"It's still sore."

She wanted to get him up to the hotel room, alone, where she would… Okay, she wasn't exactly sure what she'd do, but at least they could talk. This idea that they were going to nobly fight their attraction to each other because of Mandy and Caleb was ludicrous.

"Wrap her ankle?" Abigail asked.

"She strained her tendon dancing," said Reed. "I've been using my herb wrap."

"Crackerjack cure," said Caleb.

"You hurt your ankle?" asked Abigail.

"It's getting better," said Katrina, somewhat surprised that Mandy hadn't already shared the information with their sister.

Mandy reached out and took Katrina's hand. "Maybe you should head back to the hotel. You've probably had enough dancing."

"Sure," Katrina agreed, playing the dutiful baby sister. Then she glanced innocently up at Reed. "You'll take me back?"

His jaw tightened. "Abigail? Are you ready to go?"

"Absolutely," said Abigail, and Katrina heard her rise from her chair. "I'm exhausted."

Since Katrina and Abigail were sharing a room, there'd be no private conversation with Reed tonight. But Katrina wasn't giving up. Tomorrow, they'd all troop back to the ranches. Eventually, she and Reed would find themselves alone.

Katrina soon discovered that things Reed didn't want to happen, didn't happen. After the charity ball in Lyndon, she and Mandy had spent a couple of days at their own ranch. But her sister soon found a reason to return to Terrells', and Katrina found an excuse to go with her.

There, Reed was polite but resolute. He spent his days in the far reaches of the ranch, and his evenings in the company of Caleb and Mandy. If Katrina asked him a direct question, he answered. And he continued to wrap her ankle each evening, but he was careful never to get caught alone with her.

So she was surprised on a midday to hear his voice on the porch of the ranch house. She'd run through a workout and a few dance routines in the basement rec room this morning and was now looking for Mandy.

"It'll only take me a few hours," Reed was saying.

"That's not the point," Caleb returned. "We have hands for those kinds of jobs."

"I have no intention of spending my entire afternoon in the office."

"Once we get things set up with a manager, you'll be able to do or not do any old job you want around here."

"Good." Reed's tone was implacable. "Today I want to fix the well pump at Brome Ridge."

"You're impossible."

"Deal with it. I'll probably be late getting back tonight." His boot heels clunked on the porch, and Katrina took her chance.

She burst through the front door. "Did you say Brome Ridge?" she asked Reed.

He stopped dead, as if frozen to the floor.

"I've been wanting to get up there before I leave," she rattled on. "I've only got a couple of days left. Would you mind?" she smiled brightly.

"Forget it," said Reed.

"Take her along," said Caleb.

Reed shot his brother a glare. "It's a working trip, not a picnic."

"I won't get in the way," Katrina promised. Trapped in a pickup, Reed would have to talk to her. She'd be heading back to New York City very soon, and she wasn't ready to pretend their attraction had never happened.

"You always get in the way." Reed's glare turned on her, his gray eyes hard as slate.

"Quit being such a jerk," Caleb put in. "Go ahead, Katrina."

"Back off, Caleb."

"Which truck?" asked Katrina.

Caleb nodded. "Parts are in the back of the green one."

"She's not going," Reed ground out.

But Katrina was already on her way down the stairs, heading across the wide driveway turnaround to the green pickup truck.

She hopped in the passenger side, slammed the door shut, and watched Reed argue with Caleb a few minutes longer. Finally, he turned, stalking across the driveway toward the pickup.

He yanked open the passenger door. "Get out."

"No."

"Yes."

She nodded to where Caleb was staring at them from the top of the stairs. "Your brother thinks you've gone insane."

"You are not going to do this to me," he vowed.

"Do what?" She mustered up an expression of calm innocence. "What is it you think I'm doing here, Reed?"

He blinked, a split second of uncertainty crossing his face.

"All I want to do is talk," she pressed. "I'm going to be gone in a couple days. It may be years before I'm back. You're a nice guy. You helped me with my ankle. You built me a stationary bike. You don't want a chance to say goodbye?"

He stared at her in silence, and she could read his hesitation. He was wondering if he'd imagined her intense attraction to him, their near-combustible chemistry, the fact that they shouldn't be allowed to be alone together if they didn't want it to race out of control.

He wasn't imagining a thing. But she didn't have to tell him that.

"Do you think I can't keep my hands off you?" She kept her tone light and teasing, even though nervous energy was churning its way through her stomach. "Is your ego really that big?"

His jaw snapped tight, and he stepped back, abruptly slamming the car door.

Katrina let out a breath of relief.

He yanked open the driver's door, dropped into the seat, started the engine and peeled out of the driveway, leaving a rooster tail of dust and small stones.

Katrina rocked against the passenger door, then flew upright. She grappled with her seat belt, fastening it tight and low across her hips.

Neither of them spoke for a good half hour as they wound their way along the rutted dirt-and-grass road up through the trees to where the pastures fanned out on the higher rangelands. Reed shifted the truck into four-wheel drive, and Katrina hung on as they traversed a shallow creek.

"Is this going to be a long, silent ride?" she finally asked.

"This was always going to be a long silent ride. I expected to be alone."

"Well, good news," she announced brightly. "I can make small talk and entertain you."

He shifted to a lower gear, pointing the truck up a steep, muddy rise. "I guess the cocktail-party circuit had to come in handy at some point."

"That's where you want to go? Insulting me?"

"I don't want to *go* anywhere. And it was an observation, not an insult."

"You're lying."

"Okay," he allowed. "It was a joke."

"It wasn't funny."

He quirked a half smile. "I thought it was."

"You're not a very nice man, Reed Terrell."

He looked her way for a long moment.

She glanced to the rutted road, to Reed, and back again. There was a curve coming up. She waited for him to turn his attention to driving. "Uh, Reed."

"I'm not a nice man," he confirmed softly. "And you should remember that." Then he glanced out the windshield and made an abrupt left turn.

Katrina was forced to hold on tight again. "I'm not afraid of you, Reed."

"That's okay. I'm scared enough for the both of us."

Katrina didn't know how to respond to that. The idea of Reed being afraid of anything was patently absurd.

A long time later, the truck rocked to a halt on the dirt road, an aspen grove fanning out on the downhill side, and a steeper hill running up the other.

Reed shut off the engine. "We'll have to walk it from here."

"Walk?"

He pushed the driver's door open. "Unless you want to wait here. I shouldn't be more than a few hours."

"No, no." She reached for her own door handle. "Walking is fine." Luckily, she'd worn comfortable runners. Her midcalf, low-rise tights weren't perfect for bushwhacking, neither was her tank top, but she gamely hopped from the seat.

Reed retrieved a worn leather tool belt from the box of the truck, strapping it around his waist, stuffing a hammer, tape measure, screwdrivers, wrenches and pliers into the loops and pockets. Then he tucked some lengths of rod and pipe beneath his arm, hoisted out a battered red toolbox and turned for a trail that wound up the side of the hill.

Katrina quickly fell into step with him. "You want me to carry anything?"

He snorted. "Yeah, right."

"I was just trying to be helpful."

His long strides were incredibly efficient, and she had to work to keep up.

He glanced over his shoulder. "Let's not pretend you're going to be any use as a pack animal."

"Let's not pretend you're going to give me a break."

"You should have stayed back at the ranch house."

The trail grew steeper, and, as they neared the crest, she was forced to grasp at the branches of trees to pull herself forward. "And miss all this?"

Reed stood tall on the top of the ridge, a sloping meadow splayed out before them, falling away to a deep valley before rising to the next hilltop.

Katrina sucked in a few breaths. "There's a well up here?"

Reed pointed north along the ridgeline. "It pumps into a pond around the bend. The cattle like it up here in late summer. This meadow catches the prevailing wind and that keeps the bugs down. But if there's no water source, they have to trek all the way back to the river."

"See that, you are a nice guy."

"I'm a practical guy." His gazed scanned her. "You doing okay?"

"Perfectly fine."

"Your ankle?"

"Almost better."

"Okay." He started along the uneven ridge, quickly outpacing her and drawing away.

If she'd hoped to engage him in a conversation, it wasn't going to work out. Reed was obviously determined to keep her at a distance. Not that she knew what to say. Just getting him alone had proven so difficult she hadn't formulated much of a plan beyond that.

After hiking for nearly an hour, they came to a muddy-bottomed pond beneath a twenty-foot windmill tower. The wind had picked up, and the whirring, clunking noise of the windmill made conversation difficult.

Reed set down the toolbox and began inspecting the arms that connected the pump to the windmill. A complex series of tubes and connections ran between the two. After a few moments, he selected a wrench and pulled hard on what seemed to be a stubborn bolt. It broke free, and he disconnected the mechanism.

Now that Katrina was standing still, she began to cool off. It didn't help that the sun had disappeared behind a thick layer of cloud; they were completely exposed to the wind here on the ridge. She had to fight off the odd mosquito, but she didn't dare complain. Instead, she gritted her teeth while Reed worked his way through whatever problem he'd discovered.

When the rain started, Reed swore.

He turned to look at Katrina, then he did a double take. "Are you cold?"

"I'm fine," she responded, but her teeth were chattering.

Reed dropped a big wrench, swore again, and stalked toward her. As he'd done when he found her on the trail with her broken bicycle, he stripped off his shirt.

"I don't need—"

"Shut up."

"I'm sorry," she found herself saying, even as the warmth of his cotton shirt wrapped around her. She tugged the ends together and crossed her arms over her chest.

"Sit down," he told her. "It'll be less windy if you're low to the ground." Then he glanced up at the sky and heaved a frustrated sigh. "You shouldn't have come up here."

"I'm fine," she repeated, perching herself on a clump of meadow grass. He was right, sitting down did help to keep her out of the wind. Now, if only the rain would stop.

But the rain didn't stop, and the more it rained, the more frustrated Reed became, and the more colorful the language coming out of his mouth. As the rain turned to a downpour, the wrenches kept slipping from his hands. He was obviously having trouble seeing clearly, and he dropped something. He peered into the mud, feeling his way around the tufts of grass.

After a long search, he tossed the wrench to the ground. "Damn it! Katrina, I can't let go of this. You're going to have to help."

She came to her feet, his wet shirt hanging loosely to midthigh. "What should I do?"

He took what seemed to be a calming breath. "Look in the toolbox. Lift out the top tray and see if you can find a nut-and-bolt set. It's better if it has some washers."

"Washers?"

"Wide, round disks of metal."

"Right." Trying not to shiver from the wet and wind, she opened the lid to the toolbox. The stormy day was complicated by the fact that the sun was now sinking behind the hills.

"Can you see anything?" he asked.

"Not really." She reached in to feel her way around instead.

"Don't!" Reed shouted, and she immediately stilled.

His voice moderated. "Some of the things in there are sharp. You could cut yourself."

"I can't see," she apologized.

"It's okay. Close the lid." He waited while she closed it and flipped the catches. "Now, can you pick up the box and move it over here?"

Katrina stood, bent down and gripped the handle of the metal toolbox with both hands. Then she pulled up with all her might. Nothing happened. She screwed up her determination and tried again.

It lifted a couple of inches off the ground, and she moved it forward before dropping it down.

"Don't hurt yourself," Reed warned.

"I'm good," she gasped. She lifted again, swinging it closer. Then again. And again.

"You're doing fine," he told her.

"This is pathetic."

"For a cowboy, yeah," he agreed. "For a ballerina, we make allowances."

"Thank goodness I'm going back to New York City."

There was a breath of silence before he spoke. "Thank goodness."

"I'm almost—" Her feet slipped out from under her, and she landed in an undignified heap on the muddy ground, brown water spraying around her. "There," she finished, seriously regretting her decision to come along on this trip. Exactly *why* did she think she needed to be alone with Reed?

"You okay?" he asked.

"Define *okay.*"

"Are you injured?"

"No. Bruised, yes."

Reed stretched out his arm, his fingertips almost made it to the handle of the toolbox. Katrina gave it a hard shove, sliding the box, and he grasped the handle in his fist, lifting it and moving it to where he could search for a bolt.

"I can't believe you carried that thing all the way up the hill," she told him.

"I have size, muscle mass and testosterone on my side."

"You're incredibly useful."

"And you're incredibly pretty." He glanced at her. "Well, not right now."

She clenched her jaw. "I hate being pretty."

"What's to hate? You bat those beautiful blue eyes and the world falls at your feet."

"Is that how you see it?"

"That's not how I see it. That's the way it is."

"You think the world gives me a free ride."

His opinion didn't surprise her. She'd known all along that was how he felt, that she was some decorative plaything. He was as bad as Quentin. Though she supposed she should credit Reed with trying to keep his distance. At least he didn't think it was his right to sleep with her.

"I think your world is a completely different place than mine," he said.

"Do you think yours is better?" She honestly wanted to know.

"I think it's harder," he admitted, still searching through the toolbox. "I don't think everyone can make it out here, and I think—"

"You think it's *easy* becoming a professional dancer?"

"I didn't say that."

"You thought it."

"I was about to say, I think people stay cleaner in your world." He seemed to find what he was looking for, pulling an object out of the box and squinting at it in the dusk.

"I work hard," she told him defensively.

"You should work at getting rid of that chip on your shoulder." He returned to the repair.

"I do not have—"

"Admit it, Katrina. You think you're better than the rest of us."

"I—"

"You live in the bright lights of a big city. You dress in designer clothes. You hobnob with the rich and famous. You eat in the best restaurants. And every few years, you come back to Colorado to go slumming." He reefed hard on the wrench.

"That's not *fair.*"

"And for some reason, this time, you've decided I should be part of your down-home experience."

Katrina's jaw dropped open. Reed thought she was slumming it by kissing him? Was he crazy?

"Thanks, but no thanks, Katrina." He rose, collecting some of the scattered tools. "I'll keep my self-respect, and you can run back to those champagne-swilling dandies at your snooty cocktail parties."

Katrina lurched to her feet. "Wow," was all she managed. She stared at his slick, half-naked body, powerful and magnificent in the waning light. "Did you ever get that wrong."

He bent to fiddle with something on the pump contraption, and the piston came to life with a rhythmic, sloshing sound.

Apparently satisfied, he closed a sheet-metal cover and fastened it. He gathered up the remaining tools, shoving some of them back into his tool belt, putting others in the box and securing the lid.

He stood and looked around at the dark surroundings. "We have to get back."

He waited for her to stand and start moving, then he took the lead, making his way along the ridge, heading toward the steep trail that led to where they'd parked the truck. Thankfully, he took it slower this time, and Katrina didn't have to struggle quite so hard to keep up.

But when they came to the top of the trail, Reed stopped abruptly. The top of the bank had sloughed away, and the trail had turned to a rivulet of mud and water, coursing down in the direction of the road.

"I don't think so," said Reed, holding out his arm as a block between her and the edge of the bluff.

"What do we do now?" she asked, peering into the gloom of the aspen grove, listening to the whoosh of the water below them.

He set the toolbox down, well back from the edge, and he stripped off the leather tool belt, plunking it on top. "I'm not dragging you through the bush in the dark, that's for sure."

"I'll be fine," she assured him, wondering if it was a lie. Just how difficult would it be to make their way back through the thick woods?

"There's a line shack about a mile that way." He gestured with his head in the opposite direction of the well. "We'll wait it out there."

That seemed like an only slightly more palatable option.

"It'll be pitch-dark by the time we get there." She was already having a hard time picking her way across the uneven meadow. And she was cold and wet and miserable.

"Yes, it will. So, up you go." He scooped her into his arms.

"Hey!"

"You'd rather walk?"

"Yes!"

"No, you wouldn't. I've got leather boots and long pants, and I've been hiking these hills my entire life." He adjusted her in his arms.

"You can't carry me a whole mile."

"I could carry you twenty miles without breaking a sweat. And even if I couldn't, I'm not letting you risk your ankle."

"This is ridiculous," she huffed.

"Welcome to my world, Katrina. It can be cold, wet, dirty and unforgiving."

She wrapped her arms around his neck in surrender. "This is exactly why I went off to boarding school."

"You were right to do that." His tone was gruff. "And you're right to stay away. Colorado's a bad place for you."

Katrina didn't disagree. But for the first time in her life, it didn't feel like an insult.

Six

Inside the line shack, Reed set Katrina on her feet, instructing her to hold still while he located a box of matches to light the two oil lamps that would be sitting on the small kitchen table. He knew where everything was in the compact, single-room shack, and he didn't want her walking into the furniture.

"Will somebody come looking for us?" her voice wafted across the cool room to him.

"What do you mean?"

"When we don't come back, will they come looking?"

Reed couldn't help but smile to himself. He struck a match, lifted the glass chamber and lit the lamp's wick. The idea that Caleb would mount a rescue operation because Reed was a few hours late was laughable.

"I'm old enough to stay out after dark," he told Katrina. He quickly moved the match to the second lamp and lit it, as well. Warm yellow light filled the small room, highlighting a compact kitchen, two worn armchairs, a bed in one corner, along with the scarred wooden table and four battered kitchen chairs.

"Won't they worry?" she pressed.

"Not for a day or so."

"But we could be hurt."

"We're not hurt."

"They don't know that."

He took in her bedraggled appearance and tried not to feel guilty, reminding himself that she was the one who'd insisted on coming along. "They'll know that odds are we're stuck."

"But—"

"This kind of thing happens all the time." Next, Reed went to the small woodstove between the armchairs. There was a cardboard box nearby with old newspapers, dry kindling and split firewood. He opened the glass-fronted stove door.

"Not to me, it doesn't," Katrina huffed to his back.

He heard her make her way farther into the shack. "We'll be fine."

"I know."

He crumpled the paper. "So stop worrying."

"I'm not worried."

He laid down a few pieces of kindling. "I can tell."

"I'm not worried. Cold, maybe."

"It'll warm up soon."

"And hungry."

"You? Hungry? Who'd have guessed."

"I eat," she protested.

"About enough to keep a bird alive." Not that she was skinny. She had a killer compact figure, smooth curves, tight muscle tone. He set a few pieces of firewood on top of the kindling.

"I guess I'm an easy keeper."

He grinned at her horse reference, striking a match then tossing it into the stove, watching the paper catch and light before closing the door. "Well, I'm definitely not. I'll see what I can find us to eat."

"There's food here?"

"I hope so." It was going to be a long night if he couldn't find a can of stew or a jar of peanut butter.

"What can I do?"

It was on the tip of Reed's tongue to make a joke about how

little she could do out here, but before he could speak, he caught a glimpse of her delicate features. Her soaking, stringy hair, those wet, bedraggled clothes, and he didn't have the heart to tease her.

"Check the bureau beside the bed. Sometimes the cowboys leave dry clothes in it."

In reaction to his words, she shook water droplets from her fingertips, and took a long look down at her soaking clothes.

Reed could stand to stay wet if he had to, but he'd much rather dry off and warm up.

She headed for the far corner of the shack while he moved one of the lamps to the small countertop and checked the kitchen cupboard. He found a box of pancake mix and a bottle of maple syrup. Not exactly gourmet, but it would keep them from going hungry.

"Not much here," Katrina called to report.

He turned, squinting into the darkened end of the room.

She came toward him, into the lamplight, holding something in each hand. "Tops or bottoms?" She unfurled a pair of gray sweatpants and a large, white T-shirt.

He couldn't help being reminded of his offer to share his pajamas. He nodded to the sweatpants. "Looks like those might be a bit large for you."

"Unless I want a blanket." She tossed them his way, and he snagged them out of midair.

She shook out the T-shirt. "Can I trust you to turn your back while I change?"

"Absolutely," he vowed. "My mama raised me to be a gentleman."

"My auntie raised me to be a bohemian artist."

"I don't even know what that means."

Her blue eyes danced as she obviously fought a smile. "It means I probably won't turn my back while *you* change."

Reed fought the temptation to tease her in return. But that was a dangerous road to go down. Instead, he forced himself to turn away, concentrating on finding a bowl in the sparsely equipped cupboard. It was already going to be a very long night. "Change your clothes, Katrina."

While he whipped up the batter and heated a pan on the two-burner propane stove, she rustled her way into the dry T-shirt.

"Your turn," she told him, moving up beside him at the counter. "That smells good."

He handed her the spatula. "You know how to cook pancakes?"

She took it. "Haven't a clue."

He glanced down at her, his chest contracting at the sight. Her hair was raked smoothly back. Her face was shiny clean. And the boxy T-shirt accentuated her slim frame, showing off her shapely legs.

It took him a second to find his voice. "When those bubbles burst, flip it over."

"I can do that." She determinedly took up a position in front of the mini stove.

She'd laid out her wet tank top and slacks, along with Reed's soaking shirt, on a kitchen chair near the woodstove to dry. Reed stripped his way out of his own jeans, stepped out of his boxers and pulled on the soft sweatpants. Katrina kept her back turned. He'd known she was bluffing.

She gave a little whoop when she successfully flipped the pancake.

"Now what?" she called over her shoulder.

He draped his clothes on another kitchen chair and moved up behind her. "Give it a minute, then we'll start another."

"I'm pretty good at this," she bragged.

"Outstanding," he agreed. He retrieved a dinner plate so they could stack the pancakes.

She dumped the pancake from the pan onto the plate and placed the pan back on the stove.

"First you spoon in the batter," he demonstrated. Then he tipped the pan so that the batter spread thin.

"You're very domesticated," she noted.

"Survival instinct."

"Your mom teach you to do that?"

Reed nodded through the familiar hitch in his chest. Even after all these years, he couldn't help but react whenever he talked about his mother. Which wasn't often. "She did."

Katrina's voice lowered. "How old were you when it happened?"

He pretended to misunderstand the question. "When she taught me to cook pancakes?"

"When she died," Katrina clarified.

He kept his voice even. "Seventeen."

There was a silent pause.

"I remember she was beautiful," said Katrina.

"She was," he agreed. And she'd been kind and gentle, and far too delicate to be toiling in the wilds of Colorado ranch country. Not unlike Katrina.

"You mind talking about her?"

Reed bought himself a moment by flipping the pancake. "I don't mind," he lied.

"It must have been hard."

"It was."

"And then Caleb left."

"What are you trying to ask me?" Reed would rather get to the point and get out of this conversation.

She shrugged. "I'm not sure. How it impacted you, losing such a big part of your family all at once. If you were lonely."

"Were you lonely?" he asked her, instead of answering.

"Huh?"

"You left your family."

She nodded but didn't elaborate. A few seconds later, she wrapped both hands around the handle of the frying pan and dumped the next pancake onto the plate.

"You want to try?" he offered, relieved to move on to something more mundane.

"Sure." She accepted the spoon, doled out the batter and tipped the pan.

"Well done." He smiled.

"I was lonely," she admitted, setting the pan back down on the heat.

He clenched his jaw. So much for letting the maudlin stuff go.

"I was only ten years old," Katrina continued, eyes taking on a faraway expression. "For a while there, I really wanted to come home. But Auntie Coco talked me out of it. She was a pistol. No matter how much the other kids teased me, no matter how hard the studies or the dancing, no matter how much I missed my mom, she'd tell me to keep my chin up, my head clear and try just a little bit harder."

Reed found himself engaging. "What was the most difficult part?"

Katrina turned to face him, and it hit him just how close together they were standing. "What was the most difficult part for you?"

He gazed into her eyes, debating whether to lie. For so many years now, whenever he was asked about his father, he'd glossed over Wilton's cruelty. It was an ingrained reflex. But he found he didn't want to lie to Katrina.

"That my father was junkyard-dog mean."

Her delicate brows went up.

"He was dictatorial, demanding and ruthless. He yelled at me every day of my life, hit me and nearly worked me to death for ten long years." Reed reached around her and flipped the next pancake.

"Are you serious?" Katrina's voice was a horrified whisper.

"I am."

"But why didn't you leave? Caleb left. Couldn't you have—"

"And let Wilton win?"

Katrina paused. "So, you were taking a stand?"

"I was."

She seemed to ponder his words.

"You think I was nuts." He'd sure heard enough of that reaction from Caleb.

But Katrina gave her head a slow shake. "I'm envious." Moving in what seemed like slow motion, she reached up to brush her fingertips along his bicep.

His muscle contracted under her touch, and it was all he could do to hold himself still.

She tipped her chin and met his gaze. "I admire you. There are days when I wish I could tell the world to go to hell and back it up with brute strength."

The urge to haul her into his arms was so powerful, that he had either to move away or give in. He used retrieving the next pancake as an excuse. "Hungry?"

Her hesitation lasted only a split second. "Starving."

"Bring the plates," he instructed. "And some forks." He transferred the pancakes and the bottle of maple syrup to the small table near the center of the room. He moved the oil lamp to make room for the dishes, and its light bounced off the scars that had been gouged into the wooden tabletop over many long years of use.

She joined him, taking one of the two chairs that weren't being used as clothing racks.

He sat down and pulled in his chair. "It's not exactly the Ritz."

She gave an exaggerated pout. "You mean no caviar and champagne?"

Using his fork, he transferred two of the pancakes to her plate, then he pushed the bottle of syrup her way. "And the wine pairings leave something to be desired."

She blinked at him over the soft yellow lamplight. "You surprise me when you do that."

"Do what?" Deciding it didn't make sense to use up another plate, he moved his clean one back to the counter and shifted the serving platter with the remaining two pancakes in front of him.

She watched his movements until he sat down. "When you talk about wine pairings and Dior."

"You are such a snob."

"I'm not," she protested, hand resting on her fork, showing no signs of getting started on the meal.

Since she wasn't using the syrup, he poured some of it on his own pancakes then pushed it back to her.

"You've spent your entire life on a ranch in Colorado," she elaborated.

He cut into the tender pancake. "Do you honestly think you're making it better?"

"Okay. How do you know about wine pairings?"

He reached across the table and drizzled the syrup on her pancakes. No sense in letting the things get cold. "How do *you* know about wine pairings?"

"Fine restaurants, parties, I read a little."

He gave a chuckle. "Me, too."

"But—"

"I've been to Denver and Seattle, even as far as L.A. I once toured a vineyard in the Napa Valley. Get over it and eat your pancakes."

She ignored his instruction. "Really? You toured a vineyard?"

"Surprised they let me in?" He took a bite. He wasn't about to sit here and starve waiting for her.

"You're twisting my words."

"I don't need to twist them to make you sound like a snob, princess. You're doing that all by yourself."

"You surprised me." To her credit, she did sound contrite.

"Apparently," he allowed.

She glanced down at her plate then inhaled deeply. "These really do smell great."

"Taste them. They're pretty good."

She cut tentatively into one with her fork. "It's been years since I've had maple syrup."

"Welcome to the wild side."

"I probably don't need two."

"You probably do."

She lifted her fork to her mouth. "Here we go."

He couldn't believe she was making such a production out of it. But finally, she took a bite, chewed and swallowed.

"Oh, my," she breathed. Her eyes sparkled and her red lips turned up in a beautiful smile.

Reed instantly lost his appetite for anything but her.

"Good?" he managed in a slightly strangled voice.

"Ambrosia." She consumed another bite. "Who needs wine pairings anyway."

"You like it on the wild side?" He didn't intend it, but his tone turned the question into a double entendre.

She glanced up. Her expression stilled. Her gaze darkened. "Yes."

Reed's fork slipped from his fingertips, and his hands clenched into fists. Though his brain screamed no, his desire shouted it down. He gave in to his desire.

"Come here," he commanded.

Her expression turned serious. She rose on her bare feet, moving toward him, draped in that boxy, oversize T-shirt. Her hair was stringy and wet, makeup smudged around her eyes, yet she still managed to be the most beautiful woman he'd ever seen.

He snagged her hand, eased his chair back, pulled her into his lap and captured her lips in one smooth motion. He wrapped one arm around her gorgeous body, cradling her face with his free hand as his lips and tongue plundered her mouth. He'd missed her taste so much. How on earth had he managed to stay away?

Her body curled against his bare chest, delicate hands wrapping around his back, their warmth all but burning his skin. She returned his kisses with passion and enthusiasm.

His fingertips found her bare thigh, trailing slowly beneath the hem of her shirt. It took him mere seconds to realize she was naked beneath, and he swore under his breath.

"What?" she breathed, her rear end pressing tightly against his growing arousal.

"I'm not stopping this time." He kissed her again.

"I sure hope not." She kissed him back.

"But this is a bad idea." His mouth opened wide, and he all but devoured her.

When the kiss finally ended, she surprised him by turning in his lap, straddling him, her arms snaking around his neck, even as the tips of her breasts brushed against his chest. "I promise you," she whispered huskily, her maple-sweet breath puffing against him. "The world will still be turning tomorrow morning."

Reed didn't doubt that was true. But he feared his own world might tip on its axis and never go back to right.

Then she kissed him again, and all reason left his brain.

He acted on instinct, moving his hands beneath her shirt, sliding along her sides, pushing the soft fabric higher and higher. They didn't stop until he'd peeled it over her head, tossing it aside, gazing at her perfection for long, satisfying seconds before he wrapped her naked body in his arms.

"You are so incredibly gorgeous." He kissed the tip of her shoulder, then the tender hollow of her neck.

"Does it matter?" she asked.

"That you're gorgeous?" He brushed the pad of his thumb across her nipple.

She gasped. "Yes."

He did it again.

"I meant—"

Again.

She groaned and arched her back, and he leaned down to kiss one hard pink nipple, drawing it into his mouth, swirling his tongue, finding immense satisfaction in the way her fingertips dug into his biceps.

But he forced himself to withdraw. If he wasn't careful, they'd be making love right here on a kitchen chair. There was a bed in the shack. It wasn't much of a bed, but he was determined to use it.

He took up her mouth with his, came carefully to his feet, holding her tight, her legs still wrapped around his waist. He was never more grateful for the habitual condom tucked into his wallet.

They crossed to the bed, and he dragged back the covers, easing down until he was sitting, lying back, drawing her full length on top of him before turning enough to strip off his sweats and pull her naked body against his own.

He ordered himself to slow down their kisses, curb his wayward hands that seemed determined to experience every inch of her soft skin. Her legs were toned and perfectly shaped. Her stomach was flat, creamy skin, with a sexy sweet navel. Her breasts were exactly the right size, fitting the palms of his hands, nipples dark pink, beaded under his touch.

Her shoulders were smooth, neck long and sexy, and her blond hair splayed messily out across the pillow, beckoning his hands. He burrowed his face into it and inhaled.

"I could breathe you in all day," he whispered.

Her hands trailed across the flat of his chest. "And I could touch you forever." She turned and met his gaze. "Or kiss you," she offered, moving in on his lips, voice going lower. "I could kiss you forever."

Her words nearly caved his chest in with emotion. He cradled her face, holding her steady while he kissed her long and deeply.

She wrapped a leg over his body and his hips reflexively arched toward her. His hand slid over her breast, down her stomach, gently easing between her legs.

She flinched, and he froze, pulling back. "Something wrong?"

She shook her head.

"Katrina?"

She kissed him deeply, but something had changed. There was a tension in her body that hadn't been there before.

"You change your mind?" It might kill him, but she was entitled.

"No," she insisted, kissing him again.

"Stop," he ordered.

"You change your mind?" she asked.

"Of course not. Are you kidding me?" He drew away so that he could look her in the eyes. "Tell me."

She clamped her jaw.

He knew he should leave the bed, but he couldn't help hoping there was a simple explanation. Something other than the fact she had cold feet. Which he'd have to respect. A pithy swear word formed on his lips. But he kept it there. "You can say no, Katrina. I'll be—"

"I'm a virgin," she blurted out.

He reared back. *"What?"*

"I haven't changed my mind. I'm just a little nervous."

"What?" he repeated, unable to articulate anything more coherent.

She didn't answer, just stared at him with those gorgeous blue eyes, looking more desirable, more forbidden, sexier than he could possibly be expected to stand.

"I want it to be you, Reed," she whispered.

He tried to shake his head, but he couldn't seem to make the simple motion. A better man would walk away. A better man would have *stayed* away in the first place. Up to this moment, he'd have claimed he was a better man.

Then she reached up to touch his cheek, her fingertips trembling ever so slightly. "I *so* want it to be you."

Reed catapulted over the edge. He swooped in to kiss her, telling himself to be gentle, but losing the battle with instinct. His hands roamed the satin of her skin, lips trailing behind, kissing her everywhere, swearing to himself he was going to make it good for her, but unable to slow the pace of his desire.

He touched her again, fingers easing inside her hot, snug body, jolts of unadulterated lust ricocheting through every fiber of his being.

"I don't want to hurt you," he rasped. He couldn't stand the thought.

"You won't," she told him.

But he knew she was wrong. "I will."

"Then just get it over with."

"I don't think so." He brushed and stroked, until she relaxed, then squirmed beneath his hand. Her skin was flushed, and her breath was coming in quick pants.

Then he moved over her, didn't give her a chance to tense and swiftly pushed in solid.

She gasped and reflexively jerked away from the invasion.

But he held her fast, gritting his teeth, forcing himself to still. "Sorry."

"It's—" She sucked in a couple of breaths. "Ouch."

"Yeah." He kissed her gently, slowly, savoring the taste of her lips, holding his lust in check while he let her body get used to him.

Then she kissed him back. Her arms went around him. And her hips gently flexed.

He stroked her thighs, positioning her legs, moving slowly at first. Then, encouraged by her reaction, he increased the pace. She was hot and slick and gorgeous in his arms. Her scent surrounded him, while her breathing seemed to echo in his soul. He couldn't stop tasting her, couldn't stop touching her, as his primal brain kicked his body into an accelerating rhythm.

Heat flashed in front of his eyes, popping like colored fireworks. He braced an arm in the small of her back, tilting her toward him, as he kissed her deeply, thrusting his tongue in and out of her mouth. A roar in his ears rose like a freight train, obliterating everything else.

He barely heard her cry out his name. But her body shuddered, convulsing around him, and he surrendered to paradise.

The world came slowly back into focus, and he realized he had to be crushing her.

"I'm sorry," he shifted.

"No!" She tightened her hold. "Don't move."

"You okay?" He pushed his weight onto his elbows, freeing a hand to brush her damp, messy hair back from her face.

"I'm not sure."

"Did I hurt you?"

"Little bit."

"Little bit?" he pressed. "But not a big bit?"

She mustered a smile, and he couldn't resist kissing it. Then he braced her body against his.

"Hold still for a minute," he instructed. "Let me do the work." He gently rolled onto his back, bringing her with him until she was on top, and there was no danger of him squishing her. Her slight weight felt good against him.

"You can stay there just as long as you like," he told her.

"Really?" She pulled back far enough to look him in the eyes. Her gaze was soft on his, voice barely above a whisper. "Because that might be a very, very long time."

"No problem." He brushed the pad of his thumb across her

swollen lips. "It'll be two, maybe three days before they come looking."

He'd happily keep her in his bed that long and longer. He didn't know what had happened, or more accurately, what had *not* happened in her past: why she'd waited, or why she'd picked him. But right now nothing mattered except that she had.

"I went to an all-girls school," Katrina found herself explaining, still draped across Reed's naked body. She'd hate him to think there was something wrong with her. "From when I was ten all the way to college. I mean, we saw the boys from the affiliated school occasionally. But it wasn't as if we had time to get to know them."

"Are you saying you didn't date in high school?"

"I didn't date in high school," she confirmed.

She slowly slid from his body to his side and let her cheek rest on his shoulder.

He settled a wool blanket over them.

"And then I went to the college affiliated with Liberty Ballet," she continued. "I've been really busy with my dancing career. So, you know, even though I live in New York City, and my social life is quite active with all the events and parties—"

"Katrina?"

"What?"

"Are you apologizing for being a virgin?"

"Yes. I mean, no. I'm not apologizing." Exactly. "I'm telling you it wasn't my fault."

His body rumbled with laughter, and his lips brushed the top of her head. "You don't understand men at all."

"That's what I'm trying to tell you." The man was exasperating.

"Yeah?" His tone turned serious. "Well, listen up, Katrina. Because I understand men perfectly."

"Bully for you."

"You've got it all wrong."

"I've got what all wrong?"

"How I'm feeling. What I'm thinking."

"Okay, what are you feeling and thinking?"

He seemed to choose his words, his tone deep near her ear. "I'm feeling privileged and proud. I'm thinking someday, a long time from now, when I'm very old and very tired, and there's nothing left of my life, I'll be remembering this night, and you, and that I was the first."

Something flip-flopped Katrina's stomach. She drew back, tipping her chin so that she could gauge his expression. "That's a really great line, Reed."

"Thank you."

"Ever used it before?"

"Of course not. How can you ask that?"

So he was serious? He'd be thinking of her on his deathbed? She had no idea how to respond, so she laid her head back down on his shoulder and just breathed for a few minutes.

Reed spoke first. "But is there something wrong with all the men in New York City?"

"Not to my knowledge."

"Because I was with you all of five minutes before I realized I'd never be able to keep my hands off you."

"Five minutes?" She couldn't help but be pleased to hear that.

"Did they ask you on dates and you turned them down?"

"Five minutes?" she repeated.

"Focus, Katrina."

"I am focusing."

"The men? In New York City?"

She gave up. It was really just her ego that wanted him to admit it anyway. "Some asked for dates," she admitted. "Most I turned down. The others didn't really work out. And Quentin Foster, well he just skipped right to the proposition."

"Quentin Foster."

"Just a guy," said Katrina, regretting even saying the man's name out loud.

"Did you meet him at one of your fancy parties?"

She shook her head. "He's on the board of directors for Liberty. I've known him for a while. He's a big contributor, and people kowtow to him. I don't think he has much of a life outside the ballet company, because he's always hanging around. He comes to rehearsals. And he's forever closeted with the ballet company director discussing… I don't know what they discuss, funding, I guess."

Reed came up on his elbow. "And he propositioned you?"

She scrunched her face up in a grimace. "Yes."

"As in solicited sex?"

"Is there another kind of proposition?"

Reed blinked several times. "A man in a position of power over you actually asked you to sleep with him?"

She came up on her elbow, mirroring his posture. "Is there something confusing about the way I'm putting this?"

"You said no," Reed confirmed.

"Absolutely. Quentin had hinted around for months, and I tried to ignore him and avoid him. But then one day, he cornered me, and came right out with it, and I said no."

"Good for you."

"Thank you."

"What did he do then?"

She dropped her head back down on the pillow. "He was upset."

Reed waited.

Katrina didn't feel like lying, and she didn't feel like dressing it up, so she told Reed the truth. "He told me he could be a valuable friend, but I didn't want him as an enemy."

"When was this?" Reed's voice had gone cold.

"About three weeks ago. And then those strange things—" She caught herself. It was wild, paranoid speculation. It didn't even deserve to be said out loud.

"Strange things?" Reed's voice went cold. "You're talking about the cables and your ballet shoes."

"No," she lied.

"Then what?"

"I'm not going to tell you. It's too crazy. I'm too crazy. Everything's fine."

He laid his head down on the pillow, touching his forehead to hers. His voice went low again. "You have to tell me."

"Why?"

"This is pillow talk. All secrets are revealed during pillow talk."

"This isn't a secret."

"Good. Then there's no reason not to tell me."

"It's silly."

He shrugged. "Then who cares if you tell me or not?"

She heaved a heavy sigh. "Fine. But you can't laugh. And you can't call me a princess."

"I'm going to call you a princess whether you tell me what's on your mind or not." He brushed a few stray hairs from her cheek. "I like calling you princess. You should take it as a compliment."

"It's not a compliment. You're telling me that I'm spoiled."

"But in a delightful, exotic, sexy way."

"Ha!"

"Tell me the whole story, Katrina."

"Fine. He propositioned me a few times. And then he phoned me here and asked me if I'd thought about his offer. I told him I wouldn't change my mind."

"And when did your ballet shoe fail?"

"Why are you giving me the third degree?" It wasn't as if she'd done anything wrong.

"When did you hurt your ankle?"

"Can we back to kissing or something?" She really didn't want to talk about this.

"Give me the chronology."

"No."

Reed ignored her answer. "First, he propositions you. You say no. You narrowly miss some cables. He asks again. You say no. Your shoe fails and you're injured. He asks again. You say no…"

"That's the most far-fetched theory I've ever heard."

"No. That's what you're thinking yourself."

"There's absolutely no way—"

"Did someone check the shoes afterward?"

"I threw them away."

Reed raised a meaningful brow.

Katrina understood his suspicions. “I have a dozen pairs of ballet shoes. Nobody could have guessed which ones I’d use that day.” But she was convincing herself as much as she was convincing Reed.

He seemed to ponder that information.

She wasn’t going to buy into any kind of paranoia. “Those were accidents, coincidences.”

Reed slowly smiled. “Okay,” he agreed.

“Yeah?”

“Yeah.”

She let her body relax, trailing her fingertips across his chest. “I shouldn’t have said anything. We were having fun, and I messed it up.”

Reed slipped his arms around her, drawing her close, speaking against her ear. “You were right to say something. You should always tell me when something goes wrong. Have I mentioned that I know how to fix things?”

“There’s nothing to fix.”

“Maybe not.”

“Maybe the shoes, if I still had them.”

Reed chuckled, and Katrina forced the theory from her mind. There was no connection between Quentin and the accidents. He hadn’t even called again. Clearly, he’d given up. She could relax and stop worrying. When she went back to New York City, everything would be fine.

Seven

The next day, it took them two hours to make their way back down the washed-out trail. Then it took Reed four hours to dig the truck out of the muddy road. And they had to stop every half mile or so to remove debris from the road or winch the truck across a particularly rough patch.

All in all, as a "morning after" went, it left a lot to be desired. Though Reed continually told Katrina to wait inside the cab of the truck, she donned a pair of leather work gloves and helped as best she could. Her efforts were pathetic, and she ended up with scratches on her arms and a bruised knee.

It was nearly six in the evening when they pulled the mud-caked truck up to the Terrell ranch house. To Katrina's surprise, her brother Travis was in the yard with Caleb, loading a couple of horses into a trailer. They both waved a cursory greeting and went back to their work.

As Katrina jumped from the pickup, Mandy trotted around the barn on horseback, smiling at them as she dismounted.

"You're just in time for dinner," she called, leading the dun mare toward the truck.

"Were you worried?" asked Katrina, keeping her back to the truck, well away from the big horse.

"About what?" asked Mandy, glancing at Reed as he rounded the hood.

"We were only supposed to be gone a few hours."

"Did the rain slow you down?"

"It did," Reed confirmed, halting next to Katrina.

"Did you get the pump fixed?" Mandy asked him.

"Up and running again," he confirmed.

"So, that's it?" asked Katrina. They'd been stranded out in the wilds of the ranch for twenty-four hours, and nobody so much as blinked an eye? What if they'd been hurt? What if they'd been trampled by horses or cattle?

"You had a phone call from New York City," said Mandy. "Someone named Elizabeth Jeril."

"She's the director of Liberty," said Katrina.

"She seems anxious for you to call back."

Katrina's thoughts went to her ankle. She realized she'd barely thought about it for the past two days. Through all the hiking and climbing, it hadn't hurt at all. And the dance routines she'd tried yesterday morning had gone exceedingly well.

She was ready to dance again.

"I'll call her in the morning." Katrina couldn't help a brief glance at Reed while she spoke. He was so rugged and sexy against the backdrop of the Rockies that her breath left her lungs.

"I should probably head back home," she managed, knowing that for the first time in her life she'd have a regret at leaving Colorado.

"But I'm not ready for you to go," said Mandy, stepping forward and pulling Katrina into a hug.

Katrina hugged back, keeping a wary eye on the mare. The animal moved, and Katrina jerked away, coming up against Reed.

"Chicken," Reed teased under his breath.

"She's scared of those, too," Mandy pointed out.

"I'll take my chances with the traffic and the panhandlers," Katrina retorted.

Caleb and Travis approached, stripping off their leather work gloves.

"I'm about done," said Caleb, lifting his hat and swiping the back of his hand across his hairline.

Travis nodded at the muddy truck, and Katrina remembered to step away from Reed.

"Nice," Travis noted.

"Half the hillside came down around it in the storm last night," said Reed.

"You stay at the line shack?" asked Caleb.

Katrina braced herself, unable to look at anyone. Would they guess? Would they ask? What would Reed tell them?

"We did," Reed answered easily. "The princess was forced to eat pancakes and maple syrup for dinner."

"Hey," Katrina protested. She hadn't been the least bit snotty about their dinner last night. All in all, she thought she'd been a trooper.

"She nearly walked out on me when she discovered there wasn't a wine cellar," Reed added.

She shot him an angry glare.

Caleb laughed.

"That's my baby sister," Travis added.

"That's not why you're leaving, is it?" asked Mandy.

Katrina caught something in Reed's expression, and she suddenly knew what he'd done. He'd deflected any hint of suspicion that they might have done anything other than fight last night. She should be grateful to him, not angry.

She'd make sure she told him so later.

She turned back to Mandy. "That's not why I'm leaving. I have to get back to work."

"I suppose you do," Mandy allowed, her voice tinged with sadness.

Caleb pulled a cell phone out of his pocket. "I'll get Seth and Abigail up here. The least we can do is have a farewell barbecue."

* * *

On the back deck of his ranch house, Reed stood to one side, watching Katrina laugh with her two sisters. She seemed more relaxed on the ranch than she'd ever been, but, ironically, she looked even more untouchable. She'd showered, as they all had, and she'd changed into a simple, clingy, white knit dress. Her legs were bare, and she wore her navy suede ankle boots with a looping, blue-beaded choker and matching earrings.

Her hair was swept up in a wispy blond knot, and her face all but glowed with carefully crafted makeup. Her eyes shimmered a sexy deep blue in the waning light. If somebody were to snap a picture, there wasn't a doubt in his mind it would make the cover of *Elle* or *Vogue.*

Still, he couldn't help but wish shc was back in that ugly old boxy T-shirt, in the line shack, in his bed.

Caleb appeared beside him, and Reed shifted his attention to the river.

"I hear you're building a house," said Caleb, handing Reed a cold bottle of beer.

Reed accepted it. "You heard right."

"Been planning it long?"

"Working on the drawings for a couple of years now."

Caleb nodded.

"Waylon Nelson," Reed told his brother into the silence.

"Come again?" asked Caleb.

"You should hire Waylon Nelson."

"Who is he and why would I hire him?"

"Ranch manager," said Reed.

Caleb straightened in obvious surprise. "You read the résumés?"

"I told you I would."

"I thought you were lying to get me off your back."

"I was. But I changed my mind."

"Good. Good. That's great. Waylon Nelson. Okay. I'll take another look at him. But if he's got your vote…"

"He does. Hire him now." Reed took a swallow of the beer. "Right now."

Caleb's eyes narrowed in obvious confusion.

Reed allowed his gaze to return to Katrina. "You're going to need the help. I'm heading to New York City."

Caleb's head snapped up, and he turned to stare at Katrina. Then, immediately, his attention went back to Reed. He stepped up close, voice lowered to a hiss. "You didn't."

Reed lifted his brow in a question.

"You slept with Katrina?" Caleb accused. "You *slept* with Mandy's sister? What is the matter with you?"

Reed stared straight into his brother's eyes. "A, I wouldn't tell you if I had. And B, that's not why I'm going to New York City."

"Then why are you going to New York City?" Caleb demanded, clearly convinced his suspicions were correct, and clearly still loaded for bear.

Reed kept his gaze steady. "I'm a young single guy with fifteen million dollars to spend. There's a long list of good reasons why I'm going to New York City."

And on the top of that list was Quentin Foster.

Caleb backed off ever so slightly. "You're looking for business investments?"

"Maybe," Reed allowed, though the possibility was exceedingly slim.

"You need Danielle to meet you there? I can call her."

"How about I call Danielle if I need her?"

"But you *will* call her."

"If I need her."

"Don't go signing anything without her," Caleb warned.

"I'll be fine." Reed could sign his fist into Quentin Foster's malicious, conniving nose without any assistance from Caleb's lawyer.

"Why don't you take the jet?" Caleb offered.

"Sure."

"You can drop Katrina off."

"No problem."

Reed supposed a better man would feel guilty about misleading his brother. But he hadn't technically lied. Whether he'd slept with Katrina was none of Caleb's business. And Reed certainly wasn't heading for New York City in the hopes of having a fling with her.

He was going along to protect her. Nothing more, nothing less. Hell, once they hit the bright lights and big city, she wasn't going to look twice at a rangy, weather-beaten cowboy like him, even if he did know something about Dior and had once taken a tour of a winery in Napa Valley.

In the taxi heading into midtown Manhattan, Katrina felt as if two worlds were about to collide. In the backseat next to her, Reed looked relaxed, slouched back, seat belt loosely around his hips.

"Have you been to New York City before?" she found herself asking. She didn't think he had, but he didn't seem at all out of place, and he wasn't gawking around like a tourist at the tall buildings.

"Nope," he answered. "Anything in particular I should see while I'm here?"

"The Liberty Ballet at the Emperor's Theater."

He smiled at her joke. "Wouldn't miss that."

"What interests you?" she asked. For that matter, what was he doing here? How long was he staying? And what were his expectations?

When he'd announced he was coming, he'd made some vague statements about seeing the City, maybe doing business even. He hadn't so much as hinted that he had any intention of continuing their physical relationship. But she couldn't help but wonder. Okay, she couldn't help but hope. No. She couldn't hope. She had to leave it alone.

"I wouldn't mind meeting some of your ballet colleagues," he mentioned evenly.

"Really?" That surprised her.

The car came to a smooth halt in front of her apartment building.

Reed gave a shrug. "If you don't think I'd embarrass you."

She took in his blue jeans, plaid shirt and the folding tool strapped to his belt in a worn leather case. "You might want to rethink the boots."

"I promise I'll clean up." He leaned slightly forward. "Can you wait a few minutes?" he asked the driver.

The man nodded as he popped the trunk.

Reed turned back to Katrina. "I'll walk you up."

So he wasn't staying. Okay. It would have been odd if he had. She only had the one bedroom. Not that she wasn't willing to share. Still, he hadn't asked about being her house guest.

"I'll be at the Royal Globe Towers," he told her with a wry half smile, making her wonder if he could read her mind.

Then he hopped out of the car, meeting her on the sidewalk with her suitcase in his hand.

The doorman nodded to her in recognition, and they moved smoothly onto the elevator, riding up ten floors to her compact apartment.

"This is nice," said Reed, taking in the French Provincial chairs and love seat, the proliferation of plants and the small dining-room table tucked against the pass-through to her tiny kitchen.

"Not much of a view," she apologized. If you craned your neck, you could just barely see past the stone building next door to the street below.

"You made it nice inside." He gestured with the suitcase toward a closed door.

"Yes, please." She quickly opened the bedroom door and flipped on the bedside lamp.

Reed set her suitcase down on the bed.

"You're rehearsing all day tomorrow?" he asked, standing close.

She nodded, holding her breath. Would he touch her? Hug her? Kiss her?

"Dinner after?" he asked.

"Sure. Yes." She quickly nodded.

"I'll call you? Seven?"

She gave another nod, and her tongue flicked involuntarily across her lower lip.

He obviously caught the movement. His gaze held for a long second on her lips.

She felt them soften, tingle, part ever so slightly.

Reed cleared his throat. "I'd better get back to the car."

Disappointment washed through her.

He took a step back. "Have a good rehearsal."

"Thank you."

He moved closer to the door. "Hope the ankle holds up."

"Me, too."

He was halfway through the door when he called back. "I'll dress differently tomorrow."

She couldn't help but smile. "Okay."

"You have a favorite place?"

"Anything will do."

"Okay. Bye." And he disappeared.

She heard the apartment door shut behind him, and she let out a heavy sigh, dropping down onto the bed.

He didn't stay. He didn't kiss her. He didn't even hug her goodbye.

How was a woman supposed to feel about that?

Caleb's assistant at Active Equipment had arranged for Reed's hotel room at the Royal Globe Towers. Entering the opulent suite last night, Reed had decided his brother was getting spoiled from being so rich. What man needed a four-poster, king-size bed, a chaise lounge and two armchairs in his bedroom? The living room had two sofas, a stone fireplace and a dining table for eight, along with two dozen candles and three bouquets of flowers and a marble bathtub in the bathroom that could hold a family of six.

It was ridiculous.

He'd have moved into something more practical, but he wasn't planning to be in New York very long. And Katrina lived in Manhattan, so he preferred to stay in this part of town.

Still, he didn't want to spend his entire fifteen million in the clothing shops on Fifth Avenue. So, this morning, he'd taken the friendly concierge woman's advice and hopped on the subway to

Brooklyn. There he found a nice shopping district that seemed to cater to ordinary people.

After wandering the streets for a couple of hours, he was enticed into a small bakery by the aromas of vanilla and cinnamon. The place had only a few small tables with ice-cream-parlor-style chairs, but a steady stream of customers came in and out for takeout. He bought himself a sugar-sprinkled, cream-filled pastry and a cup of coffee from the stern-looking, rotund, middle-aged woman at the counter and then eased himself gently into one of the small chairs.

The doors and windows were open, letting the late-morning air waft through. The staff were obviously busy in the back, smatterings of English and Italian could be heard, bakers appearing occasionally as the middle-aged woman and a younger assistant served customers.

Reed could hear a truck engine cranking through the open door to the alleyway behind the store. There was a sudden clang of metal, followed by a male voice shouting in Italian. The bakery went silent for a brief moment, then the customers laughed a little. Reed didn't understand the language, but it didn't take much to get the gist.

The older woman marched away from the counter, through the kitchen hallway, sticking her head out the open door and shouting at the man.

Reed thought he could figure that one out, too.

The man shouted back, and she gestured with her hand, scowling as she returned to the counter. The last of the current customers took their paper bags and moved out onto the sidewalk, leaving the bakery empty.

"Engine trouble?" Reed asked the woman, wiping his hands on a paper napkin as he came to his feet.

At first, he thought he was going to get an earful himself.

"The delivery truck is ancient," she offered rather grudgingly.

Reed gestured to his empty plate, giving her a friendly smile. "That was fantastic." It was easily the best pastry he'd ever tasted. Same went for the coffee—it'd been strong but flavorful.

She nodded an acknowledgment of his compliment, but still

didn't smile in return. The younger woman, however, gave him a broad, slightly flirtatious grin.

Then another bang reverberated through the alley, and both women jumped. It was followed by a deafening clatter and clang, and another string of colorful swearwords.

Reed moved swiftly and reflexively around the glass display case, down the short hallway, past the heat and bustle of the kitchen, past stacks of boxes, buckets and bins, and out the back door.

The alley was narrow and dusty. Stained, soot-covered brick walls rose up on either side. The awful noise was coming from the engine of a five-fifty panel truck, with Gianni Bakery written on the side in chipping blue paint, that blocked the alley.

A balding man sat in the driver's seat with the door propped open.

"Shut it down!" Reed called, making a slashing motion across his throat.

The man shot him a glare.

"Shut it down," Reed repeated, striding forward. "You've dropped a valve."

"Always takes her a few minutes to warm up," the man responded with confidence.

Reed reached in and turned the key to Off.

"What the—"

"It's dropped a valve," Reed repeated. "If you keep it running, you'll blow a connecting rod."

"You a mechanic?" the man asked.

"Rancher," said Reed, stepping back. "But I've worked on plenty of diesels in my time. Some older than this."

"I've been limping her along for a few months," said the man.

"Does it idle a lot?" asked Reed, knowing that was the most likely explanation.

"In the winter," the man said, reaching for the key.

"Don't do that," Reed warned. "You need to call a tow truck."

"I don't have time to call a tow truck."

"If you try to start it you'll only make it worse."

The man clamped his jaw, rocking back in the worn, vinyl driver's seat. "We've got deliveries to make."

"Do you have a backup? Another truck maybe?"

This one wasn't going anywhere anytime soon, and probably never. Even on the ranch, where they jerry-rigged pretty much anything back together, they knew when it was time to put something out to pasture. There wasn't much point in replacing the engine in a twenty-five-year-old truck.

The man shook his head. "I've been looking for another truck for six months. The used ones are as worn out as this, and the new ones cost a fortune."

"Tough break," Reed commiserated.

"Irony is, these days, I need two trucks."

"Business that good?"

The man rubbed his hands along the steering wheel. "Walk-in business is slowing."

"Doesn't seem very slow today," Reed observed.

"It's slowing," the man reiterated. "We need to strengthen distribution to other retail outlets. We also need to diversify." Then he stuck out his hand. "Nico Gianni."

Reed shook. "Reed Terrell."

"You from Brooklyn?"

"Colorado."

"On vacation?"

"More business than pleasure." Reed's interest had been piqued by Nico's words, not to mention by his own experience sampling the bakery's wares. "You're saying you've got enough orders to run two trucks?"

"If I had two trucks, I'd bring my nephew in on nights, and run the kitchen twenty-four hours. The walk-in traffic may be going down, but catering, now there's some expansion potential. Expensive parties, weddings, dances. The rich don't stop getting richer."

"True enough," Reed had to agree.

Nico seemed to have a good handle on the industry, and he seemed to have a plan for his business. Reed sized up the building. "You own this place?"

"Me and the wife."

Reed couldn't help but wonder if this was what Danielle meant by buying a percentage of a business. This wasn't exactly a start-up. Though, for Reed's money, it seemed less risky than a start-up.

"So, you're saying with a little capital for a new truck or two, your business would be in a position to expand."

"It would," Nico confirmed.

"You ever think about taking on a partner?"

Nico blinked.

"I mean a minor shareholder. A silent partner."

"I don't understand."

Reed rested his hand on the top of the open truck door, assuming a casual pose. "One of the reasons I'm in New York is possibly to invest in some business opportunities."

"You're interested in a bakery?"

"Maybe. Do you know what the real estate's worth? Have the annual gross and net handy?"

"Is this some scam?"

"No."

"You an eccentric rich guy?"

"No. I'm a rancher. But if we can make a deal, I'll kick in enough cash for a couple of new trucks. You cut me in for an appropriate percentage, and maybe we both win."

"So you're looking to diversify?" Nico nodded thoughtfully.

"I'm looking to diversify," Reed agreed. "I've got this sharp, prissy lady lawyer who wants me to sit in her office and review balance sheets all day long."

Nico grinned.

"But I don't want to invest in companies," said Reed. "I'd rather invest in people. And I'd rather invest in your pastries, Nico. They're damn fine."

"It's a secret family recipe."

"I'm not surprised."

"Come inside and take a look?" asked Rico.

"Absolutely," Reed agreed. "And, can you give me the name of a good tailor who works fast?"

Rico grinned and hopped out of the truck. “Salvatore’s. Around the corner. He’ll fix you up.”

Salvatore turned out to be one heck of a tailor. And he had a business-expansion idea that sounded as promising as Nico’s. So Reed left the store with two new suits, half a dozen dress shirts and another potential business investment.

Back at the Royal Globe Towers, he called Danielle, and her assistant put him straight through.

“Good afternoon, Reed,” her crisp voice came on the line. “How can I help you?”

“I just spent half a million dollars.”

“On a sports car?”

“No.” Reed unzipped one of the suit covers as he talked. “A bakery and a tailor shop.”

There was a long moment of silence. “Reed?”

“Yes?”

“I have a law degree from Harvard, but you’ve got me confused.”

Reed retrieved the charcoal-gray suit. Salvatore had told him he could dress it up with a white shirt or down with steel blue and a diamond-pattern tie. “I need the money to buy a percentage of a bakery and a tailor shop in Brooklyn.”

“Oh. Okay. Give me the company names. I’ll start an investigation.”

“I don’t need some bureaucratic investigation. I just need a check.”

“I don’t follow.”

“I met the guys today. I saw their operations. I looked into their eyes and shook their hands. The deal’s done. Gianni Bakery and Imperial Tailors.”

“How did you meet them?”

“I was hungry.”

“You’re losing me again, Reed.”

“Nico sells some excellent pastries, but he needs a new delivery truck. Well, two new delivery trucks.” Reed stripped off the plastic covering and stepped back. He really did like this suit.

"You ate a pastry today, and now you want to invest in his business?" Danielle confirmed.

"Pretty much."

"Reed, wandering around Brooklyn is not a reasonable investment strategy. You can't do things that way."

"It appears I can."

"Reed."

"Danielle, it's my money."

She gave a long-suffering sigh. "Fine. Okay. I hear you. But I'm looking at their financials before we cut the check. That's not negotiable. And if you're going to spend any more than this, you have *got to talk to me.*"

"Sure," Reed agreed easily, holding the diamond-patterned tie against the steel-blue shirt then the white one.

"You keep saying yes, and then you go ahead and do whatever you want."

"Funny how that works." Reed decided to go with the blue.

"You are impossible."

"Know any good restaurants in Manhattan?"

"Dozens. What do you have in mind? Please tell me you're not buying one."

"I'm eating at one."

"Good. Steak? Seafood? Greek? Thai?"

"What about French?" French was elegant. Then again, he was going with the blue shirt. "Greek. Make it Greek."

"What part of town?"

"Midtown."

"Try…Flavian's. It's near the Park, around Sixty-Fourth."

"I will. Thanks, Danielle."

"You're keeping me awake nights."

He chuckled and hung up the phone, then stripped off his cotton shirt and headed for the enormous shower that had two massive showerheads in the ceiling and six more jets in the walls. Ridiculous. He didn't think any man needed to be that clean.

He stripped down, adjusted the water temperature and chose a small bottle of shampoo. There were still a couple of hours before he was meeting Katrina, but his stomach hitched in anticipation. He couldn't help hoping she liked his suit.

On the other hand, he couldn't help hoping she'd restrain herself with her own wardrobe. If she looked too good, it was going to be an awfully long night keeping his hands to himself and his promise to Caleb. Though, he supposed, it was going to be an awfully long night no matter what she wore. Katrina would look sexy in a burlap sack.

Katrina was gratified by the way Reed's eyes darkened to gunmetal when he took in her red dress. She'd been hoping he'd like the short, clingy, off-the-shoulder number. It was made of lustrous silk with hundreds of black beads sewn into the low neckline and in a swirled pattern down one side. She'd paired it with spiky-heeled black shoes and a matching clutch.

Her hair was loose, flowing in waves around a pair of dangling onyx earrings, with a chunky bracelet and matching choker.

"We may have to upgrade the restaurant," he told her, his gaze sweeping from her hair to her shoes and back again.

"You clean up good, too," she teased, impressed as always by his athletic physique beneath the cut of his suit.

He was freshly shaved. His hair was neat, his shirt perfectly pressed, and his tie was in a smooth knot. He'd even forgone cowboy boots for a pair of polished loafers.

"What's your favorite restaurant?" he asked her, stepping back in the hallway to make room for her to exit her apartment.

"Did you make a reservation?" As far as she was concerned, there was no need to change his plans.

"Danielle suggested Flavian's."

"Who's Danielle?" Katrina fought a spurt of jealousy at the mention of another woman's name.

"Caleb's lawyer."

"She lives in New York?"

"Chicago."

Katrina was confused. "And you called her for a restaurant recommendation?"

"It's a long story."

Katrina waited, but he didn't elaborate.

"Flavian's is fine," she told him. "The ballet company goes there a lot. They have a nice deck."

She pushed down her curiosity and told herself to quit being jealous. Danielle was likely just a friend, a business acquaintance at that. In fact, it sounded as if she was a business acquaintance of Caleb's rather than Reed's. Which didn't explain why Reed would call all the way to Chicago for a restaurant recommendation.

"Will you be warm enough if we eat outside?" he asked, gazing critically at the little dress.

Katrina determinedly put Danielle from her mind. She reached for the black wrap she'd hung on a hook near the door and draped it over her shoulders, tucking her small clutch purse under her arm.

"They have outdoor heaters on the deck," she told him. Then she stepped into the hallway and pulled the apartment door closed behind her.

He lifted the door key from her hand and secured the dead bolt for her. "You do know there's something fundamentally wrong with the dress code."

"What dress code?" As far as she knew, Flavian's didn't have a dress code.

"New York City's dress code."

She raised her brows in a question.

He pressed the key into her palm then held out his arm. "You're going to freeze, and I'm going to swelter."

She replaced the key in her purse and tucked her hand into the crook of his elbow as they started toward the elevator. "That's so you can be a gentleman at the end of the date and let me wear your jacket."

"You think this is a date?" he asked. There was a level of unease in his voice.

"What else would you call it?"

He came to a halt at the elevator and pressed the call button.

It pinged in response, and the mechanism whirred behind the closed door.

Reed peered down at her, his gray eyes narrowing for a moment before he finally spoke. “I didn’t come to New York to sleep with you, Katrina.”

She held the gaze for a long moment, working up her courage. “Well, that’s disappointing.”

He sucked in a breath. “Don’t look at me like that.”

“I think of you like that,” she dared.

“Katrina,” he warned on a growl.

“What? It’s not like you can take my virginity a second time.”

“My brother is marrying your sister,” he repeated for what was probably the third time. “We’re going to be in each other’s lives from here on in. I wouldn’t feel right about having a fling.”

“As opposed to having a one-night stand?”

He didn’t seem to have an answer for that, and the elevator doors slid open to reveal a distinguished-looking sixtysomething couple whom Katrina vaguely recognized.

“Good evening,” Reed offered smoothly, gesturing for Katrina to enter first.

“Evening.” The couple nodded in response.

Katrina moved into the elevator, turned and stood next to Reed. The doors closed, and the car descended.

When the doors reopened, they crossed the compact lobby and went out through the glass exit door, where a massive, white stretch Hummer limousine waited at the curb.

There was a trace of laughter in his voice. “Your ride, princess.”

She stopped short, taking in the polished luxury vehicle from hood to trunk. “That’s a lot of money to shell out just to mock me.”

“You think I’m mocking you?”

“Absolutely.” Why else would he order such an expensive car? They were only going a few blocks, and he clearly wasn’t trying to seduce her.

“I’m not mocking you,” he insisted. “The owner is a friend of Salvatore’s. I guess he’s trying to treat me well.”

"Salvatore?" Reed knew someone in New York City?

He tugged pointedly at the sleeves of his suit jacket and squared his shoulders. "A tailor I met in Brooklyn this morning." He turned slightly sideways to give her a view.

She took in the crisp outfit and straightened his already perfect tie, but it gave her an excuse to touch him. "You went all the way to Brooklyn to buy a suit?"

The uniformed driver opened the door and stood back to wait for them.

"I did," said Reed.

"You do know your hotel is mere blocks from Fifth Avenue?"

"I do know that." He gestured to the open limo door.

She didn't move. "And did you know Fifth Avenue is famous the world over for fine shopping?"

He raised a brow. "You don't like my suit?"

"I like it just fine."

"Then don't be such a snob about Brooklyn. You going to get in or what?"

"I've got nothing against Brooklyn."

"Good to know." He moved past her to stand opposite the driver.

Katrina moved forward, accepting Reed's hand and, sliding onto the limo seat, made room for him to join her.

The driver shut the door and the inside lights dimmed. Subtle violet floor lighting glowed beneath their feet while tiny white lights glowed in a scattered pattern across a black ceiling. A small wet bar was illuminated powder-blue.

"Is this how you normally travel?" Reed asked, a teasing note to his voice.

Katrina crossed her bare legs. "Beats a battered pickup truck covered in mud."

"Anything beats a battered pickup truck covered in mud."

She bumped her shoulder playfully against his arm. "Are you coming over to the dark side?"

"Maybe," he allowed.

"That was quick."

The limo pulled away from the curb, the lights of Fifty-Ninth Street changing the shadows inside.

"Champagne?" He leaned forward and retrieved a tiny bottle of champagne from a recessed ice bucket.

"Yes, please." She gestured an amount with a small space between her index finger and thumb, deciding to relax and enjoy herself, even if Reed was going to keep his distance.

He pulled off the wire holder and neatly popped the cork, taking two delicate flutes from the polished wood rack above the counter.

She stopped him at an inch, wanting to save room for a glass of wine with dinner. And he poured the remainder of the bubbly, golden liquid into his own glass before discarding the bottle.

He raised his champagne in a toast. "To…?"

She let herself drink in his handsome features, her tone becoming reflexively husky. "To the finer things in life."

He touched the rim of his glass to hers, his warm gaze melding with her own. "To keeping them in context."

"What's out of context?"

"I am."

The stirrings of desire whirred through her limbs. As far as she was concerned, in this moment, he was in perfect context. "You worry too much."

"No." He shook his head slowly. "I worry exactly the right amount."

She loved the way his mind worked, the practicality, the cool logic, his straightforward confidence. He wasn't a maybe kind of guy.

"What are you worried about now?" she prompted.

"The dinner bill."

She couldn't help but grin at that. "We're not splitting it?"

"As if," he coughed out a laugh.

"So it is a date."

His mouth twitched in a moment of uncertainty, and she laughed at him.

"Got you that time." She took a sip.

"It doesn't have to be a date for me to be a gentleman."

Katrina decided to leave it alone. They both knew she'd scored a point.

"So, how do you like New York City?" she asked instead.

"I like it fine so far." He took a drink of his own champagne. "It's a lot different from Colorado."

"It's cleaner."

"Yes, it is."

"Noisier."

"True."

"Quite tasty." He took another drink.

"Don't forget shiny."

His glance went pointedly to her shimmering red dress, the glossy beads and the glimmering jewelry. "You people like to be noticed."

She frowned. "Was that an insult?"

"Are you trying to tell me you don't expect to be noticed in that dress?"

Only by him. But she couldn't very well own up to that. "It's ordinary for New York City," she lied.

The car rolled to a halt in front of the brightly lit restaurant, and a doorman paced smartly across the sidewalk toward them.

"I'm not sure there's anything ordinary about New York City," Reed mused.

"An ordinary dress, in an ordinary city, for an ordinary evening," she lied again.

The doorman opened the door of the limo.

Reed exited first and immediately turned to hold out his hand for her.

Katrina took the hand, turning in the seat, feet together, knees tight, rising gracefully, just as she'd been taught by the Liberty PR staff.

A flashbulb went off, and then another, and she glanced up to see a small crowd of people had gathered on the sidewalk. It was highly unlikely they realized who she was. The huge limo telegraphed a false sense of celebrity.

"Just an ordinary night?" Reed muttered in her ear as his arm slipped protectively around her waist.

"Smile and keep walking," she mumbled back. "It's the car, not us."

"Are you sure?"

"I'm sure." Though she'd been on a billboard or two in the past month, she wasn't particularly recognizable, certainly not by the general public who might happen to be on the sidewalk outside a midtown restaurant. It was the fancy car, that was all.

Luckily, they were only steps from the glass entry doors. A second doorman swiftly ushered them inside to a compact, octagonal, high-ceilinged foyer where a maître d' was positioned next to a set of oversize, oak interior doors.

"Reservation for Terrell," Reed informed the maître d'.

"Of course, sir." The man responded with professional deference, barely glancing at the small computer screen in front of him. "Would you care to dine inside or on the balcony tonight?"

Reed looked to Katrina. "Were you serious about the balcony?"

"Yes, please." She nodded. She loved a warm evening, watching the bustle of the street below, feeling the breeze, hearing the sounds of the city.

"You're not worried about reporters with long lenses?"

"Cute," she drawled, giving him an eye-roll.

"I can put you behind a privacy screen," the maître d' put in without missing a beat.

"Not necessary—"

"Katrina?" The voice from behind her was recognizable as Elizabeth Jeril's, the Artistic Director of Liberty Ballet Company.

Katrina turned to greet her boss, and was swept quickly into a light, expensively perfumed hug combined with two air kisses.

A former ballerina, Elizabeth was slightly taller than Katrina, dark haired with dark eyes and close to forty-five. Though she didn't dance professionally anymore, she was still trim and athletic.

"We didn't get a chance to talk after rehearsal today," Elizabeth noted, pulling back. "But you looked fantastic. Did Dr. Smith check your ankle?"

"He did. It's fine," Katrina assured her. It had been sore immediately after the dancing, but the pain was nearly gone now.

Elizabeth's gaze shifted to Reed, curiosity clear in her expression.

"Elizabeth Jeril," Katrina obliged. "This is Reed Terrell. Reed is from Colorado."

"A souvenir?" Elizabeth teased, grinning as she held out her long-fingered, red-tipped hand.

"It was either me or the tacky T-shirt," Reed played along, taking Elizabeth's hand gently in his larger one.

"I like him," Elizabeth told Katrina, eyeing Reed up and down.

There wasn't much about Reed a woman wouldn't like, Katrina silently acknowledged. "Elizabeth is Liberty's Artistic Director," she finished the introduction.

"You do choreography?" Reed asked Elizabeth.

"Planning, logistics, business management. I get to worry about the money. What little we have of it."

"I understand that's a common problem with arts organizations," Reed acknowledged.

Katrina wasn't sure what Reed knew about arts organizations, but she was quickly distracted from the question as Brandon Summerfield arrived. He stopped next to Elizabeth and tucked his phone into his suit-jacket pocket.

"There you are," Elizabeth acknowledged his presence, placing a hand on his arm. The two weren't officially a couple, but they'd been good friends and colleagues for years. There was an ongoing betting pool at Liberty over when they'd take their relationship to the next level.

"Nice to see you back, Katrina," Brandon told her. He gave her a perfunctory hug.

When they separated, Reed offered his hand. "Reed Terrell. I'm in town to visit Katrina."

Brandon shook. "Brandon Summerfield. Good to meet you."

Elizabeth continued the introduction. "Brandon is the CEO of Seaboard Management, one of our most generous donors."

"Real estate," Brandon elaborated, "mostly commercial and industrial."

"Ranching," Reed responded, "mostly barns and toolsheds."

Brandon grinned, and Katrina couldn't help but smile at Reed's easy joke.

"Will you join us for dinner?" Brandon offered, surprising Katrina. Liberty Ballet Company didn't exactly operate on the class system, but dancers didn't often mingle socially with the donors outside official functions.

She was momentarily speechless.

"Oh, please do," Elizabeth echoed.

Katrina tried to gauge the woman's expression, not sure if she should accept or decline.

Reed gave her a look that said the decision was up to her.

"Okay," Katrina decided.

Elizabeth seemed sincere. And Brandon was an important player in the Liberty organization. With Quentin out there stirring up trouble, Katrina might need all the help she could get.

Eight

It turned out to be a wonderful dinner. Katrina was impressed with how Reed had held his own with Elizabeth and Brandon. He'd asked questions about the ballet company and had seemed genuinely interested in Brandon's business ventures. She hadn't realized he took such an interest in state politics or was so knowledgeable about international commerce and the impact of commodity and energy prices on global trade.

The more she hung around him, the more depths of his personality became apparent. For a guy who'd barely left Lyndon Valley, he seemed surprisingly worldly.

After dinner, they'd said goodbye to Elizabeth and Brandon and decided to take a walk along a pathway at the edge of the park. A canopy of trees arched over them, obscuring the streetlights and muting the sounds of traffic.

"I assume this is the part where I give you my jacket?" Reed asked, even as he shrugged his way out of it.

"This would be the time," she agreed.

He draped it over her shoulders, and the warmth from his

body seeped from the satin lining into her bare shoulders and arms.

He tugged the knot loose from his tie, popping the top button. "That was a nice restaurant."

"Danielle didn't steer you wrong."

"I guess not."

Katrina couldn't help but be curious. Though she told herself to shut up, she couldn't seem to stop the question from pouring out. "Why was it that you called her to ask about restaurants? I mean, it's not like she's a New Yorker."

"The call was on an unrelated matter." He removed the tie, turned to walk backward and looped it around her neck. "There. Now you're accessorized."

"Unrelated how?"

"As in, I didn't call her specifically for a restaurant recommendation."

He sure wasn't making this easy.

"You called her on…business? Pleasure?" Katrina pressed as they made their way along the mostly deserted swath of concrete.

"Business." He pointed through a gate to a bench overlooking the tulip gardens.

"Oh." She shouldn't feel so relieved. "Ranch business?"

"New York business."

She altered her course. "You have business in New York?"

"I own part of a tailor shop and part of a bakery." He waited for her to sit on the bench.

"Really?" Why hadn't he mentioned that before? It seemed an odd thing to leave out, given their past conversations. "So, that's why you're here? To check on your businesses?"

He sat down beside her, slow to answer. "I'm here for a lot of reasons."

The lamppost put him in light and shadow. His face was rugged, all angles and strength. His eyes were dark as they watched her.

She tried not to hope he was also here for her, but she couldn't help herself. She had it bad for Reed Terrell, and no amount of reason or logic was going to change that. "Tell me the others."

He shook his head. "I don't think so."

She shifted closer to his big body, and his arm moved to the back of the bench, creating a crook of space.

She tipped her chin to look at him. "Am I one of them?"

"Not in that way."

"What way is that?"

"The way where you blink your baby-blue eyes, and part those cherry-red lips and make me forget I'm a gentleman."

His words sent a hitch of desire through her chest.

"Am I doing that?" she asked.

"Don't play coy."

"I am coy. Or at least I was coy." She tucked her hair behind her ears, lowering her voice to a tease. "Quite innocent, really. Until a couple of days ago."

He fixed his gaze straight ahead. "Don't remind me."

"Why not?" It was only fair that he share her frustration. "I've been thinking about it constantly, reliving every minute, especially while I lay there alone, in my bed—"

Reed swore between clenched teeth.

"Tell me you miss it, too."

He swore again.

She boldly put her hand against his chest.

His arm tightened around her shoulders, tugging her close while his lips came down, covering hers possessively. Her body responded with instant desire, kissing him back, twisting and pressing against him. Her arms wound around his neck, anchoring her as she tipped her head to better accommodate his overwhelming kisses.

After long, hot, sexy minutes, he rasped, "This is crazy. You're crazy. *I'm* crazy. We're playing with fire."

"We're adults," she pointed out.

"Barely."

"I can legally vote, drink and make love in any state in the Union."

"Bully for you."

"Reed. Get real. A fling is no different than a one-night stand."

He went silent.

She took it to mean he didn't have a rebuttal.

"I've had this fantasy most of my adult life," she dared to say.

"I don't want to hear this."

She took one of his hands between hers. "It was about losing my virginity. I imagined it happening in a big bed, with fine linen, maybe flowers and candles."

Guilt seemed to tighten his features. "Instead, you got me in a broken-down old line shack."

She nodded, faintly surprised at her own willingness to play that particular card. "The *you* part was fine. But I wasn't crazy about the line shack." She screwed up her courage again. "We did it on your turf, Reed. Don't you think it's fair we do it again on mine?"

He gazed at their joined hands. "You think you can reason your way into making love again?" But his expression had softened. There was even a hint of a reluctant grin.

"Yes."

"You're impossible."

"And you're stubborn."

He came to his feet. "I'm trying to be respectful."

She stood up, rounding to face him and placing a hand on his arm. Going for broke, she lowered her voice and put every ounce of vamp she could muster into her expression and tone. "Do me a favor, Reed. Respect me all night long."

His gray eyes darkened, and the half smile disappeared. "And when I leave you in the morning?"

"I'll probably jump off the balcony in sheer anguish and despondency." She came up on her toes and kissed him. The first one was quick, but then she kissed him longer, and he responded, and once again they were wrapped in each other's arms.

This time, when he set her away from him, he grasped her hand, tugging her to his side. They began walking silently back to the sidewalk, setting a beeline for the nearby Royal Globe Towers.

They crossed the opulent lobby, entered the elevator and were whisked to the top floor. Along the way, Katrina was afraid to speak, afraid to even look Reed's way for fear of breaking the spell.

She shouldn't have worried. The minute the suite door clicked shut behind them, he swept her into his arms. Even as he kissed her, he was pushing his jacket from her shoulders, tossing it, along with her purse, onto a nearby bench. The tie followed, and his lips roamed their way across her bare shoulder.

He hugged her tight, the heat of his body penetrating her silk dress. His hand closed over her breast, and sensation zipped its way through the center of her body, bringing a gasp to her lips.

He captured the sound with his mouth.

"You're amazing," he whispered, pushing the dress farther down her shoulder. "Gorgeous." He kissed her mouth. "Delicious." He cupped her cheek, the pad of his thumb stroking as the kisses continued. "Exquisite."

A heady sense of power tripped through her. She felt for the buttons on his shirt, popping them through the smooth holes, desperate to feel his skin against hers.

She separated the halves of his dress shirt, tugging it from his slacks. Her dress slipped down to her waist, and she wrapped her arms around him, pressing her breasts against his smooth chest.

He immediately lifted her into his arms, kissing her deeply and thoroughly, as he settled her against his chest, striding through the big suite, making his way into the master bedroom. The four-poster bed was turned down and a dim lamp glowed soft yellow in a far corner.

Reed set her on her feet, smoothing back her messy hair. "You want some champagne?"

She shook her head, pushing her dress to the floor.

In response, he slipped off his shoes. "A whirlpool bath?"

"No." She stepped out of the silk in nothing but a pair of tiny, lacy, black panties, her shoes and the onyx jewelry.

His hand went to the button on his pants, flicking it open and dragging down the zipper. "Some music?"

She trailed her fingertips along the six-pack of his rock-hard abs. "What are you doing?"

"Romancing you." He kicked off his pants along with everything else. He was beyond magnificent.

"Consider me romanced." She sat down on the bed, lifting her foot, presenting him with the delicate sandal.

He slipped off one and then the other. He let her foot drop gently to the floor as he bent forward, taking her mouth with his, running his hands from her hips, to her breasts, splaying his thumbs across her peaking nipples as he gently laid her back on the bed.

He rolled onto his back then, so that she was on top. He stroked his hands down her spine, dipping below her panties, palming her bottom and rolling the delicate fabric down her legs.

She kissed his chest, tasting the salt of his skin, inhaling his smoky, masculine scent. Her hands roamed his chest, working their way down his body. She'd been nervous in the line shack, uncertain of whether to touch him or how or where. But now she was curious. She followed the contours of his body, his strong shoulders, thickly muscled arms, flat nipples, the indent of his navel and lower still.

After the briefest of moments, he sucked in a breath and captured her wrist, moving her hand from him.

"Hey," she protested.

He turned her onto her back, trapping her other arm while his free hand began its own exploration.

"Not fair," she complained on a guttural groan.

"Deal with it," he advised, kissing her swollen mouth, his tongue delving deep while his caresses left scorching heat in their wake.

He moved from her nipples to her stomach, inching ever lower, finding more sensitive places until her breath was coming in gasps and her body arched.

"Reed," she gasped. "Please."

He reached for a condom.

Then he wrapped his arms fully around her, moving between her legs, gazing deeply into her eyes and gently kissing her brows, her lids, the corner of her mouth. He flexed his hips, pushing ever so gently inside.

"I don't deserve this," he groaned.

She tried to tell him he did, but her answer was swallowed by another deep, lingering kiss.

Instinct clouded her brain, while sensations radiated out from where their bodies were joined. He started slowly, but she urged him on with growing impatience. She wasn't exactly sure how this was supposed to go, but slow definitely wasn't working for her.

She clung to him, arms wrapped around his neck, her body rising to meet his while she kissed him frantically, moving from his mouth to his chin, before burying her face in the crook of his neck, sucking the taut skin, savoring the taste of him with the tip of her tongue. His hand went to the small of her back, lifting her to him, changing their angle, sending blinding sparks shooting through her body.

She gasped his name over and over again, wrapping her body around him, feeling them meld to one.

He picked up the rhythm, and she rode the crest of his wave, rising higher and higher, until a guttural groan was torn from her throat. Reed cried out her name, and fireworks went off behind her eyes, bursting over and over in impossibly vibrant colors.

An hour later, Reed had banished his guilt and self-recrimination to a far-flung corner of his brain, allowing himself to absorb the experience. Katrina was still naked, submerged now beneath the roiling water in the cedar hot tub on the hotel suite's deck. The scattered lights of Central Park fanned out behind her, while the midtown towers rose up in the distance—a beautiful city framing a beautiful woman.

"So, what do you think of my world?" she teased, voice soft and sexy, tone melodious. A wineglass dangled from her polished fingertips. Her face was flushed and dewy, her hair mussed in a soft halo.

"It's a pretty great world," he responded, popping a rich dark truffle into his mouth.

Leafy green plants surrounded them, placed in huge, ceramic pots on the floor of the deck and in smaller containers on a variety of wooden shelves. A lattice screen delineated the hot-tub deck, offering privacy. Candles flickered on polished wood, on occasional tables and on nooks and crannies in the shelves around them.

He slid his calf along her smooth leg. He wished she'd come closer. He didn't like her sitting so far away.

"View's nice over here," he told her.

"Is that a hint?"

"Absolutely."

"Promise you won't feed me another truffle?"

He shook his head. "Nope."

"What does that mean?"

"It means, you like truffles, and I'm going to feed them to you."

She crossed her arms over her chest, mulishly screwing her face. "Then I'm not coming over there."

"Oh, yes, you are." Reed leaned forward, wrapping his hands around her rib cage, easily lifting her, pushing a wave through the tub ahead of her as he moved her to his lap.

"Hey!" She held her glass of merlot out to one side to keep it from spilling.

He settled her. "That's better."

The water sloshed back to level, and he retrieved his own glass of wine.

"You are impossible," she huffed.

"Not my fault," he defended, giving in to temptation and placing a soft kiss on her hairline. "I did try to talk you out of this."

"The hot tub?"

"All of this. Coming to my hotel room. Making love again."

"Oh, that." Her body relaxed, curling into his. "I guess that was my first mistake."

He loved it when she cuddled against him. She felt custom-made to fit his arms. Her hair held the subtle scent of wildflowers. Her skin was petal-soft. Her face was as beautiful as an angel's.

"Or maybe it was my second mistake," she mused, kissing his wet shoulder. "The first was forcing you to take me up to Brome Ridge to fix that broken pump." She rubbed the water droplets on his bicep. "Then again, I suppose I never should have looked into your eyes that first day I came home. That's where it all really started." Her tongue followed her fingertips, swirling against his heated skin.

"You were attracted?" he asked, curious.

She nodded. "I could feel the sparks from across the room."

"I was pretty much a goner then, too." He sighed. "Why did you have to turn out so beautiful?"

Though *beautiful* didn't even begin to describe her. She was smart and sassy and funny, and she messed with his hormones simply by breathing.

"It's an anthropological defense mechanism," she offered. "If I can't accomplish any hard work, I can at least be decorative."

"Stop that," he told her gruffly.

"Stop what?"

"Quit insulting yourself. You work damn hard dancing."

She gazed up at him, apparently unaffected by his angry tone. "Do you think you might be just a bit biased?"

"No."

Some of the light went out of her blue eyes. "It's not the same thing as being productive."

Wanting to be clear on this, he sat up straight, moving her to face him.

She sorted her legs out and straddled his lap.

"It's exactly the same thing. You're an incredibly accomplished woman, princess. Your family, any family anywhere, should be thrilled and proud to have you as a member."

A smile grew on her face, and she reached up to touch his cheek. Her hand was warm from the water. Her breasts rose above the frothy surface, nipples peeking in and out.

"Yet, you still call me princess."

"Do you hate it?"

She shook her head. "Not when you say it."

"Good." He liked having a special name for her. He'd once meant it as derogatory, but those days had long since passed.

She gave a poignant smile. "You're not at all what I expected."

"Neither are you." He'd thought she was spoiled, frivolous, skipping merrily through life on her looks, never giving a thought to anything beyond her own sphere of luxury. She was anything but that. She was a hard worker, a deep thinker, emotionally sensitive, easily hurt and acutely aware of the negative opinions ignorant people formed about her.

Their gazes met, and he couldn't seem to stop himself from kissing her. The kiss deepened and his arms wound around her. Her smooth body pressed intimately against his, heat building between them, tantalizing him, making him ache for her all over again.

He drew back sharply, his breath ragged, frightened by how close he was to throwing caution to the wind. "I am *not* making love to you without a condom."

She downed the rest of her merlot, setting aside both of their glasses.

To his surprise, her eyes danced with amusement. She stroked the pad of her thumb across his lips. "Reed, darling," she purred. "You have *got* to stop telling me things you won't do."

"You're like a spoiled child." But he didn't mean it. He didn't mean it at all.

Despite her rebellious words, she obviously took pity on him, turning in his lap, sitting sideways, still tempting, but not nearly as dangerous.

"We'll do it your way," she agreed, looping her arms loosely around his neck and placing a soft kiss on his cheek. "Because I know we can't make love right now. And I like it here with you." Her voice dropped to a whisper. "But I want to make love. I *really* want to."

"You're killing me, Katrina."

She sighed against him. "Get used to it."

And that was the biggest problem of all. He was already used to it. He liked it here, too. The merlot was delicious, the truffles delectable, the view memorable and, if he had his way, he'd hold Katrina naked in his arms forever.

"You said they didn't know who you were," Reed challenged from where he stood in the glassed-in atrium of the harbor-tour cruise ship.

He was staring at the small magazine rack, the Statue of Liberty visible through the glass behind him.

"They didn't," she assured him, peering at the small square photo on the bottom corner of the tabloid newspaper. It had been taken last night as they exited the limo.

"Well, not last night, anyway," she allowed "They must have looked it up later."

"Katrina Jacobs on the town," he read. "You want to buy it and read the story?"

"I don't need to read the story. I was there, remember?"

"You think they caught us kissing in the park?"

"Do you care?"

"Not at all. Well, maybe if Travis saw it. He'd sure be ticked off. But to these anonymous New Yorkers?" Reed waved a dismissive hand. "I'm the guy who kissed the prima ballerina. I can strut."

"I'm a principal dancer."

He gave a mock frown. "That doesn't sound nearly as exotic."

She wrinkled her nose. "Quit complaining. I had to kiss a cowboy."

He leaned in close and snagged her hand, voice gravelly. "You did a hell of a lot more than kiss him."

The words spurred a hot shiver of remembrance. But she couldn't act on it in public.

Then a family entered the atrium, adding to the crowd, and Reed gently urged her toward the glass door. It slid smoothly open, and they exited onto the windy deck, finding an empty place at the rail.

"You going to come and watch me dance tonight?" she opened. She wished she dared ask him how long he was planning to stay in the city. That was what she really wanted to know. But she'd promised herself she wouldn't push.

"Am I invited?" he asked in return, his gaze fixed on the Manhattan skyline, growing closer as their two-hour tour came to an end.

"Absolutely."

"Then I'll be there."

"I have to be at the theater a few hours early, but I'll leave a ticket at the box office." She tried not to let her excitement rise at the thought of Reed in the audience, but her heartbeat deepened and her chest felt fuzzy. She'd dance for him tonight. It would be all for him.

"You can come backstage afterward," she offered.

He was silent for a long moment.

"If you'd like," she added, growing uncomfortable.

"Sure." There was no inflection in his tone.

Had she made a misstep? It was impossible to tell, and the silence stretched between them.

"New York really is different from Colorado," he observed.

"Taller buildings?" she asked, not really caring. Did he want to come backstage or not? Did he want to see her after the performance? Would he invite her back to the hotel? Or was he already searching for a way to let her down easily?

"Taller buildings, more noise, more people, more…I don't know…life, I guess."

She turned to study his profile. "Is it that bad?"

He shrugged his broad shoulders. "I can't imagine what it was like for you at ten years old."

"I didn't see it all at once," she remembered. "I saw the airport, then Auntie Coco's apartment. I knew there was a lot of traffic on the streets, but I never guessed how far the city sprawled."

"Were you frightened by the crowds?"

She shook her head. "Ironically, I was lonely. But I liked the dancing, and I liked the sparkling lights." She smiled to herself.

"I particularly liked the sidewalks. I liked that you could sweep the dirt away, and they were clean and smooth."

"I like dirt," said Reed.

"Is that a joke?" She couldn't tell.

"It's life," he said. "The dirt is what starts everything. You add seeds, and they grow into plants that get eaten by animals. And at the end of a day, if you're dirty and sweaty, and you smell like the outdoors, you know you've done good. You've worked hard. Something that wasn't there that morning now exists. It could be a stack of hay bales, a fence, a working motor, some clean tack. It doesn't matter what it is. Just that you did it."

"I hate getting dirty," Katrina reaffirmed. Not that Reed would be surprised by that statement. It was the constant dust on her clothes and the grit in her hair that had made her most crazy growing up.

"You're such a girl," he teased.

"Good thing I'm pretty."

His smile disappeared. "You're more than just pretty." He looked as though he was about to say something else. But then he stopped. He drew a breath. "Ever been to the Empire State Building?"

"I have."

"You want to go again?"

"With you?" Her chest hitched.

"Tomorrow?"

She gathered her courage. "So, you're staying a little longer?"

"I was invited to a party on Saturday night."

At the restaurant last night, Elizabeth had extended an invitation to Reed for Liberty's largest annual fundraising gala.

"You were noncommittal. I thought that was your polite way of turning her down." Truth was, Katrina had also thought he was signaling to her his intention to leave before the weekend.

He chuckled. "Do you think she cares if I'm polite?"

"She liked you," Katrina told him honestly. She'd rarely seen Elizabeth warm up to someone the way she'd warmed up to Reed. It was obvious enough that Katrina had felt a little jealous at the time. Maybe that's why she'd pushed him so hard to sleep with her last night.

Oh, wow. That wasn't particularly admirable.

Then she let herself off the hook. Sleeping with Reed had nothing to do with Elizabeth. Katrina simply wasn't ready to let go of the intimacy they'd found together in the line shack.

He was a great guy and an amazing lover. And she couldn't imagine herself with anybody else. Which meant, once this was over, lovemaking was over for her for a very, very long time.

"I liked her, too," said Reed.

"So, you're coming to the party?"

"Sure." He shrugged. "I wouldn't mind meeting a few more of the Liberty Ballet notables."

"You're going to need a tux. This is a pretty high-end affair."

"No problem. I'll go see Salvatore."

"You're going back to Brooklyn for a tux?"

"I like Salvatore. Besides, I own part of his company now. He'll have to give me a good price."

"Just out of curiosity." Katrina turned and leaned her back against the rounded metal rail, asking a question that had nagged at her since last night. "How did you decide to buy into a tailor shop in Brooklyn?"

He shrugged. "Instinct more than anything. I was in Brooklyn yesterday, and Nico recommended Salvatore. We got to talking about his business. He needed some help, and it made sense to me to help him out. In the end, I looked him in the eyes. I liked him, and I liked his business."

"Who's Nico?"

"The guy who owns the bakery I'm buying into."

Katrina got a bad feeling in the pit of her stomach. "Are you saying this all happened yesterday?"

"While you were rehearsing."

She was dying to ask him how much he'd invested. She was terrified that Nico and this Salvatore character had seen Reed coming. "How do you know he didn't rip you off?"

"I'm a good judge of character."

"Maybe in Colorado. But this is New York City."

"Are you questioning my judgment?"

"Yes," she answered honestly.

The muscles in his neck went tight, and she braced herself.

But when he finally spoke, his tone was neutral. "Don't worry about it."

"How much—" She stopped herself. "Never mind. None of my business."

"That's right."

"I'm sorry."

The wind whistled past them.

"I have a plan," he said.

"Do tell."

"The baker. The tailor. And the limo guy. They all have the same problem, great little businesses, solid work ethic, and short-term cash-flow issues."

"Oh, Reed, no." Not the limo business, too.

"They're good guys, family businesses that have been around for generations. I make a few more of these small investments, and when they pay off, I reinvest the profits in the next person."

"And what if there are no profits? What if you lose? Reed, this is a very big city. Con artists are everywhere."

"In a small bake shop in Brooklyn with a broken-down delivery truck, just waiting for a guy like me to come along and bail him out?"

Okay, that did sound far-fetched for a sting operation. But it didn't mean these guys weren't opportunistic.

"I'm not going to lose, Katrina," said Reed. "I'm willing to bet people are people just about anywhere. Some good, some bad, most just trying to get by."

"I didn't know they taught philosophy at Lyndon Valley High School."

His jawline set, and his eyes turned to charcoal, and she knew she'd gone too far. Then, his voice went hard as steel "Well, I'd already guessed they taught snobbery at the Upper Cavendar Dramatic Arts Academy."

Regret shot through her. "Reed, I didn't—"

"We're docking," he pointed out, turning on his heel to head for the gangway.

Sitting in row G, center orchestra, in the opulent Emperor's Theater, Reed's anger had long since disappeared. Katrina's ballet performance had blown him away, and he felt like the biggest jerk in the world for barking at the ethereal angel who'd held the audience enthralled throughout the evening. He wondered how quickly the well-heeled crowd would turn on him if they knew how he'd behaved.

Mere minutes into the performance, he'd found himself transferring his anger to her family. Why had he never heard she was this good? Why weren't they shouting it from the rooftops and dropping everything to rush to New York City and watch her dance?

Supported by rows of other dancers, she was the center of attention, all ribbons and tulle. Her skirt was gauzy mauve, her hair neatly upswept, woven with flowers and jewels as she spun gracefully across the stage, toes pointed, arms outstretched, all but floating to her partner, who lifted her as the orchestra built the music to a final crescendo.

Reed held his breath through the leaps and turns and lifts, until they finally held their position. The orchestra cut, and the crowd burst into thunderous applause.

The company gracefully repositioned themselves on the stage, lining up for a bow. Katrina's chest was rising and falling with deep breaths as she smiled at the audience. Her bright blue gaze seemed to stop on Reed's, and emotion shot through his own chest. It was all he could do not to leap from his seat and carry her off in his arms.

But the curtain came down. The applause finally died, and the audience made their way toward the aisles on either side of him. He sat still for a long moment, wondering if he was still invited backstage. After the harbor cruise, he'd fumed in the cab all the way to the Emperor's Theater, where he'd dropped Katrina off in midafternoon.

She'd tried to apologize numerous times, but he'd cut her off. He wasn't sensitive about his education or his background. What he hated was when she reminded him of their vastly different lifestyles. Still, he sure didn't have to be such a jerk about it.

She was probably still angry with him, and rightly so. Then again, was he going to let that stop him? She'd invited him backstage. She hadn't uninvited him. He could easily play dumb and show up, and then apologize for his behavior and hope she'd forgive him.

All he had to do was figure out exactly where backstage was in this huge place.

He glanced around at the rapidly emptying theater, looking for an usher. Instead, he spotted Elizabeth Jeril down near the front, in a conversation with a man. The seats beside him were empty, so he quickly exited the row and made his way down to her.

"Reed." Elizabeth greeted him with a wide, welcoming smile.

The stranger next to her turned to give Reed a suspicious once-over.

Elizabeth showed no such hesitation. She reached out her arms and all but floated toward him in her full-length silver gown. "I hope you enjoyed the performance."

Reed gently returned the hug. "Very much," he told her honestly.

"Are you coming backstage to see Katrina?"

"I'd like to."

"Good. Reed, this is one of our major donors and a member of the board of directors, Quentin Foster."

Reed's senses went on instant alert. But he schooled his features and faced the man.

"Quentin," Elizabeth continued, oblivious. "This is Reed Terrell. Reed is a friend of Katrina's."

"A close friend," Reed added, holding out his hand to shake, meeting the muddy gaze of Quentin's light brown eyes square on.

Foster was slightly short, slightly balding, with a narrow nose and a haughty, supercilious smile. He held out his own hand, pale and thin-skinned.

"A pleasure," he told Reed in a tone that said it was anything but.

Reed squeezed a little too firmly. "Katrina's spoken of you," he told Quentin.

Quentin's nostrils flared for a split second, uncertainty crossing his expression before he quickly withdrew his hand. "Katrina's dancing is coming along nicely."

"She looked great to me," said Reed.

"You're an aficionado?" Quentin challenged.

"I know what I like," Reed returned evenly.

Quentin gave a fake laugh. "The subtleties of the ballet are usually lost on the masses."

Reed dropped the conversation and spoke to Elizabeth. "Can you point the way?"

"Absolutely." She linked her arm with Reed's and led him along the front of the stage to a small door, subtly recessed into the wall paneling.

They passed through single file to a dimly lit narrow hallway and staircase.

Reed kept his footsteps and his tone measured as he chatted inconsequentially about the weather and the sights of New York City. Inside his head, he was cataloging his instincts.

Now that he'd met Foster, every fiber of his being told him to protect Katrina. Slamming the man into the nearest wall and reading him the riot act seemed like an excellent start. But he restrained himself as they passed through another door and came out into a wide, bustling corridor.

"There she is," said Elizabeth, gesturing down the hallway.

Reed's attention immediately fixed on Katrina as she emerged from a doorway. She'd changed into a simple black sheath dress with black leggings, high-heeled shoes and a short purple open cardigan. Her hair was in a wavy ponytail, and her face was free of makeup.

"Thanks," he told Elizabeth absently, already winding his way through the performers and crew clogging the hall.

When he appeared next to her, Katrina was startled, obviously surprised to see him. But he didn't pause to talk, simply slipped an arm around her waist, and gently eased her into a walk in the direction opposite to Foster.

"You ready to go?" he asked.

"Where are we going?"

"I don't care. Is this the way out?"

She settled in to his pace. "Aren't you still mad at me?"

"I was never mad."

"Liar."

"Okay, a little bit mad. But I shouldn't have been mad. I guess I'm psychologically delicate. Are we going the right way?"

"As if," she scoffed. "Take the next right."

He steered them around a corner into an empty hallway.

The other voices disappeared behind them, and he noticed they were alone. He impulsively backed her into the wall. He searched her expression, finding her more beautiful than ever. "You were amazing out there."

A genuine smile grew on her face. "You liked the performance?"

"I can't wait to watch you dance again."

Still grinning, she scoffed, "There's no need to go overboard, Reed."

Instead of responding, he cupped her chin, stilling her motion. He leaned in. "I'm hooked," he whispered, a split second before his lips touched hers.

Their kiss was instantly passionate, and he pressed his body to hers. Her arms wound around his neck, and he pulled her into a tight full-body hug.

"Reed?" she gasped, clearly struggling for breath.

He forced himself to let her go. He hadn't meant to maul her in public. "Sorry."

"It's okay."

"Are you hungry?" he asked, dredging up some manners. She had to have used up a lot of energy out there tonight.

"I am." She nodded.

"What do you want to eat?" He'd take her anywhere. They could do anything she wanted, as long as it was together.

She blinked once, her dark lashes covering her deep blue eyes, momentarily expanding her pupils. "Room service?"

Everything inside him stilled, then his hand sought hers, tugging her away from the wall, leading her farther down the corridor.

At first, they walked in silence.

"You really liked the performance?" Her tone was slightly hesitant. "Like, truly?"

"I truly loved it," he answered.

"As in, you'd watch another ballet?"

"If you were in it." Then he shrugged. "Or if you came to watch with me."

Though it wasn't something he'd ever given a moment's thought to, he'd honestly enjoyed the ballet. He admired the dancing, the choreography, the lighting, the costumes. He liked to think he recognized hard work when he saw it.

"What about the opera?" she asked.

"I've never been to the opera."

"Would you try one?"

"Is this some kind of a test? Are you setting me up for a joke?"

She frowned at him. "Not at all. I like opera."

"Why?"

They made their way up a back staircase, and a door came into view at the end of a short hallway.

"The music, the pageantry, the stories."

"Aren't they in Italian?"

"It doesn't matter."

"I don't speak Italian."

"Quello è sfavorevole."

He tugged her against his side. "You are *such* a showoff."

"Unlike you? Who turned my bike into an exercise machine and laughed at me because I was afraid of chickens?"

He paused a beat. "Being afraid of chickens is pretty comical."

She tipped her head sideways against his shoulder. "You sure you want to mock the woman who's coming back to your hotel room?"

He leaned down to whisper in her ear. "Let me tell you exactly what I want to do to the woman who's coming back to my hotel room."

Nine

Every time Reed thought Katrina couldn't possibly get any more beautiful, she surprised him. Even tonight, at the Liberty Ballet fundraising gala, among the richly dressed, she stood out like a beacon.

Across the room, her updo was smooth, her honey-toned shoulders bare, her slender arms ringed in delicate white sapphire bangles. She wore a matching necklace, gold inset with a trail of tiny white sapphires, while small studs sparkled in her ears. Her dress was snow-white, with a tight bodice liberally trimmed in deep purple piping. It topped a generous tulle skirt adorned with purple appliqué that made her look even more like his princess, or maybe his bride.

He let that image swim around his brain. It was preposterous, of course, but he couldn't help liking it.

"Enjoying the party?" Elizabeth asked, standing by his side.

"Very much," said Reed, telling the truth. He'd met a lot of interesting people, many from New York City, but a surprising number from other parts of the country. All seemed well-traveled, and some had visited Colorado.

Reed took advantage of the opportunity. "I heard Katrina had trouble with a ballet shoe."

"Terrible luck that," said Elizabeth. "I'm glad she's healed so fast. It was a bizarre accident, but we're not taking any chances."

"How so?" Reed prompted, determined to catalog whatever information he could gather.

"We've changed the standards, shortened the wear period."

"Katrina told me she had a dozen pairs of ballet shoes." Reed would love to get his hands on the others. If Katrina was right, and there was no way to know which pair she'd choose on any given night, then Foster might have sabotaged more than one.

"We replaced them all."

Destroyed the evidence. "And whose idea was that?"

"A board recommendation. Overkill in my opinion, but I suppose it's a PR move if you need one. You don't have a drink."

"I'm pacing myself."

She linked an arm with his. "An admirable quality."

He glanced down to where her fingertips trailed flirtatiously along his bicep. "You know you don't mean that."

Her laughter tinkled. "Sorry. Ingrained habit." She disentangled her arm. "You can catch more flies with honey than with vinegar."

"You catching flies tonight?"

"Liberty Ballet doesn't survive without donations. No offense to your gender, Reed. But men are more likely to pull out their checkbook for a vivacious woman."

"Do you ever get tired of doing that?"

"Of course not."

"Liar."

She shrugged. "It's my job." Then she pointed with her champagne glass. "See that man over there, white hair, glasses, laughing?"

"I see him."

"He donated a substantial sum last year. His business manager called today to say they'll have to cut that in half. My job tonight is to change his mind."

"Good luck with that," Reed offered.

"Thanks."

"I could probably intimidate him for you."

Elizabeth's laughter tinkled again. "That would certainly be a change in tactics."

"Can't flirt with him though," Reed noted.

She looked him up and down. "There is one wealthy widow here tonight, Mrs. Darwin Rosamine—"

"Not a chance," said Reed.

Elizabeth shrugged. "You look very sexy in a tux. Seems a shame to waste it."

"What about Foster?" Reed put in. He'd spotted the man a couple of times, and he was waiting for an opportunity to confront him.

"Quentin? I don't think we should send Quentin to flirt with Mrs. Rosamine."

"I meant his donation."

"He donates every year."

"A lot?"

"One of our top donors."

"Would you be willing to give me a number?"

Elizabeth drew back, her expression changing from animated to thoughtful as she considered Reed. "That would be unethical."

He returned her level gaze. "And?"

"And I could get in a lot of trouble for revealing that kind of information."

Reed waited, but she didn't cave. He had to admire that. "Hypothetically speaking, a ballpark number, what would you consider to be a top donor to Liberty Ballet?"

Elizabeth's even, white teeth came down on her bottom lip, and she smiled as she shook her head. "Hypothetically speaking, I consider a top donor to be in the range of two hundred to three hundred thousand a year."

Reed nodded. "That's a lot of money."

She took a sip of her champagne. "I can smile through almost anything for that kind of money."

"Are you saying you have problems with Quentin?"

"Nothing serious." She glanced from side to side and lowered her voice. "The biggest problem I have with him is that he's boring. He's way too fond of the sound of his own voice, and tends to corner me at parties."

"Boring how?"

"Loves to name-drop and brag about all the important events he's attended. For a skinny man, he's fairly obsessed with menus—who served which caviar, that the shrimp was overdone, that the Kobe beef wasn't, and that the pastry chef was subpar."

Reed nodded. It was annoying, but nothing compared to what Quentin had done to Katrina.

"By the way—" Reed took the opportunity "—if you ever need a good bakery, I know a great one in Brooklyn."

"I don't entertain much in Brooklyn."

"They do deliver." Reed signaled a passing waiter and chose a glass of red wine. "If I could get you a discount, would you be willing to try someone new?"

She arched a sculpted brow. "Are you serious?"

"I am. I own a small percentage of one that would like to break into the upscale catering market."

Elizabeth gave a small shrug. "Send me the information. We can talk."

"I'll have them send you some samples. Thanks."

"No problem." She nodded across the room. "I see Katrina's wearing Asper Emily tonight."

Reed watched Katrina laugh with two tuxedo-clad guests. He tried not to let jealousy creep in. "Is she securing donations?"

"One never knows who will decide to participate financially." Elizabeth paused. "You know, Katrina has a fantastic future ahead of her with Liberty." She took a sip of her champagne. "Assuming she stays in New York City."

Confused, Reed asked, "What makes you think she won't?"

Elizabeth's smile was sly. "You."

Reed laughed at that.

"I've seen the way she looks at you."

"Don't worry about it. She hates Colorado a whole lot more than she likes me."

"She must really hate Colorado then." Elizabeth wound her arm through his once more. "Walk me over to the piano. I need to speak with Samuel Wilcox, and I don't want Quentin to snag me along the way."

"Yes, ma'am."

Several people greeted Elizabeth from a distance as they walked, but none approached her directly. Reed could see Foster out of the corner of his eye, tracking their progress across the ballroom.

"Thank you," said Elizabeth as Reed handed her off to Samuel Wilcox.

Reed didn't wait for an introduction, but quickly withdrew and made his way to where Foster stood alone near one of the bars. He ditched the wineglass on the way, wanting both hands free.

"Foster." He nodded, coming to a halt.

The man's dirt-brown eyes narrowed. "Have we met?"

Reed scoffed out a laugh. "Right." If that's the way the guy wanted to play it, fine by him.

Reed put his back to the polished bar and set his tone low, though nobody was particularly close by. "My message is short. I know you propositioned Katrina. I know about the shoes. And I know where you live—"

"I haven't the faintest idea what you're talking about," Foster sputtered. But his face had flushed ruddy.

"I can also easily access your social calendar." Reed straightened, noting the bead of sweat that had formed on Foster's brow. "If you hurt Katrina, if you threaten Katrina, if you lift one finger to harm her career, I will hunt you down and wipe you off the face of this planet."

Foster pulled himself taller, his voice going shrill. "Even if I did know what you were talking about, I do *not* respond to threats."

"Yeah? Well, you might want to make an exception in this case."

"Uncivilized thug," Foster spat.

"When it comes to Katrina, absolutely. You'd be smart to remember that, too." Message delivered, Reed walked away.

Katrina was determined to avoid Quentin. The last thing she wanted was to be forced to rebuff him all over again. He'd been watching her for several minutes now, and he was headed her way. She started for the other side of the ballroom, deciding avoidance was her best strategy.

She couldn't help but wish Reed was at her side. But last time she'd seen him, he was engaged in what had looked like a serious conversation with Elizabeth. Katrina had to admit, she was rather surprised at how adroit Reed seemed to be at managing the party without much help from her. She'd never had a date give her so much space before.

She saw a chance and entered a conversation with another dancer and two of the guests, hoping it would keep Quentin at bay. Unfortunately, they were just saying good-night, and she was quickly on her own again. And her stop had given Quentin a chance to get closer.

She skirted along the edge of the ballroom toward the back, thinking Reed might have gone to one of the bars for a drink.

She didn't make it.

"Katrina?" Quentin called to her.

Caught, she heaved a sigh and pasted a polite smile on her face. "Hello, Quentin."

"You look lovely tonight." Though he uttered the words, there was a distinct insincerity to his tone.

His smile was there, if a bit fake. And there was a tenseness in his posture, a tightness at the corners of his mouth. Like he had a right to be angry with her. If anything, it ought to be the other way around.

"Thank you," she responded calmly, letting her smile fade. It was one thing to be cordial if he was trying to keep up appearances, but if he wasn't even going to make the effort, she certainly saw no reason to pretend.

His gaze moved insolently from her face, to her breasts and down the length of her body. "Putting it out for someone special tonight?"

She ignored the rude question and started to leave. "Excuse me. But I'm on my way to get a drink."

But as she began to move, he grabbed her by the arm. His grip was tight enough to be painful.

Before she could react, he stepped up close, his voice a growl. "You call him off."

"What? Let go of me." Had he lost his mind?

"That pit bull of a junkyard dog—"

Suddenly, Reed appeared. He grabbed a handful of Quentin's shirtfront and pushed him backward ten full paces, slamming him into the wall.

"Reed," Katrina gasped.

"Did you think I was bluffing?" Reed demanded in a harsh voice that carried. *"Did you?"*

Quentin's mouth moved, but no sounds came out.

Katrina moved swiftly toward them, praying nobody else was paying attention. "Reed, *stop.*" She could handle this herself, discreetly and quietly. The last thing in the world Liberty Ballet needed was a sordid scene played out in full view of their donors.

But he only pushed Quentin harder against the wall. "I meant every word I said."

Quentin gasped for breath.

"Let him go," Katrina begged, glancing around.

Instead, Reed pointed a stiff finger close to Quentin's nose. "Every word."

"Security!" somebody called out from behind her.

Katrina groaned in mortification.

Quentin managed a pained but triumphant smile. "Better let me go."

"It'll take them at least five minutes to get here," Reed warned. "I can do a lot of damage in five minutes."

"You'll go to jail," Quentin wheezed.

"Do I look like I care?"

"Reed," Katrina pleaded, her panic growing.

He glanced her way. "You don't need to see this."

"*Everybody's* seeing this."

He turned back to Quentin, his enunciation slow and deliberate. "What's it going to be?"

The two men glared daggers at each other.

Finally, Quentin glanced away, giving a tight nod of acquiescence.

Reed abruptly let him go, stepping back just as the security guards came into view. Reed backed off farther, straightening his jacket. Then he turned and walked casually toward her, while Katrina stared at him in abject horror.

She felt dozens of pairs of eyes come to rest on her. This story was going to race through the dance world like wildfire. Katrina would be a laughingstock. Whatever Quentin might have done to try to harm her career, Reed had outdone the effort and then some.

Reed stopped in front of her, and she felt her eyes sting with mortification. She didn't say a word, but dashed blindly for the exit. Ignoring the curious and pitying stares of the other guests, she made her long and painful way to the foyer.

Once there, she went directly to the elevators.

Reed was right behind her. "Katrina, I'm sorry you had to—"

"You're *sorry?*" She gasped for breath, barely finding her voice. She couldn't bring herself to look at him. "You think *sorry* cuts it?"

"He had it coming."

"It was a party, Reed. A civilized party."

"What does that have to do with anything?"

"At a *civilized* gathering, you can't just beat people up because they annoy you."

Reed stepped closer, his voice low but no less menacing. "He tried to hurt you. He *did* hurt you. He sabotaged your shoe."

"We've been through that. It doesn't make sense." She wasn't going to let the fear in.

"It makes perfect sense. Elizabeth said the board replaced every pair of your shoes."

"So what?"

"It was a *board* decision. Foster tampered with the others and—"

"Stop right there. He's an opportunistic jerk, but that's it. And I could have handled it myself."

"You shouldn't have to handle it."

"Why? Because you fix things?"

"Because he doesn't get to do that to you. Nobody does. I confronted him. I warned him. And he ignored me."

"Did he confess?"

"No. But I looked him in the eyes—"

"And you shook his hand? And you're such an oracle when it comes to judging people that you felt entitled to try and convict him without a shred of evidence?"

"He did it, Katrina."

She closed her eyes and counted to five. There was a broader point.

"This isn't Colorado, Reed."

He coughed out a laugh. "No kidding."

"Can you at least take this seriously?"

"I *am* taking this seriously."

She poked a finger against his chest. "This isn't the Wild West."

Reed didn't answer, simply set his jaw.

"You threatened to hurt him," she accused.

"I did not."

"You're lying."

"I'm not lying."

"I *heard* you." There was no other explanation.

A beat went past, and then another, before Reed finally spoke. "I didn't threaten to hurt him. I threatened to kill him."

Katrina staggered back.

She couldn't have heard right. Reed had seemed so urbane these past few days, so civilized. He knew how to order a good wine. He was intelligent, well-read. He could make small talk with just about anyone. But it was all a facade.

"So, that's it?" she croaked through an aching throat, more to herself than to him.

"What's it?" he asked.

"You. Underneath it all, you're still just an uncouth Colorado cowboy."

He didn't flinch. "I'll always be an uncouth Colorado cowboy."

Her stomach cramped in pain. This had all gone so horribly wrong. "I should have listened to you," she whispered.

"Yeah," he agreed. "You should have listened to me."

She felt tears build again, hot and heavy, trapped behind her eyes, making her voice quaver. "You tried to warn me."

"I never meant to hurt you, Katrina." His eyes were storm-cloud gray. "The last thing in the world I wanted to do was hurt you."

"Well, you did."

"I know."

"You have to leave." She was going to break down any second. She fought her anguish with anger. "Leave now. Leave New York City. Go back to those sawdust-covered honky-tonks where guys like you can make a point with your fists."

"I'll take you home." He reached out his hand.

"No." She determinedly shook her head, backing away. "I'm not going home. I'm going back to the party."

He jerked up his chin. "Oh, no, you aren't."

But she had no choice. "I can face them now, or I can face them tomorrow. And I want to get this over with."

"I meant you can't go back to Foster. He's still inside."

"I can deal with him."

"No, you can't."

Katrina felt a red haze form inside her brain. "This is my problem, Reed. It's my life. You need to leave now."

There was no way he was going to agree. She could see his intense frustration. She could see him considering options. She was suddenly frightened that he might haul her bodily from the hotel for her own good.

She took another step back, quickly turning away, pacing as fast as she could toward the ballroom.

Reed would leave New York City. He'd do it quickly and quietly and without bothering Katrina again. But there was one thing he had to take care of first. And Elizabeth Jeril was the person to help him.

At the Liberty Ballet administration offices, she closed her door and gestured to one of the guest chairs in front of her maple-wood desk. "My receptionist just warned me you were dangerous."

"Was she at the party?" Reed was sorry his behavior had marred the event. But he wasn't sorry he'd confronted Foster. He'd done what he had to do.

Elizabeth laughed, rounding her desk. "She heard the story this morning. Everybody in Manhattan heard the story this morning."

Reed waited for her to sit. "I have a hard time believing it was that interesting."

She plunked down on the padded burgundy leather chair, definitely seeming more amused than angry. "Most exciting fundraiser I've ever attended."

Reed took his seat. "Sorry about that."

She waved a dismissive hand. "Not to worry."

Fair enough. He'd forget the party and get straight to the point. "I need a favor, Elizabeth."

She squared her shoulders and folded her hands on the desktop. "What kind of a favor?"

"I need Quentin Foster out of Katrina's life forever."

Elizabeth's brows knitted in obvious confusion.

"And that means I need him out of Liberty Ballet forever."

She began shaking her head. "Reed, it's not going to be possible for me—"

"How much?" he asked.

"Excuse me?"

"How much will it take to get rid of Foster?"

Elizabeth blinked.

"I have a proposal for you." Reed saw no point in pussyfooting around. "I'm prepared to set up a foundation for the benefit of the Liberty Ballet Company. The endowment would provide stable funding to the organization into perpetuity."

He tightened his grip on the arms of the chair. "My only condition is that Quentin Foster is immediately kicked off the board of directors, banned from ever contributing to Liberty Ballet, and banned from ever attending any of their fundraisers. If I thought I could keep him from buying tickets, I would ask for that, too."

Elizabeth's gaze probed Reed's expression for a long minute. "What did he do?"

"Nothing that's provable."

Her eyes narrowed.

Reed didn't blame her for being confused, even suspicious. He made up his mind to put all his cards on the table. "I tell you this in confidence, and only to protect Katrina. I couldn't care less about that jackal. Foster wanted to sleep with her, and when she turned him down, he pressured her again. Then the cables appeared and her shoe malfunctioned, and he was pivotal in replacing her other shoes before anyone could look at them. I warned him off at the party Saturday, but I don't trust him. I can't trust him. I need him gone."

Elizabeth came halfway out of her chair. "Are you *kidding* me?"

"I am not."

"He used his access to the company as a board member to solicit sex with a dancer?"

"Yes," Reed answered shortly.

Elizabeth reached for her phone. "I'll turf him for that alone."

"That doesn't solve the money issue."

She paused with her hand on the receiver. "No, it doesn't solve the money issue. But I'm not throwing Katrina to the wolves for any amount of money."

"Put down the phone."

"But—"

"Elizabeth, I can solve the money issue."

She looked genuinely sympathetic. "You have no idea what you're saying."

"Why do people keep doubting me? I'm not a rocket scientist, but I do manage to clothe and feed myself on a daily basis. I'm aware of what I'm offering."

"Reed."

"Ten million dollars."

Elizabeth's jaw went lax.

"The Sasha Terrell Endowment Fund will start with ten million dollars in seed money."

"Who is Sasha Terrell?"

Reed couldn't help but grin. "*That's* your question?"

"That's my first question."

He softened his tone. "My mother."

Elizabeth nodded, then she nodded again, then she blinked rather rapidly. "That's nice. That's very nice."

"Your other questions?" he prompted.

"I can't think of any." She laughed unsteadily, covering her lips with her fingers. "Is this real?"

"It's real." Reed reached for his cell phone, dialing Danielle.

Elizabeth sat in astonished silence while Danielle's office put his call straight through.

"Reed?" came Danielle.

"It's me."

"Not another bakery?"

"Can you come to New York City?"

"When?"

"Now."

There was a long silence on Danielle's end, followed by a worried, "Why?"

"Probably better if I tell you when you get here."

"No way. I'll have a coronary en route worrying."

Reed chuckled. "I'm about to set up a ten-million-dollar endowment fund to the benefit of the Liberty Ballet Company of New York City. I want you to manage it."

To her credit, Danielle kept her cool, her tone professional. "I generally advise people to target twenty-five percent of their net worth to charitable endeavors."

"Yeah?"

"Yes."

"Have I ever taken your advice before?"

"No."

"Let's assume I won't be starting now."

"I'll be there in two hours."

"Perfect." If this was the only thing left he could do to protect Katrina, he was going to do it right.

Two days later, and Katrina still couldn't stop thinking about Reed. Riding the bike at her gym reminded her of him. Sitting in the whirlpool reminded her of him. Eating, drinking, even sleeping all brought back memories of his simmering gray eyes, his rugged face and his killer body that she could swear she felt around her every time she closed her eyes.

In her gym's locker room, she shut off the shower taps and reached for her towel. Her workout was finished, but she didn't have it in her to head home and stare at her four walls and feel lonely. So instead, she dried off and dressed, heading for the juice bar that fronted on the sidewalk on the facility's main floor.

She found a table on the deck near the rail and ordered a raspberry smoothie. At least smoothies didn't remind her of Reed. And neither did pedestrians or taxicabs. Well, as long as she stayed away from the park.

A long white Hummer limo cruised past, and her chest contracted. She blinked back tears and took a sip of the sweet, icy beverage.

"Katrina Jacobs?" a woman's voice inquired.

The last thing Katrina wanted to do was to sign an autograph or pose for a picture. But she put on a smile. "Yes?"

The tall, dark-haired woman held out her hand. "Danielle Marin. I'm a lawyer from Chicago. I work for Caleb Terrell, and I've met your sister on a number of occasions."

"Mandy?" Katrina asked in surprise, taking the hand the woman offered.

"Yes. Mandy. She's fantastic. I think we're on the way to becoming good friends."

Katrina looked Danielle up and down. She was neatly dressed, with a chic, short haircut, perfect makeup and a highly polished veneer. It was kind of hard to imagine her as good friends with Mandy.

Danielle glanced meaningfully at the empty chair on the opposite side of the small round table.

"Would you like to sit down?" Katrina felt obligated to offer.

Danielle smiled broadly and took a seat. "Thank you." She placed her small purse at the edge of the table and ordered an iced tea.

"Are you in New York on business?" Katrina opened, telling herself that at least the conversation might distract her from her depressing thoughts.

"I am," Danielle answered. "I'm also doing some work here for Reed Terrell."

Katrina couldn't tell if it was her imagination, but Danielle seemed to be watching her closely as she spoke his name.

"The bakery?" Katrina guessed, trying desperately to keep her features neutral. Then it hit her. "You're Danielle?"

"Yes."

"The restaurant reservation. Flavian's."

"That was me." Danielle smiled. "I didn't know it was you. Did you enjoy yourself?"

"Yes," Katrina managed. Then she swallowed hard. She didn't want to think about that night.

"Reed's a very nice man."

Katrina wasn't ready to speak, so she nodded instead.

"Does that mean you and he are…involved?"

"No," Katrina quickly replied. "I mean, we went out a couple of times, sure. But he was only here for a few days, and then—" She forced out a laugh. "You know what Coloradans are like. Couldn't wait to get back to the dust and sweat."

"Didn't you grow up there?"

"I haven't lived there since I was ten."

"Ah."

The waitress arrived with Danielle's iced tea.

She squeezed in a slice of lemon and concentrated on stirring. "You could always go visit him."

"I don't get to Colorado very often. It's really never been my favorite place."

"But, with Reed—"

"It's nothing like that," Katrina assured her, scrambling for a way out of the conversation. She and Reed were past tense, done, over.

"He's a very handsome man."

A thought hit Katrina. "Are you interested in Reed? I wondered when he called you for the restaurant recommendation—"

Danielle laughed lightly. "It's nothing like that for me, either. But it seems like you and he—"

"No."

"You're blushing, Katrina."

"I am? Well..."

There was a combination of pity and curiosity in Danielle's eyes. Reed had obviously shared something with her.

"You know more than you're letting on, don't you?" Katrina asked.

"I know he took you to dinner. And I can see that you're blushing. And he seems to have left town in a bit of a...hurry. That only adds up to so many things."

Katrina felt her face grow even hotter.

"And now it occurs to me that Caleb and Mandy's relationship has the ability to make things complicated for you."

"It's no problem." Though Katrina was struggling to keep her composure.

"I don't mean to pry." But Danielle's mixture of concern and curiosity somehow invited confidences.

"It never should have happened." Katrina gave up pretending.

"I hear you," Danielle agreed with what seemed like genuine sympathy.

"We're completely unsuited. Our lives are a million miles apart. And yet there was this chemical thing." Katrina stopped herself.

"I've experienced that chemical thing myself," said Danielle with a self-deprecating laugh.

"You have?" Katrina hated to admit it, but her misery felt a little better with company.

"A guy named Tr—Trevor." Danielle stabbed at her iced tea for a moment, and it looked as if she might be blushing. "He was from Texas."

"Did you sleep with him?" Katrina instantly checked herself. "I'm sorry. That was completely inappropriate."

"Not at all. I don't mind. We didn't. Oh, he tried hard enough. And he was quite a charmer. But I managed to say no."

"Reed was the opposite," Katrina confessed. "He tried to talk me out of it. But I wouldn't listen, and I— Good grief, I can't believe I'm telling you this."

Danielle reached across the table and covered Katrina's hand. "When was the last time you saw him?"

"Saturday night."

"So, the wound is fresh."

Katrina nodded miserably.

"Then you need someone to talk to." Danielle glanced around. "Do they serve martinis here?"

"You know, that actually sounds tempting."

Danielle waved to the waitress.

"I bet you're glad you said no," Katrina ventured in a low voice. If she hadn't slept with Reed, maybe she wouldn't have such a burning pain in her chest. Maybe the world wouldn't feel as if it was crushing her with its weight. Maybe she'd be able to sleep. And maybe tears wouldn't feel as if they were mere seconds away every moment of the day and night.

"Not necessarily," said Danielle, her expression going soft. "I lay awake at night wondering what it would have been like."

"Was he really great?"

"He was conceited and pig-headed and irrepressible and rash.

He was also the sexiest guy I've ever met, and I know deep down in my soul that he'd have been an extraordinary lover."

"Maybe you should go back to Texas."

The waitress arrived and Danielle ordered two vodka martinis. Katrina had never tried one, but today she was game.

"Don't think I haven't thought about it," said Danielle.

Katrina heaved an empathetic sigh. "But you'd end up with regrets either way."

"Afraid so."

"It's not fair. It's just not fair." If Katrina hadn't slept with Reed, she'd be just like Danielle, wondering what she'd missed. At least she had those few nights. At least she'd lost her virginity to a man she—

Oh, no.

The waitress set down the martinis, and Katrina grabbed one, downing a healthy swallow.

Her throat burned, and she gasped and coughed and wheezed.

"You okay?" Danielle asked, while the waitress frowned.

"Fine," Katrina managed. The warmth of the alcohol spreading though her veins felt good. "Just fine," she finished.

Danielle thanked the waitress, and the woman left.

"So, how does Reed feel about you?"

The question struck Katrina as odd. But then the entire conversation was odd. She shrugged. "Angry. Very, very angry."

For some reason, the answer seemed to surprise Danielle. "You fought?"

"And how. I told him to leave New York City, and basically never to come back again."

"Ouch."

"It's for the best." Katrina nodded, ordering herself to believe it. She took another experimental sip of the martini, and it went down better this time.

"Do you think he'll come back anyway?" Danielle asked softly.

Katrina shook her head, long and slow, lifting her glass.

"Do you think he might have fallen in love with you?"

The drink sloshed over Katrina's hand. *"What?"*

Danielle shrugged. "It's a possibility."

"It's preposterous," Katrina blurted.

"He tried to talk you out of sleeping with him."

"That's because he's a gentleman, a cowboy."

"My cowboy tried to talk me *in*to sleeping with him."

"Yours is from Texas."

A funny expression crossed Danielle's face.

"Reed knew all along it would turn out badly for us if we slept together," Katrina continued. "He's had relationships end before. He's had experience with ex-lovers."

"And you haven't?"

Katrina immediately realized what she'd given away. "Haven't what?" She played dumb.

But Danielle was too shrewd to let it go. "Had experience with ex-lovers."

Katrina didn't answer, but her face heated up again.

Danielle closed her eyes for a long second. Then she opened them. "Katrina, is there any chance you've fallen in love with Reed?"

Katrina's stomach turned to a block of lead. "No," she intoned. "Never. Not a chance." What kind of a colossal disaster would that be? She downed the rest of the martini. "But I will have another one of these."

"You should call Mandy."

"Why?"

"To talk to her about this."

Katrina dismissed the notion. "I really don't know Mandy that well."

"She's your sister."

"We're not close."

"Well, if I had a sister, and if she was as nice as Mandy, and if I was feeling the way you are, I'd be calling her in a heartbeat."

Katrina felt as if she were listening through cotton wool. "Say again?"

"Call Mandy, Katrina."

"Maybe." But what would she tell her? What could she say? That she was in way too deep with Mandy's soon-to-be brother-in-law, and that she could never come home again?

Ten

Back home on his ranch, Reed knew he had to forget about Katrina. He had to restart his regular life and put the surreal week in New York City far behind him.

Starting right now.

But as he stared at the barbecue grill on the back deck, he couldn't seem to rouse himself to light it. Instead, while the sun descended, he lifted the half-empty bottle of beer from the table next to him and took a desultory sip of the tepid liquid.

"The door was open," came Danielle's unexpected voice from the kitchen doorway.

"Always is," Reed responded without turning.

Her high heels clicked on the deck as she made her way to him.

"I get why you did it," she told him without preamble. "What I don't get is why you did *that.*"

He set down the bottle. "You want to toss a few nouns into that sentence?"

"You're obviously in love with Katrina."

Reed wasn't about to deny it. Danielle was his lawyer, after all. It wasn't like she could tell anyone.

"That's why you wanted to help her," she finished.

"Go to the head of the class."

She waited for him to elaborate. When he didn't, she stepped into the silence. "But why such a huge gesture. Ten million dollars? Were you hoping to win her back?"

"Hoping to win who back?" asked Caleb from the same spot where Danielle had just appeared.

Reed twisted his head at the unexpected sound of his brother's voice.

"Hi, Danielle," Caleb added. "What are you doing here?"

"Hey, Danielle," said Mandy as she breezed past Caleb onto the deck. Then she grinned at Reed. "You're back." She dropped a quick kiss on his cheek before plunking down in one of the four empty Adirondack chairs.

"So are you," Reed responded to Mandy, hoping against hope they hadn't overheard Danielle's revelation. "How was Chicago?"

"Noisy. How was New York?"

"Noisier."

She chuckled.

"Get who back?" Caleb repeated, glancing from Reed to Danielle.

Reed knew there were parts of the situation that shouldn't stay a secret, and parts that couldn't stay a secret. He decided now was as good a time as any to get the basics out of the way.

"Danielle helped me out with some investments while I was in New York," he opened.

Caleb's glance went to Danielle. "Yeah?"

She nodded.

"That's great." Caleb's posture relaxed. "Anybody else need a beer?"

Mandy raised her hand.

"What the heck?" said Danielle, moving to sit next to Mandy. "I'll take one."

Caleb disappeared, while Reed tried to bring some order to

the riot of emotions coursing through his body. He was normally cool under pressure, calm under stress. He could hold his own under physical danger and in the toughest of arguments. But his feelings toward Katrina took him to uncharted waters.

"How's Katrina doing?" Mandy asked. "Did you see her dance?"

"I did," Reed responded as Caleb returned, passing beers to the two women.

Then Caleb held his up in a toast to Reed. "Welcome to the world beyond Lyndon Valley."

Reed couldn't help a harsh chuckle at that. The world beyond Lyndon Valley hadn't worked out so well for him.

"So, tell me about these new investments."

Reed looked his brother square in the eye. The bakery, the tailor and the limo service were irrelevant. "I set up the Sasha Terrell Endowment Fund with ten million dollars."

Caleb blinked.

"It's for the benefit of the Liberty Ballet Company," Reed continued.

Mandy reached over and grasped his upper arm. "For Katrina?"

"For Katrina," Reed confirmed, reaching for his warm beer, swallowing it against his dry throat.

Caleb's eyes narrowed. "What did you do?"

"I just told you what I did."

"Reed, are you sure?" asked Mandy, sitting forward in her chair and leaning toward him. "I mean, it's great and all. And what a wonderful tribute to your mother. But that's a whole lot of money."

"You slept with her?" Caleb accused.

"Back off," said Reed.

Caleb paced across the deck. "What is the matter with you? I specifically—"

"It's to protect her," Reed stated.

"From you?"

"Give me a break." Reed rocked to his feet. "She doesn't need protection from me."

"Then why the ten million?"

Reed was tired of having his motives questioned. "There's a guy in New York, Quentin Foster. He's made a lot of large donations to the ballet company, and he seems to think it gives him the right to sleep with Katrina."

"What?" Caleb demanded.

"What?" Mandy echoed.

"That's why I went to New York," said Reed, owning up to at least part of the truth. "I told him to back off. Threatened to kill him, actually. But he wouldn't listen."

Caleb's jaw had turned to steel. "He didn't..."

"He's still breathing," said Reed. "So, no. He didn't. He asked. She turned him down, but he wouldn't take no for an answer. He's the guy who caused her ankle accident."

Mandy rose distractedly. "I have to call Katrina." But she didn't move any farther.

"The Sasha Terrell Endowment Fund will replace all of Foster's donations," said Reed, still looking directly at his brother. "And then some. He's out. We're in. And Katrina is perfectly safe."

"Now I understand," said Danielle.

Mandy's shoulders slumped in relief. Then she took the two steps that brought her to Reed and she enveloped him in a hug of gratitude.

"Thank you," she whispered, her throat obviously clogged.

Reed hugged her back. "Happy to do it."

"Why didn't you come to me?" Caleb asked.

"Didn't need to."

"She's going to be my sister-in-law. And I have a lot more money than you do."

"It's handled," said Reed, releasing Mandy. A couple of tears had leaked out of the corners of her eyes, but she was smiling.

Caleb cocked his head to one side. "But why not—"

"Leave it," said Reed, glaring at his brother.

But then comprehension dawned on Caleb's face. "I'll be damned."

"What part of 'leave it' didn't you understand?"

"What?" Mandy looked back and forth between the brothers.

Caleb shook his head in obvious bewilderment. "How long have you been in love with Katrina?"

"You don't have to answer that," said Danielle.

Caleb turned to her. "What? We're in a court of law now?"

Mandy looked to Reed, her brows knitting together. "Did I miss something?"

"She's safe, Mandy." He told her. "That's all that matters."

"But—"

He moved toward the door, wanting nothing more than to get very far away from this conversation.

"How does she feel about you?" Mandy called after him.

He paused, his respect for Mandy at war with his instinct for self-preservation. "She's in New York City. I'm here. End of story."

"Is she upset? Did you hurt her?"

Reed knew his answer was going to make Mandy angry. He regretted that. He regretted it a lot. But it was always going to end this way. He'd tried to tell that to Katrina, and he'd certainly known it himself. "She understands that our lives are completely separate."

"But you slept with her anyway," said Caleb.

"That's still none of your business." Reed started for the kitchen door.

Caleb put an arm out to stop him. Surprisingly, there was no anger in his tone. "A very wise man once told me that when a Jacobs woman sleeps with you, it means she loves you."

Reed remembered their conversation perfectly. But that was a different time, a completely different circumstance. "That doesn't bring Katrina any closer to Colorado."

"You think that's your only answer?"

Reed ignored his brother and began moving again, increasing his pace.

"That Katrina comes to Colorado?" Caleb called. "You can't go to New York City?"

Reed smacked his hand on the doorjamb as he rocked to a halt.

"There are two possible solutions," said Caleb.

Reed turned, enunciating carefully. "My world is here. I have a house to build and kids to raise and a mother to honor."

"You think Mom would want you to give up Katrina?" Caleb stepped closer.

"I think Mom would want Katrina to be happy," Reed answered with total honesty. There were more than a few parallels between the two women. And he would never, ever do to Katrina what his father had done to his mother.

"So do I," Caleb said softly, stopping directly in front of Reed. "I think Mom would want you to make Katrina happy, on Katrina's terms, in Katrina's world."

Reed opened his mouth to argue.

But Caleb wasn't finished. "I know your plan, Reed. And I understand why you're doing it. But you're wrong, dead wrong. You don't honor Mom by staying in Lyndon Valley. You honor Mom by honoring Katrina."

Reed couldn't wrap his head around it. "You're suggesting I move to New York City?" Was Caleb saying their mother would want him to move to New York City? The idea was preposterous. He was a cowboy. His life was here. He was about to dig the foundation for his house.

"Imagine," Caleb continued, voice controlled, but Reed could see the anger simmering in his eyes. "If Wilton had once, even once in his miserable, toxic life, given a damn about Mom? What she wanted, what she needed, what would make her happy instead of him?"

Reed got where his brother was going with this. "It's not just geography, Caleb."

"Then, what is it?"

Reed wished there weren't quite so many witnesses, but he supposed there was no point in backing off now. "The last thing she said to me was, no matter how I dressed up, I'd always be an uncouth Colorado cowboy."

Caleb shrugged. "So change."

Reed snapped his fingers. "Just like that?"

"Just like that."

"I'm not going to stop threatening to kill any man who hurts her."

A grin spread across Caleb's face. "Yeah? Well, maybe you could stop telling her about it."

Danielle spoke up. "But you already did that, Reed."

Reed looked at her. "Already did what?"

"You didn't kill him. You found another way." She gave a shrug. "Maybe the tux and the tie rubbed off on you. Because instead of killing Quentin Foster, you outsmarted him. That was very civilized."

It was Mandy's turn to step in, and she was fighting a smile. "Honestly, Reed, I can't see Katrina objecting if you threaten to outsmart any man who hurts her."

Danielle nodded her agreement.

"It's not quite as satisfying," Caleb allowed.

"It was pretty satisfying," Reed admitted. The only thing he'd regretted was not being able to watch Elizabeth deliver the news to Foster.

"She misses you," said Danielle, her tone softer, more thoughtful than normal. "I went to see Katrina while I was in New York City. I was trying to figure out if you'd lost your mind. You hadn't. And she misses you."

The only time Katrina didn't miss Reed was while she was performing. Being on stage took all of her concentration and she was thankful that, if only temporarily, the effort blocked him out of her brain. But as soon as the curtain fell, her chest would hollow out again and her stomach would start to ache.

The applause from tonight's audience had barely died down. She was pacing her way along the hall to her dressing room, and her tears were once again close to the surface. She'd picked up her phone about a hundred times in the last few days, longing to call him and hear the sound of his voice. She wasn't ready to let him go. Not yet. Not so soon.

She'd concocted all kinds of wild schemes to eke a few more hours out of their brief relationship. Maybe he could come back to the city for a day or a week. Or maybe she could go to Colorado for another visit. Maybe it wouldn't be so bad there, if she was with Reed.

But deep down inside, she knew none of the plans made any real sense. It would still be temporary, and she'd get her heart broken all over again. Reed was like a drug, and her only hope was to go cold turkey.

She made it to the privacy of her dressing room. But before the door could close behind her, Elizabeth appeared.

"Another full house," she told Katrina, breezing inside, letting the door fall shut, taking one of the two armchairs in the compact room.

Katrina dropped down on the padded bench in front of the lighted mirror, automatically pulling the decorations from her hair.

"That's great news." She forced herself to smile, catching Elizabeth in the reflection.

"Have you heard from Reed today?" Elizabeth asked.

Katrina's fingers fumbled, and she dropped a small jeweled comb. It clattered onto the table and down to the floor.

"From Reed?" she asked stupidly, as she reached down to retrieve it. Could she have misheard? Why was Elizabeth asking about Reed?

"I left a message for him this morning, but he hasn't gotten back to me. That doesn't seem like him."

Katrina picked up the comb, her fingers slightly numb, mind scrambling to find some logic in Elizabeth's words. "You left Reed a message?"

"Yes."

"Why?"

"Just some more paperwork we need to sign. Danielle couriered it over, but I'm not clear on some of the tax sections."

Katrina blinked at Elizabeth. "Tax sections?" she parroted. What on earth would Elizabeth have to do with Reed's taxes? Or what would Reed have to do with Elizabeth's taxes? And what was Danielle doing in the middle of it?

Katrina knew she couldn't let herself be jealous, but she

simply couldn't help it. She wanted to be the person Reed called. It wasn't fair that it was Elizabeth and Danielle.

"Just details," Elizabeth said brightly, coming to her feet and putting her hand on the doorknob. "If he calls, can you make sure he has my cell number?"

"Certainly." Not that Reed would call. For a wild moment, Katrina thought of using this as an excuse to call him. But she dismissed the idea. It would be so transparent.

"So you met Danielle?" she asked Elizabeth.

Elizabeth laughed lightly. "We've been talking every day. Ten million dollars needs a lot of babysitting."

"Ten million dollars?"

Elizabeth stilled. Her expression faltered. Her hand dropped from the knob, and she stared at Katrina. "You don't know?"

Katrina didn't answer.

"How can you not know? Have you *talked* to Reed?"

Katrina swallowed a lump. "Not in a few days. We, well, we left things on bad terms after the gala."

Elizabeth sat back down in the chair, her hands going limp. "The gala? You haven't talked to him since the gala?"

"No," Katrina replied.

"She didn't tell you?"

"Elizabeth?" Katrina tried to tamp down her anxiety.

"Before he left New York. Before… Reed set up an endowment named the Sasha Terrell Fund. It's for us. It's for Liberty. It's ten million dollars."

The breath whooshed out of Katrina's body.

"His only stipulation," Elizabeth continued, "was that we kick Quentin Foster off the board and out of the organization forever."

"What?"

"I thought…" Elizabeth gave a helpless laugh. "I assumed. I mean, a man doesn't do something like that for just anyone. And after his performance at the gala. Well, if a man stepped up for me the way Reed stepped up for you…"

Katrina's hands started to shake. What had Reed done? Why had he done it?

"I was embarrassed," she confessed in a small voice. "At the gala. I was mortified by his behavior. I told him to leave, to get out of the city. I told him to go back to his sawdust-covered honky-tonks where he could make a point with his fists."

Elizabeth's jaw dropped open.

Katrina's stomach churned.

Elizabeth cleared her throat. "I, uh, guess he did this instead."

"What was he *thinking?*"

Elizabeth cocked her head sideways. "I guess he was thinking he wanted to protect you. And he didn't appear to care what it cost him."

Guilt washed over Katrina. Ten million dollars? He'd spent *ten million dollars?* "Who does that, Elizabeth? Who *does* something like that?"

"Apparently, cowboys from Colorado."

"I hate Colorado." But Katrina was blinking back tears. "Okay, I don't exactly hate it. But I don't want to live there."

"Reed's there," Elizabeth offered softly.

"I love Reed," Katrina admitted her worst fear out loud. "I *love* Reed. But my life is here."

Elizabeth moved to the bench, tucking in beside Katrina and taking her hand.

"I need to apologize."

Elizabeth squeezed. "I hate to ask this. It seems terribly insensitive. But is there any chance you could do it by phone?"

Katrina gave a watery laugh. "I don't think so."

"We've got sold-out performances for four more nights running."

"I know." Katrina wouldn't walk out on Liberty. "Maybe Monday? Caleb, my sister's fiancé, has a jet. Maybe I could talk to him about flying—"

The dressing-room door swung open. The two women all but jumped up as Reed's form filled the doorway.

Katrina froze, her stomach going into a freefall.

"Hello, Katrina." His deep voice reverberated around her, exactly as she remembered it.

She opened her mouth, but she couldn't seem to make any words come out.

Elizabeth recovered first, coming smoothly to her feet and moving toward the door, pausing beside him. "May I talk to you later on, Reed? About the paperwork?"

His gaze never left Katrina. "Sure. I'll call you."

"Thanks. See you both later then."

Reed moved in as Elizabeth moved out, and the door clicked shut behind him.

Katrina came shakily to her feet, steadying herself on the dressing table. She was still in her costume, her hair half up, half down.

All she could muster was a whisper. She swallowed. "Elizabeth just told me about the endowment."

Reed opened his mouth, but Katrina shook her head. She moved forward and touched her fingertips to his lips to silence him.

"Why did you do it?" She blinked against the stinging in her eyes. "I mean… No, that's not what I mean. I mean, thank you. And I'm sorry."

"I'm the one who's sorry." Reed spoke around her fingertips.

She shook her head again. He had nothing to be sorry about. He'd been right all along.

"I'm sorry I threatened to kill him," said Reed. "Okay. That's a lie. But I'm sorry it upset you. And I honestly would have killed him if he'd come after you. But I outsmarted him instead. And Mandy and Danielle tell me that's a more civilized solution."

Katrina smiled through the tiny tears that leaked out the corners of her eyes. "I can't believe you did that. Reed, you spent all your money."

He reached for her hand, enclosing it in his, pulling her close. "Don't cry."

"But—"

"It's not *all* of my money."

His hand was warm and strong and secure. She moved

against him, closing her eyes and absorbing the feel of his body and the scent of his skin. "I missed you so much."

"I missed you, too." He held her tightly and sighed. "You feel so good."

She fisted her hands into his shirt, voice raw. "I don't know if I can let go of you again."

"I know."

"Oh, Reed," she whispered, then drew a shuddering breath. "What are we going to do?"

"I hope we're going to love each other."

"How?" she sniffed.

He touched his index finger to her chin, tipping it up. His eyes were warm and rich, and his smile was soft. "I thought we'd start with real estate. Maybe a nice place in Brooklyn. Though I could be talked into Manhattan."

"Huh?"

"And after that I was planning to propose to you."

Katrina didn't understand. What was he saying? He couldn't mean what she thought he meant. "You're..."

"Moving to New York City?" He nodded. "Yes, I am."

"You can't do that."

"Turns out I can."

"But the ranch. Your family. Your new house. Your heritage."

"I want you to be my family." He smoothed back her hair. "I love you, Katrina. And I think my mother would love to know she had little ballerina granddaughters going to fine arts school in New York City. I think she would love that a lot."

"Oh, Reed." Katrina's heart swelled. She couldn't believe this was happening. She couldn't believe he would do such an amazing thing for her. She pressed herself tighter into his arms. "I love you. I love you *so* much."

"That's good. Because it turns out I can't wait on this. I'm proposing right now." He drew back again. "Will you marry me, Katrina?"

She nodded. Then she nodded faster. "Yes. Yes, I'll marry you, Reed. And I'll learn to ride horses, and I'll befriend the chickens. And we can spend weekends and holidays in Colorado with our families."

"That's my girl." He kissed her hairline. "I sure wish I had a ring. I shouldn't be doing this without a ring."

"There's a Tiffany's around the corner," she teased. Then she paused. "Or we can go to Brooklyn. Would you rather buy a ring in Brooklyn?"

"Sweetheart." He hugged her tighter. "You can have any ring you want. You can have any *thing* you want. As long as you'll stay with me for the rest of my life."

Katrina stopped in her tracks halfway between the Terrells' farmhouse and their barn. "I thought you said I could have anything I wanted."

"You can," Reed cajoled, taking her hand in his.

She snatched it back. "But I *don't* want *this*."

"That's not the same logic."

"Close enough."

"You'll love her," said Reed, slipping an arm around Katrina's shoulders and urging her forward. "She's twenty-two years old, has raised nine foals. She's as gentle as a kitten."

"She's as big as a house." Katrina complained, trying to shrink back as they approached the dapple-gray mare tied to the hitching post in front of the corral.

"She's maybe fifteen hands. Her name's North Star."

"Can't I start with a pony?" Not that Katrina had any desire to get up on a pony, either, but at least it would buy her some time. Maybe she could hide while Reed was looking for a pony.

"You promised you'd try," he admonished.

"I lied."

He laughed. "I'm not going to let anything happen to you."

"No offense, Reed. You're big and strong and capable, and all. But you're a human being. She's a horse."

"And she knows who's boss."

"Well, it's sure not going to be me."

"Katrina."

"What?"

"Buck up."

"That's your pep talk? 'Buck up'?" They were drawing closer to the mare by the second. She fought an urge to squeeze her eyes shut.

"I don't think you want to hear the alternative."

She wanted to be brave. She really did. Deep down inside, she knew this was an irrational fear. Very few people were killed by horses each year. And those that were tended to be in the rodeo or ride in steeplechases.

But an irrational fear didn't normally respond to logic, and so she was stuck with it. "I think I'm going to pass out."

"Katrina," he told her firmly. "Quit being such a wuss."

"You quit yelling at me."

"I am not yelling."

North Star snorted and shifted.

"You're scaring the horse," Katrina complained.

"So now you care about the horse?"

"Absolutely I care about the horse."

They'd stopped about five feet away from the hitching post.

"You'll make her sad if you don't ride her," said Reed.

"Nice try."

"Just look at those big brown eyes." Reed left Katrina behind and moved around the hitching post to stroke North Star's neck. "She loves teaching new riders."

"She does not."

"Want to bet?" He scratched the mare's nose, and she gave a couple of long, slow, obviously contented blinks.

Katrina didn't blame her. Reed did have magic hands.

"I've had six-year-olds on her back," Reed offered in smooth, honey tones. "She's a mama through and through. She won't let anything happen to you."

North Star was gazing at Katrina now. She did look rather gentle. In fact, she looked quite friendly.

"You want to come closer?" asked Reed.

"Not really." Katrina was tempted, though. When Reed had proposed back in New York, she had told him she'd learn to ride. She wanted to keep that promise. And if she could force herself to get on the horse's back, it would be one less thing to be embarrassed about while she was in Colorado.

And they were definitely going to spend time in Colorado. Reed had been amazing about offering to move to New York City. The least she could do was try to meet him halfway.

She glanced at him.

His expression had turned loving, one of understanding and patience.

She wiped her damp palms across the front of her blue jeans and took a step forward, then another and another.

When she came up beside Reed, North Star swung her head to look. But her movements were slow and calm, not at all threatening.

"Pat her neck," Reed suggested. "Firmly, or you'll tickle her."

"I don't want to tickle her." Katrina reached out. She patted the mare's neck three times. It was hot and wiry under her touch. A small puff of dust came up.

The horse didn't move at all.

"She's all saddled up," said Reed.

"I'm terrified," Katrina confessed in a whisper.

"I'll hold the lead rope. We'll walk her in the round pen."

"Inside the pen?" That would be easier.

"Until you're ready to go out."

Katrina screwed up her courage. She nodded. "Okay. But only inside the pen." It had to be safe enough. Surely to goodness, Reed wouldn't let her die before the wedding.

He kissed the top of her head. "Back here." He moved. "Put your hand around the saddle horn."

She reached up to grab the hard protrusion of leather.

"Foot up in the stirrup. I'm going to grab your butt."

"You're not allowed to enjoy this," she warned.

"I'm allowed to enjoy it all I want. Let me know when you're ready, and I'll give you a boost."

Katrina braced herself. "One, two, three." She pulled and Reed lifted, and before she knew it, she was perched on top of North Star. The mare hadn't moved a muscle.

"See how easy it is?"

Katrina adjusted her seat. "I'm awfully high up here."

"Put your other foot in the stirrup. And relax. You're not going anywhere."

He released the lead rope from the hitching post, and the horse shifted under her. Katrina gave out a little whoop of surprise.

"Go with the motion," Reed advised. "Don't fight it. We both know you have good balance."

Katrina tried to relax. Reed was right. She did have good balance. In that, she was ahead of the game.

He opened the gate to the round pen and led the horse inside. North Star's gait was slow and smooth beneath Katrina. The horse's barrel was warm against her legs. Its breathing was somehow soothing. And having Reed close by certainly helped.

He stopped North Star then moved back and released the reins that were looped around the saddle horn. He reached into the back pocket of his worn jeans and produced a pair of small, leather gloves.

"Put these on."

The gloves were soft against Katrina's hands, warm from Reed's body.

He placed the reins across her palm, showing her how to hold them. Then he backed away, holding a long length of the lead rope while North Star started forward, moving in a big circle.

It took a few minutes for Katrina to realize she wasn't afraid. A little while later, she felt as if she'd found her balance. And when Reed asked if he could take off the lead rope, she found herself agreeing.

He stayed in the middle of the round pen while North Star, who apparently knew the drill, paced around the perimeter with Katrina on her back.

"You're doing great," Reed told her.

She braved a look up from North Star's back. She smiled at Reed, and he smiled back, strong, sexy and confident.

The sun was high in the sky above him, the snow-capped mountains rising behind, a knife edge against the crackling blue sky. Wildflowers fanned out in the field, and aspen leaves blew in a gentle breeze. Even the cattle looked bucolic grazing on the hillside, while robins, chickadees and bluebirds flitted from tree to tree.

Katrina's heart lurched, and for the first time in her life, she felt at home in Lyndon Valley.

A pickup's engine rumbled in the distance, growing closer. The truck pulled into the yard, and North Star glanced over her shoulder, but otherwise didn't pay any attention to the interruption. A few moments later, Mandy and Caleb appeared and moved toward the fence.

Reed paced his way over to Katrina and North Star, stopping the horse with a hand signal and a low word.

"Probably don't need an audience yet," he told Katrina. Then he helped her down from North Star.

She was grateful for his understanding.

Reed took the mare, and she waded her way through the deep, loose dirt, back to the round-pen gate. Mandy opened it, beaming.

"You did it!" She laughed, pulling Katrina into her arms.

"I did it," Katrina agreed happily.

Reed had been right. North Star was gentle as a kitten, but she felt proud anyway. She hadn't been scared, and she hadn't fallen off, and she was actually willing to try it again.

"Caleb and I have been talking," said Mandy, linking arms as they started toward the house.

A stable hand took over North Star, and Reed and Caleb fell into step behind.

"About?" asked Katrina. She pulled off the leather gloves and twisted her new engagement ring back into place. The band was a stylized tension wave, platinum, holding a round diamond solitaire, with two small emeralds embedded in the outsides of the band.

She and Reed had found it at a funky jewelry store in Brooklyn. Katrina had loved it on sight. An hour later, she had her ring, and Reed had bought into the jewelry business.

"Why don't we have a double wedding?" Mandy asked in a breathless, animated voice.

Katrina blinked in surprise at the unexpected suggestion.

"Katrina doesn't want to get married in Lyndon Valley," said Reed.

"It doesn't have to be in Lyndon Valley," Mandy responded.

Reed moved up next to Katrina. He took her free hand and placed a kiss on the back of her knuckles. "I think she wants a New York City wedding. And I've promised her anything she wants."

"We'll be living in New York City," Katrina put in. Not that she wanted to get married in Lyndon Valley. But Reed had certainly made one huge concession. She could do the same.

"What about Chicago?" Caleb suggested. "That's halfway in between."

Katrina glanced at Reed. She kind of liked the idea of a double wedding with her sister and Reed's brother. But Chicago didn't mean anything to either her or to Reed.

"Denver," said Mandy, with conviction. "It's Colorado, but with skyscrapers and beautiful parks and five-star hotels."

"It doesn't have to be a double wedding," said Reed.

"I like Denver," said Katrina, her heart warming to the idea. "It's a nice compromise."

"You sure?" asked Reed, concern in his voice.

Katrina let go of her sister and turned to Reed, slowing to a stop, taking his hands and looking deep into his eyes. Her chest was tight, her heart full. "I'm sure," she told him. "After all, I am marrying Colorado."

"Yes, you are," said Reed, drawing her into his arms, holding her close while Mandy and Caleb got farther ahead. "And I'm marrying the very best thing in all of New York City."

"Our children can ride bareback to the Met," she teased.

"Or wear a Versace dress to a barn dance."

"I can't wait to see that."

He paused and the sounds of the ranch filled the spaces around them. After a minute, he stroked the rough pad of his thumb across her cheek. "I'm an ordinary cowboy, Katrina. As ordinary as they come. How'd I ever deserve someone as amazing as you?"

He had it all wrong. But she didn't know how to explain. "You're the one who's amazing," she tried. "And I love you so much."

"Oh, sweetheart." He leaned down for a kiss, his voice turning hoarse. "I'm going to love you forever."

* * * * *